COMMA

**200 OF THE FINEST NEEDED!
DEFEND THE FAITH OF CENTURIES!**

PAY GUARANTEED

Colonel Sten, late of His Imperial
Majesty's Third Guards Assault
Division, needs 200 elite soldiers to
assist in the protection of one of the
Empire's most respected social and
theocratic orders.

Only the Best Need Apply!

NONHUMANOID FREELANCES CANNOT BE CONSIDERED DUE TO RELIGIOUS CONDITIONS*

The Lupus Cluster and the Faith of
Talamein are under attack by a godless
mercenary horde which is attempting to
destroy some of the sector's most
beautiful and desirable worlds.
Required individual equipment:
sidearms, cold-weather suits, space-
combat armor. Combatants should
expect little ground leave...

*An Equal Opportunity Employer,
exempted under E.E.C. 12 (a) 1.c

Also by Allan Cole and Chris Bunch
Published by Ballantine Books:

STEN

THE WOLF WORLDS

ALLAN COLE and CHRIS BUNCH

A Del Rey Book

BALLANTINE BOOKS • NEW YORK

DEDICATED TO
Kathryn and Karen
...for the usual godzilla reasons
and
The real *Alex Kilgour*
..."Who Cares Who Wins..."

A Del Rey Book
Published by Ballantine Books

Copyright © 1984 by Allan Cole and Christopher Bunch

Library of Congress Catalog Card Number: 83-91218

ISBN 0-345-31229-5

Manufactured in the United States of America

First Edition: March 1984

Cover art by David B. Mattingly

BOOK ONE

ABSENCE OF BLADE

CHAPTER ONE

THE GQ SIRENS ululated through the Jannisar cruiser. The thunder of crashing boots died away. The ship's XO nodded in satisfaction as the STATIONS READY panel winked to green. He made a mental note to assign extra penance to one laggard ECM station, then spun in his chair to the captain. "All stations manned, Sigfehr," he reported.

The captain touched the relic that hung under his black tunic, then opened his intercom mike. "Bow, ye of the Jann, as we make our prayer to Talamein.

"O Lord, ye who know all things, bless us as we are about to engage the unbeliever. We ask, as our right due, for your assistance in victory.

"S'be't."

The chorus of "S'be't" echoed through the ship. The captain switched to a double channel.

"Communications, you will monitor. Weapons, prepare launch sequence, LRM tubes two, four, six. Target onscreen. Commercial ship. Communications, establish contact with target ship. Weapons, we will launch on my command, after surrender of enemy ship. This is bridge, clear."

The cruiser's prey appeared to be just another obsolescent *Register*-class mining survey ship wildcatting through the galaxy's outer limits.

Its oval hull was patched, resprayed, corroded, and even

rusty from its very occasional atmospheric landings. Its long, spindly landing legs were curled under the ship's body, and the mining grab claws were curled just below the forward controls.

It resembled nothing so much as an elderly crab fleeing a hungry shark.

Actually, the ship was the IA *Cienfuegos*, an Imperial spy ship, its mission complete and now speeding for home.

Extract, Morning Report, II Saber Squadron, Mantis Section:

> The following detached this date, assigned temporary duty Imperial Auxiliary Ship *Cienfuegos* (x-file OP CAMFAR):
>
> STEN, (NI), Lt. OC Mantis Section 13, weapons;
> KILGOUR, ALEX, Sgt., NCOIC, Demolitions;
> KALDERASH, IDA, Corporal, Pilot & Electronics;
> MORREL, BET, Superior Private, Beast Handler;
> *BLYRCHYNAUS*, Unranked, Anthropologist, Medic.
> Team detached with Indiv Gear, Units 45 & 46.
> NOTE: OP CAMFAR under dir O/C Mercury Corps, subsq. entries t/b cleared thru Col. Ian Mahoney, Commander Mercury Corps.

Sten stared approvingly at the nude woman strobe-illuminated by the hydroponic lights. He walked to the edge of the plot and gently picked his way past the two huge, black-and-white Siberian tigers.

One of them opened a sleepy eye, emitted a low growl of recognition. Sten ignored it, and it returned to licking its mate's throat.

Bet turned then frowned, seeing Sten. Sten's heart still thumped when he saw her. She was small, blonde, and muscles rippled under her smooth, tawny skin.

She hesitated, then waded through the waving plants to the edge of the plot and sat beside him. Sten was only slightly taller than Bet, with black hair and brooding black eyes. He was slender, but with the build of a trained acrobat.

"Thought you were asleep," she said.

"Couldn't."

Bet and Sten sat in silence for a moment—except for the

purrs of Munin and Hugin, Bet's two big cats. Neither Bet nor Sten was particularly good at talking. Especially about . . .

"Thought maybe," Sten tried haltingly, "we should, well, try to figure out what's going on."

"Going wrong, you mean," Bet said softly.

"I guess that pretty well is it," Sten said.

Bet considered. "I'm not sure. We've been together quite awhile. Maybe it's that. Maybe it's this stupid operation. All we've done for a long time now is sit on this clottin' ship and play tech."

"And snarl at each other," Sten added.

"That, too."

"Look," Sten said, "why don't we go back to my compartment? And . . ." His voice trailed off. Very romantic approach, his mind snapped at him.

Bet hesitated. Considering. Finally she shook her head. "No," she said. "I think I want things left alone until we get back. Maybe—maybe when we're on R and R . . . maybe then we'll go back to being like we were."

Sten sighed. Then nodded. Perhaps Bet was right. Maybe it was best—

And the intercom sang: "If we aren't disturbing the young lovers, we seem to have a small problem in the control room."

"Like what, Ida?" Sten asked.

The tigers were already up, ears erect, tails swimming gently.

"Like a clottin' great cruiser haulin' up on us from the rear."

Bet and Sten were on their feet, running for the control room.

A relatively short man, about as wide as he was tall, scanned the display from the ship's *Janes* fiche and grunted. Alex was a heavy-worlder with steel-beam size bones and super-dense muscles. And his accent—Scots because of the original settlers of his homeworld—was as thick as his body.

"Naebody w'knae th' trawble Ah seen," he half sung to himself as he glanced over the description of the ship that was pursuing them.

Sten leaned over his shoulder and read aloud: "619.532. ASSAULT/PATROL CRUISER. Former Imperial Cruiser *Turnmaa*, *Karjala* class. Dim: 190 meters by 34 . . . clottin' chubby ship . . . Crew under Imperial manning: 26 officers, 125 men . . ."

"Four of us, plus two tigers, against 151 troops," Ida broke in. The Rom woman mused over the odds. She was as chubby as she was greedy. Ida had her fingers in every stock and futures market in the Empire. "If anyone's taking bets, I'll give odds ... against us."

Sten ignored her and read on: "Armament: Six Goblin antiship launchers, storage thirty-six in reserve ... Three Vydall intercept missile launchers, storage forty-five in reserve ... four Lynx-output laser systems ... usual in-atmosphere AA capability ... single chain gun, single Bell-class assault laser, mounted unretractable turrets above A deck. Well-armed little bassid. ... Okay, now, speed ..."

"Ah'm kepit my fingers linkit," Alex murmured.

"Clot," Sten said, "they can outrun us, too."

It was Ida's turn to grunt. "Clottin' computer, all it tells us is that we're swingin' gently, gently in the wind. Any data on who those stinkin' bad guys are?"

Sten didn't bother to answer her. "What's intercept time?" he snapped.

Ida blanked the *Janes* display and the screen relit: AT PRESENT SPEED, TURNMAA WILL BE WITHIN WEAPONS RANGE IN 2 SHIP SECONDS FOR GOBLIN LAUNCH. CONTACT WILL BE MADE IN—

Bet cut the readout. "Who cares? I don't think those clowns want to shake our hands." She turned to Sten. "Any ideas, Lieutenant?"

Ida's board buzzed. "Oh-ho. They want to talk to us." Her hand went to the com switch.

Sten stopped her. "Stall them," he said.

There was a reason for Sten's caution. The problem wasn't with the control room—the *Cienfuegos* was indeed an Imperial spy ship—but except for its hidden super-computer, a rather sophisticated electronic suite, and overpowered engines, it still was pretty much the rustbucket inside as it was on the outer skin.

The problem was its crew: Mantis section, the Empire's super-secret covert mission specialists. Mantis troopers were first given the standard one-year basic as Imperial Guardsmen, then, assuming they had the proper nonmilitary, nonregimented, and ruthless outlook on life, seconded first to Mercury Corps (Imperial Military Intelligence) and then given the two-year-long Mantis training.

Clot the training, Sten thought while trying to come up with a battle plan that offered even a one-in-ten chance of survival. The problem was really the team's physical appearance: Munin and Hugin, two four-meter-long mutated black-and-white Siberian tigers. One chubby Scotsman. One fat woman wearing a gypsy dress. One pretty woman. And me, Sten thought. Sten, Lieutenant, commanding Mantis Team 13, suicide division.

Whoopie, he thought. Oh, well. Sten motioned to Doc while Ida fumbled with the com keys, making confused responses to the cruiser.

Doc waddled forward. The tendriled koala's real name was *BLYRCHYNAUS*, but since no one could pronounce his Altarian name, they called him Doc. The little anthro expert (and medic) held all human beings in absolute contempt. Though he was mostly considered a pain in the lower extreme, he had two indispensible talents: He could analyze culture from small scraps of evidence; and (as one of the Empire's most formidible carnivores) he had the ability to broadcast feelings of compassion and love for his adorable self and any companions.

"Any idea who they are?" Sten asked.

Doc sniffed. "I have to *see* them," he said.

Sten signaled Ida, who had taped a crude frame to the com pickup so that she would be the only creature visible on the ship.

"Once more onto the breach of contract," she said and keyed ANSWER.

Three stern faces stared at her from the screen.

"G'head," Ida yawned. "This is *Hodell*, Survey Ship P21. Ca' Cervi on."

"You will cut your drive instantly. This I order in the name of Talamein and the Jannisars."

Out of sight of the Jann captain, Doc studied the man. Noting his uniform. Analyzing his speech patterns.

Ida gave the captain a puzzled look. "Talamein? Talamein? Do I know him?"

The eyes of the two men beside the captain widened in horror at her blasphemy. The senior officer glared at Ida through the screen.

"You will bring your vessel to an immediate halt and prepare for boarding and arrest.

"By the authority of the Prophet, and Ingild, his emissary in present-time. You have entered proscribed space. Your ship will be seized, you and your crew conveyed to Cosaurus for trial and execution of sentence."

"Y'sure got yourself a great justice system, Cap'n." Ida rose from her chair, turned, and planted her bare, ample buttocks against the pickup. Then, modestly lowering her skirt, she turned back to the screen. She noted with pleasure she'd gotten a reaction from all three black uniforms this time.

"And if nonverbal communication ain't sufficient," she said, "I'd suggest you put your prophet in one hand and your drakh in the other and see which one fills up first."

Without waiting for an answer, she broke contact.

"A wee bit d'rect, m'lass?" Alex inquired.

Ida just shrugged. Sten waited patiently for Doc's analysis.

The bear's antenna vibrated slightly. "Not pirates or privateers—at least these beings do not so consider themselves. In any case authoritarian, which should be obvious even to these odiferous beasts of Bet's."

Hugin understood enough of the language to know when he was being insulted. He growled, warningly. Doc's antenna moved again, and the growl turned into a purr. He tried to lick Doc's face. The bear pushed him away.

"I find interesting the assumption of absolute authority, which would suggest either a fuehrer state of longstanding or, more probably, one of a metaphysical nature."

"You mean religious," Sten said.

"A belief in anything beyond what one can consume or exploit. Metaphysics, religion, whatever.

"My personal theory would be what you call religious. Note the use of the phrase 'In the name of Talamein' as a possible indicator.

"My estimation would be a military order, based on and supporting a dictatorial, puritanical religion. For the sake of argument, call this order the Jannisars.

"Note also that the officer has carefully positioned two aides to his either side. Neither seemed more than a bodyguard.

"Therefore, I would theorize that our Jannisars are not a majority in this . . . this Talamein empire, but an elite minority requiring protection.

"Also note the uniforms. Black. I have observed that in the human mind this indicates a desire for the observer to associate the person wearing that uniform with negativism—fear, terror, even death.

"Also, did any of you notice the lack of decoration on all three uniforms? Very uncharacteristic of the human norm, but an indicator that status is coupled with the immaterial—in other words, again, an indicator that we're dealing with metaphysical fanatics."

Doc looked around, waiting for appaluse. He should have known better.

"Ah a'ready kenned they wa' n'better'n a lot'a Campbells," Alex said. "The wee skean dubhs th'had slung a' they belts. No fightin' knives a man wae carry. D'ble-edged, wi' flat handles. A blade likc tha's used for naught but puttin' in a man from the rear."

"Anything else, Doc?" Sten asked.

"The barrel that walks like a being said what I had left out," Doc said.

Sten rubbed his chin, wishing, not for the hundredth time, that Mantis had been able to assign them a battle computer before the mission. Finally he looked up at everyone. "The way I see it, we have to let them play the first card."

CHAPTER TWO

"ON MY COMMAND," the Jannisar captain said harshly. "Goblin tubes two, four, six, prepare to launch. Launch."

Metal clanged as the three long-range missile tubes lifted above the cruiser's outer skin. Oxygen and solid fuel boiled from the tubes as the Goblins fired.

"We have a launch on missile six and missile two . . . launch on missile four . . . missile four, misfire."

"Attempt reignition," the captain said.

"Reignition attempted," the weapons officer droned. "Attempt unsuccessful. Missile failed to ignite. Primary ignition circuits defunct . . . secondary ignition circuits defunct, missile failed to self-arm."

A Jannisar will never show emotion, the captain thought. He cut off the weapons room circuit, then looked at his executive officer. His expression was also blank. Malfunctions weren't, after all, that unexpected. By the time an Imperial warship was sold, it had generally seen a lot of combat. But still, the captain thought furiously, with the proper tools, what we Jannisar could do in the name of Talamein!

Then he refocused his attention on the missile tracking screen, as the two 5kt missiles homed on the fleeing *Cienfuegos*.

"Guess he told me," Ida said. "They've launched missiles."
"How long?" Sten asked.

"Impact in . . . eighty-three seconds. We've got a whole lifetime."

"Not funny," Sten managed as he dropped into a weapons seat and tugged on the helmet.

Into a gray half-world. Part of him "saw" the ghost-images of the other soldiers in the control room. But suddenly he was the missile.

The weapons control system was, of course, no different from the feelies. The helmet's contact rested on the base of the skull and induced direct perception to the brain. The operator, using a standard joystick and remote throttle, kamikazied the missile directly to the target.

Sten "saw" the port open before him . . . a froth of air expired . . . then the streaked blackness as his CM missile launched. He flipped another switch on the panel and launched "himself" again. He kept the second antimissile-missile on a slave circuit, holding a path to his flank.

Sten dimly heard Bet, from another panel, snap, "Gremlin flight nine launched . . . all ECM A-A-A operational . . . waiting for contact . . . waiting for contact."

The Gremlins were small antimissiles that provided a false target signature identical to the *Cienfuegos*. Dead silence, waiting either for the Gremlins to divert and explode the Goblins or for Sten to close his own missiles into range.

Alex noticed that sweat had beaded on Ida's lip hair. Then blinked as salt droplets roll down his forehead, into his eyes. He deliberately looked over at Doc, Hugin, and Munin.

The tigers were pacing back and forth, their tails lashing. Doc sat perfectly still on the tabletop.

"I have a diversion on missile one," Bet called suddenly. "The bassid's turnin' . . . come on, you. Come on . . . right on and . . ." She blanked her pickup as one Goblin, idiot sure its mission was accomplished, blew a meter-long diversionary missile into nothingness.

"Dummy," Bet said triumphantly, pulling off her helmet.

Sten suddenly muttered obscenities, yanked stick and controls back: "Stupid missile's got a misfiring engine . . . no way to get a track on it."

The second Goblin arrowed straight into Sten's vision— and Sten desperately stabbed at the manual det switch.

The small nuclear head on his missile fireballed . . . but Sten had already switched "himself" to the second countermissile, spun it on its own axis, and pushed full drive.

"You have a negative hit on that," Ida said, keeping her voice calm.

Sten didn't answer. He was slowly overhauling the Jann missile. He closed in . . . and his helmet automatically switched him from radar to realtime visual.

Gotcha . . . gotcha . . . gotcha . . . he thought as the blackened drive tubes of the Goblin grew visible.

"Seven seconds till contact," Ida said, wondering how her voice stayed level.

And Sten fired his missile.

Another atomic fireball.

"I still have a—nope, I don't. Radar echo. We got 'em all, Lieutenant, old buddy."

Sten took off the helmet; he blinked around the control room. He'd stayed with his missile right until det point—and his mind insisted that the explosion had temporarily flare-blinded his eyes. Slowly the room went from negative to overexposed to normal.

Nobody applauded. They were, after all, professionals. The only comment was Alex's: "An' noo y'ken whae a Scotsman wearit kilts. It's so he noo hae to change trews when aught like this happens."

"Fine," Sten said. "First problem out of the way. With only two long-range launches, that's probably all they've got. Which means they'll close with us in . . ."

"Four hours," Ida said.

"Four hours. Perfectly lovely. Find us a place to hide. Preferably some nice world about 6AU wide with one hundred percent cloud cover."

Ida swung the scope console down on its retracting arm and started scanning the space-globe around them.

"Here's the plan. Ida'll find some world where we can go to ground," Sten said, in his best command voice. "Maybe we'll be able to reach it before the bad guys catch up with us. We'll go in-atmosphere, set it down—"

"Set *this* clunk down in-atmosphere?" Ida asked.

"—then we'll sit on what hopefully is a tropic isle until they get tired of lurking and we can go home."

"You call that a plan?"

"Doc, you got an alternative to sitting around up here and dying a lot?" Sten asked.

The team got to work.

* * *

"The enemy ship has diverted course, Sigfehr," the Jann XO said. "Probability is they are plotting landfall on Bannang IV."

Involuntarily the captain started, then composed himself. "That ship cannot be from any world in Lupus Cluster."

"Obviously not, sir."

"That increases my interest. An out-cluster ship, with enough antimissile capability to deter even us. Obviously a ship with what must be considered a valuable cargo. What is our closing rate?"

"We will be within intercept missile range in three hours, sir."

"And Bannang IV?"

"They could in-atmosphere at approximately the same time."

The captain allowed himself a smile. "Were I not interested in their cargo, it would be tempting to allow them to land on Bannang. It is true—Talamein will revenge his own."

"Your orders, sir?"

"Unchanged. Continue the pursuit. And destroy them."

"It ain't much of a world," Ida said, "but it's the best I can do."

Sten eyed the screen, half-consciously read it aloud: "Single solar system. Sun pretty much G-one yellow dwarf...five worlds...That's too close to the sun. Desert world...two methane giants."

"Unknown IV looks like home," Ida put in.

"Unknown IV it is. Let's see...about twelve thousand km on the polar axis. Spectograph—where the hell—okay: Acceptable minims on atmosphere. Grav's a little lighter'n normal. Mostly land...acceptable bodies of water...single source of electronic emission."

"So it's inhabited," Bet said from the galley area.

"Which is where we won't put it down. Maybe they're related to these clowns on our tail. You're right, Ida. That's our new home."

"*Maybe* it's our new home," Doc said. "Both screens, you will note, show about the same figure. We'll reach your Unknown Four just about the same time as the *Turnmaa*. The suspense should be most interesting." He pulled a chunk of raw soyasteak from Munin's plate and swallowed it.

* * *

Sten itemized: ground packs, weapons, surface suits, survival gear, first-contact pouches . . . as ready as possible.

The computer clacked and spat out seven small cards. Each duplicated the data held in the *Cienfuegos'* computer—the data the spy ship had been dispatched to gather, an analysis of a mineral found on a world in the now-distant Eryx Cluster.

Sten wondered if he'd ever find out why the Emperor was so interested in the gray rock that sat on the mess table in front of him. His but to do, keep from dying, and not ask classified questions.

He distributed the cards to the team members and tucked one each into Hugin and Munin's neck pouches.

"Ah hae to admire a mon wi' organization," Alex said. "Noo a' wha Ah hae to worry aboot is splittin' yon sample. Ah gie it a whirl an hour ago."

"And?" Sten asked curiously.

"Two iridium drills, two shipsteel crystals, an' one scratch in m' mum's heirloom diamond. It's hard, it is."

Sten's hand dropped, fingers curled. From the sheath in his arm a crystal knife dropped into his hand. Sten had grown it on Vulcan while doing time in the deadly industrial Hellworld for labor sabotage.

Double-edged, with a skeleton grip, the knife had a single purpose. To kill. There was no guard, only grooves on the end of the haft. The knife was about 22cm long and only 2.5cm thick.

Its blade, however, was barely 15 molecules wide. Far sharper than any razor could be. Laid against a diamond, with no pressure, it would cut smoothly through.

Sten carefully held the ore sample in one hand and started cutting. He was somewhat surprised—the blade met some resistance.

"Aye," Alex said. "Ah nae ken whae we're doin' aie this. A substance ae tha' . . . it's price is beyond reckon."

"Worst abortion anybody's ever seen," Ida said proudly.

"Worse than that," Doc added. "Ugly. Misshapen. Improbable. It should work just fine."

While the others in the team were readying themselves for landing, Doc and Ida had been building the decoy, three Gremlin antimissile missiles. The first was rebuilt to broadcast a radar echo like the *Cienfuegos*. The second was modified to provide an extremely eccentric evasion pattern, and the third was to provide diversionary launches, much as the *Cienfuegos* would under direct attack.

Finally the entire team stood around the three welded missiles, deep in the cargo hold of the ship.

"Pretty," Sten said. "But will it work?"

"Who the hell will ever find out?" Bet said. "If it does, we're fine. If it doesn't . . ."

She turned and headed for the bridge. Hugin and Munin paced solemnly behind her.

"Closing contact," the Jannisar XO reported.

The captain ignored him for a moment. He was running tactical moves through his brain—the enemy ship will (a) engage in combat . . . and be destroyed; (b) surrender . . . impossible; (c) launch a diversion and enter atmosphere.

Only possibility . . .

"ECM room," he called up. "Report readiness."

The delay was long. "Most units in readiness, Sigfehr. Interdiction system standing by, target/differ system plus/minus forty percent, blocking at full standby."

His screen broke: 32 MINUTES UNTIL INTERCEPT . . . 33 MINUTES UNTIL TARGET BREAKS ATMOSPHERE.

The crab *Cienfuegos* continued its so-far-successful scuttle.

Inside the control room, Mantis troopers were tightly strapped down—including the tigers who, isolated in their capsules, were somewhat less than happy about the state of the world. The battle was, from then on, in the hands of whatever gods still existed in the fortieth century.

Except for the tigers, all were clad in the phototrope camouflage gear of operational Mantis soldiers. They wore no badges, no indication of rank, just the black on their left collar tabs and the flat-black Mantis emblem on their right.

Three screens glowed dully—the proximity detector locked on the Jann cruiser, the main monitor on the upcoming world, whose atmosphere had already begun to show as a hazy glare, and Ida's central nav-screen.

Doc provided the needless and somewhat sadistic commentary: "Sixteen minutes until atmosphere . . . 15 minutes until the *Turnmaa* is in firing range . . . 15 minutes/fourteen minutes . . . 14.90 minutes . . . 14.30 minutes, congratulations, Ida, you've picked up a lead."

Alex broke in. The tubby three-gee-world Scotsman was

lying on his accel couch. He'd insisted that if he were going to die, he was going to die in uniform. And the others agreed.

"It wae back ae Airt...ane, b'fore the Emp'ror, even. In those days, m'ancestors wae called Highlanders, aye."

"Twelve minutes, even, and closing," Ida announced flatly.

"Now, in th' elder days, tha' Brits wae enemies. E'en tha, we Scots ran th' Empire tha had, wi'out tha' known it."

In spite of the tension, Sten got interested.

"Howinhell, Alex, can anybody run an empire without the boss knowing about it?"

"Ten minutes to atmosphere," Doc said.

"Ah 'splain thae some other time, lad. So, one braw day, there's this reg'mint ae Brit guards, aw braw an' proud in their red uniforms an' muskits. An' th' walkin' along thro' this wee glen, wi' they band playin' an' drumits crashin' an singin' and carryin' on, an' all ae sudden, they hears this shout frae th'crags abouve 'em. 'Ah'm Red Rory a' th' Glen!'

"An' th' Brit general 'e looks up th' crag, an' here's this braw enormous Highlander, wi' his kilt blowin' an' his bearskin o'er one shoulder an' aye this braw great claymore in his hand. 'E has this great flowit beard on him.

"An' yon giant, 'e shouts just again, 'Ah'm Red Rory a' th' Glen! Send oop y'best pickit man.'

"An' so the Brit gen'rl turns to his adj'tant an' says, 'Adj'tant! Send up our best man. Ah wan' tha' mon's head!'"

"Hold on the story," Ida cut in coldly. "We're on launch."

Dead silence in the control room...except for the increased panting of the lashed-down tigers.

Consider three objects, the target/goal, the pursurer, and the pursued. Seconds...now milliseconds in the light-year chase...as the *Cienfuegos* tries to hide in-atmosphere. Three factors in the equation. And then an unexpected fourth as the decoy-missile launched.

"Captain! I have a double target!"

"Hold course. Repeat, hold course. ECM room, do you have a selection?"

"Negative, captain. We have a negative...Talamein help us...all systems lost in ground-clutter."

The captain closed the com circuit. Forced down the sailor oaths that rose unasked in his regimented memory. Substituted a prayer. "May the spirit of Talamein—as seen in his only true prophet Ingild—be with us. All stations! Stand by for combat!"

The Jann cruiser suddenly looked more like a dolphin school as the Vydal close-range ship-to-ship missile stations fired. Fired, cut power, and looked around for a target.

VYDAL-OPERATOR INPUT: TARGET...NO TARGET...CLUTTER...ECHO...HAVE TARGET...TARGET...TARGET...DOUBLE TARGET...DOUBLE LAUNCH...FIRST TARGET NONACTIVE...FIRST TARGET POSSIBLE POWER...TARGET...I HAVE A TARGET...HOMING...ALL SYSTEMS HOMING...ALL OTHER UNITS SLAVE TO HOMING...HOMING...

New, the Vydal-series missiles were not the brightest missiles the Empire ever built. After twenty years' hard service, several in the less-than-adequate maintenance the warriors of the Jann used, they were no longer even what they had once been.

Most of the Vydals obediently followed the tarted-up decoy launch as it blasted into deep space. But one, more determined, more bright, or more iconoclastic than its brothers, speared flame from its drive tubes and homed on the *Cienfuegos*.

In the Jann cruiser, its operator cursed as he tried, without success, to divert the Vydal to its "proper" target. But the lone missile detonated barely 1000 meters from the *Cienfuegos* as the ship began the first white-hot skip into the atmosphere of the unknown world.

Ida had been trying to bring the *Cienfuegos*—a vehicle with the glide characteristics of an oval brick—successfully in-atmosphere for a landing, but the one kt detonation of the Vydal put paid to the plan. The *Cienfuegos* flipped, turned, spun. No problem in deep space—down was only where the McLean generators defined it—but entering a world?

The explosion crushed the *Cienfuegos'* cargo holds and flipped the crablike ship a full 180 degrees. Top-to-bottom, of course, since disaster never comes as a solitary guest, just as the *Cienfuegos* finally hit solid atmosphere.

Doc was the only being who might have found the situation humorous as the craft spun wildly out of control, beyond the skew-path Ida had plotted, beyond even a conventional dive, beyond any kind of sanity.

But Doc was not chuckling. He was, after all, seconds from death.

As were Sten and the other members of Mantis.

The ship crackled out of the skies and plunged into the upper atmosphere. Sensors sniffed wildly for surface . . . any kind of molecular surface at all.

Figures danced and swirled across the ship's computer screen and Sten shouted strings of changing numbers at Ida. Her fingers flowed across the controls, tucking in the impedimenta of the mining ship, sliding out two stubby wings. She tensed, as she felt the beginnings of atmosphere. Brought the nose down gently . . . gently . . . The ship hit the first layer of air and spun wildly.

Ida slammed on the right thruster, a short violent flare, then off again. Hit the left. And slowly brought the ship back under control. Nose in again. Just right. Slicing deeper into the air a degree at a time. Then the ship settled out, behaving like a ship again.

Sten glanced around. Bet was pale in her seat, but steady. Alex was flexing excess gees out of his muscles. And Doc had the fixed stare in his teddy-bear face that he got when he was plotting revenge on someone. Ida shot a grin over her shoulder.

"Now let's find a place to hide," Sten said.

She just nodded and turned back to the controls.

Suddenly the jet stream hit them at twice the speed of sound. On the *Cienfuegos* girders bent and groaned. Cables snapped and whipped, sparking and hissing like electric snakes.

The massive air current tossed the *Cienfuegos* again, further out of control and driving it helplessly down toward the surface of the unknown planet.

Ida cursed and fought the control board, trying not to gray out. One viewscreen flashed a possible crashlanding site, then blanked out.

Ida jammed out everything the ship had that resembled brakes, from the stubby emergency landing foil to the landing struts to the atmosphere sampling scoops.

The ship juddered and jolted as the little winglets bit into the atmosphere, and Ida punched the nose thrusters, momentarily pancaking the *Cienfuegos* into something resembling control.

A moment later the *Cienfuegos* topped the high walls of the huge volcanic crater Ida had targeted on and then was booming low over a vast lake, sonic blast hurling up waves.

Everything not fastened down hurtled forward as Ida reversed the Yukawa-drive main thrusters and went to emergency power.

A prox-detector screen advised Ida that the current landing projection would impact the *Cienfuegos* against a low clifflet rimming the lake's edge—something that Ida was quite aware of from the single remaining viewscreen.

Ida did the only thing she could and forced the *Cienfuegos* into a 10-degree nose-down attitude.

The ship plowed into the lake, slashing out a huge, watery canyon.

And Sten was back on Vulcan, running through the endless warrens after Bet, Oron, and the other Delinqs. The Socio-patrolmen were closing in on him and he shouted after his gang to turn and fight. Help him.

Something stung at him beyond dream pain and Sten was clawing his way back up into bedlam. Every alarm on the ship was howling and blinking.

Doc was standing on Sten's chest, methodically larruping him across the face with his paws. Sten blinked, then wove up to a sitting position.

The other Mantis soldiers were scrambling around the room, in the careful frenzy that is normal Mantis-emergency.

Alex was lugging gear to the open port—wrong, Sten realized, it was a gaping tear in the ship's side—and hurling it out into bright sunlight. Bet had the tigers out of their capsules and was coaxing the moderately terrified beasts out of the ship. Ida was piling up anything electronic that was vaguely portable and self-powered.

Alex lumbered over to Sten and slung him over one shoulder. With another hand he grabbed Sten's combat harness and rolled through the tear in the *Cienfuegos*' side.

Alex dumped Sten on the pile of packs and went back for another load. Sten staggered to his feet and looked at the *Cienfuegos*. The ship was broken almost in half longitudinally, and various essentials like the winglets and landing struts had disappeared into the lake mud. The *Cienfuegos* would never fly again.

Sten battled to clear the fog from his brain, trying to conjure up a list of the supplies they'd need. He stumbled toward the rent in the ship.

"Wait. We should—"

But Alex ran out with more gear then spun Sten around, turning him away. "W' should be hurrin', lad. Tha wee bugger's aboot t'blow."

Within seconds, the team was assembled, packs shouldered, and stumbling up the low clifflet.

They had barely passed over its crest when, with a rumble that echoed around the vast crater walls, the *Cienfuegos* ceased to exist save as a handful of alloy shards.

CHAPTER THREE

THE EGG-SHAPED CRATER they had crashlanded in was huge, almost seventy-five kilometers long. The lake itself filled about half of the area, even though it was obviously drying rapidly, from the "big end" of the egg toward the "point," where Ida had glimpsed a break in the crater's walls.

The ship had cashed it in about ten kilometers from the gap, leaving the team with a nice hike to clear their still muddled brains.

By now they'd taken stock of their situation, which bore a close resemblance to dismal. They'd lost almost all their gear in the wreck, including emergency protective suits and breathing apparatus. They did have their standard ration/personal gear/water filtration packs that, rumor had it, no Mantis soldier would walk across the street without.

The arms situation was equally bleak. The only weapons they'd brought out were their small willyguns, a sufficiency of the AM2 explosive tube magazines for those guns, and their combat knives.

No demo charges. No hand-launched missiles.

A slackit way f'r a mon, Alex mourned to himself. Ah dinnae ken Ah'd ever be Alex Selkirk.

"Does anyone have any plans?" Bet asked mildly as she pushed her way through a clump of reeds. "How the clot are we gonna get off this world?"

21

"Plans could be a bit easier if Ida would tell us where she committed that landing."

"Beats me," the heavyset woman growled. "If you recall, I didn't have much time for little things like navigation."

"Regardless," Bet put in. "It's all your fault."

"Why?"

"It always has to be somebody's fault," Bet explained. "Imperial Regulations."

"An' who better'n the wee pilot?"

Alex should have kept his mouth shut. It had been a very long day for Ida, and she decided the joshing was no longer funny. She turned on Alex.

"I'd push your eyes out," she said, "except it'd only take one finger, you bibing tub of—"

And Sten stepped in before tempers could in fact heat up. "Words. Just words. They don't cross klicks."

"Leave them be," Doc suggested. "At the moment, a little spilled blood would cheer me enormously."

Alex whistled suddenly. "Willna y'have a lookit this!"

They'd broken out of the reeds and were crossing an open section of terrain. Here the ground had once been covered by fine, volcanic ash, which had hardened over eons into solid rock.

Alex was pointing at a cluster of enormous footprints, bedded deeply into the rock surface. Sten followed the prints with his eyes: They came out of what must've been the lake's edge, moved about twenty meters along it, then the being who had made them stopped for a moment—the prints were deeper there. Then they turned, hesitated as if the being had looked at something, then went on, disappearing gradually.

Sten stood in one of the humanlike prints and raised an eyebrow. It was at least twice as large as his own foot.

"I hope we don't meet his cousin," he said fervently.

Ida turned her little computer on, measured the rock. She laughed and snapped it off again.

"You're safe," she said. "Those footprints are at least a million years old."

Sighs of relief all around.

"I wonder who they were?" Bet asked.

"The People of the Lake, obviously," Doc answered.

Alex gave him a suspicious look. "An' how w'ye be knowit thae, y' horrible beastie?"

Doc shrugged his furry shoulders. "What else would a being call itself if it lived on the shores of a lake this size?"

"Doc," Ida said, "if I were a gambling woman—which I am—I'd say you just outfoxed yourself. You couldn't possibly know something like that."

Everybody chortled in agreement.

Doc trudged on without comment.

The spectacle from the top of the low rise was interesting enough, Sten admitted as he frantically scrabbled the willygun off his shoulder.

First was the slow descending of the crater walls as the crater opened out to flatlands and brush.

Second were the tiny thatched knots of huts scattered around the crater's opening—possibly two or three hundred of them, clustered in knots and hidden on tree cover.

But far more significant was the solid wall of warriors. Lined up, almost shoulder to shoulder, were hundreds of beings, each nearly three meters tall. Evidently Ida was wrong and the beings that'd left the mooseprints in the rock were still alive and quite healthy.

Also hostile.

They were huge, slender creatures, with straw-colored skin like the savannah around them. They wore bright-colored robes, caught at one shoulder with elaborately carved pins.

And each was armed with a spear that towered even higher than himself.

"What was that you said about being safe, Ida?"

"I haven't been calling them very well lately, have I?"

"What do we do?" Bet asked.

"I think somebody's coming to tell us." Sten nodded in the dierction of one warrior who was advancing up the hill.

Guns came up, level.

"Put 'em down," Sten hissed. "We don't want to look threatening."

"Threatenit? Ah dinna ken who threatenit who, Ah must mention."

The being stopped about ten meters away. Closer up, he was even more formidable. His height was accented by an impossibly long, narrow face, with flowing, feathery eyebrows and hair greased high into a tan helmet shape. He was carrying a bundle of what appeared to be weapons.

The group jumped involuntarily as he hurled the bundle toward them. It dropped in front of Sten.

"/Ari!cia! /Ari!cia!" the being shouted, pointing at a low grove of trees lining one side of the hill.

"What's he want, Doc?" Sten asked.

Doc shook his head.

"Except for the fact that he is speaking a heavy glottal-stop language, I haven't the faintest idea."

"/Ari!cia!" the being shouted again.

Then he turned and strode back down the hill and disappeared into the trees.

"Projection," Doc theorized. "Given a primitive culture . . . warrior-herdsmen. No longer nomadic, their wars have most likely become raids and meetings of champions."

"Oh." Sten got it and walked forward. He knelt and took the weapons from their hide wrap. There was quite an assortment: one short spear; one atlatl, throwing-stick; one medium-size club; one long war spear; and one hand-shaped and polished curved chunk of hardwood. A throwing-club, Sten theorized, wondering about the open vee at one side.

"We have been challenged," Doc continued. "One of us is supposed to face him in that grove. If our champion loses, our lives shall all be forfeit.

"If we win, they will call us brothers and try to fill us with whatever mind-altering potion these primitives have been able to create." Doc preened at his own instant synthesis.

"The question is," he continued, "which one of us heroes will enter that grove? I might suggest . . ."

Guard—and Mantis officers—are trained to lead from the front. By the time Doc had begun his suggestion, Sten had already shed his combat harness, picked up the weapons, and begun sprinting down the hill toward the grove.

His sprint became a dead hurtle as Sten hit the treeline at a run as behind him he heard the eerie ululating cheers of the warriors on the savannah outside.

Brush smashed up at Sten, and he flat-dove over a bush, twisted in midair, and hit the ground in a left-shoulder roll. Ground scraping, and then knees under him and don't do that as Sten did a fast bellyskid to his right.

The air hissed and a short spear did a stomach-high death-dance in a tree where he would have been.

Sten stayed down. Diaphragm breathing. His hands running over the weapons. Trying for some kind of familiarity. He remembered something from Mantis Section's thoroughly hateful primitive weapons instructor—if you have to even think about it, troop, you're dead.

Don't think. Automatic. Listen. See. A soft breeze, carrying the scent of unknown flowers, and a soft rustle. Dead ahead, Sten thought, sweeping his head from side to side, tracking the sound of the warrior moving away from him, deeper into the grove.

Sten was on his feet, the short spear notched into the atlatl.

Move forward. Deep shadows became masses of vines and ancient tree roots. Silence became the rustling of small animals and insect buzzings.

Half crouched, Sten moved after his challenger. Ah. A snapped twig. The warrior had waited at *that* spot.

Nothing else—and then the frantic buzz of an insect and a blur as Sten snapped back the throwing-stick, hurled, and dove away in one motion.

Sten almost felt his enemy's spear bury itself in the ground next to him. He heard a muffled yelp of pain—satisfaction, hit—and was on his feet again and plunging forward, the war club coming up to strike.

He smashed down at a tangle of brush. Nothing.

Wrong, and Sten spun behind a tree for cover.

Waiting.

If you will not come to me, he thought, and went flat, belly-crawling forward under that bush he'd clubbed. Not that far wrong—there was bruised vegetation, immense footprints in the soft soil, and a rusty smear of what he assumed was blood.

But from the amount, Sten was sure he'd done little damage. He scanned the area, looking for a sign. Grudgingly Sten had to admire his opponent. How could a creature that size disappear without a trace?

Up, and slowly moving deeper into the grove.

"/Ari!cia!"

It was a muffled shout.

"/Ari!cia," it came again.

Sten had been listening to the shout for nearly fifteen minutes. And for at least five of those, he had been trying to figure out what to do.

He gently parted a few stems and peered out. The warrior was standing at one end of a large glade smack in the middle of the grove. A large, *well-tended* grove, where, Sten was sure, many beings had met and fought and died before. The warrior had dropped all of his weapons except for the huge, woodenlike war boomerang. He was brandishing it and yelling "/Ari!cia!" for Sten to come out to fight.

Sten had quietly circled the grove twice, trying to logic out the warrior's game. Obviously this trial by combat, or whatever it was, consisted of formalized rules: creepy-crawly through the grove and then if everyone survived that, another test in the glade. One on one, one weapon at a time. At the moment it looked like it meant they were supposed to stand out in the open and hurl boomerangs at each other.

Sten had several problems with this proposition. First off, although this was obviously a fight to the finish, he was sure that the being's many friends, relatives, and stray drinking acquaintances wouldn't be too pleased if Sten cut the warrior's head off. Sure, it was probably a great way to get invited to a drinking feast, but leaving alive afterward might be a problem. Second, there was the problem with the boomerang. Sten hefted it for the eighteenth time. He had thrown such things during primitive-weapons training, but they were all built for beings pretty much Sten's size, give or take a quarter meter or so. This weapon, on the other hand, was built for three-meter-high beings. Sten could barely pick it up, much less throw it in his enemy's general direction.

Sten ran his troubles through his mind a few more times. And kept on coming up with the same answer. He grunted and walked out onto the glade.

The warrior spotted him instantly and the shouting stopped. What could only be an enormous grin split his face. To Sten it looked like it might be a relieved grin, as if the warrior had been worried that Sten wouldn't be much of a contest.

The warrior went into a crouch, holding the boomerang edge-on in front of him. Sten, feeling like a damned fool, tried to copy the stance.

The attack came without warning. It was an explosion of motion, like a huge coiled steel cable whipping out. The throwing-club snicked out, knee-high across the grass, and Sten leaped upward, almost clawing the air to get higher. And then to his horror, he saw the boomerang slowmotion upward in a molten-edged glide. Sten was tumbling over in midjump . . . a numbing shock as something crashed into his arm and he thudded into the ground.

Sten rolled up to his feet spitting earth and grass. He checked to see where he had been hit, what was left him, and then he heard the hooting laughter of his opponent. At Sten's feet lay his own boomerang neatly splintered in two.

A slight bloom of anger as Sten realized that his enemy was laughing because Sten had nothing to throw back, as if that would have done any clotting good, and the weird duel was dead-even again.

The warrior snatched up his huge spear and came running at Sten like an enormous cat. Sten ignored his own war spear, curled his fingers, and felt the tingling response and then a coldness in his hand as the knife leaped into his waiting fingers.

He stalked across the grass, bracing for the leap and the slash as the warrior hurtled toward him. Just before the collision, the warrior spun his spear end over end and then suddenly . . . he wasn't there.

Instinctively Sten dropped flat and rolled. And in that instant of the roll, he saw the most incredible thing: The warrior had pole-vaulted over him. Sailing, sailing, like a giant heron, over Sten's body . . . hitting the ground . . . spinning and laughing back all in one motion.

Sten back-somersaulted. And again and again like some mad tumbler, leaping more than two meters with every turn.

Stop.

Forward somersault, dodging under the spear, slicing over and downward with his knife.

And the warrior was standing there, in an instant of helplessness, gaping at his half spear. Sten tackled him, trying to put all his weight into the fall, and he heard the warrior's breath woosh out, and then Sten was astride the warrior. Knees locked on each shoulder. His knife at his enemy's throat. A long hesitation.

"/Ari!cia!" Sten finally said, pressing knife against skin.

The warrior looked up at him. Panting. And then a long, slow, grin. "/Ari!cia," he gasped. "Clotting hell! You won!"

If the warrior had taken advantage of Sten's amazement, he could have killed him on the spot.

CHAPTER FOUR

"MY FRIEND, THE gourd is with you."

"Wanna 'nother drink?"

"Clot me! Am I not circumcised? Must I wail like a woman when the elder passes?"

"Gotcha. Ya wan' 'nother drink?"

Ida took a long draw off the gourd, burped, and passed the gourd to Acau/lay. It was a neat trick, since they were sitting across a fire from each other, about a meter and a half apart. But Acau/lay, Sten's former enemy, simply hiccuped, grabbed, and chugged.

Sten had to admire the being. When you are three meters high, you have a helluva drinker's reach, among other advantages. Speaking of reach, Sten plucked the jug from his new old buddy Acau/lay and took a deep swallow, passed it on, and bleared at the scene.

Prior to his present drunkeness, Sten had learned several things. To begin with, his hard-found friends were one of many tribes on this planet. They called themselves the Stra!bo. Which translated into The People of the Lake. Recalling Doc's mocking laughter over that discovery, Sten winced.

The postcombat celebration was being held in the Stra!bo tribal hall, which was a single chamber the size of a warehouse. The circular "building" was made of an enormous bush. As near as Ida could tell, the bush was a single plant, thousands of years old. As generations passed, the outer edge of the bush had expanded to its present enormous size, while the inner area died back, leaving bare ground—one huge bald spot. The Stra!bo had only to put a thatched roof in place to provide themselves a feasting hall.

The place was crowded with partying Stra!bo. Males and females all getting drunk on their thin (but highly alcoholic) grain beer and telling lies about what great warriors they were.

Acau/lay thumped Sten in the ribs and passed him a big, foul-smelling pot. Sten took it, raised it to his lips, and smothered a gag. The pot was filled with a grayish-pink matter with large globules of stringy red floating and bubbling about.

"The drink of life," Acau/lay said by way of encouragement.

Sten contemplated his own life and liver, then sipped. The smell and flavor hit him like a missile.

"Thanks," Sten croaked to Acau/lay, and passed the pot to Doc, who looked at him with pleading in his eyes.

For a moment Sten almost sympathized. Then he remembered the mocking laughter and gave Doc a grin. "Delicious," he said.

Doc suppressed a shudder and drank. And a remarkable thing happened: For the first time since they'd met, Sten saw Doc beam. Beam without benefit of tragedy or gore. Doc took another gulp. Nem!i, the Stra!bo chieftain, almost had to rip the pot away to enjoy his own "drink of life."

"What is that stuff?" Sten whispered.

"Blood and milk," Doc said with unseemly satisfaction. Then he smacked his lips.

"You're . . . smapsolute . . . I mean . . . absoluteshly . . . Clot it. You're right. It's delushhious."

Doc burped and grabbed the pot back from his host, Nem!i. Guzzled the vile mixture down.

Sten was in awe. Doc was drunk. From the blood. Then he understood. As one of evolution's most perfect carnivores, Doc was in butcher's heaven. The blood was hitting him like 200-proof alcohol.

"Sm-watch schmiling at you . . . foul hu . . . hu . . . human?"

Doc glared at Sten and turned to Nem!i. Patted him on the knee with a tiny paw.

"Ya' know," Doc said, "you're not too . . . uh . . . bad . . . for a life-form. Now gimme that pot back."

* * *

"Aye, and it must be a lone life y' be livint, lass. Herdin' thae bloody great coos, wi' nae boot the wind in y'r ear ae company."

Alex placed a sympathetic hand on the tawny knee of Di!n, one of the Stra!bo women. She patted his hand back, her palm engulfing even one of Alex's huge meat hooks. She was thanking him for his understanding.

"What is a woman to do?" she asked. "Hour after hour staring at the buttocks of beasts. Once in a doublemoon I get to practice my javelin throwing on a hungry Tsar-cat . . ."

She drank deeply. Wiped away a tear. She lowered her voice to a soft whisper.

"But I have dreams," she said.

Alex smiled, moved closer.

"You promise you will not laugh if I tell you?"

Alex nodded a solemn promise. Fingers tracing the knee a little higher.

"I dream that somewhere, someplace, there is a strong and handsome enemy. An enemy just for me. Who will love me and I can love in the killing."

She gave Alex a deep soulful look. Alex slowly pulled his hand away.

"Do you think," she began, then: "No. I could never ask. I am still an unblooded warrior. How could a man like you . . ."

Alex tried to be kind.

"Nae, lass, it cannae be. Ahm beit sorry, but we must be friends noo. Nae more."

Di!n sighed a maidenly sigh of disappointment, belched, and passed the gourd back to Alex to drink.

"Fascinating," Bet said. "Fascinating."

She politely covered a yawn. It wasn't just the beer, although beer had always made Bet sleepy. It was the beer plus her companion, Acau/lay.

The warrior Sten had defeated was the tribe's champion. And as champion, it was also his duty to be the Stra!bo historian. Just then he was giving Bet a thrust-by-parry account of the tribe's beginnings.

The history of Stra!bo was its wars. Normally there was nothing Bet liked better than war stories. But some time ago, the Stra!bo and the other tribes had realized that the millennia of slaughter had to stop. Still, there remained the problem of how young warriors could be blooded, to become adult men and women. Thus the creation of the highly formalized champion-against-champion combat.

The ritual, Bet guessed, had begun about two hundred thousand years ago. And Acau/lay knew the details of each combat. It was a strange kind of a Jacob begat whomever history.

". . . And then in the year of the burning grass," Acau/lay droned on, "Mein!ers slew Cal/icut and there was a great feasting. . . . In the following year, Ch!intu slew the Stra!bo champion, Shhun!te, and there was a great mourning . . ."

Bet glanced over at Sten for possible help, then cursed to herself. He was pointedly staying out of it, drunkenly babbling to the chief.

". . . And in the year of the rains, the Trader's champion . . ."

Bet came wide awake.

"Traders?" she asked. "What traders? And when?"

Acau/lay was delighted at her sudden display of interest. He had at one point begun to suspect his guest was bored, but on reflection dismissed the thought for the silliness it was.

"Just traders," he said. "Beings like you. It was—perhaps five hundred combats ago. Our champion defeated theirs. We exchanged many presents, and they left.

"Let me see now, I think their champion's name was—"

"Never mind that," Bet broke in. "Do the traders still come?"

"Of course," Acau/lay said with some surprise. "They come very regularly. Are we not friends? Do friends not wish to visit often and exchange gifts?"

"How often do they visit?"

"About every thirty days. In fact, they were here not long ago."

Acau/lay took a slurp from the gourd. "We thought you were their rivals."

Bet jabbed Sten.

"These . . . traders," Sten asked carefully. "Different, you say." He hiccuped. "Are you sure they aren't just from another part of this world?"

"Could I, Nem!i, chief of all the Stra!bo"—he belched—"become that confused?"

"Drinkin' this yak-pee," Bet said, "easily." Acau/lay had already passed out beside her.

"Do herdsmen have gray rafts that float in the air instead of the water? Do herdsmen have their huts shaped like fish, that can also fly through the air?"

"Offworlders," Sten said with satisfaction.

"And will you take us to these traders?" Bet asked. She sounded almost sober.

"For my new friends, who have been blooded by the rites of the Stra!bo . . . tomorrow or the next feast day I will send you, accompanied by my best warriors."

"We thank you, chief," Sten said, realizing he was starting to sound about as formally drunk as Nem!i.

"It is, I must say," the old chief wheezed, "a long and hard journey of some thirty risings and settings of the sun."

"Nem!i, what're the hazards that . . ."

Bet stopped. Nem!i had sagged gently against Sten and started snoring. Sten and Bet looked at each other. Bet shrugged and picked up another gourd.

"Well," Bet said, "I guess we'll be able to get off this . . . charming world and not have to spend the rest of our days drinking blood and pushing calcium critters around. So shall we follow the example of the noble Nem!i?"

"Why not," Sten said, and took the gourd. It seemed as good an idea as any other.

CHAPTER FIVE

STEN CAME AWAKE to the glare of an evil, yellow sun that was hurling spears through the cracks of the hut. He moaned gently and shut his eyes.

His head felt like a thousand—no, two thousand—ungulates had hooved through his brain, then paused to graze and defecate on his tongue.

Someone stirred next to him.

"I think I'm gonna die," he said, holding his eyes tightly shut.

"You are," Ida answered.

"Shut up, Ida. I'm not kidding."

"Neither am I. We're all gonna die."

Sten came fully awake. Sat up and stared through bloody eyes at the rest of the group already up and glooming around the sleeping hut.

"For once," Bet said, "Ida isn't exaggerating. We've got some kind of bug. And it's gonna kill us in about . . ."

"Twenty days," Ida said.

"Clot on that," Alex said. "At the moment Ah need a wee bit of the dog that gnawed the dirty Campbell if Ah'm gonna see the end of this day."

Sten ignored this. "Would you mind explaining what's going on?"

Ida flicked her hand scanner on Medic-probe and gave it to

33

Sten. He peered at the tiny screen. And found another creature staring back at him with DNA hate in its single-glowing protein eye.

The Bug, as Bet had called it, was a rippling blue ribbon with the thinnest of green edges to mark the boundaries of its form. Spotted about its perimeter were tiny, bright red dots, like so many gun nests.

"What the clot is is?"

"Some kind of a mycoplasm," Ida said. "Note, it is a cell, but it has no cell walls. It's probably the oldest life-form in the Galaxy. It's mean, lean, and hungry. And we've been breathing in millions of them since we landed. Interesting that mycoplasms do occur in areas of volcanic activity."

"I'm not interested in its lifestyle, Ida. What about our own?"

"Like I said, Sten, twenty days."

"No prophylaxis?"

"None—except getting offworld."

"Twenty days," Bet mused. "Which puts us ten days short of the traders' post."

Sten rubbed his head, which was moving from the gong solo to the tympani section of the program, then looked back up at his equally gloomy friends.

"Fine news. Now what else can go wrong?"

And above them the air split open with a blinding shriek. The hut shook, and a cloud of insects from the thatched roof floated down about them.

Sten and the others ran outside, to see the Jann ship scuttling across the sky.

Alex turned to Sten, smiling oddly. "Y'beit tha luckiest lad Ah'm knowit," he said, then pointed up at the *Turnmaa* as it climbed, then banked back toward the Stra!bo village, braked, and settled for a landing.

"If die we mus', tha wee beastie'll hae to stàn' in line."

CHAPTER SIX

"IN THE NAME OF TALAMEIN WE DEMAND THAT YOU
DELIVER UP THE OFFWORLDERS."

The Jannisar captain's voice boomed across the savannah,
drowning out even the chants of a thousand warriors drawn up
before his ship.

A forest of spears shook back in defiance.

"It's bloody foolishness," Alex said.

Sten, Alex, and the others were hiding in a small grove of
trees watching the confrontation.

Sten had to admire the Janns' efficiency. They were very
well trained soldiers. The ship had landed. Before the dust of
the ship's landing had a chance to settle, the Janns had swarmed
out, dug in, sandbagged, and set up their squad automatic
projectile weapons.

On the ship itself, the top-turret chain-gun moved back and
forth, tracing the line of warriors.

It reminded Sten of the volcanic mycoplasm hunting in their
veins. The mycoplasm with its hateful DNA swinging back
and forth, waiting for the pounce.

"IN THE NAME OF TALAMEIN . . ."

"We can't let this happen," Bet said, rising to her feet. The
others—even Doc—rose with her. Sten started out of the trees
first.

And then they heard Acau/lay's cry for combat.

35

"/ARI!CIA!"
"/ARI!CIA!"

Acau/lay stepped away from the crowd and stalked toward the ship. He was carrying the bundle of weapons—a gift for the enemy he would slay with love in the grove.

"/ARI!CIA!" He cried again. Coming to a stop in front of the waving turret of the chain-gun.

"S'BE'T," the Jann captain's voice boomed back.

Acau/lay hurled the bundle of weapons down on the ground. Drew back, pointing at the grove of trees and urging the ritual combat.

"/ARI!CIA!"
"/Ari!. . ."

And the chain-gun boomed out. Cutting off Acau/lay's final cry to fight. The projectiles stitched across him, literally cutting him in half.

As one body, the warriors hurled themselves forward, and all the Jann guns opened up instantly, cutting and spewing fire. Before the Mantis team could move, a hundred Stra!bo were dying on the ground and the others were fleeing.

In a crazy moment, Bet remembered Acau/lay telling her of the Stra!bo pride. In their two-million-year history they had never broke and run.

The tear-runnels had dried, but still marked Nem!i's cheek-bones. He and Alex lay below the crest of the low hill over-looking the Jann cruiser.

"If these men are beyond custom, then they are beyond the law," the alien whispered.

"Y'ken right," Alex said. "Ae Ah said b'fore, they're naught better'n ae scum a' Campbells."

Sten lay on the hilltop, binoc-lenses carefully shielded from reflection, staring down at the cruiser.

"If they do not have the law, then we cannot surrender our friends to them," Nem!i continued his careful analysis. He was still deeply shocked by Acau/lay's murder. "So this will mean . . ."

Sten clicked the binocs off and back-slithered down the hill beside them. He'd overheard the last of Nem!i's whisper.

"This will mean," he interrupted flatly, "that at night's fall we kill them. We kill them all."

As the sun was occulted by the crater wall, an exterior speaker crackled:

"Evening stand-to. All bow. Talamein, we thank thee for thy recognition of our might. We thank thee for our strength as Jannisars and for proclaiming our duty on this world of unbelievers."

There was no movement around the cruiser as the black-uniformed troops listened to the prayer, except the endless, automatic sweep of the chain-gun's turret atop the ship.

"We thank you in advance," the captain's voice rasped on, "for the boon which you will grant us on the morrow as our due for pursuing these unknown raiders. S'be't."

The soldiers moved quietly into their nightwatch positions.

"Why did your Sten not pick one of us, one of the Stra!bo, to begin the attack?" Di!n asked furiously.

Bet deliberately kept stroking Hugin, even though both tigers had been given their instructions and should have been on their way. Ida didn't volunteer, either.

"Because Sten respects your customs," she finally improvised. She picked herself up and eyed the ranked formation of Stra!bo warriors, hidden deep in the battle grove.

"Knowing little of your laws, he felt that perhaps his methods—the methods of our team—might violate your customs."

Di!n grunted in satisfaction. She returned to the endless stropping of her spearblade on the leather strap curled around her fingers.

Bet looked down at the tiger. "Munin. Hugin. The cattle. Now."

The tigers spun and bounced off into the gathering dusk, bounding deeper into the grassland that led out of the crater.

Ah, nae ye're bonnie wee boys, Alex thought, watching the five-man Jann patrol approach the clump of brush he was flattened in,

Ye hae not jus' the wee perimeter laddies, but rovin' patrols goin' to an' fro throughou' the night.

Aye, an' here they come. Point mon, all alert an' strikit...patrol leader...aye, two weapons mons, an' th' wee tailgate.

C'mon, laddies. Alex's waitin'.

The patrol crept through the now almost total blackness past his clump of brush. Kilgour shouldered out of his weapons harness. Waiting.

Eyes awa' fr'm 'em, he needlessly reminded himself. Dinna

be lookin'... ah, they be passin'. Pass on, pass on horseman, his mind misquoted.

The patrol, moving at a well-trained slowstep, silently passed the clump.

And Alex came up and fell into step behind them.

Step an' step an' y'ken we're in rhythm... an' now comin' up behind yon laddie...

Alex's enormous fist, three-gee-world muscles bunched behind it, smashed into the back of the rearguard's neck. The Jann dropped without a sound. Alex caught him, eased him to the ground.

There was no sound. The patrol eased forward, and Alex continued his creep.

Nae, these twa'll be linked by th' weapons belt. A nit tricket if y'can solve it. His fist went flat at belt level, flashed forward, into the base of the fourth man's spine.

He contorted, back broken, and fell. Alex pivoted around the falling corpse and sideslammed one meaty paw into the base of the third man's neck. Then swore to himself as the loosely held squad weapon crashed to the ground from the dying man's shoulder.

The Jann noncom had time to whirl and start his weapon up, finger coming back on the trigger. Alex one-handed the weapon away, the barrel cracking, and his open palm went straight into the man's throat.

Gettin' a wee sloppy, m'boy. Cartilage crackle and a gurgle, his mind reprimanded as Alex flat-dove forward. Hit the ground in what looked like a curled bellyflop as the point man heard his noncom's deathrattle, came around, and Alex was rolling, his legs thrashing, and the man came crashing down, his weapon flying a meter away.

The pointman scrabbled for a knife, and Alex, now moving almost slowly, brought his knee up and then crashing down into the man's ribcage. He heard the dull sound of ribs crunching, and the Jann contorted and was dead.

Alex held, flat. Waiting. Nothing. Up on his hands and knees, and looked back down the path.

Y'mum'd be proud, lad. Five for five. Ah, well. Roll on demob.

And Alex went back down the path to wait for the attack to begin.

* * *

Nem!i had never seen so small a being run so fast. He and Doc had taken position about one kilometer outside the crater's mouth, deep in the grasslands. Between them and the craters, the Stra!bo cattle moved leisurely toward the corrals.

Doc was crashing through what was to him a jungle of grasslands, holding a heavy—again for him—bag of powder carefully to one side.

The ripped corner of the bag was trickling powder onto the ground. Doc looked up, saw that he was parallel with the crater's far wall, turned, and—still at a dead heat—dashed back toward the Stra!bo chief.

Came to a halt. The small bear and the tall chief looked soberly at each other.

"A being such as yourself deserves the highest respect," Nem!i said soberly. "To these eyes, you were an elder advisor to your youths. But now to find that you are yourself still a warrior, in spite of your advancing years. And that your body can still function, even though you are as fond as I of feasting—it is an amazing sight."

Doc ground his sharp little teeth and wished that the Empire hadn't done such a good job of conditioning him out of killing people who thought well of him.

"I thank you, Nem!i," he managed. "Your pleasure can only be exceeded by mine, when I see you personally lead the charge against the black ship."

Nem!i shook his head sadly. "I am afraid not, my friend. Men of my age are fit only for the mopping up and to congratulate the young warriors after their success. I will not be able to seek battle this night."

Doc swore six words Alex had taught him and touched the toggle switch.

And the powder caught, flashing high into the night. The tinder-dry grasslands roared into life, and, almost instantly, the two-kilometer arc of savannah outside the crater was a crescent-inferno, burning straight into the crater.

The cattle caught the scent of the flames and lowed nervously. Their amble became a trot. Behind them was wildfire—a prairie firestorm.

Burning brands flew high into the night, and the fire began overleaping itself, almost burning itself out.

A blazing clump of bushes landed on one emasculate bellwether's back. He howled in dismay and broke into a gallop.

The panic spread, and the ground thundered as the herds of the Stra!bo stampeded directly toward the crater's mouth.

Hugin yowled nervously across the crater gap. Educated and mutated he may have been, but part of his tiger genes remembered what happened when large cats stood in the way of buffalo herds.

Munin coughed back, comfortingly. Then squatted and urinated. Hugin, too, followed orders.

The herd was just beginning to turn, unable to channel into the narrow crater pass, when the lead animals caught the scent of urine. What little ideas they had vanished in the acrid smoke and the scent of a hunting animal.

Hugin and Munin had not only channeled the stampede into the crater but almost doubled the stampede's drive forward.

Into the crater.

Directly toward the Jann cruiser.

The Jann com center was a confusion of gabble:

"Negative observation on firestart"..."Alpha patrol, this is base. Alpha patrol, do you receive this station?"..."In the name of Talamein, stop them!"..."All stations...all stations to General Quarters"...and then a long, blood-chilling shriek from one speaker.

The shriek came from the lone Jann soldier on observation point as the charging cattle broke through the savannah and reached his position. He held the trigger back to full automatic on his projectile weapon, and three animals rolled and were swallowed up as the rest of the herd boiled over the Jann.

The cattle thundered on. Even though they had heard the rush of the charge, the men in the weapons pits outside the floodlit glare had little time. To a man, they died under the axe-sharp hooves of the herd.

The Jann cruiser was barely twenty meters ahead of them. There was no way or time for them to turn.

Sten, crouched high in one tree in the grove closest to the cruiser, didn't even have time to finish his flashed-curio equation:

To calculate the changes in velocity of a body (the *Turnmaa*) when a certain force is applied (stampeding cattle), the formula is—clottin' hell!

That solid black wave of cattle hit the equally solid Jann cruiser . . . and the stampede kept on coming.

And like a wave, it crested higher as animal dove over dead animal into the cruiser.

Fifty meters away, Sten could hear the alarms roar inside the cruiser.

The huge ship tottered on its landing jacks . . . rocked . . . and one small phalanx of animals slammed into it.

The Jann cruiser rolled, jack supports bending and snapping, and crashed to the ground.

Sten could feel the smash, even over the rolling thunder of the stampede.

Which was . . . just below him.

And, of course, the animals broke neatly, dividing around the trees, and continued their panic run off into the blackness.

Sten dropped out of the tree and hurtled toward the cruiser, clambered over the dead and dying animals, just as the *Turnmaa* settled on one side. The weapons in the top turrets were parallel to the ground.

Sten's willygun came off his shoulder, and he scrabbled up the cruiser's side, feeling a fingernail tear and break away. The turret hummed into life, just as Sten shoved his willygun's muzzle into the shrouding around the chain-gun's barrels.

He yanked the trigger all the way back and held it.

The willygun contained 1400 rounds. Each "bullet," while barely 1mm in diameter, was made of Antimatter Two, the same substance used to drive starships. Each "bullet" was in its individual Imperium shield, and laser-fired.

One round, on impact, would have about the same explosive force as a twentieth-century handgrenade.

It took twenty rounds to sledgehammer through the shrouding, into the turret's inside. And then:

Picture liquid dynamite exploding. Picture the heart of a fusion reactor, *sans* lethal radiation.

The picture of hell.

Sten let 500 rounds whisper/and/crash into the turret, then dove straight down, as the explosion boiled up, spraying the steel of the turret out the gun mounting.

Sten tuck-rolled in midair, then thunked down on a fairly convenient steer. He whirled as footsteps thudded up and:

"Ah tol' you there be naught ae useful like ae coo," Alex said, helping him onto his feet.

And then the world turned into chaos as:

Di!n, Bet, and the Stra!bo warriors roared out of the darkness; Hugin and Munin, seemingly enjoying themselves immensely, loped out to join the Lake People's charge; Doc panted up, muttering unintelligibly, and . . .

Ida was standing beside them, her willygun spitting out measured bursts as Jann warriors tried to retake the turret, and:

"Ah'm Red Rory a' th' Coos," Alex bellowed, and leaped straight up the cruiser's side. Caught hold of some ripped hull plate and dove into the hole where that turret had been.

Sten, somehow, was right beside him, and then they were inside.

Flashing moments of red gore:

Di!n, a fixed smile on her face, as she slowly spitted a Jann officer against a bulkhead;

The whistle of spears wailing down a long corridor into a knot of panicked Jann troops;

Alex ripping a compartment door off its dogs and spinning it into squad weapon as its gunner tugged uselessly at a jammed tripod;

Ida calmly snapping shots as a platoon of Jann, assembled in one hold, maneuvered forward;

Bet, on the back of not particularly pleased Hugin, Munin soaring ahead of her, smashing down three Jann.

And then silence.

The red fog faded, and Sten looked around.

They were in the ship's control room. Bodies were scattered across the room, and blood seemed to trickle everywhere.

On one side, a handful of Stra!bo warriors, spears ready. The cats. The Mantis troopers. Sten.

And, his back to the semicircular main control panel, the Jann captain.

In full uniform.

"Talamein spoke against us," the captain said. "We have not found favor in his eyes."

Sten didn't answer, just walked toward him.

"You are the leader of this rabble?" the captain asked.

He took Sten's silence for assent.

"Then it is only right and fitting," the captain said, slowly drawing the saber at his side. "I shall fight a warrior worthy of my stature."

Sten considered. Suddenly Di!n was beside him, pressing a spear into his hand. She nodded—yes. You.

Sten hefted the spear, then dropped it, and, in one motion, lifted his willygun and fired twice.

The rounds caught the captain in the head, splattering his skull back across the twin view panels.

Sten turned away, holstering the gun. Nem!i was looking shocked, and then his expression cleared. He smiled.

"Ah," he said gently. "For Acau/lay. You do understand our culture."

"Is it gonna lift, Ida?" Bet asked, slightly worried.

"Of course it is," the Rom woman snorted. "So we've got half the ship sealed against leaks, we're taking off with no landing gear, there's a bad fuel leak, and I haven't had a bath in a week."

"No problem for a lass like you," Alex agreed.

Her thunder somewhat stolen, Ida snorted and hit keys. Maneuver drive belched, hiccuped, snorted, and the *Turnmaa's* nose lifted.

"Now, as long as I can keep this computer from realizing what I'm doing . . ."

And she slammed both drive pots full forward.

Somehow both Yukawa drive units caught at once, and the *Turnmaa* clawed its way upward, searing the ground as the ship lifted for space.

Below it, only a handful of the Stra!bo were watching. They'd buried their dead, held their feast, and life went on.

Di!n, at the head of her phalanx, watched the *Turnmaa* flame upward and out of sight, silently thinking her own thoughts for many minutes after the last wisps of exhaust floated away and became indistinguishable from the clouds.

BOOK TWO

GARDE

CHAPTER SEVEN

THE MAN IN the river appeared to be in his mid-thirties. His long fishing rod was bent in an almost complete half-circle and the near-invisible line sang out from the reel almost to the growling rapids a few dozen meters upriver.

The man was muttering a steady stream of curses, half under his breath—curses and almost-prayers.

"Run on me again like that, y'clottin' guppy, and I'll turn you loose. Come on, salmon. Come on back down. Come on."

Suddenly the salmon broke water, a silver arc flashing in the gray spring sunlight, and came downriver.

The curses doubled as the man touched the wind button on his reel, one thumb held on the reel itself to prevent over-winding.

The meter-long fish torpedoed directly at the fisherman, and he stepped hastily back, swayed as his rib-booted foot slipped on a rock and he almost went under.

Then the salmon was past him and running again.

He flipped the reel switch and now let line run out, braking with an already seared thumb on the line.

Mahoney cut the power on the combat car and it dropped gently to the moss-covered ground. He stepped out of the wind-screened sledge and eyed the grove of soaring redwoods with extreme skepticism. Perfectly safe, the logical side of his mind said. The other side, the side that had kept him alive on half a thousand primitive worlds, insisted there be ghosties and ghoulies and four-pawed critters with appetites inside.

As usual, he listened to that part of his mind and fished a combat harness from the back of the seat, slid the shoulderstraps on, and buckled the belt. On it hung a mini-willygun, a grenade pouch, and his combat knife.

"So if I'm wrong I'll feel like a clottin' fool," he subvocalized, and grabbed the small daypack from the floor of the car.

Looking cautiously about him, he paced very deliberately forward into the trees.

And, quite suddenly, standing in front of him was a small, bowlegged, muscular man wearing the mottled brown uniform of a guardsman and a rakishly-tilted bellman's cap with a chinstrap. The soldier's willygun was slung across his back.

Held in his right hand, at a forty-five-degree port-arms, was a fourteen-inch-long knife that looked like a machete, but its blade flared to double its size at the tip. The soldier's left hand held, almost caressingly, the back of the knife.

"Lieutenant-Colonel Ian Mahoney. Mercury Corps. On His Imperial Majesty's service," Mahoney said, being very careful not to move, trying to remember when and why he'd had himself hypnoconditioned to speak Gurkhali.

The soldier was perfectly motionless. Very cautiously Mahoney extended his right hand, palm down.

The guard took his left hand from the knife and unclipped his remote sender. Half-stepped forward and ran the computer's pickup over the back of Mahoney's wrist.

The computer read the implant and fed it back to the guard company's watch-computer. A beat, and then one light glowed green.

The Gurkha stepped back and brought his kukri to the salute. Mahoney returned it and walked deeper into the woods.

He was very, very glad there hadn't been a glitch—he'd once been permitted to attend the praetorian unit's birthday and seen one soldier, no taller than the meter-and-a-half trooper who'd challenged Mahoney, lop a bullock's head off with one stroke, using the long ceremonial knife.

He half grinned, remembering the drunk that had followed the religious ceremonies and the blessing of the unit's weapons. Tradition. How long, he wondered, had the short mountain men from Earth's Nepal served as soldiers? Perhaps, he thought, longer than even the Eternal Emperor.

And then the roar of the river was loud in his ears, and he stepped through the scrub bush and stood looking down the sloping bank at the fisherman.

It was quite a sight. The man had the rod held high and horsed back. The salmon writhed in the rolling water around the man's knees.

"Ah, if I had one more hand... get in here, you clottin' fish."

The problem, Mahoney decided, was that the fish wouldn't fit the landing net the fisherman held in his other hand. The fisherman turned the chill air a little bluer, dropped the net to dangle from its waist-strap, pulled from his back pocket something Mahoney thought was remarkably like a sap, and smacked the fish.

The salmon convulsed and went limp.

"That's all you needed," the fisherman said with satisfaction. "A priest to administer the last rights."

He swung the creel from his back, opened the top, and started to stuff the overlength fish into it.

"Nice to see a man happy at his work," Mahoney said dryly.

The fisherman froze, then turned and eyed Mahoney with a very cold eye.

"Is that any way to speak to me?"

Mahoney ceremoniously doffed his beret and knelt. "You are of course correct. Accept my most humble apologies, and allow me simultaneously to apologize for disturbing your vacation and to greet His Imperial Majesty, the Eternal Emperor Lord of Half the Universe and All Its Worshipful People, including that half-dead aquatic in your purse."

The Eternal Emperor snorted and began wading toward the bank.

"I have always appreciated," Mahoney went on, "serving a man who, in spite of his position, appreciates the simple pleasures of life."

The Emperor stopped dead in the calf-deep water.

"Simple, you clottin' idiot? Do you know what this clottin' salmon cost me? Three hundred years, you oaf. First I must convince Earth's government that granting me a small vacation spot would in no way interfere with their local half-wit ancestral policies."

He clambered out of the river and began walking toward the campsite.

"Next I purchase from the province of Oregon the whole clottin' Umpqua River. Then I purchase the towns up and down the river and relocate each and every yahoo to the world of his choice with a proper pension.

"Then I spend several million credits cleaning up the pollution and programming these clottin' fish to swim up it to lay their clottin' eggs.

"Nah. Do not give me a simple."

Mahoney followed the Emperor, smiling to himself. It was obvious the Emperor was having an excellent vacation. He hoped he'd be as happy once he finished Sten's report.

It was quite a campsite. A low, staked-down vee-tent almost into the bushes. A half-decayed log had been muscled up to a flat boulder. Stones had been piled nearby to form a three-sided fireplace.

Other than that, there were no signs that the Emperor had been camping in this spot for more than fifty years.

In the fireplace was tinder under a teepee-shaped collection of wood that went from twigs to some fairly sizable logs. The Eternal Emperor walked out of the brush, whistling softly. He was deftly bending a green sapling into a snowshoe-shaped grill. As he passed the fireplace he took out a disposable firestick, fired it, and pitched it at the wood. It roared into a four-foot pillar of flame.

"See that, Colonel? Good firebuilding. Woodsy lore and about half a gallon of petroleum. Now we wait for the fire to burn down, and I clean this here monster."

Mahoney watched curiously as the Emperor took out a small knife and deftly cut the fish from below its gills to venthole. He carried the fish guts into the brush, then walked over to the riverbank to wash the now degutted salmon.

"Why don't you have one of the Gurkhas do that, sir?" Mahoney wondered.

"You'll never make a fisherman, Colonel, if you ask that question." Almost without a beat: "Well?"

"The rumors were right," Mahoney said, suddenly sober.

"Drakh!" the Emperor swore as his hands, seemingly moving with their own will, slit the salmon down its back and split it neatly into two halves.

"The samples the Mantis team procured from the Eryx Cluster match, according to preliminary analysis, all the capabilities of Imperium-X."

"You can ruin a man's first vacation in ten years, you know, Colonel."

"It's worse. Not only is this X-mineral able to replace Imperium-X for shielding purposes, but it evidently occurs in close to a free state. Of the four worlds surveyed by my team, this X-mineral is present on at least three of them."

"I hear the sounds of a gold rush," the Emperor muttered. "And I'm starting to feel like John Sutter."

"Pardon, sir?"

"Never mind. More of the history you refuse to learn."

"Yessir. You want the capper?"

"Go ahead. By the way . . . did you bring a bottle?"

Mahoney nodded glumly. He fished a bottle of what the Emperor had synthesized and dubbed scotch from the pack and set it on the boulder between them.

"Too good," the Emperor said. "We'll start on mine."

He walked to his tent and came back with a glassine jar full of a mildly brownish liquid. Mahoney looked at it suspiciously. One of the problems of being the Emperor's head of Secret Intelligence—Mercury Corps—and his confidant/aide/assassin was being subjected to the Imperial tastes for the primitive. Remembering a concoction called "chili," he shuddered.

"They called this 'shine," the Emperor explained. "Triple-distilled, which was easy. Run through the radiator of something those hillpeople called a fifty-three Chevy, which I never bothered finding out about. Then aged in a carbonized barrel for at least a day or so. Try it. It's an experience."

Mahoney lifted the jar. He figured the less the taste, the better off he'd be, and poured a straight gurgle down his throat.

He realized he'd never noticed that the river was a nova and that he seemed to be standing in the middle of the fireplace. But somehow he didn't drop the jar. Eyes watering, seeing double, he still managed to pass it to the Emperor.

"I see you're wearing a gun," the Emperor said sympathetically "Would you mind holding it on me while I have a drink?" Mahoney was still gasping as the Emperor chugged a moderate portion.

"Continue, Colonel, with your report. You are planning to stay for dinner, aren't you?"

Mahoney nodded. The Emperor smiled—he *did* hate to eat

alone, and his Gurkha bodyguards preferred their far simpler diet of rice, dhal, and soyasteak.

"I ran a computer project, sir," he went on. "We can supress the existence of this X-mineral for perhaps two, possibly three E-years maximum. And at that time every footloose wanderer and entrepreneur in the Galaxy will start for the Eryx Region to make his fortune."

"As I said, a gold rush," the Emperor murmured. He was busy dressing the fish. He'd picked a handful of berries from a bush on the outskirts of the clearing and a small clump of leaves from each of two bushes nearby.

"Juniper berries—they grow wild here; two local spices, basil and thyme, that I planted twenty years ago," he explained. He rubbed berry juices on both sides of the split salmon, then crushed the leaves and did the same.

Mahoney continued with his report. "Per your orders, sir, I instructed my Mantis team to take the most direct way back from the Eryx regions toward Prime World."

"Of course—that'll be the route all my eager miners'll follow if word gets out."

"The plot led through the Lupus Cluster," Mahoney said.

"What the hell is that?"

"A few hundred suns, planets . . . mostly inhabited . . . back of beyond."

"Inhabited by whom, might I ask?" the Emperor said.

"My team's ship got jumped by one of your majesty's ex-cruisers. The *Turnmaa*."

"Are they all right?" the Emperor asked tersely. All pretense of casualness was gone.

"They're fine. The cruiser starting shooting, my team put down on some primitive world. The *Turnmaa* came after them. So they took the ship. Two hundred dead black-uniformed crewmen later, they came home in the *Turnmaa*."

"Hostile group of boys and girls you breed over there in Mantis," the Emperor said, relaxing. "Any idea why these baddies jumped my ship? It was supposed to look like a tramp miner, wasn't it?"

"They started out by screaming In the Name of Talamein," Mahoney said, as usual preferring the indirect explanation.

The Emperor slumped down on the log. "The Talamein! I thought I put a stake through their heart ten generations ago!"

*   *   *

No psychohistorian has ever been able to explain why, throughout human history, waves of false messiahs come and go. Never one at a time. Witness, for example, the dozens of saviors, from 20 B.C. until A.D. 60, who gave the Romans a rough road to go.

A similar wave had swept the Galaxy some four hundred years previously. Since the Emperor knew that a culture must be allowed religious freedom, he could do little until a particular messiah would decide he was the Entity's final fruition and declare a jihad. Until then, all the Emperor could do was try to keep the peace and endure.

There was much to endure.

Such as the Messiah of Endymion VI, who decided that all women on the planet were his sole property and all the men were unnecessary. The first item of interest is that the entire male population, believers all plus or minus a few quickly sworded atheists, suicided. Even more interesting is that the Messiah was impotent.

There was an entire solar system that believed, like the early Christian Manichees, that all matter, including themselves, was evil and to be destroyed. The Emperor never learned how they managed to blackmarket a planetbuster nor how they managed to launch it into their sun, producing both a solar flare and a sudden end to the movement.

A dozen or so messiahs preached genocide against their immediate neighbors, but were easily handled by the Guard once they off-planeted.

The messiah of one movement took a fairly conventional monotheism system, added engineering jargon, and converted several planetary systems. The Emperor had worried about that one a bit—until the messiah absconded to one of the Imperial play-worlds with the movement's treasury.

One messiah decided Nirvana was a long ways off, so his world purchased several of the old monster liners, linked them together, and headed for Nirvana. Since their plot showed Nirvana to be somewhere around the edge of the universe, the Emperor quit worrying about them, too.

And then there was the faith of Talamein. Founded in reaction to a theology in decay, a young warrior named Talamein preached purity, dedication of life to the Entity's purpose, and putting to the sword anyone who chose not to believe as he did.

The old religion and the new were at gunpoint when the

Emperor stepped in. He offered the Talameins and their Prophet enough transport to find themselves a system of their own. Overjoyed, the warrior faith had accepted, boarded ships, and disappeared from mortal man's consciousness.

The Emperor was fairly proud of his "humanitarian" decision. He had interceded not because he particularly cared who would win the civil war but because he knew that (a) the old, worn-out theocracy would be destroyed, (b) the people of Talamein would have themselves close to a full cluster as a power-base, and (c) that faith would inevitably explode out into the Galaxy.

The last thing the Eternal Emperor needed, he knew, was a young, virile religion that would ultimately find the Emperor and his mercantile Empire unnecessary. The result would be intragalactic war and the inevitable destruction of both sides.

Not only did the Emperor defuse the situation, but he also guaranteed that if the faith of Talamein survived, he would always be thought of as Being on Their Side.

All this the Emperor remembered. But, being a polite man, he listened to Mahoney's historical briefing.

"More fish, Colonel?"

Mahoney burn-cured a slight case of the hiccups with a shot from their second jar then shook his head.

After the birchwood fire'd burned down to coals, the Emperor had put the salmon on the sapling grill. He'd left it for a few minutes, then quickly splashed corn liquor on the skin-side and skillfully flipped the slabs of fish over. The fire flared and charred the skin, and then the Emperor had extracted the fish. Mahoney couldn't remember when he'd eaten anything better.

"So the people of Talamein ended up in this—this Lupus Cluster," the Emperor said.

He smiled to himself, remembering that when he had picked out the system for the young fanatics, a court wag had translated it "The Wolf Worlds." How appropriate, he thought, thinking of the attack on his Mantis team.

"Then, following them, it seems as if every renegade, degenerate, and bandit warlord in their sector headed for the Lupus Cluster and sanctuary because they, of course, were True Believers in the Faith of Talamein all along."

"Tell me more," the Emperor said. "I'm morbidly fascinated on how much worse things can be."

* * *

Things were, indeed, much worse.

About 150 years before, the Faith of Talamein itself had split, conveniently ending with the Talamein A people on one side of the roughly double-crescent-shaped cluster, the Talamein B fanatics on the other.

Talamein A had the "True Prophet," the man who claimed the most direct descent from Talamein himself. But this "original" faith deteriorated into opulence, schismatic politics and a succession of less-than-prescient Prophets. This not only split the faithful, but the real power came to rest with a merchant council.

The council was made up of most of the baronial trading families, who were more than willing to provide leadership in the confusion. Each family, of course, secretly felt that the council was only temporary, until it managed to seize full power for itself.

So this "True Prophet" of Talamein A was indeed a figurehead, but was also the only thing keeping one crescent of the Lupus Cluster from absolute anarchy.

On the other side were the "renegades" of Talamein B, who had vowed a return to the purity of their original warrior faith. Purists need proctors, so the "False" Prophet of Talamein B had created a ruling class of warrior-priests. Black-uniformed, they publicly eschewed worldly goods though their bleak fortresses were known to "store" many "for the common good." Such were the Jannisars. The Jann had needed barely one generation to become the rulers of the people of Talamein B.

"So on one side," the Emperor said, "we have these merchant princes. The top man is..."

"A rogue named Parral. He currently heads the council."

"His Prophet is?"

"Theodomir. When he was young he massacred a few lots of disbelievers then settled down to his real interests, which seem to be bribes, antiquarian art, and the martyrs of the faith. Sanctus—the homeworld and the capital—is sometimes called the City of Tombs."

"Who's the Jannisars' Prophet?"

"A killer named Ingild. Among other things, my agents report, he's addicted to narcotics."

The Emperor put both hands to his temples and rubbed slowly, thinking.

"Our analysis—"

"Enough, Colonel Mahoney," and suddenly the Eternal Emperor was cold sober and his voice shifted into the metallic command tone.

"Here is your analysis," he said. "First, there is no way to mine this X-mineral without the word getting out. Second, when word *does* seep out, all those rich-miners-to-be will move straight through the Lupus Cluster. Third, either the merchants will turn privateer or the Jann will become bandits. Fourth, there will be a monstrous slaughter of those rushing to the gold fields. Open the scotch, Colonel."

Mahoney passed the Emperor the bottle.

"Fifth, the bloodbath will force me to send in the Guard— to keep the spaceways open and all that drivel. Sixth, it will be interpreted as the Eternal Emperor's violating his most sacred word and supressing a religion. Here, have a drink.

"Sixth—no, I did that. Seventh, before word of this discovery gets out, the entire Lupus Cluster must be under the control of one entity. By the way, does Theodomir the Vacillating have much longer to go?"

"He's probably got another one hundred years under him, boss," Mahoney said. "His main heir's named Mathias. About thirty years old. Thinks religion and politics don't mix. Unmarried. Lives a pure life. Thinks the faith of Talamein is sacred."

"Uh-oh," the Emperor murmured.

"Nope. He thinks the faith of Talamein is for the vastnesses—he did say that, 'cause I can't pronounce that word— and so he's got a small troop of young men. They spend their time in manly sports, hunting animals, fasting, retreats, and so forth."

"Mmm." The Emperor was deep in thought again.

"What's the problem, boss?"

"I can't remember whether I was on seven or eight."

"Eight. I think. Can I have the bottle?"

"Royalty has its privileges," the Eternal Emperor said, swallowing twice before he handed the jug to Mahoney.

"Eighth, we want the cluster controlled by one entity, but one that's . . . amenable to reason. Which means he'll listen to me without my having to send in the Guard. Nine, these Jannisars are impossible. No way am I going to be able to keep a bunch of thug priests under control."

"Uh, you're saying you want ol' Theo to come out on top?"

"Not at all. I want somebody on his side to come out winners."

"Anybody in particular?"

The Emperor shrugged. "Hell if I care. You pick a winner, Colonel."

Mahoney felt himself sobering up. "Obviously this is to be a deniable operation?"

"Brilliant, Colonel. Of course I don't want the hand of the Emperor to be seen meddling in a cluster's private politics."

Mahoney chose to ignore the sarcasm. "That means Mantis."

"By the way," the Emperor said, neatly plucking the bottle from between Mahoney's feet. "That team that took the samples?"

"Yessir. Team Thirteen. Lieutenant Sten commanding."

"Sten?"

"He's handled some difficult assignments for us in the past, sir."

"Give him a couple of medals, or something," the Emperor said.

"Or something," Mahoney said.

"Any decision, Colonel?" the Emperor asked. "Before we get thoroughly drunk—which Mantis unit do you intend to use?"

Mahoney took the bottle back and drained it. Oddly, when he was drinking or angry, he spoke with the faint whisper of what used to be called a brogue. "Could I be troublin' you for some of your 'shine, Emperor? And in answerin' your question, indeed, I think I have just the lad in mind."

CHAPTER EIGHT

IT TOOK A while for Sten to hunt down the rest of his team members to let them know he was being detached. They'd scattered across the Guard's Intoxication and Intercourse world as completely as they could.

Bet, true to their agreement, had gone her own way— picking up a hunting guide and disappearing into the outback with Hugin and Munin. Sten had given her the message briefly, over a com in Mantis voice-code, then gotten clear. He wasn't sure he was that sophisticated yet.

Ida had been easy; she'd been comfortably ensconced in a casino, trying to see if her beat-the-game system would bankrupt the casino before the officials threw her out.

Doc had disappeared into the wilds of the recworld's only university and was finally located growling contentedly at anthropology fiches in the media center. Before him was a flask of Stra!bo blood-milk drink that he'd conned a slightly revolted Guard tech to put together for him.

Detached service wasn't unusual for Mantis soldiers. But this was the first time it had happened to Team 13 and to Sten. But the Emperor orders, and man can but obey.

Sten was feeling a little homesick-in-advance and he was puzzled about how one man could accomplish what Mahoney had ordered. Meanwhile he was scouring bibshops. He knew he would find Kilgour in one of them.

He heard Alex before he saw him, as the voice boomed out the screen opening of the shop. "So the adj'tant sae 'Sah,' an' dispatchit thae best Brit sol'jer, who fixit his bay'nit . . ."

"What's a clottin' bayonet?" another voice asked.

"Y'dinnae need to know. Jus' keepit silent an' list'n. So this braw Brit sol'jer goes chargint opp yon hill. An' in a wee second, his head come bumpit, bumpit, bumpit back down.

"An' then yon giant skreekit e'em louder, 'Ah'm Red Rory ae th' Glen! Send opp your best squad!'

"Ah the Brit gen'ral, who's turnit purple, sae, 'Adj'tant! Ah wan' that mon's head! Send opp y'best squad.' An' th' adj'tant sae 'Sah!' an' opp go thae regiment's best fightin' squad.'"

And Sten, wondering if he'd ever hear the end of the Red Rory saga, walked into the bar.

Alex saw him, read the expression, and grunted to the two totally swacked guardsmen who were pinned against the wall by the table. "Ah gie y' a wee bit more ed'cation some other time. Be on wi' ye, lads."

He pulled back the table, and, relieved, the two guardsmen stumbled away. Sten slid into an empty chair.

"Gie me th' worst, lad. An kin handl't."

And Sten repeated Mahoney's briefing, the anti-tap pak on his belt turned up to high.

"Ah wae wrong! Ah noo can handl't," Alex moaned. He was even too depressed to order more quill.

"Whae m'mither sae i' she findit out Ah been cashier't frae th' Guard?"

"It's just a cover, dammit. Your mother'll never hear."

"Y'dinnae ken m'mither." Alex groaned. "Ah whae y'be't, lad, if Ah'm a busted-out Guards RSM?"

"Obvious. I would like you to meet ex-Captain Sten, Third Guards, decorated, wounded, mentioned in dispatches, and cashiered for committing nameless atrocities."

Alex groaned again, brought a paw out in what Sten thought would be mock-salute, and turned into a grab for Sten's mug.

"Ah knewit, Ah should'a stayed Laird Kilgour." He sighed.

CHAPTER NINE

ACCORDING TO CHURCH dogma, Talamein had ordered his fleet of émigrés to set down on Sanctus because a vision told him that the water-world was particularly blessed by the spirit of the cosmos.

Actually, Talamein had diverted for the first E-normal world that swam onto the scopes since he was faced with near-mutiny and his people were developing a moderate case of the cobblies.

Sanctus had one major city—the City of Tombs—a few minor fishing villages, one minor port, and hundreds of villages. Its population was composed of those in the theocracy, those who exploited the pilgrims to the World of Talamein, and peasants—fisherfolk or farmers.

And Sten.

He shifted uncomfortably on the stone bench and massaged the stiff place in his neck. A cold breath of air needled his spine. The Prophet's guardsman eyed Sten just as coldly as the breeze caressing his spine. Sten grinned at him and the guard turned away.

He had been sitting on that bench for three hours, but patience was a virtue learned quickly on Sanctus. Especially in the City of Tombs, with its drab bureaucratic priests, massive monuments to the long-dead, and ghostly cold spots.

Not exactly soft duty, Mahoney, Sten thought, looking around the ancient anteroom in pure boredom. Like everything else in the City of Tombs, it was constructed of yellowing stone that had once been white. The chamber was enormous, decorated here and there with chiseled faces, gilded statuary, and elaborate tapestries.

And the room was thick with the scent of incense.

But like everything else on Sanctus, everything in the room was worn and threadbare. The tapestry had been torn and then mended, the gilded figures chipped.

Even the guard, with his ceremonial halberd and unceremonial projectile weapon, was threadbare, his uniform far from clean and patched many times.

Sten, on the other hand, wore the brown undress of the Guards division, his chest hung with the decorations he and Mahoney had decided were appropriate. Conspicuously absent was a Guards Division patch on the sleeve—but there was a dark patch where it might have been ripped off following a court-martial. He stood out in the poverty that was Sanctus.

Money was the number-one problem on the World of Talamein, far more important than the state of a being's soul. Bribery, Sten had learned, was a surer path to salvation than prayer.

Fortunately, Mahoney had supplied Sten with more than enough credits. He had already been a week on Sanctus, humbly seeking an audience with Theodomir the Prophet, but it had taken awhile to grease his way up the chain of command.

A helluva way to run a religion, Sten thought.

He had paid a last big bribe the day before to purchase a bishop. So far the bishop had kept his promises.

Sten had been ushered through the streets of the "awesome" City of Tombs, with its vast monuments and towering chimney-like torches. A few of the torches spouted huge columns of flame. They were turned on, like fiery praywheels, when the families of the very rich made their offerings for the recently departed.

To Sten, the city looked like a huge valley of factories in mourning.

Sten eased himself down the bench another half meter to escape the cold. Besides the tawdriness of the place, the cold spots were one of the first things Sten noticed. They seemed to be scattered all through the long hallways and chambers, rising strangely from seemingly solid stone. Careful, Sten warned himself, or pretty soon you'll start seeing Talamein ghosts.

He heard a *click click click* in the distance and looked up just as the guard snapped to attention. The clicking footsteps stopped for a moment, and then a huge door boomed open. And Sten rose to greet the man his bribe had bought.

"Welcome. Welcome to Sanctus."

And Mathias, son of the Prophet, strode over to greet Sten. Even though Sten had studied his fiche, Mathias' appearance was a surprise. In a world of fishbelly-pale ascetics, the tall young man had the ruddy look of an outdoorsman. He wore an unadorned red uniform that smacked more of the military than the priesthood.

And, more interestingly, he greeted Sten with the palm-out gesture of equal meeting equal.

Sten hesitated, then muttered the proper greetings, trying to get a measure of the young man, as he found himself taken by the arm and escorted down a long, dark hallway.

"My father is most anxious to meet you," Mathias said. "We have heard much of you."

Of me and my money, Sten thought a little cynically.

"Why did you not approach us straightaway? The Faith of Talamein is most ready to accommodate a man of your . . . abilities."

Sten mumbled an excuse about wanting to look around Mathias' delightful city.

"Still. You should have come direct to the palace. To me. I have been hoping to meet a man such as yourself."

It occurred to Sten that Mathias meant what he was saying and, possibly, knew nothing about how one bribed one's way into the Presence.

"I hope my father and yourself reach an—an understanding," Mathias said.

"As do I."

"Perhaps . . . if such is the case . . . you will find time to meet some of my Companions. My friends."

"That would be interesting," Sten said. Prayer meetings! The things a man must do to kick over a dictatorship.

Mathias suddenly smiled, warmly, humanly. "I suspect you are thinking my friends sit around by the hour and drone from the Book of Talamein?"

Sten looked away.

"We are familiar with the words of the Prophet. But we find our faith is . . . best realized . . . away from the cities. Trying to teach ourselves the skills that Talamein used to find freedom.

Nothing professional, of course. But perhaps you might offer us some pointers."

He stopped as they stopped at the end of the corridor, and the double doors thundered open.

And Sten found himself standing in what could only be described as a throne room. Threadbare, for sure, but a throne room just the same. Here the tapestries were much thicker and (originally) richer. And it was crammed with statuary. And at the far end, nestled in thick pillows on a huge stone chair, was Theodomir, the Prophet. Behind him was a huge vidmap of the water-world that was Sanctus. With the single island continent that was the Talamein Holy of Holies. A large ruby glow lit the location of the City of Tombs. The picture was framed by two immense torches—the cleansing symbol of the religion.

Suddenly Sten realized Mathias was no longer standing beside him. He glanced downward. The young man was on his knees, his head bowed in supplication.

"Theodomir," he intoned. "Your son greets you in the name of Talamein."

Sten hesitated, wondering if he should kneel, then settled for a courteous half bow.

"Who is that with you, Mathias?"

The Prophet's voice was thin and rasped like sawgrass.

Mathias was instantly on his feet and urging Sten forward. "Colonel Sten, father. The man we have been speaking of."

Sten blinked at the sudden promotion, then stepped toward the throne, all parade-ground military. He clicked his heels and semirelaxed into a parade-rest stance.

"A poor soldier greets you, Theodomir," Sten intoned smoothly. "And he brings a humble soldier's gift."

There were gasps around the room, and Theodomir went pale as Sten's hand went in his tunic and came out with a knife. Out of the corner of an eye he saw a guard start forward, and Sten laughed to himself, as he very carefully and very ceremoniously laid the knife at the Prophet's feet.

The knife was very valuable and very useless. It was made of precious metals and inlaid with gleaming stones. Sten glanced at Theodomir's frayed robe and wondered how quickly the Prophet would put the gift up for sale. If the fiche was correct and Theodomir's tastes were as earthly as it indicated, Sten figured it would take about an hour.

Theodomir recovered and motioned for a cupbearer to hand

him a chalice of wine. He took a long, unholy gulp and then burst into laughter.

"Oh, that's very good. Very good. Slipped it past security, did you? Through the scanners and skin search."

The laughter stopped abruptly. The Prophet turned a yellow eye at an aide cowering nearby. "Have a word with security," he said softly.

The aide bowed and scurried off.

The Prophet took another gulp of wine, then began chortling again. He turned his head to a curtain beside him and toasted the shadowy recess.

"Well, Parral. What do you think? Can we make use of our clever Colonel Sten?"

The curtain parted and a small, thin, dark-faced man stepped out. He gave Theodomir a slight bow and then turned to Sten, smiling.

"Yes," Parral said. "I think we should have a little chat."

They sat in a small, dusty library. The chairs were cracked and ancient, but quite comfortable, and the walls were lined with vidbooks. Sten couldn't help but notice that the dust lay thick on the religious works and reference texts. A few well-worn erotic titles caught his eye.

Mathias refilled their cups with wine—all except his own. The Prophet's son preferred water.

"Yes, we are indeed quite fortunate to find a man of your talents, Colonel Sten," Parral said smoothly. He took a small sip of his wine.

"But I can't help but think we might be too fortunate. By that I mean you appear, shall we say, overqualified for our remote cluster. Why is a man with talents in the Lupus Cluster?"

"Simple," Sten said, "like all things military. After I, ah, resigned from the Guard . . ."

"Ah. Perhaps cashiered would be a better word?"

"Don't be rude, Parral," Mathias snapped. "From what we've heard of the colonel's background, the Empire appears to hold in low esteem a soldier who fights to win. The details of his leaving Imperial Service are immaterial to us."

"I apologize, Colonel," Parral said. "Continue, please."

"No apologies necessary. We are, after all, both businessmen." Sten raised the glass to his lips, catching the startled looks around the room. "You are in the business of trading. I am in the business—and I mean business—of fighting."

"But what about loyalties? Don't soldiers fight for causes?" Theodomir asked.

"My loyalties are to the men who hire me. And once the contract is signed, as a businessman, I must keep my word."

He gave Parral a conspiratorial merchant-to-merchant look. "If I didn't, who would ever buy what I sell again?"

Parral laughed. A cold bark. He leaned across the table. "And what exactly do you have to sell, Colonel?"

"To you, a vastly expanded business empire. The first trading monopoly in the Lupus Cluster."

Sten turned to Theodomir. "To you, a church that is whole again."

After a moment, Theodomir smiled. "That would accomplish my grandest wish," he said dreamily.

Parral remained unconvinced. "And where is your army, Colonel?"

"Within reach."

"To topple Ingild—and to destroy the Jann—would require an enormous force."

"You have beautiful forests on Sanctus," Sten replied obliquely. "I imagine with very tall trees. Trees that die, but still stand. How much force does the woodsman need to exert to topple that tree?

"Where my force excels," Sten said, "is knowing, just as the woodsman knows, where and how to exert the proper force."

"To destroy Ingild," Theodomir whispered. "All those worlds would be mine again. That's quite a lot." He turned to Parral. "Don't you think so, Parral? Don't you think that's quite a lot indeed?"

To Theodomir's delight, Parral nodded his agreement.

"Since you come so well, ah, provisioned," Parral said dryly, "I assume you have a budget describing the costs of your operation?"

Sten took the fiche from his inside tunic and passed it to the merchant.

"Thank you, Colonel. Now, if you'll excuse us, the Prophet and I shall discuss your terms."

Sten stood up.

"Although," Parral said quickly, "I'm sure we'll have no difficulty meeting them."

"I will show you to your rooms," Mathias offered. "I assume you will be willing to move into the palace?"

Sten smiled his thanks, bowed to Theodomir, and followed

Mathias. The door had hardly closed before Theodomir poured down the rest of his wine and started worriedly pacing the room. "What do you think, Parral? What do you really think? Can we trust him?"

Parral shrugged and refilled the Prophet's glass. "It really doesn't matter," he said. "As long as we watch our backs."

"Oh, I'd love to see it," Theodomir said. "I'd love to see that idol-worshipper Ingild chased down and crushed—Do you really think we can do it? Is it worth the risk?"

"The only thing we can lose," Parral said, settling back in his seat, "are a few of my credits and the lives of his men."

"But if Sten wins—if he wins, what do we do with him?"

Parral laughed his cold laugh: "What you always do with a mercenary."

Theodomir smiled. And then he joined in the laughter. "I'll find a nice little tomb for him," he promised. "Right beside the place I'm going to put Ingild."

CHAPTER TEN

THE JANNISAR STOOD quaking by the missile launch tube. Sten could see his eyes rolling in fear above the big wad of stickiplast slapped across his mouth. His hands were bound behind him. His knees buckled and the two hulking figures on either side of him jerked him up.

The Bhor captain lumbered forward, his harness creaking in the silence. The bloodshot eyes of fifty crewmen swiveled, following him, as he paced up to the Jann and stopped. Otho peered up at his victim through the two hairy bushes the Bhor called eyebrows.

"S'be't," he mocked.

He turned to his crew and raised a huge hairy fist, holding an enormous stregghorn.

"For the beards of our mothers," he roared.

"*For the beards of our mothers*," the crewmen shouted back.

In unison, they drank from the horns. Otho wiped his meaty lips, turned to the Bhor tech waiting by the missile bay door. He raised a paw for the command and Sten could hear the Jann squeak through the stickiplast. He almost felt sorry for the poor clot, guessing what was coming next.

"By Sarla and Laraz," Otho intoned. "By Jamchyyd and ... and ... uh ..."

He looked at an aide for help.

"Kholeric," she stage-whispered.

Otho nodded his thanks. "Bad luck to leave a clotting god out," he said.

He cleared his throat, belched, and continued. "By Jamchyyd and Kholeric, we bless this voyage."

He brought his hand down, and the Bhor tech slammed the BAY OPEN switch. The doors hissed apart, and the two Bhor guards lifted the wriggling Jann prisoner into the tube. Otho roared with laughter at his struggles.

"Don't fear, little Jann," he shouted "I, Otho, will personally drink your heathen soul to hell."

The crew hooted in glee as the doors slid shut. Before Sten could even blink, the tech slammed the MISSILE FIRE switch and the ship jolted as air blasted the Jann into vacuum. He barely had time to moan before his body exploded.

The ship's metal floor thundered with the footsteps of cheering Bhor crewmen as they rushed and battled for room at the porthole to watch the gory show.

Sten fought back a gag as a smiling Otho heaved himself over to him. His breath whooshed out as the Bhor slapped him on the back, a comradely jackhammer blow.

"By my mother's beard," he said, "I love a blessing. Especially"—he thumbed toward the missile bay doors and the departed Jann—"when it's one of those scrote."

He bleared closer at a pale Sten. "Clot," he cursed at himself, "you must think me a skinny, stingy being. You need a drink."

Sten couldn't argue with that.

"It is good," Otho said, "that the old ways are dying."

He poured Sten a horn of stregg—the pepper-hot brew of the Bhor—and heaved his bulk closer.

"You won't believe this," he said, "but the Bhor were once a very primitive people."

He'd caught Sten in mid-drink, and he nearly spewed the stregg across the table. "No," Sten gasped, "I wouldn't."

"The only thing left now," Otho said, "is a bit of fun at a blessing."

He shook his huge head. Sighed. "It is the only thing we have to thank the Jann for. Before they came along and started killing us, it had been . . . in my grandfather's time that we last blessed a voyage."

"You mean, you only use Jannisars?" Sten asked.

Otho frowned, his massive forehead beetling.

"By my father's frozen buttocks," Otho protested, "who else would we use? I told you, we are a very civilized people.

"We had almost forgotten the blessing until the Jann arrived with their clotting S'be'ts. But when they slew an entire trading colony, we remembered. We clotting remembered."

He drained his horn, refilled it. "That scrote we just killed? He was one of fifteen we captured. What a treasure trove. We shared them out among the ships. And one by one we used them in the blessing. Now, I must admit a small regret. He was the last."

Sten understood completely. "I think I can solve that for you," he said quietly.

The captain belched his agreement. Pushed the jug of stregg away. "And now, my friend, we must discuss our business. We are three days out from Hawkthorn. My fleet is at your disposal. What are your orders after planetfall?"

"Wait," Sten said.

"How long?"

"I assume that the credits I have already paid will hold you for quite a while."

The Bhor raised a hand in protest. "Do not misunderstand, Colonel. I am not asking for more . . ." He rubbed thumb and hairy forefinger together in the universal gesture of money. "I am merely anxious, my friend, to get on about this business."

Sten shrugged. "A cycle at the most."

"And then you go to kill Jannisars," Otho asked.

"And then we kill Jannisars," Sten said.

Otho grabbed for the stregg again. "By my mother's beard, I like you." And he filled the horns to overflowing.

The Bhor were a wise choice in allies. If ever there was a group noted for fierce loyalties, fiercer hatreds, and the ability to keep a single bloody goal in constant sight, it was they. They were the cluster's only native people, the aborigines of a glacier world, an ice planet pockmarked with a thousand volcanic islands of thick mist and green.

In times of legend, the Bhor lived and died in these oases. Growing what little they could. Bathing in their steaming pools. And, when they became brave enough, hunting on the ice.

At first, it was really a question of who was hunting whom. No one knows what the streggan looked like in those days. But Bhor stories and epic poems describe an enormous, shambling beast that walked on two legs, was nearly as intelligent as a

Bhor, and had a gaping maw lined with row after row of infinitely replacable teeth.

Starvation drove the Bhor out on the ice. A dry professor in a room full of sleepy students would say it was merely a need for a more efficient source of protein.

Tell that to the first Bhor who peered over an ice ledge, considered the streggan crunching the bones of a hunting mate, and thought fondly of the empty—but safe—vegetable pot back home.

It must have been an awesome sight when the first Bhor made the historical decision. Compared to the streggan he would have been a tiny figure. Compared to a humanoid, however, the Bhor was solid mass. Short, with a curved spine, bowed but enormous legs, splayed feet, and a face only a "mother's beard" could love. His body was covered by thick fur. A heavy forehead, many cms thick. Bushy brows and brown eyes shot with red.

Although about only 150cms tall, the average Bhor is one meter wide—all the way down—and weighs about 130 kilograms. As far as mass equivalent, this equals the density of most heavy-worlders like Alex.

And so what the streggan was faced with was enormous strength in a small package. Plus the Bhor ability to build cold-heat-tempered tools. All the Bhor had to figure out was how to club the streggan down.

There were many mistakes. Witness the gore of early Bhor legends. But, finally, somebody got it right and the streggan became a major source of that missing protein.

There was an early error, quickly corrected. The first thing a Bhor did at a kill was to rip out the liver and devour it raw. With a streggan, the Bhor might as well have been consuming cyanide. The lethal amount of vitamin A found in a streggan liver would be double that of an Earth polar bear (also lethal) or that of a century-old haddock. Eating the liver of your enemy was the first of the Old Ways to go.

Before they could expand offworld, the Bhor first had to master the ice of their native world. With the streggan at bay, the Bhor then learned to trade. With that came the ability to kill their own kind. After all, what else was left to brag about in the drinking hall?

Unlike those of most beings, Bhor wars over the centuries were small and quickly settled into an odd sort of unity through combat.

Basic principle of Bhor religious emancipation: I got my gods, you got yours. If I get in trouble, could I borrow a couple?

When the Bhor first began expanding their "oases" by melting the glacier ice, the great cry came to "Save the Streggan." The Bhor had killed so well that their previous Grendel of enemies was nearly extinct. Today the only examples left are in Bhor zoos. They are much smaller (we think) than before, but still fierce. Enough for a Bhor mother to still use them for traditional boogey-men.

The streggan are now as much a legend as the saying "By my mother's beard." All Bhor have a great deal of facial hair to hide their receding chins. The females have slightly more than the males. In ancient times, it was a long, flowing beard for their children to cling to when mother was gathering veggies—or was faced with a shot at pure-protein streggan.

By the time the streggan were nursery legends, the Bhor had already established themselves as traders throughout the Lupus Cluster. Even though the People of Talamein—both sides—were moderately xenophobic, they knew enough to leave the Bhor alone.

As long as the Bhor kept to themselves and stayed within the trading enclaves, there was no trouble as the humans expanded through the cluster. The Bhor did not think much one way or another of most people anyway, so coexistence was possible.

Until the Jannisars decided they needed an Enemy. Which put the rogue, one-god fanatics against casually pantheistic armed trader-smugglers.

When Sten met them, the outnumbered Bhor were as headed for extinction as their old enemies, the streggan. But with no one to drink their souls to hell.

CHAPTER ELEVEN

"HAWKTHORNE CONTROL, THIS is the trader *Bhalder*. Request orbital landing clearance. Clear."

Otho closed the mike and looked over the control panel at Sten. "By my mother's beard, this be an odd world. Last time we put down here there were three different landing controls." Otho rumbled slight merriment. "And they swore great oaths that if we followed anyone else's landing plot they'd blow us out of the atmosphere.

"Enough to drive a Bhor to stregg, I tell you." He grinned huge yellow teeth at Sten. "Of course, that doesn't take much doing."

Sten had noticed.

The speaker garbled, then cleared. "Vessel *Bhalder*. Give outbound plot."

"This is the *Bhalder*. Twenty ship-days out of Lupus Cluster."

"Received. Your purpose in landing?"

"My chartermate is hiring soldiers," Otho said.

"Vessel *Bhalder*, this is Hawkthorne Control. Received. Welcome to Hawkthorne. Stand by for transmit of landing plot. Your approach pattern will be Imperial Pilot Plan 34Zulu. Caution—landing approach must be maintained. You are tracked. Transmission sent."

"And if we zig when this pilot plan says to zag," Oth grumbled, "we'll be introducing ourselves to interdiction missiles."

Even mercenaries have to have a home—or at least a hiring hall. Hawkthorne was such a "hiring hall" for this sector of the Galaxy. Here mercenaries were recruited and outfitted. Hawkthorne was also where they crept back to lick their defeats or swaggered back to celebrate their victories.

It was a fairly Earth-normal world around a G-type star. Its environment was generally subtropical.

And Hawkthorne was anarchic. A planetary government would be created by whatever mercenary horde was strongest at any given time. Then they'd be hired away and leave a vacuum for the smaller wolves to scrabble into. Other times the situation would be a complete standoff, and total anarchy would prevail.

The mercenaries hired themselves out in every grouping, from the solo insertion specialists to tac-air wings to armored battalions to infantry companies to exotically paid logistics and command specialists. The only coherence to Hawkthorne was that there wasn't any.

The *Bhalder* swung off final approach leg, Yukawa drive hissing, and the flat-bottomed, fan-bodied, tube-tailed ship settled toward the landing ground.

Weapons stations were manned—the Bhor took no chances with anyone. The landing struts slid out of the fan body, and the *Bhalder* oleo-squeaked down. A ramp lowered from the midsection, and Sten walked down, his dittybag in one hand.

A dot grew larger across the kilometer-square field and became a gravsled jitney, Alex sitting, beaming, behind the tiller.

Alex hopped out of the jitney and popped a salute. Sten realized the tubby man from Edinburgh wasn't quite sober.

"Colonel, y'll nae knowit hae glad Ah be't t'sae y', lad."

"You drank up the advance," Sten guessed.

"Thae, too. C'mon lad. Ah'll show y' tae our wee hotel. It's a magical place. Ah hae been here n'more't aye cycle, an' thae's been twa murders, aye bombin' an' any number't good clean knifint's."

Sten grinned and climbed into the gravsled.

* * *

Alex veered the sled around two infantry fighting vehicles that had debated the right of way and now blocked the dirt intersection with an armored fenderbender.

The main street of Hawkthorne's major "city" was a marvel, filled with heavy traffic, which consisted of everything from McLean-drive prime movers with hovercraft on the back to darting wheel-drive recon vehicles to a scoutship doing a weave about forty feet overhead.

The shops, of course, sold specialty items: weapons, custom-made, new or used, every conceivable death tool that wasn't under Imperial proscript (which of course meant the Guard-only willyguns, as well as some other exotica). Uniform shops. Jewelers who specialized in providing paid-off mercs with a rapidly convertible and portable way of carrying their loot and accepting on pawn whatever jewels a loser needed to hock.

And through the chaos marched, swaggered, stumbled, crawled, or just lay in a drunken babble the soldiers. All kinds, from the suited pilots to the camouflage-dressed jungle fighters to the full-dress platoons that specialized in guarding the palace.

Then Sten noticed a very clear area on one side of the street. It was a small shop, with the dirt walk neatly swept, the storefront freshly painted. The sign outside read:

JOIN THE GUARD!
THE EMPIRE NEEDS YOU!

Sten glanced in the door at the recruiting post's only occupant, a very dejected, lonely, and bored Guards sergeant, wearing his hashmarks, medals, and unhappiness for all to see.

"Ah nae understand't our Guard," Alex said, seeing Sten's gaze. "Dinnae thay ken half ae thae troopies ae deserters in the first place an' in the secon't place men whae na sane army'd hae in th' first place?"

Sten nodded glumly. Alex was quite correct—Hawkthorne was quite a place. Mahoney, Sten thought, was a jewel. Here, son. Go hire a few hundred psychopaths and crooks and topple two empires.

And see if you can't get it done before lunch. . . .

But that was the way Mantis Section worked. Sten probably wouldn't have wanted it any other way.

CHAPTER TWELVE

COMMANDOS!
200 OF THE FINEST NEEDED!
DEFEND THE FAITH OF CENTURIES!
PAY GUARANTEED

Colonel Sten, late of His Imperial Majesty's Third Guards Assault Division, is hiring 200 elite soldiers to assist in the protection of one of the Empire's most respected social and theocratic orders.

NONHUMANOID FREELANCES UNFORTUNATELY CANNOT BE CONSIDERED DUE TO ABOVE RELIGIOUS CONDITIONS

Only the Best Need Apply!

The Lupus Cluster and the Faith of Talamein is under attack by a godless and mercenary horde, attempting to invade and destroy some of this sector's most beautiful and desirable worlds, inhabited by peace-loving people. Needed individual equipment: individual weapons, cold-weather suits, space combat suits. Combatants should expect little ground leave.

A SHARP SHOCK NEEDED!

Colonel Sten, highly regarded in the Guard both for his extensive combat experience (18 major planetary assaults, numberless raids and company-size actions), is noted for having the lowest casualty rate in the Third Guards.

THOSE ACCEPTED WILL BE PROVIDED
WITH USUAL SURVIVOR'S INSURANCE
PROVEN COMBAT EXPERIENCE NECESSARY

To include covert operations, lifts, jugular raids, smash-and-grab, ambush, harassment, and diversionary. Background in following units preferred: Imperial Guards, Trader Landing Force, Tanh, some specific planetary forces allowed (please check with recruiter).

CONDITIONS OF DISCHARGE
WILL NOT BE INQUIRED INTO
Standard Contract

Individual acquisitions by proficient individuals or units will not be logged, provided point of origin is *not* from friendly forces.

Commando-qualified soldiers, individuals or units, should apply Colonel Sten, Breaker House, WH1 . . .

Sten read the onscreen ad and winced slightly.
"You wrote this?"
"Aye," Alex said, upending his half liter of quill.
"It's gone planet-wide?"
"Aye."
"You think you're pretty clottin' funny, don't you?"
"Aye," Alex agreed smugly and keyed for another drink.

CHAPTER THIRTEEN

STEN LOOKED AT the man across the bar table from him and decided he was potentially lethal. About two cms taller than Sten, a kilo or two heavier. Part of his hawkface moved stiffly— a plas reconstruction, Sten guessed.

The man probably had a hideout gun trained on Sten, under the table. And I really hope he doesn't think about using it, Sten thought, eyeing Alex, who slumped, seemingly half asleep, on a stool nearby.

"It's all what they used to call a crock, you know," the hawkfaced man said cheerfully.

Sten shrugged. "What isn't?"

"I've got seventy-eight men—"

"Seventy-two," Alex broke in, without opening his eyes. "Twa b'hospital, one kickit y'stday, three in a wee dungeon an' y' wi'out th' credits to gie 'em oot."

"Good men," the man went on, seemingly unperturbed. "All with battle experience. About half of them ex-Guards, some more used to be Tanh, and the others I trained myself. You can't ask better than that, Colonel." He carefully put quotation marks around Sten's rank.

"I'm impressed, Major Vosberh," Sten said.

"Not from the contract offer you're not," the lean mercenary officer said. "I read the fiche. Religious war. Two clottin'

77

Prophets. Council of merchants, for hell's sakes. And these—these Jannisars."

"You did understand the fiche," Sten agreed.

"And you expect me to commit my people into that maelstrom for a clotting *standard* contract?"

"I do."

"Not a chance."

Sten leaned forward. "I want your unit, Major."

"But you won't get it at those prices."

"I will. Item—you signed on for Aldebaran II; your side lost. Item—Kimqui Rising; the rebels won and you offplaneted without most of your hardware. Item—Tarvish System. They signed a truce before you got there. You're broke, Major. As my sergeant-major said, you can't even afford to bail your troopies out of jail!"

Vosberh rose slowly, one hand moving, very casually, toward his tunic button.

"Don't do that, Major," Sten went on. "Please sit down. I need your soldiers—and I need you alive to lead them."

Vosberh was startled. Sten hadn't moved.

"All right. I apologize for my temper."

Sten nodded wordlessly, and Alex got up and headed for the bar. He returned with three liter glasses. Sten sipped from one.

"Say I'm still in the market," Vosberh said, after drinking. "The job's to take out these Jannisars and their boss, right?"

Sten grunted.

"Ah," Vosberh said, interested in something he must've caught in Sten's expression. "But we'll get back to that in a minute. How do we do it? Specifically."

"I haven't chosen specific targets yet. We'll base on a planet named Nebta, which should make your troops happy."

Alex handed Vosberh a fiche, which the man pocketed.

"No major campaigns. No advisory. Assassination. Nitpick raids. No land-and-hold. Get in, get out, few casualties."

"They always say few casualties." Vosberh was starting to relax.

"Since I'll be with the landing forces, I have certain personal interest in keeping the body count low," Sten said.

"Okay. Say I take standard contract. How's it paid?"

"Half in front, to the men's accounts."

"I handle that."

Sten was indifferent.

"How's the payment handled?" Vosberh continued.

"A neutral account on Prime World."

"Prime World? What about the Empire?"

"I checked. They don't even know where Lupus Cluster is. Private war. No Imperial interests in the cluster. Believe me, I looked."

Vosberh was getting steadily friendlier. "When's the pay-off? When this Ingild gets crucified?"

"When the job's finished."

"We're back to that, aren't we? Maybe . . . maybe, Colonel-by-the-grace-of-this-Theo-character Sten has some plans of his own? Maybe when the Jann are history there'll be another target?"

Sten took a drink and stayed silent.

"A forgotten cluster," Vosberh mused. "Antique military and a religion nobody takes seriously. This could be very interesting, Colonel."

He drained his glass, stood, and extended a hand. Sten stood with him.

"We accept contract, Colonel." Sten shook his hand, and Vosberh was suddenly, rigidly, at attention. He saluted. Sten returned the salute.

"Sergeant Kilgour will provide you with expense money. You and your unit will provide yourselves with all necessary personal weapons and equipment and stand by to offplanet not later than ten standard days from this date."

CHAPTER FOURTEEN

STEN LOWERED THE binocs and turned to Alex, more than a little puzzled.

"If this Major Ffillips is the clottin' great sneaky-peeky leader you say she is, how in the clot did she get herself this pinned down?"

"Weel," Alex said, thoughtfully scratching his chin, "yon wee major makit ae slight error. The lass assumit whan sh' nae pay h' taxes, th' baddies'd show up, roll a few roun's, an' then thae'd g'wan aboot thae bus'ness. Sh' reckit wrong."

Sten gaped. "You mean those tanks down there . . . are tax collectors?"

"Aye," Alex said.

Below the hillock they lay on was a wide, dusty valley. At one end the valley narrowed into a tight canyon mouth, barely twenty meters wide.

In the valley were ten or fifteen dozen infantry attack vehicles—laser- and rocket-armed, five-meter-long tracks, each carefully dug in. In front of them were infantry emplacements and, Sten's binocs had told him, a very elaborate electronic security perimeter.

"Taxes ae Hawkthorne," Alex continued, "be't a wee complex. Seems ae mon whae sayit he be th' gov'mint—if he hae enow firepower to backit hae claim, well, tha' be what he be."

"So when this instant ruler asked for credits, Ffillips told him to put the tax bill where a laser don't shine, and then they put her under seige?"

"Aye, yon Ffillips 'raps is a wee shortsighted ee her thrift," Alex agreed.

"And all we have to do is break through the perimeter, get inside that canyon, convince Ffillips that we can pull her tail out, and then break the siege?"

Alex yawned. "Piece ae cake, tha."

Sten took out a cammie face-spray and wished desperately that he'd been able to bring two sets of the Mantis phototropic camouflage uniforms with him.

"What Ffillips dinnae ken we knowit," Alex mentioned, "is tha twa weeks ago, sappers infiltrated her wee p'rimeter an' blew her waterwells to hoot."

Sten eyed the tubby man from Edinburgh and wished, for possibly the ten thousandth time, that he wouldn't hold *all* the intelligence until the last minute.

A piece of darkness moved slightly and suddenly became Sten, face darkened, wearing a black, tight-fitting coverall. Behind him slipped Alex.

In front of them were the manned and the electronic perimeters. They'd passed the emplaced tracks easily—armor soldiers traditionally believe in the comforts of home. Which means when night comes they put on minimal security, electronic if possible, button up all the hatches, turn on the inside lights, and crack the synthalk.

Sten and Alex had moved forward of the armor units walking openly, as if they belonged to the tax-collecting unit.

The manned post to their left front was no problem. The two men behind the crew-served weapon were staring straight ahead. Of course there was no need to watch their rear.

The problem was the electronics.

Sten dropped flat as his probing eyes caught an electronic relay point. He moved his hand forward, closed his eyes, and finger-read the unit. Clot me, he thought in astonishment. This thing's so old it's still got transistors, I think!

Alex passed him the Stealthbox. Sten touched it to the relay and the box clicked twice. Then a touchplate on the stealthbox warmed, signaling to Sten's hand that the relay would now send OK OK OK NEGATIVE INTRUSION even if a track ran over it. The two men crawled on.

Sten and Alex were barely fifteen meters in front of the

manned position when, without warning, a flare blossomed in the night sky.

Freeze . . . freeze . . . move your face slowly away . . . down in the dirt . . . wait . . . and hope those two troopies back in the hole aren't crosshairing on your back.

Blackness as the flare died and crawl on.

The second line of electronics was slightly more sophisticated. If Sten and Alex didn't need to crawl back out, it would have been simple to put a couple of "ghosts" into that circuitry, so that the perimeter warning board would suddenly show everything attacking, including Attila's Hordes.

Instead Sten took a tiny powerdriver from his waistbelt and gently—one turn at a time—backed off a perimeter sensor's access plate. The stealthbox had already told him there were no antishutdown sensors inside.

Sten set the access plate down on the sand and held one hand back. Alex gingerly fished a very dead desert rodent from his pouch and passed it to Sten. Sten shoved the tiny corpse nose-first into the sensor. That sensor flashed once and went defunct.

Sten then carefully bent the access plate to appear as if the rodent had somehow wormed its way inside. He reinstalled the plate on the box and all looked normal again.

As they crawled past the now-dead electronic line, Alex suddenly tugged at Sten's ankle.

Sten froze, waiting.

Alex slithered past him and sabotaged a second, independent-circuit alarm. Then he swept the area in front of it with his stealthbox. Finally he took a small plastic cup from his pouch and positioned it, open end down, over the pickups for a landmine trigger.

Sten glanced at him. Alex yawned ostentatiously and waved Sten onward.

"I agree, Major," Sten said politely. "You and your force would be a valuable addition. I've never had the chance to operate with three-man commando teams and I'd like to see them in action."

Ffillips was a short, muscular woman with ramrod military posture. She was middle-aged, with silvery hair as immaculate as her uniform. She had cold, assessing eyes that warmed now as she boasted about her troops.

"Trained 'em myself," Ffillips said proudly. "Took the best

I could find from the planetary armies. Gave them pride in themselves. Taught 'em to look like soldiers. And, I tell you frankly, without bragging, they're very damned good. Think of 'em like my own children, I do. I'm like a mother to them."

Ffillips' people did look pretty good, Sten had to admit, even though he and Alex had been able to penetrate the canyon and infiltrate Ffillips' camp without being challenged. Sten's mild egotism was that there wasn't another soldier in the Galaxy who could see a Mantis soldier until the knife went between the third and fourth ribs. Sten was probably right.

The canyon opened up into a broad, green, high-walled valley. Caves dotted the cliff walls, and there had been possibly half a dozen natural artesian wells in the valley.

Ffillips' troopers, broken down into their three-man (or -woman) squads, were strategically positioned. Antitrack positions lined the canyon and the high walls probably had dug-in antiaircraft positions.

And the valley was now completely dark, from the fighting positions to Ffillips' own headquarters-mess cave. Good light discipline.

Since no track or soldier could attack down that narrow canyon, Ffillips' mercs could have held the position for a century, assuming they weren't hit with nukes or human wave assaults.

Except that their wells had been destroyed.

Ffillips finished reading the contract by hand-cupped penlight and shook her head.

"I think not, Colonel. Frankly, I could not, in all conscience, offer my young men and women an offer as penurious as this one."

Sten shrugged and looked around the cave. He saw a fist-sized boulder, picked it up, and walked over to a nearby well.

He let go, and they all heard the echoing thuds of the rock as it clattered down into dryness. Sten walked back and sat down across from Ffillips. Alex was looking very interestedly at one canyon wall, trying to keep from laughing.

Finally the silver-haired woman said, with obvious reluctance, "Lift the siege for us. Then give us three days to resupply."

Sten smiled.

Sten's first analysis was that mercenaries work for pay, or for beloved/feared/respected leaders, or possibly even for idealism. Ho. Ho. Ho. None of the latter two applied to these tax collectors.

Second analysis, as he and Alex crouched in the brush behind the "tax collector's" headquarters, was that no matter how high they promoted him, he better never get so lazy, luxury-loving, and sloppy.

The setup was pretty plush. Five tracks, which should've been on line, were semicircled in front of the headquarters. The headquarters unit was three com tracks, two soft-skinned computer vehicles, one security-monitor half-track, and one extended-base track that was the unit leader's quarters.

Most of the tracks had their rear ramps dropped, and light gleamed through the small camp. What perimeter human guards there were had been positioned well within the light circle, so Sten knew they'd be night-blind.

Sten kicked Alex's outstretched foot. "Time to take the palace, Sergeant." Alex rolled to his feet, and the two cat-footed forward toward the headquarters.

Sten was within two meters of the first guard when he was spotted. The man's projectile weapon came off his shoulder—on his clottin' shoulder!—to somewhere between present and port arms.

"Halt." Bored challenge.

Sten didn't answer.

Simultaneous: guard realizing two men were coming in on him/his weapon coming down/hand toward trigger/Sten inside his guard.

Very smoothly . . . step in . . . right hand back, left forward. Hipsnap and Sten's cupped right hand shot forward. It crashed into the sentry's chin, and his head snapped back. The man was probably dead, but Sten continued the attack, one sidestep and the edge of the hand straight across the man's larynx. Catch the body and ease it to the ground.

And then they were both running.

Alex rolled a fire-grenade into the security-monitor half-track, flat-dove as another sentry fired a burst into his own camp, rounds whining off armor, and was back on his feet just as an alarmed tech peered out of one of the computer vehicles, saw Alex, and yanked the door closed.

Alex's fingers grabbed the door, centimeters from slamming, and three-gee muscles yanked. The door *skrawked* completely off its hinges and went spinning away.

One of the techs inside was grabbing for a pistol. Alex one-handed a console through the air at him. It crunched the man's chest, and he sprawled, blood spurting and shortcircuiting the main computer. Lights flashed and then the inside of the vehicle was plunged into darkness.

"Cask? Cask?" The other tech's terrified whisper.

Ah, wee lad, Alex thought. M'moon's in benev'lence, an' Ah lie y' t'livit.

And he was out the door, moving toward the second vehicle. He picked up its ramp and slammed it sideways into the track's now-clamped-shut door. Door and ramp gave way at the same time. Bullets seared out, and Alex flattened to one side.

Ah c'd use m'willygun ae thae very moment, he thought, and then saw what looked like a hydraulic jack nearby. Alex rolled to it, took the meter-long handle in both hands, and twisted. The handle, only half-inch mild steel, snapped off cleanly.

Alex rose to his feet, hefted the handle, then hurled it through the vehicle's door. Followed it with a thermite grenade. A howl gurgled down and then sparks began flashing and Alex could see flames crackle.

He picked himself up, dusted his knees, and looked around for something else to demolish. The headquarters was in chaos— it seemed as if everyone was shooting. But not at Alex.

Since panic spreads, the line units opened up. Alex wondered idly what they thought they were shooting at, then wandered over to see if Sten needed any help.

He didn't.

Alex started to enter the command track, then checked himself. "Ah'm wee Alex a' th' Pacifists," he said softly.

Sten chuckled and emerged from his lurking place just inside the track's entrance. He wiped his knife-blade clean and slid the knife back into his arm.

The two men stood, slightly awed by the high explosive and pyrotechnics on the plain around them.

"C'mon, laddie. Thae clowns'll be ae it a' night, an' Ah'm thinkit Ah buy y' a wee brew."

And, as silently as they came, Sten and Alex disappeared back into the night.

"Ah dinnae like to tell the wee laddie no," Alex explained.

"PREEEEE-SENT . . . HARMS!"

And the ragged formation of beings brought their weapons up. At least those that had them did.

"Aw," Alex said, entranced, "ae likit ae wave an' all."

"You," Sten said, "have even a lousier sense of humor than Mahoney."

"HIN . . . SPECTION . . . HARMS!" A bucket-of-bolts clatter as the assembled hopeful mercenaries snapped their bolt-carriers open. The young man wearing captain's bars, khaki pants, and a blue tunic managed a salute.

"Unit ready for inspection, Colonel," he said.

Sten sighed and started down the line. He stopped at the first person, who was trembling slightly. Sten snapped out a hand for the man's rifle. The prospective merc didn't let go.

"You're supposed to give it to me when I want it," Sten explained. The man released the rifle. Sten ran his little finger around the inside of the firing chamber, then wiped off traces of carbon. He glanced down the corroded barrel and gave the weapon back. Then he moved on to the next person.

The inspection took only a minute.

Sten walked back to the captain. "Thank you, Captain. You may dismiss your men."

The captain gaped at him.

"But, uh . . . Colonel . . ."

All right. He wants an explanation, Sten thought.

"Captain. Your men are not trained, are not experienced, are not combat ready. Their weapons—those they have—are ready for recycling, not for killing people. If I hired your unit, I'd be . . ."

"Like takit wee lambkins t'slaughter," Alex put in. Both Sten and the captain wondered what the hell he was talking about.

"I'm sorry, Captain," and Sten started away.

The young officer caught up with Sten, started to say something, reconsidered, then began again.

"Colonel Sten," he finally managed. "Sir, we . . . my unit . . . need this assignment. We're all from the same world, all of us. We grew up in the same area. We've used all our savings just to get here. And we've been on Hawkthorne for five cycles, and so far, well . . ." He suddenly realized that he sounded like he was begging and shut up.

"Thank you for your time, Colonel," he finished.

"Hang on a second, Captain." Sten had a thought. "You and your men are stranded, yes? Zed-credits? And nobody, justifiably, will hire you?"

The captain nodded reluctantly.

"Captain, I can't use you. But in the center of the city there is a man who can."

The man's expression grew hopeful.

"He's an old sergeant, and you'll find him at Imperial Guard Recruiting. Now, here's what he'll want to see from you . . ."

Sten ignored the boy sitting across the mess table from him and glowered at Alex.

"Another joke, Sergeant?"

"Nossir. Ah dinnae ken whae tha' lad comit frae."

The boy was about nineteen years old. About Sten's height and possibly fifty kilos in weight with an anchor tied around his ankles. Even in the daylight Sten could see the glitter of the boy's surgicorrect lenses.

"*You* want to enlist?"

"Certainly," the boy said confidently. "By the way, my name's Egan. And I'm speaking for twelve colleagues."

"Colleagues," Sten said amazedly.

"Indeed. We would like to sign on. We've read your contract and accept the terms for the duration of service."

Sten moaned to himself. It was turning out to be a very long day.

"If you read my, uh, proposal, you'd have seen that—"

"I saw that you want a hardy crop of killers. Daggers in their teeth or wherever you people carry them."

"Then why—"

Again an interruption. "Because you can't fight a war without brains."

"I assumed," Sten said, "that I could possibly provide those."

"You? Just a soldier?" It was Egan's turn to sound amazed.

"I manage."

"Manage? But you need battle analysis. You need projections. You need somebody to run logistics programming. You need somebody who can improvise any ECM system you might require. You need—Colonel, I'm sorry if I sound cocky. But you really need us."

"Not a chance. You and your friends—I assume they're like you?" Sten tried another, somewhat more polite tack. "First of all, how can I tell if you're really the brain trust you say?"

"Possibly because I know your payee account on Prime World is 000–14–765–666 CALL ACCOUNT PYTHON, account depositor one Parral, world unnamed, and your current balance, as of this morning, was $72,654,080 credits."

Very silent silence. Sten decided he was getting tired of gaping. It was time to start laughing. "Howinhell," he managed, "did you find that out? We are operating through cutout accounts."

"You see why you need us, Colonel?"

Sten didn't answer immediately. Oh, Mahoney, his mind went. Why did you put me out here by myself? I don't know what the clot kind of people you need to run a private war. So far all I've done is fake it. I wish I were back with Bet and the tigers and doing something simple like icing some dictator.

Stalling, he asked, "Egan. One question. Who are you and your friends?"

"We . . . up until recently, we were advanced students at a lycée."

"Which one?"

Egan hesitated, then blurted, "Prime World."

Both Sten and Alex looked impressed. Even soldiers knew that the Empire picked its brightest to attend the Imperial Home World Lycée.

"So what are you doing here?"

Egan looked around the mess. No one was within earshot. "We were experimenting one night. I built a pickbox—that's something you use to get inside a computer—"

"W'ken whae i' be," Alex said.

"And I guess it seemed like a good idea at the time, but somehow we ended up inside the Imperial Intelligence computer."

Sten, carefully keeping a straight face, held up a hand for silence. Egan shut up. Sten motioned to Alex. They rose and walked to the far end of the mess, both automatically checking for mikes.

"D'ye ken whae yon wee but wickit lad done? He an' his boyos got aeside Mahoney's files. Ah nae wonder wha' thae b'doint ae Hawkthorne. Espionage's good frae ae penal unit f'r life." Alex chuckled.

"What, good Alex, do you think of our Colonel Mahoney right now?"

"Ah'm thinkit h' beit puttin' us in ae world ae drakh. Ae this momit, Ah nae b'thinkit kindly ae th' boss."

"So we hire these kids?"

"Frae m'point, Sten lad, there be nae ither choice."

* * *

Computer printouts littered the room. Sten dragged a paw through his now-longish hair and wondered why the clot anybody ever wanted to be a general in the first place. He never realized how much paperwork there was before you got to say Charge!

Alex was sprawled on the couch, placidly going through a long, fan-folded report, and Egan hunched over the computer keyboard. He tapped a final series of keys and straightened.

"Ready, Colonel. All units are on standby."

"Aye," Alex agreed, tossing the logistics printout to one side and reaching for a nearby bottle.

"Sten's Stupidities," Sten said, coming to mock-attention and throwing a salute to the winds. "Ready for duty, saaah! I have two hundred who're—"

"Two hundred and one," the voice rumbled from the corner of the room.

Alex was on his feet, pistol ready, as Sten hit attack stance.

The voice shambled forward. Sten decided the man must be both the ugliest and most scarred humanoid he'd ever seen.

He held both hands up, palms forward, waist level, in the universal I-bear-no-arms symbol. Sten and Alex relaxed slightly.

"Who the drakh are you?"

The man looked down. Picture a giant, two-and-a-half meters tall, looking hunch-shouldered and shamefaced.

"Name's Kurshayne," he said. "I want to go with you."

Sten relaxed and grabbed the bottle. "We closed recruiting yesterday. Why didn't you apply then?"

"Couldn't."

"Why not?"

"I was in the clink."

"Nae problem wi thae," Alex said, trying to be friendly. "All ae us bin thae. E'en m'mither."

"But I ain't with any mob," Kurshayne said. "There weren't nobody to stand my bail."

"If you're solo, what are you doing on Hawkthorne?" Egan asked.

"Lookin' for work."

"Any experience?" Sten asked.

"I guess so," the giant answered. "I got this."

He pawed through his waistpouch, dug out a very tattered and greasy fiche, and reluctantly handed it to Sten.

Sten took it and dropped the card into the pickup. It started as a standard Guard Discharge Certificate:

THIS IS TO CERTIFY THAT THE BEARER IS
KURSHAYNE, WILLIAM
PRIVATE
TERM OF ENLISTMENT: 20 YEARS
ASSIGNMENT: FIRST GUARDS ASSAULT
MILITARY SCHOOLS: NONE
DECORATIONS AWARDED: NONE
HISTORY: 27 Planetary Assaults, First wave. 12 Relief Expeditions, 300 support assaults (TAB X1 FOR DE-TAILS), Brought up for following awards: Galactic Cross, four times; Imperial Medal, eight times; Titanium Cluster, sixteen times, Mentioned in Dispatches, once. Reduced in rank, 14 times (TAB X2 FOR DETAILS).

The fiche continued scrolling. Sten looked up at the giant with considerable awe. Four times this Kurshayne was up for the Empire's highest medal? And . . .

"Why'd you get busted fourteen times?"

"I don't get along with people."

"Why not?" Egan asked.

"Dunno, really. I guess I like 'em okay. But then—then they do things. Things that don't look right. And I gotta do something about it."

I have more than enough troubles, Sten thought, and took the man's fiche out of the pickup. He handed it back to the man.

"Kurshayne, if we weren't fully manned . . ."

"Beggin't y'r pardon, Colonel." Alex.

Sten held. Alex paced slowly around the giant.

"Ah knae ye," he said, very, very softly. "Y'r a mon whae knowit th' right, but y' dinnae ken whae thae be't betters'n y' Aye, Kurshayne, Ah knae y'ilk."

Kurshayne glowered down at the rotund sergeant.

"Nae, Ah proposit ae wee game," Alex said silkily. "Y' ken aye punch?"

"I know one punch, little man," the giant said. "Do you want to play it with me?"

"Aye. Ah do thae," Alex said.

"You go first."

"Nae, m'lad," Alex said, a grin flickering across his broad

face. "Y'be't thae applicant. Ah be't thae mon. Gie i' y'best shot."

Without warning Kurshayne swung, an air-whistling round-house punch that caught Alex in his ribs. The punch tumbled him, rolling and spinning back against the couch, the couch crashing over, and then Alex slammed flat against the wall. He lay motionless for a moment.

Then he picked himself up and came back. "Aye, tha be ae braw slug, m'lad," he said. "B'nae i' be't mae turn.

"An' Ah be't fair. Sportin', likit. Ah gie y'warnin'. Nae likit yae, wha hie me ae sucker punch ae i' y'be't ae Campbell. Nae, Ah w'hit ye, mon.

"But since Ah want ye in m'troop, Ah nae will damage y' severe't. So Ah tell y' whae Ah'll be hittint y'. Ah be strikit y' ae th' center chest. Light-like, f'r Ah nae want y' hurt."

Sten had never heard Alex's dialect so thick. Correctly, he figured Kilgour was angry. Sten decided he was sorry for what was about to happen. Illogically, he was starting to like the dumb giant.

Kurshayne braced for the punch.

Instead, Alex delicately reached forward and picked Kurshayne up with . . . clottin' hell, one hand, Sten realized . . . and lifted him clear of the ground. And then, seemingly casually, threw Kurshayne.

Two hundred kilos of Kurshayne, as if the laws of gravity had been put on hold, flew through the air. Hit the wall—two meters off the ground—and the wall went, crumbling into plas destruction in the corridor outside.

Kurshayne pinwheeled after the wall, out into the corridor. And, moving very, very fast, Alex went after him. He bent over the semiconscious relic and near whispered.

"Nae, nae, y'wee mon. Y'hae ae job, Ah reck. But y'll no playit thae game twice, Ah reck."

Kurshayne fogged his way to his feet. "Nossir."

"Ah'm nae sir. Ah'm nae but aye sergeant. Yon Sten, h'be't sir."

Kurshayne struggled into rigid attention. "Sorry, Sergeant."

"Ah ken y'be't sorry, lad," Alex crooned. "Nae, y'be't off aboot i', an' Ah wan' y'back here in ten hours, clean't up an' ready t'fight."

"Sir!"

And Kurshayne saluted and was gone. Sten and Egan were still gaping as Alex turned.

"W' noo hae 201 soldiers, Colonel Sten," he said. Then staggered to the console and snagged Sten's bottle.

"Clottin' hell!" Alex groaned. "Yon lad nie near kilt me! Th' things Ah do't frae th' Emp—th' cause!"

CHAPTER FIFTEEN

AND I HAD a great future as a cybrolathe operator, Sten thought mournfully, looking at his assembled troops. They were standing in what could only be called Parade Motley on the landing ground, just in front of the *Bhalder*.

Oh, Mahoney, I will get you, Sten groaned. There were Vosberh's troops. Unshaven, unbathed, but well armed and, Sten conceded, fairly lethal.

Beside them, giving many hostile looks, were Ffillips' commandos. Spit and polish.

There were other one or two at a time pickups and Egan's crew of studious-looking Lycée kiddics.

Why me all the time? Sten wondered.

Beside Sten were flanked Vosberh, wearing a simple brown uniform, Ffillips in her personally designed dress uniform (suspiciously close to Guards full-dress), Alex, and Kurshayne.

Kurshayne had evidently decided he was cut out to be Sten's personal bodyguard and had equipped himself with what he thought was an ideal weapon.

As far as Sten could tell, since Kurshayne refused to let anybody examine it, it was a full-auto projectile weapon, with about a one-gauge barrel.

Sten knew that no human could fire it without being destroyed by the recoil. Whether Kurshayne could do it was still a moot point.

Oh, Mahoney, Sten thought again.

Then, business. One pace forward.

"UNIT..."

"COMP'NEE...COMP'NEE..."

The shouts rang across the wind of the landing field.

"Unit commanders. Take charge of your troops. Move them into the ships.

"We're going to war!"

And then nothing but the howl of the wind and the drumbeat of bootheels.

And then nothing but Sten looking at Alex and both of them knowing why they'd chosen the profession they did.

And so, without banners, without bugles, they went off to war....

BOOK THREE

TAKING THE BLADE

CHAPTER SIXTEEN

THE JANN CITADEL hugged the plateau crest of the high, snow- and ice-covered mountain. Three sides of the mountain dropped vertically. Only the fourth featured a machine-carved road that S-snaked up toward the crest. A road with manned and electronic guardposts every few dozen meters.

The Citadel was more than just the theological center of the warrior faith/caste—it was also the training ground for all Jann cadets. And it was Sten's first target.

The Citadel had been located on a not especially welcoming world, near the tip of a northern continent. It promised, by its very appearance, monastic dedication, asceticism, and lethality—quite an apt summary of the Jann beliefs, in fact.

Sten and his 201 mercenaries had been able to insert easily, using the talents and the ground-lighters of the Bhor.

Now they lay crouched at the foot of one vertical precipice, the sheerest that Sten could pick from the vidpics aerial recon had taken. The sheerest and the least likely to be guarded, especially now.

Far above him, atop the crest, the Citadel itself sprawled on the plateau. It closely resembled a black cephalopod, with its humped center section and, finger-sprawling out from the central bulk, the four tube barracks that held the Jann cadet cells.

Lights were on in the barracks, red against the snow. And,

in Sten's mind, he could see the top of the "hump"—the massive building containing the temple itself, gymnasium, arena, and administrative offices, see its weather membranes "breathing" in and out as they adjusted and readjusted the environment within. Even from the base of the cliff, Sten could see one of the membranes, glowing yellow-red from the lights inside and gently moving in and out like a living thing.

He pushed out of his mind the fear response that the entire Citadel was a living, brooding entity—an entity one of the mercenaries had immediately dubbed "the Octopus."

Snow crunched behind Sten as Alex moved beside him. A second crunch as the ever-present Kurshayne snow-crawled up on his heels.

Sten tapped Alex on his shoulder and passed him the night glasses, then turned to check the rest of the mercenaries on the rock-strewn hillside behind him.

The 200 men and women wore white thermal coveralls and were snuggled deep into snowbanks. Sten's practiced eye could pick out a movement here and there, but only because he knew where to look. Not only were the troops white-cammied, but so were their weapons and faces.

Which is why Sten started slightly when Alex lowered the night glasses and looked at him, peering through large, white eyes. White-camo contact lenses were very hard to get used to.

Sten smiled about the obvious joke about holding your fire until you can see . . . Alex raised a questioning eyebrow over a pure white eyeball. Sten covered, smile gone. He didn't think even Alex would appreciate the joke under the circumstances.

Which were: the Citadel. A deadly octopus in profile. On top of a sheer mountain. With black spots of soft shale where even snow couldn't stick. And where it did, the rock was old and rotten. Blanketed with ice and snow. Sten wasn't worried about the crumbling rock. That he could handle. But the ice sheets were waiting, ten-meter-long razorblades.

Sten shuddered.

Alex took one more look at the kilometer-high cliff. Leaned close to his side.

"Ah dinna lovit tha heights," the heavy-worlder confessed in a whisper. "Aye lads bounce whenit tha fall. Th' Kilgours squash."

Sten chuckled and Alex whispered into his throat mike for Vosberh and Ffillips to come forward.

Expertly the two swam-crawled through the snow until they were on either side of him. Sten gave his last instructions. He was pleased when the two professionals didn't even raise an eyebrow as they saw the climb that faced them. Ffillips, however, put in a word for bonus money, and Sten shushed her.

"I want to hit them where it hurts," he reminded. "The chapel. A legitimate target. Torch it. Melt it.

"Ffillips? Your group has responsibility for the chapel. Vosberh—the barracks. They should be empty now. Blow them to hell for a diversion.

"If you see an officer—a teacher—in your way, kill him." He paused for emphasis.

"But if you can help it, don't kill any cadets."

Vosberh hissed something about baby roaches growing up to be . . .

"They're kids," Sten reminded. "And when the war's over, I'd rather face some ticked-off diplomats than angry parents, or brothers and sisters with short-range murder in their thoughts."

Vosberh and Ffillips—very much the professionals—remembered wars they had won and coups they had then lost, and agreed with Sten's reasoning.

The cadets —unless some got in their way—were not valid military targets.

There was a thump at Sten's boot. He looked back and saw Kurshayne. The man had Sten's pack of climbing gear. Sten sighed. Accepted.

"All right, you can come with me," he said.

Still, as he crawled forward to begin his climb, he felt a little bit better.

CHAPTER SEVENTEEN

IT WAS A temple of guttering torches. Deep shadows and oiled gold. A thousand young Jann voices were lifted in a slow military chant generations old. And the thousand-cadet procession moved in measured, slow-motion paces through the temple. The cadets were dressed in ebony-black uniforms, with white piping.

At the head of the procession was the color guard, carrying two heavy golden statues. One was of Talamein. The other was Ingild, the man the Janns called the True Prophet. Mathias and his father, Theodomir, would have called him many other things. True, or Prophet, even, would not be among them.

The procession was in celebration of the Jann Sammera: the Time of Killing. In Lupus Cluster history, it was a revenge raid by a small band of Jann. They hit one of the small moons off Sanctus that keep the potentially great tides in check, and slaughtered everyone. And then, trapped, they waited for the inevitable reprisal from Sanctus. When it came, there were no Jann survivors. A bloody historical note of which the Jann were immensely proud.

The procession moved through the temple, past enormous statues of Jann warriors and the flags of the many planets the Jann had converted or destroyed. The temple was the Jann holy of holies.

The cadets moved out of the temple, and huge metal doors

slid closed as the last row of men passed. Then the cadets slow-marched down a hallway so enormous that in the summer months humidity brought condensed "rain," into an equally huge dining room.

In the dining room, the color guard marched straight forward down the main aisle, toward the huge stage and podium where the black-uniformed guest of honor and the school's military faculty waited.

The others shredded off and wove black and white ribbons through the long aisles created by the dining tables set for a thousand young men who were soon to join the Jann.

As the color guard approached the stage, General Khorhea—the guest of honor—and the hundred or so faculty members rose. From the wall behind them came a *hiss* as a twenty-meter-wide flag dropped from the ceiling. It was black with a golden torch.

Gen. Khorhea raised a hand. "S'be't."

And the color guard bowed, wheeled, and then began the slow march back to the chapel. Where they would return the statues to their positions and then quietly filter back for the celebration.

General Suitan Khorea despised personal ostentation. Except for silver-threaded shoulderboards and a thin silver cord on his left arm, he wore no clues that he was the head of the Jannisars. In his prayers he reminded himself often of the line from one of the chants of Talamein—"O man, find not pride of place or being/But gather that pride onto the Glory that is Talamein/For only there is that pride other than idle mockery."

Mostly Khorea was proof that, even in a rigid theocratic dictatorship, a peasant can rise to the top. All it takes is certain talents. In Khorea's case, those talents were an absolute conviction of the Truth of Talamein; physical coordination; a lack of concern for his own safety; total ruthlessness.

Khorea had first distinguished himself as subaltern when a Jann patrol ship had stopped a small ship. Possibly it was a lost trader, more likely a smuggler.

Khorea's commander would have been content merely to kill all the men on the ship as an object lesson. But before he could issue orders, Khorea's boarding detachment had slaughtered the crew and then, to guard against accusations of profiteering, had blown up the ship.

Fanaticism such as that earned its reward—a rapid transfer by Khorea's unsettled CO to an outpost located very close to the "borders" of Ingild's side of the cluster, a transfer probably made in the hope that Khorea would make himself into a legend in somebody else's territory. Hopefully a posthumous legend.

But luck seems to select the crazy, and, in spite of the best efforts of the Janns' enemies, Khorea survived, even though he inhabited a body that looked as if a careless seamstress had practiced hemstitching on it for a few months.

In his rise, Khorea had gathered behind him a group of young Jann officers, either as fanatical or as ambitious as he was.

Eventually Khorea ended as ADC to the late General of the Jann, who one evening had confessed to Khorea that he was struggling against a certain...desire...for one of his own orderlies. Before he finished speaking, the man was dead, Khorea's dress saber buried in his chest.

Khorea faced the court-martial with equanimity. The officers on the court were trapped. Either they executed Khorea, which would make him a convenient martyr for his following, or they blessed him and...

—And there were no likely replacements to head the Jannisars.

The answer was inevitable.

Khorea returned to the court-martial room not only to find his dress saber's hilt pointing at him (point would have meant conviction), but lying beside it the shoulderbars of a Jann general.

Now the Jann priest's voice droned on. He was nearing the end of the traditional reading of the Book of the Dead, the list of the casualties of Sammera. The cadets were drawn up at attention. Except for the priest's voice, the hall was silent. Finally the priest finished and closed the ancient, black-leather-bound book.

General Khorea stepped forward, a golden chalice in his hand. He raised it high in a toast. As one, the thousand cadets wheeled to their tables and raised identical chalices high.

"To the lesson of Sammera," he roared.

"To the Killing," the cadets roared back.

The liquid in the chalices burst into flames, like so many small torches. And, in unison, Khorea and the cadets poured the flaming alcohol down their throats.

Sten craned his neck back, looking up the sheer cliff of ice that towered above him. It was a near-impossible climb and therefore, Sten reasoned, the route where the Jann were most vulnerable.

He looked at Alex and shrugged, as if to say: "It ain't gonna get any easier."

Alex held out one hand. Sten stepped into it, and the heavy-worlder lifted him straight up. Sten scrabbled for his first hand-hold, found a crack in the ice, jammed a fist into it and the spiked crampon points into the ice, and began his climb.

The most important thing, he reminded himself, was rhythm. Slow or fast, the climb had to be constant steady motion upward. After all these centuries, science had done little to improve the art of climbing. It was still mostly hands and feet and balance. Especially on ice. His eyes scanned for the next hold, so he would always know where he was going before he committed himself. If Sten trapped himself on the cliff, with no way down, in the morning, when the Jann troops found him, he would be a very embarrassed corpse.

Then he reached the first nasty part of the climb, a yawning expanse of glass-smooth ice. He looked quickly about, searching for handholds, already making his decision and digging out the piton gun.

Sten aimed the gun at the ice and pulled the trigger. Compressed air hissed as the gun fired the piton deep into the cliff face. Quickly he snapped the carabiner onto the piton, laced the incredibly lightweight climbing rope through it, and spooled the rope from his climbing harness down to Alex.

Climbing thread would have been far easier to manipulate, but it was not suitable for a main rope 203 men would have to use. Alex clipped his jumars onto the rope and slid up after Sten.

Sten set the next piton, and then another, weaving his way up the cliff. By the time he reached the end of the sheet ice, he was tiring. But he kept climbing, thankful for the massive amount of calories he'd choked down before landing.

Sten found a long, slender crack in the ice and jammed his way into and up it. He took advantage of the brief respite to suck in huge gulps of air to steady his trembling muscles. Still, he was constantly watchful, making sure that he kept his weight balanced over his feet. Behind him, he sensed Alex and Kurshayne.

And then it happened. Just as he was reaching up for the next handhold... straining... straining... one spiked boot broke through rotten ice and Sten was scrabbling for a hold and then he was falling . . . falling . . . falling. He tried to relax, waiting for the shock when the rope brought him up short of the first piton.

There was a jolt. And then a *ping* as the piton pulled out, and then he was falling again and . . . and . . . Crack. The next piton held, and Sten was slammed up against the face of the cliff.

He hung there, dangling, swaying, for a long time, momentarily numb. Then he recovered, ignoring the pain of bruised muscles and doing a quick inventory of his body parts. Nothing broken. He peered downward and saw Alex's anxious face looking up at him. Which immediately broke into a smile, when Sten flashed him a weak grin and gave him a thumbs-up sign.

Sten spun around on the rope and looked up at the cliff's mass looming over him. He took two shuddering breaths and started climbing again.

Sten chinned himself on the cliff's summit. He kept tension in his fingers and shoulder muscles so that he could finally relax most of his body and turn the problem over to his eyes and brain.

The main body of the Octopus humped up at him black and glowing in the snow. The Citadel was merely a building constructed for a purpose. But it was a live thing. It was an animal that had to do animal things. It had to eat fuel, it had to breathe, and its enormous body had to retain heat and expel cold.

The last function was the constantly moving weather membranes. Sten's way in.

Sten checked the plateau in front of him, hummocky ground rolling slightly uphill toward the Citadel. Even though it was impossible for any intruder to attack the Jann from this side of the mountain, they obviously put little faith in the impossible. The hundred meters or so of rolling ground between the cliff edge and the first building was thoroughly covered by sensor-activated guns.

The multibarreled lasers constantly swept the area, looking for movement. Sten slithered over the clifftop and snow-crawled forward, thankful, for a change, that he had hired Egan and his Lycée kids.

Sten halted just outside the first sensor's pickup point. He fingered open his pack and slid out a powerdriver and a little metal box with dangling wires and heat clips. Sten dug into the snow and found the plate that guarded the sensor control system from the elements. He hesitated at the screws that held the plate in place and reminded himself of potential boobytraps. He placed the driver's bit into the first screw and flicked the button for reverse. The first screw whirred out smoothly and Sten was alive.

He quickly removed the plate, fused in the heat clips, and then glanced at the nearest sensor guns that were "sniffing" at the night.

It was an illusion, of course. The guns didn't do anything but shoot. However, buried across the landscape were very efficient sensors that ignored the stray rodent but ordered the guns to cremate anything approximating man-size.

Sten turned the dial on the box until it told the sensor he'd just become a small furry creature, not worthy of a killing burst from the guns.

He stood up. And the guns kept searching. Ignoring him for larger game. The Lycée kids were right.

"Come on up, Alex," he said in a perfectly normal voice. He braced himself for the hiss of the guns. Nothing. And he knew again that he was safe.

Alex effortlessly lifted himself over the cliff. "Y' be takit tea oop here f'rit sae long?" Then he glanced at the scanning guns. They didn't react even to Alex's body mass. "Aye" was his only comment.

Alex turned to throat-mike the orders down to the rest of the mercenaries.

Kurshayne was the first up with all of Sten's equipment, then Egan and his Lycée crew, who moved out and began permanently defusing the sensor guns. Next came Vosberh and his boyos. As Sten walked toward the curving hump of the Citadel, he consciously shut off any worry about his troops. He had to assume they were professionals. And that everything Sten had in mind would work.

CHAPTER EIGHTEEN

KHOREA BOWED TO the Citadel Commandant and stepped to the forefront of the podium. He had prepared a speech for this graduating event. But then he felt the movement deep in his mind—a feeling that he *knew* was the spirit of Talamein.

It could have been described more prosaically as a result of alcohol drunk by a near-teetotaler, adrenaline-response, and egotism. It was, however, doubtful that any Jann psychologist would have had the temerity to do so.

Khorea forgot his prepared speech and began: "We are being tested today. Tested as we, the Jann, have never been tested before."

He looked out at the thousand before him and thought that the officers would be the most important graduates the Citadel ever produced. He also sensed that most of them would be dead in not too many months.

"It is fitting," he continued, "that while we celebrate the Killing and your acceptance as Jann I tell you of the trials that we shall face.

"Trials which we shall only overcome by strength. Our strength, the strength of our arms, our minds, and our Faith in Talamein."

The cadets stirred. The speech was quite different from what they had expected and from what they were accustomed to hearing from their cadre.

"These trials I shall now warn you of. They have been building for time. We know the babblings of the madman Theodomir. And we know how dearly he would love to destroy the flame of truth, so it could be perverted into his own ashes."

More like it. The cadets relaxed, and a few of them even smiled grimly. They were quite used to Theodomir diatribes.

"But the madman has gone beyond ravings. He has determined to try us by force of arms."

Large smiles from some of the cadets—in their final training cycle most of them had participated in raids against the poorly trained, ineffectual levies of Theodomir. Khorea understood their smiles.

"This night you will become Jann. And then you will go out to face the armies of Theodomir. But be warned—these are not the rabble you have known.

"Theodomir has chosen mercenaries. Men who have trained to the peak of killing madness in the gold-souled ranks of the Emperor of the Inner Worlds."

Khorea ceremoniously spat.

"Mercenaries. But a mercenary can fight, regardless that he defends an evil cause. This then is the trial you will face, Jann-to-be.

"At this moment Theodomir, the False Prophet, is raising an army against our peaceful worlds. An army that does not believe. An army that, if it conquers, will ensure that the Truth of Talamein and we, his servants, will cease to exist. If they win, it shall be as if we had never existed.

"Tell me, Jann-to-be—to keep that from occurring...is that not worth the Death? My death, your death—the death of every man in this room?"

Silence. And then one cadet came to his feet. Khorea automatically noted him proudly as the cadet screeched:

"Death! Long live death!"

And the cadets howled, the long, enraged howl of hunting beasts.

Sten whirled the fusion grapnel twice, then cast it straight up. The line coiled at his feet disappeared upward, into the obscuring snow, and then the head of the grapnel hit the outer skin of the Citadel about twenty meters up and instantly melted itself into bond.

Sten gave a tug. Solid contact. He began catwalking his

way upward, keeping his body almost ninety degrees out from the curving surface of the Octopus.

When he reached the grapnel's head, he braced himself against it and hurled a second grapnel upward. Even with the crampons, he almost slipped and fell, before the grapnel hit, skidded, and then caught.

Sten leaned back onto the rope then began the next stage of the climb to the roof of the Jann sanctuary.

Below him Alex, Kurshayne, and Ffillips' commandos began swarming up the awesome curve of the Octopus like so many ice flies. Grapnel, gloves, and boots found every protuberance in the smooth surface to keep from coming off.

Sten was the first to reach the weather membrane. He peered down through its red glow into the chapel below. It was empty. Alex pulled up behind him and tapped Sten's boot.

Sten reached back for the blister-charge, and Alex, panting after the climb, slid it into his gloves. Sten gave one fast look at the charge, thanked the whizkids again, licked the charge, almost freezing his tongue in the process, and slapped the charge to that "breathing" membrane. Then, still in one motion, he slid back down the rope.

The charge fused to the membrane, glowed, and then the whole membrane surface began a slow melt. It peeled back and up, leaving a gaping hole directly into the heart of the Jann Citadel.

Sten took yet another grapnel from Alex, anchored it on the edge of the hole, and then unreeled the line down into the chapel below.

Then he descended, hand over hand, into the Citadel. Alex, Kurshayne, and Ffillips' men and women followed. They landed, then spread out through the chapel, checking for intruders and setting up security.

Sten stood in the middle of the room. It was awesome. Sten could almost feel evil flowing from the walls. In the flickering torchlight, the huge military statues loomed at him like gargoyles, about to leap through the forest of wall-hung regimental banners. It was indeed a temple—a temple for the worship of violent death.

Behind him Sten heard Alex's breath hiss. His friend shivered. "Ah nae hae seen aught s'cold," he whispered. Sten nodded, then looked over at Kurshayne.

"Blow it," he ordered.

* * *

The Jann cadets were eating in silence. On the huge stage, the officers were also at their meal. General Khorea nibbled politely at each dish, then pushed it away. He refused when a servant offered to refill his wine glass.

Khorea looked around at the cadets and felt a great stirring of pride. Soon, he thought, all these young men would be joining him in the great Jann cause. Many would die, he knew. He also wondered if one of these young men at the tables would someday be a general like him.

And at that moment there was an enormous, soul-shattering explosion. For one of the few times in his life, Khorea felt an instant of fear. The enemy had struck where no Jann had ever believed possible. The Citadel was under attack.

Vosberh and his men raced toward the barracks. Minutes later, Jann guards, reacting to Vosberh's diversionary blast, poured out of the barracks and died as Vosherh's men sprayed them with a withering fire.

Vosberh snapped a command and his fire team hustled forward. Quickly they set up the tanks of the flamethrower, twisted the controls, and a sheet of flame gouted out.

The first barracks complex exploded into fire.

Kurshayne hustled up to a statue and draped a heat-pack on one huge metallic arm. Around the chapel Sten, Alex, and Ffillips' men were doing the same.

Sten slapped his last heat-pack into place, whirled, and ran for the huge door. He and Kurshayne were the last men out. Sten barked an order, and Kurshayne hit the det button while still on the run. Behind them in the chapel the heat-packs detonated, one by one.

The fire began as a slight red glow, gradually growing larger and larger, and then a blinding flash of white.

Each pack was like a miniature nova. The heat radiated out, farther and farther, with white glow blending into white glow, until the whole chapel was blinding white.

The drapes and regimental banners were the next to go, crisped in the instant fire-storm. And the golden statues began to bubble and then melt. A molten river of gold streamed across the floor as the statues melted like so many giant snowmen.

Air howled through the hole in the roof and the open door like two tornadoes as atmosphere rushed to fill the semivacuum created by the fire.

And then, with a roar, the entire temple exploded.

That second blast shook the Citadel to its foundation. It hit the dining room like an earthquake, flinging Jann to the floor.

The enormous room was in chaos. Men shouted meaningless orders that no one was heeding anyway. On the stage Khorea dragged himself out from under the table, pawing for his weapon. He was appalled at the hysteria raging about him. A wild-eyed Jann officer ran toward him, waving his gun. Khorea grabbed the man, but the officer struggled free and ran on.

Khorea grabbed for a mike. In a moment his voice boomed through the huge dining-hall speakers, demanding order. It was a voice trained on a hundred battlefields and brought almost instant response. Men froze in place, recovered, and then turned to stare up at him.

But before he could issue any orders, the main doors blew open and Sten's killing squad waded in. They punched through the unarmed cadets, ignoring them, and fanned out across the room in three-man teams, firing into the Jann officers on the stage.

A young cadet lunged at Sten with his ceremonial dagger. Kurshayne grabbed the boy with one hand and hurled him across the room. Behind Sten, Alex lifted an enormous table and threw it into a group of charging cadets. It sent them reeling back, effectively out of the fight.

Sten flipped a pin grenade into a group of officers, and they disappeared in a hurricane of arms and legs and gouting blood. The wall beside him exploded, and he whirled to see a Jann officer getting ready to fire again.

Kurshayne swung that monster shotgun off his shoulder and triggered it. The officer shredded in the hiccuping boom of the cannon.

Ffillips plunged forward onto the stage itself just as Sten and his team got moving again, up the other side.

Sten spotted Khorea instantly, recognizing him from Mahoney's briefing. He slashed his way forward, going for the ultimate target. But there were dozens of men between him and the general. They died bravely, but they died just the same, trying to protect their general.

And Khorea saw Sten and instinctively recognized him as the leader of the attack. Khorea clawed his way forward. He wanted desperately to kill Sten.

A group of Khorea's aides rallied, grabbed the general, and, ignoring his shouts of protest, did a flying-wedge toward the rear of the stage. Sten had one last, fleeting look at the man's white, spitting face as the aides carried him through the rear door and disappeared.

Then Sten went down under a pile of bodies.

They punched and kicked at him, fighting each other in their blind fury for revenge. Sten slashed and slashed with his knife. And still they kept coming. Sten could feel numbness spread through his body.

Alex and Kurshayne fought desperately to get to him. For fear of killing Sten, they had to use their hands. Hurling men away, smashing skulls, and literally ripping limbs from bodies.

And suddenly they were there. There was no one in front of them but a battered and torn Sten, bleeding from a dozen superficial cuts.

Alex pulled him to his feet. They looked around for more Jann to kill. There was nothing but pile after pile of black-uniformed bodies and Ffillips' commando teams, grimly making the same search.

Sten spotted Ffillips across the stage. She gave him a large smile and a thumbs-up sign. It was over. Before the Jann cadets could rally at the loss of their cadremen, the mercenaries were moving across the stage and out a side door.

Outside the Citadel, the mountaintop ran with rivers of fire. Vosberh had done his job well. All the barracks were crackling and exploding.

Sten, Ffillips, and their people linked up with Vosberh and Egan's troops at the start of the exit roadway. They were in loose formation, ready to move out.

"Casualties," Sten snapped.

"Three killed. Two stretcher cases. Ten walking wounded. It was a walkover," Vosberh reported.

"None," Egan said proudly.

Ffillips looked mournful. "Seven dead. Twelve more wounded. All transportable."

Sten saluted his subcommanders and turned to Alex, pointing at the downward S-curving roadway.

"We'll walk this time."

"Ah'm w'y', lad," Alex said. "M'bones ae t' oldit to play billygoatgruff wi' again."

The mercenaries moved out briskly.

Behind them, the Citadel and its dreams of death and glory flamed into ruin.

CHAPTER NINETEEN

THE DOCTORS HOVERED over the wriggling, leechlike creatures, waiting for them to shoot their potent narcotics into Ingild the Prophet's veins. They were the perfect parasites for an addict, creatures who traded euphoria for a few calories. Ingild waved at the doctors impatiently, and they carefully coaxed the tiny bulbous monsters free of his skin.

Ingild sat up and motioned the men away. The doctors scattered, not bothering with their usual professional bowing and posturing. The "False" Prophet (as Theodomir would have called him) was in a snit. He glanced around the throne room at his guards, trying to compose himself before the comforting ego-drug took effect.

A little over half the guards in the throne room were black-uniformed Jann. Ingild fought back instinctive paranoia, even though he knew that in this instance it was a correct psychosis. The Jann guards, he realized, were more interested in watching Ingild than in protecting him from possible assassins. The rest of the guards were members of Ingild's own family, which made him relax a little. He pushed aside the thought that there was an excellent possibility they had been subverted by the Jann.

The symbiotic narcotics began to filter through, and he felt a faint wave of relief.

He *was* Ingild, and before him all men owed allegiance.

Ingild, like his counterpart and opponent Theodomir, was a middle-aged man, not too far into his second century. But unlike Theodomir, he looked as if he was near the end of his time. Ingild was wizened, his skin blotched and peeling. His head featured a bald dome with unhealthy strings of hair dangling from the sides.

A traveling medico had given him the reasons for his scrofulous appearance many years ago. The doctor had said that Ingild's deep-seated fears counteracted the benefits of modern longevity drugs. Ingild had the man executed for his advice, but had kept the compu-diagnoses and scrolled through them several times a day for insight.

A Jann guard walked over to him, very correct and military, but Ingild could sense the contempt.

"Yes," Ingild said.

"General Khorea," the guard announced.

Ingild covered the wave of fear and nodded at the guard. Khorea entered, made a slight bow, and strode over to the throne couch.

The ego-drug cut in for an instant, and Ingild did a mental sneer at Khorea's appearance. The man had not even bothered to change, he thought, after the debacle at the Citadel. His uniform was torn and there were streaks of dried blood on the exposed skin.

Khorea drew up before him and snapped a very respectful salute. Ingild just nodded his acceptance. Then Khorea shot a look at the guards, made a signal, and, to Ingild's horror, all of them withdrew.

When the last man had gone, Khorea sat on the edge of Ingild's couch. Ingild fought back an angry scream. Instead he smiled at Khorea and gave him a fatherly pat on his arm.

"At last, my general," he said, "you have returned to me. I have prayed for your safety."

Khorea made an impatient motion. "Listen very carefully. I have had an address prepared. It minimizes the damage to the Citadel.

"Basically it says we fought back a cowardly surprise attack. We drove the enemy away and killed many of them."

"But," Ingild protested, "your report—"

"Forget my report," Khorea snapped. "That was for my officers." Then, almost as an afterthought: "And for you."

Ingild swallowed his indignation.

"You will emphasize the casualties to the cadets. They were mere children, after all."

Ingild looked at him in surprise. "But there were few cadet casualties."

Khorea gave him a withering look, and Ingild bit back any other protest.

"Everything is ready for your system-wide address," Khorea continued. A small pause for effect. "My speechwriters have appended an appropriate prayer."

"What do we do next?" Ingild blurted, hating himself for it.

Khorea smiled.

"We fight," he said. "Total war. These are only mercenaries, after all. They will collapse after a few engagements.

"Especially when this amateur Sten, who leads them, is proven only to be lucky and not in fact a qualified leader at all."

"Who is he?"

Khorea grimaced. "Ex-Imperial Guards. Court-martialed and thrown out. Hardly a worthy opponent."

Khorea stood up. "But Sten and the mercenaries are the worry of the Jann. You must see that the faith of our people is behind us.

"I wouldn't advise any more stimulants before your address," he warned.

Ingild shivered, but involuntarily nodded obedience.

Khorea smiled his cold smile again, drew himself up, and delivered a perfect salute. Followed by a low, mocking bow. "The Jann will await your further orders, O Keeper of the Flame."

He wheeled and marched out. Ingild looked after him, hating the clicking heels and the ramrod back.

A moment later, his guards drifted back in.

CHAPTER TWENTY

EVEN PIONEER CLUSTERS, settled by dissidents, fanatics, and malcontents, and crippled by two warring religions, can have a minor Eden.

Such was Nebta, the temporal version of Sanctus. Parral's power base.

The Nebtans controlled mainstream trade, which meant whatever merchanting the Bhor weren't able to wangle, connive, blackmail, or smuggle.

Nebta was a very rich and very beautiful world, a world where even the poor were rich—at least compared to the other habitable Lupus Cluster planets.

Nebta's oceans were slightly salty and its minor moon provided gentle tides. It swam in a perpetually mild climate, and most of its small continents were located inside the planet's temperate region.

The ugly necessaries of warehouses, landing fields, and brokerage houses had been sensibly located on the large, equatorial, desertlike main continent.

Nebta's merchant princes preferred their mansions, luxury, and indolence to the realities of trade. Sten had wondered how long it would take Ida to own the entire planet if she were there.

The government of Nebta was based on strength. Each of

the merchant princes had his private army and generally confined himself to his own fortified city and fortress mansion.

Nebta was "ruled" by a council of these merchant princes, a council that had been suborned, subverted, and threatened into acquiescence by Parral many years before.

Inside the fortified cities lived the clerks, shipping specialists, bankers, and such. The farmers lived outside the cities and were, by mutual agreement, kept out of the constant political connivings of the merchants.

Parral's own fortress-estate was actually a series of mansions, covering more than 150 square miles of hand-manicured parkland. Grudgingly Parral had housed Sten and his mercenaries in one of those mansions, a sprawling marble monstrosity the mercs were happily turning into a cross between a barracks and a bordello.

After the astonishing rapier stroke against the Jann Citadel that had opened the war, Parral had decided a masque was in order.

According to Parral's social secretary, those invited were the best, the most beautiful, and the brightest men and women from Nebtan high society.

Plus, slightly reluctantly, the guests of honor. This did not mean all 201 mercenaries: This portion of the guest list was restricted to Colonel Sten, his executives Ffillips and Vosberh, and, at Sten's insistence, Alex. And at Kurshayne's insistence, Kurshayne.

Sten and Alex had decided the monster's protectiveness was going too far. They didn't know if telling Kurshayne no party would produce tears or a battle royal. Besides, it was just a party.

But, Sten admitted as the five soldiers walked up the sweeping steps to Parral's main mansion, past too many rigid guards, it might be quite a party.

The invitation had specified uniform, so Sten had tucked himself into the Third Guards' blue full-dress and shako that his cover identity required. Ffillips was also in Guards uniform, wearing medals that Sten knew damned well she wasn't entitled to.

Vosberh moved behind them, wearing a neat, undecorated brown uniform that Sten theorized was of his own design.

Kurshayne's uniform, on the other hand, *was* his Guards parade uniform. The sleeves still had the thread-patterns where rankstripes had been laboriously sewn on and then ripped off a dozen times. He wore none of his campaign ribbons, having explained, worriedly, that he'd hocked them all for quill and was that a problem?

Sergeant Alex Kilgour was the glamour, though.

Somewhere—Sten didn't think it'd been in his kit, although he never knew exactly what Alex chose to lug around in that elderly, battered leather trunk—Alex had put together the following: flat, low-heeled, very shiny black shoes; knee-high, turned-down stockings of a horrible, clashing-colored pattern of squares; a black, silver-mounted, jeweled dagger tucked in the right silk-flashed stocking. Above that Alex wore a hairy skirt in the same pattern as the stockings. In front of his groin a pouch made from the face of an unknown animal hung from silver chains. The chains were attached to a broad, silver-buckled leather belt, with a diagonal support strap running over one shoulder.

Suspended from the belt was not only the pouch, but a half-meter-long, single-edged, hiltless dagger on the right as well as a long, basket-hilted broadsword.

Sten didn't know if Alex thought he was going to a party or an invitational massacre.

To continue: Under the belt was a black doublet and vest, both with silver buttons. At Alex's throat was a ruffled silk jabot and, at his wrists, more lace.

Over that was another couple of meters of the hairy, colored cloth, belted to Alex's belt in the rear and then attached to his left shoulder with a silver brooch.

Finishing off the outfit was what Alex called his bonnet— looking a bit like an issue garrison cap, but with more silver and some kind of bird-feather pluming rising from it.

Also, Sten knew, tucked out of sight in that pouch was a nasty little projectile pistol.

Sten couldn't decide exactly what was going on and wasn't sure he wanted to ask.

Naturally, all of the sentries outside the mansion saluted Alex and ignored the others. Only Ffillips seemed upset by the error. They went into the hall.

Just inside the door Sten gratefully parked the shako and walked into the central ballroom.

The first thing he saw was a woman wearing nothing else but a quiver of arrows with a bow tucked beside it taking three glasses of some beverage from a servibot.

Startled, he looked around the ballroom. From the nude Amazon on, his impressions became a little chaotic.

The princes of Nebta seemed to have a vague idea about uniforms but a very definite idea about making these uniforms unique.

Sten saw a pastiche of every army that had ever fought in the thousand years of the Empire and the prehistory before it.

Sten thought he recognized about one tenth of the uniforms. But just barely. There was, for instance, a podgy, red-faced man wearing the fighting cloak of the Thanh, but under it was an aiguelette-crowded purple tunic. There was someone wearing a skirt like Alex's, but of common cloth, with a broad, short-bladed sword, hammered metal helmet, greaves, and shoulder-plate, and even somebody wearing a full metal suit.

He turned to Ffillips in puzzlement.

"That's called armor, Colonel," Ffillips said as she passed Sten a glass.

"But . . . those holes in the facemask? Wouldn't it leak in space?" Ffillips laughed for some reason and Sten decided to quit showing his ignorance.

Then Parral was standing in front of him, in a costume as fantastic as any of his guests: a long, embroidered robe, a square hat, a huge sword—swords were evidently very popular—and slippers.

"Welcome, gentlemen," Parral silked. "Since this fete is in your honor, we are delighted."

"The pleasure is ours," Ffillips replied smoothly. "We can only hope that our campaign is successful enough to provide many other occasions as wonderful."

Parral looked at Ffillips, then ostentatiously turned his attention to Sten.

"Colonel, there are a few minutes before the meal. Perhaps you and your . . . underlings would care to circulate?"

Sten nodded stiffly.

Sten's ideal party was a certain amount of quill, beer, four or five congenial companions, and a bright woman he hadn't bedded yet. Certainly not this kind of panoply—there must've been a thousand people milling around the ballroom.

But Sten smiled his thanks to Parral and then moved slowly off through the crowd, flanked by Alex and the silent, non-drinking Kurshayne.

"It ain't the heavy haulin' that 'urts the 'orses 'ooves," Alex murmured, "hit's the 'ammer, 'ammer, 'ammer on the 'ard 'ighway."

"What are we doing here?"

"Bein' heroes," Alex said. "An' gie'in these wee parasites a chance to dress up."

"Oh," Sten said, and set his untouched glass back on a passing tray.

"W'll lurkit around here until they feed us, makit our 'pologies, an' gie back to our wee homes an' gie drunk like civilized sol'yers," Alex said. "Dinnae tha' be a plan?"

Sten agreed and started looking at his watch.

The merchant princes of Nebta religiously held to a pattern for the banquet. Dinners were multicourse—a twenty-course meal was regarded as vaguely bourgeois. Each course consisted of a main dish, the cooked barley that had originally sustained the first settlers on Nebta, coupled with a highly exotic side dish.

Of course the princes ignored the barley side dishes and concentrated on the goodies.

Sten had decided the only way to survive terminal obesity was to nibble a lot. He sampled something strange from a dish, then nodded to his waiter, who promptly removed the dish.

He wasn't much impressed by the supposedly exotic dishes. In Mantis he'd relentlessly eaten anything that didn't (a) poison his skin when rubbed on it; (b) move too much; or (c) try to eat him.

The waiter bowed up with the next sample, and Sten tried to behave the way he thought an experienced ex-Guard officer, experienced in affairs of state and the gut, would behave.

Kurshayne hulked behind him. He'd not only refused drink but food as well. Sten thought he was taking this bodyguard thing entirely too seriously.

Alex, on the other hand, was enjoying himself. And eating most of everything in sight. His table area looked a little like ground zero on a very sloppy nuclear test. Sten could not understand where the man was putting all the food—perhaps in that pouch.

The waiter removed the dish. Sten waited. And then heaved a sigh of relief, when he saw other servitors removing the plates. At last it was over.

A few more minutes, listen to some speeches, and then Sten

for the mercenaries' mansion and bed. He did, after all, have an appointment to keep a few hours before dawn....

Parral hissed politely for silence, and the conversational hum in the room died away. Parral stood and lifted his glass.

"I thank you, honored guests, for joining me as we, the defenders and supporters of the True Faith of Talamein, celebrate the victors of the battle of..."

And Sten shut his ears off. He was sure this speech would not tell him anything he already didn't want to know.

And the speeches went on, and the toasts went on. Sten barely touched his glass to his lips at each toast.

And then, mercifully, Parral finished, there was applause, and, from some unseen niche, music began.

"Colonel Sten," Parral said. The man had an odd ability to materialize unseen. Not that Sten noticed, because beside the prince stood a young woman. About Sten's own height, close-cropped dark hair that Sten could already feel on a pillow beside him. She would have been nineteen, perhaps twenty years old.

Her costume was not a uniform; instead it was a high-necked, dark-colored tunic skirt, very conservative until you noticed the hip-high slit up one side of the skirt and until the lights caught the dress.

It turned translucent under certain lighting and at certain angles, suddenly promising flashes of the tanned, smooth skin underneath.

Sten would have thought that his suit radio was suddenly malfunctioning with a static-rush—but he was not wearing a suit.

Dimly he heard Parral: "This is my youngest sister, Sofia. She expressly wanted to meet and congratulate you."

Sofia extended a soft hand. "I am honored, Colonel." Her voice was low and throaty and full of promises.

Sten stumbled his return greetings, realizing he sounded like an utter clot. He couldn't help staring at her, and then he realized with a start that she was staring at him too. Sten was sure it wasn't true, but it seemed as if she was just as taken as—

"Perhaps," Parral broke in, "you would do Sofia the honor of dancing with her."

Sofia blushed.

"I've never—I don't—" and Sten shut up, because he suddenly knew he was going to learn how to dance in record time.

He took Sofia by the hand and led her around the table.

Trying not to look at her, trying to eye the moving feet of the dancers already on the floor. Hell, it can't be that hard, he reasoned/rationalized. First they move a foot to the side, then the other comes up beside it and—what was the Bhor prayer?... By the beard of my mother, don't let me blow it.

Then, somehow, it was all natural as Sofia was all softness melting into his arms. He could smell the perfume in her hair, and Sten, who had never cared much about music, felt something in the dance and was floating across the floor with her. He felt a building tightness in his throat as he found himself drowning in intense deer-eyes staring solemnly up at him.

"Are you enjoying the party?" she whispered to him.

"Not until now," he said. It was a statement, not a flirt.

"Oh," she said, blushing again.

Then, if it was possible, she was snuggling closer in his arms. Sten thought he had died and gone to whatever heaven was sanctioned in this part of the Empire.

Suddenly, nearby, he heard a table crash over. Sten spun, Sofia forgotten, his right hand started to curl to bring the knife out.

The center table was overturned and, standing in the rubble was Alex and a young, heavily muscled man that Sten vaguely remembered as being Seigneur Froelich.

"I do not challenge underlings," Froelich was saying. "I merely wished to convey my compliments to your superior, express my admiration for his abilities, and then to allow my considerable dismay that he had decided to company the lady Sofia."

Sten was across the dance floor, costumed Nebtans scattering before him.

"Sergeant!"

"Beggin' your pardon, Colonel." Alex's voice was down into that deep brogue and almost whisper. "Ah hae a wee bit a business ae th' moment."

Sten, properly, shut up. And then there was a tap at his shoulder. He turned, and fingers flicked across his face.

Momentarily blinded, Sten dropped into attack stance, clawhand coming out to block-feint... and then he caught himself.

Another man was there, someone who looked enough like Froelich to be his twin. It was Seigneur Trumbo.

"As Seigneur Froelich's cousin, I must also confess to being offended. I also wish to extend my compliments."

Sten caught a glance of Sofia as the crowd gathered around. Very interesting, he flashed. In a dueling society like Nebta, she doesn't seem delighted. She looks scared. For me? Come on, Sten, he reprimanded himself. Shut your clottin' glands off.

And now Parral. "This is becoming an interesting evening," he said. "Colonel, perhaps I should explain some of our customs."

Sten shook his head. "Don't bother. These two bravos want to fight. S'be't," Sten mocked.

"Then, tomorrow," Froelich's cousin began. . . .

"Tomorrow I am very busy," Sten said flatly. "We fight now. Here."

A murmur floated through the crowd, and then eyes brightened. This would indeed be a fete worth talking about.

"As first challenger, then," Froelich said, "I believe I have precedence, if you'll excuse me, Seigneur Trumbo?" He bowed to his cousin.

"Ye hae a problem, lad," Alex said. "Ye'll nae b'fightin' m'colonel. It's be me."

"I have already told you that—"

And the great sword hung in Alex's hand and then crashed down, splitting the thick overturned table down the middle.

"Ah said ye'll be fightin' me. Ah challenge you, as Laird Kilgour ae Kilgour, frae ae race thae was noble when your tribe was pullin' p'raties in ae wasteland. Now ye'll fight me or ye'll die here ae y'stand."

Froelich paled, then recovered, smiling gently.

"Interesting. Very interesting. Then we shall have two bouts."

The dance floor was cleared and sanded in a few minutes, and the Nebtans ringed the fighting area. Alex and Sten stood fairly close together at one side of the floor, Trumbo and Froelich across from them. The two soldiers were flanked by Vosberh, Ffillips, and the still-unworried Kurshayne.

Since Sten and Alex were the challenged parties, they had choice of weapons as well as location and time.

Alex, of course, had chosen his claymore, and Parral had been delighted to provide Froelich with a basket-hilt saber that nearly matched the Edinburghian's weapon.

Sten had thought wistfully of his own ultimate knife, then discarded the notion. He was, after all, supposed to be a bit of a diplomat as well as a soldier, and he figured that Parral would not be overly thrilled by having one of his court bravos butchered two seconds into the fight.

So he'd picked poignards—long, needle-tapered, double-edged daggers, almost 40cm long. Parral had lovingly selected a matched pair from his own extensive collection.

Sten hefted the weapon experimentally—it was custom-built, of course, and made of carefully layered steel, in the eons-old Damascus style. To compensate for the blade-weight and consequent imbalance, the maker had added a weighted ball pommel. It would do.

Alex padded softly up beside Sten. "How long, wee Sten, d'Ah play't wi' th' castrati t'makit appear bonnie?"

"Give him a minute or two, anyway."

Alex nodded agreement and walked to the center of the floor. Froelich stood across from him, testing his saber's temper by tension-bending the blade. And trying to look deadly, dashing, and debonair.

Alex just stood there, blade held casually in eighth position. And then Froelich blurred forward, blade slashing in on a high attack. Alex's hand crossed over, point still down, and blades clanged.

"Ah," he murmured. "Y'fight th' wae ac mon should, wi'out skreekit an' carryint on."

But Sten could tell by the expressions of the Nebtans that Froelich had already broken etiquette. Probably, he guessed, there was supposed to be some kind of formal challenge, offer to withdraw, and all the rest of the boring business. So? All Froelich was doing was shortening the time span before he became wormfood.

Froelich went back on guard. Alex still waited patiently. The next attack was a blinding flurry of strokes into first and third. Or at least it was supposed to have been. Alex locked hilts with Froelich's second stroke in a *prise de fer*, forced the man's saberhand up level, and then shoved.

Froelich clattered back, falling, rolling, coming up, quite respectably fast, Sten thought, and then going on guard. Breathing hard, he closed in, cautiously clog-stepping forward.

And now Alex attacked, brushing past Froelich's parry with a strong beat and flicking the claymore's blade. The tiny cut took off most of Froelich's ear. Froelich riposted and back-handed across Alex's gut—which was no longer there.

Alex had leaped backward, almost ten feet. Again he stood waiting. As Froelich, leaking blood and reddening, howled and came in, Alex flicked a glance at Sten. Now?

Why not? Sten nodded back, and Alex's blade snaked out, clashed Froelich's saber out of the way and then Alex, seemingly in slow motion, brought the claymore's hilt back almost to his neck and hewed.

Froelich's head, gouting blood, described a neat arc and splashed into the punchbowl. The corpse tottered, then collapsed. Alex sheathed his claymore and strode off the floor to dead silence.

"You might really be Laird Kilgour," Sten whispered.

"Aye. Ah might be," Alex agreed.

Parral, looking a little shaken, walked up to the two soldiers. "That was, uh, quite a display, Sergeant."

Alex gravely nodded his thanks.

"Colonel? Seigneur Trumbo? I should caution you, the man is one of Nebta's best. He has fought more than a score of duels and operates his own *salle*."

Sten kept silent.

"I am in a bit of a quandary. You should be aware," Parral went on, "that this man goes for the kill. On one hand, I do not wish to lose the able captain of my mercenaries."

"But on the other?"

"The Trumbo family and mine have somewhat of an alliance. His death would be equally inappropriate."

"The question then, Seigneur Parral," Ffillips said quietly, "is which death our colonel would find least appropriate then, is it not?"

Parral had the good grace to smile before walking to the center of the dance floor as a servitor finished sweeping the last of the gore aside and sprinkling fresh sand. The body was being lugged out by two of Froelich's long-faced retainers, who must've bet on their ex-leader.

"It would appear," Parral said, relieved at finally being able to go through the rigamarole, "that both challenged party and challenger are unable to settle their differences except by blood. Am I correct?"

Sten nodded, as did Trumbo as the two men walked toward each other, each gauging his opponent.

"Then blood is the argument," Parral intoned, "and by blood it shall be settled." He bowed twice and backed off the floor.

Trumbo went on guard. At least he wasn't holding his poignard like an icepick. Instead he had his left hand flattened out in front of him, fisted into a guard and held chest-high. His poignard was held low, pommel lightly resting on his left hip. He crab-walked toward Sten.

Sten stood nearly full-on, with right hand, fingers curled, held forward, waist high. His poignard was held slightly to the rear and slightly lower than his right hand.

Sten, too, began crab-walking, trying to move to Trumbo's offside. Come on in, friend, he thought, eyes carefully wide open. Come on. A bit closer. And who trained you, clot? as Trumbo's eyes narrowed and predictably he lunged, going for Sten's chest.

But Sten wasn't there to meet the blade. He sidestepped and snapped his right palm into Trumbo's temple. The man staggered back, then recovered.

And came in again. And Sten's knife flicked out, flashing under Trumbo's guardhand, into the flesh of his knifewrist. Blood started dripping slowly as Sten went back on guard.

Trumbo was becoming canny. First thing in a knifefight is try for the cheap kill. But if you're facing an experienced man, the only way of winning is to bleed your opponent to death.

And so he next tried an underhand slash, coming straight up for Sten's knifehand. Sten easily parried the stroke, arm-blocked the blade, and stepped close inside Trumbo's guard. The razor tip of his poignard sliced Trumbo's forehead open.

And Sten doubled back, ready position, moving, moving, shuttling from side to side. Trumbo closed in again and . . . oh, clottin' amateur . . . tried the old knife-flip, tossing the knife from his right to his left hand. The maneuver should've thrown Sten off-guard, and Trumbo would have continued his lunge, driving the poignard deep into Sten's gut.

But somewhere between Trumbo's right and left hand was Sten's snap-kicked foot, and the poignard pirouetted high into the air, gleaming blade flashing reflection, and Sten reversed his grip on the poignard and smashed the pommel into Trumbo's chin.

Trumbo thudded back, stunned. Sten waited for movement, then flipped his own poignard into the air. It thunked, point-first, into the dance floor. The fight was over.

Sten bowed to Parral, who was again looking surprised, and started back toward...

"No!" was the scream from what Sten thought/hoped was Sofia, and he was crouched, head-down, duck-spinning as Trumbo came off the floor, grabbing Sten's poignard and driving it forward, and Sten's fingers scooped, his own knife came out of his arm and he overhanded a slash from his knee.

His knife blade hit the poignard's keen steel and cut through it like cheese.

Trumbo's eyes gaped at the impossible and then Sten back-rolled and was on his feet, Trumbo still stumbling forward as Sten sidestepped, whirled, and slashed again.

The knife neatly parted Trumbo's skin, ribcage, heart, and lungs before Sten could pull it free. The body squished messily to the floor.

Sten sucked in air that tasted particularly sweet and decided he'd try another bow to Parral.

CHAPTER TWENTY-ONE

"YOU DISAPPOINT ME, Colonel," Parral said gently.

"Ah?" Sten questioned.

"I thought all soldiers were hard drinkers. Poets. Men, I believe someone wrote, who have an appointment with death."

Sten sloshed the still-untouched pool of cognac in the snifter and smiled slightly.

"Most soldiers I've known," he observed dryly, "would rather help someone else make that appointment."

Parral's glass was also full.

The two men sat in Parral's art-encrusted library. It was hours later, and the fete had broken up with excited buzzings and laughter. Parral had let Alex and Sten freshen and change in his chambers and then had wanted to talk to Sten alone.

Reluctantly Alex, Kurshayne, Ffillips, and Vosberh had left the mansion. After all, Sten had pointed out reasonably, I'm in no particular danger. No one except an absolute drakh-brain would kill his mercenary captain before the war's won.

"I find you fascinating, Colonel," Parral observed, touching his glass to his lips. "First, we in the Lupus Cluster are . . . somewhat isolated from the mainstream of Imperial culture. Second, none of us have had the advantage of dealing with a professional soldier. By the way, aren't you rather . . . young to have held your present office?"

"Bloody wars bring fast promotions," Sten said.

"Of course."

"The reason I asked you to stay behind is, of course, primarily personally to compliment your prowess as a warrior . . . and to gain a better knowledge of what you and your people intend."

"We intend winning a war for you and for the Prophet Theodomir," Sten said, being deliberately obtuse.

"No war lasts forever."

"Of course not."

"You assume victory, then?"

"Yes."

"And after that victory?"

"After we win," Sten said, "we collect our pay and look for another war."

"A rootless existence . . . Perhaps . . . Perhaps," Parral continued, staring intently into his snifter, "you and your men might find additional employment here."

"In what capacity?"

"Do you not find it odd that we have two cultures, both very similar, at each other's throats? Do you not find it odd that both of these cultures espouse a religious faith that you— a sophisticated man of the Galaxy —must find somewhat archaic?"

"I have learned never to question the beliefs of my clients."

"Perhaps you should, Sten. I know little of mercenaries, I admit. But what little my studies produce is that those who survived to die without their swords in hand became . . . shall we say, politically active?"

Parral waited for Sten's comment. None came.

"A man of your obvious capabilities . . . particularly a man who could develop, let us say, personal interests in his clients, might find it more profitable to linger on after his contract was fulfilled, might he not?"

Sten stood and walked to one wall, and idly touched a gouache of a merchant's tools—microcomputer, money converter, beam scales, and a projectile weapon—that hung on the wall, then turned back to Parral.

"I gather," he said, "that the key to success as a merchant is an ability to fence with words. Unfortunately, I have none of that. I would assume, Seigneur Parral, that what you are asking is that, after we destroy the Jannisars, you would wish us to remain on, with a contract to remove Theodomir."

Parral managed to look shocked. "I would never suggest such a thing."

"No. You wouldn't," Sten agreed.

"This evening has run extremely late, Colonel. Perhaps we should continue the discussion at a later date. Perhaps after more data have become available to you."

Sten bowed, set his full glass down on a bookcase, and walked to the door.

CHAPTER TWENTY-TWO

STEN WALKED DOWN the steps and yawned broadly at Nebta's setting moon. A very long night, Sten, he thought to himself. And you still have four hours to go until you make contact.

"You look tired, Colonel," came the silken voice from the shadows.

Kill a man, love a woman, Sten hoped. It could turn out to be an interesting evening. He nodded to Sofia as she rose from her seat on the balustrade.

Not to mention interesting things like my dawn meeting yet to come, not to mention Parral's wanting me to sell out the Prophet, not to mention this incredible woman who I do not believe wants to make love to me because of the cut of my hair.

And I will momentarily ignore the fact that my gonads are suggesting it's perfectly proper to sell out Emperor, mercenaries, Theodomir, and Uncle Tom Dooley for this woman. He smiled back at Sofia.

"You provided quite an entertainment," Sofia said.

"Not my idea of an enjoyable evening."

"After they removed your opponents, I looked for you."

"Thought it best to leave, Sofia. I do not think it's proper to dance with a woman with blood up to your elbows."

Sofia was surprised. The script was not going as it should.

"The only thing I could be sorry about," Sten improvised,

131

"is that my late friends intervened before I could tell you how lovely you are."

Sofia brightened. Things might proceed. And Sten suppressed an urge to laugh. *MANTIS SECTION/COVERT OPERATIONS*: Instruction Order Something, Clause I Forget, Paragraph Who Remembers: "When approached on a sexual level, covert operators should remember that they have not necessarily been found attractive beyond the moon and the stars but rather that the person making the approach is allied with the opposition and attempting to subvert, to maneuver into a life-threatening situation, or to provide the opposition with blackmail material. In any event, until a life-threatening situation occurs, it is recommended that operatives pretend to be seducible. Interesting intelligence has been produced in such situations."

And so Sten stepped very close to Sofia, lowered his voice, and gently touched a finger to her cheek.

"Perhaps we might walk. Perhaps I might have a chance to tell you what I wasn't able to."

Sofia's smile vanished. Then it returned to her face. Very interesting. The woman is an amateur, Sten concluded. Parral, you should never have sent your little sister to do a whore's work.

Then, arm in arm, the two walked down the steps into Parral's sprawling garden.

CHAPTER TWENTY-THREE

IT WAS QUITE a garden.

At one end—almost a kilometer from the castle—the garden narrowed, then spread into a soft meadow where a gentle river flowed.

And of course there was a small dock in midmeadow.

And of course there was a boat.

You aren't that far removed from Imperial technology, Sten thought as he stood on the dock, romantically put an arm around Sofia, and looked at the boat.

It was clear plas, with an illuminated strip to mark its gunwale. No sign of power, no oars, just several soft cushions.

What a setup, Sten thought.

And so he kissed Sofia.

And again the world went soft around the edges as her lips caught him and brought him in. At that moment, Sten was having trouble remembering who was seducing whom.

He gently broke the kiss and touched her lips at the corners with his, twice. Then bent, took off her shoes, and stepped her down into the boat.

Noiselessly, the boat moved along the river. Above them hung the waning moon, and below them, Sten could see the luminous flash of fish as they slept below him.

And so we will round this bend in the river, Sten thought, and then the boat will dock itself in a lovely grotto. And what will I find there besides taps? Assassins? Kidnappers? Parral working a badger game? And good luck to 'em all. Sten bent over and kissed Sofia again.

It was a helluva grotto, Sten realized as the clear boat silently touched the grassy bank. Rocks had been sculpted to form a secluded hideaway. And down over them splashed a waterfall, illuminated with what Sten guessed were a couple of low-powered meth/HC1 lasers, lasing from UV down toward yellow in the spectrum.

A helluva trap, too, as he lifted Sofia in his arms out of the boat, ready to peg her into the arms of any waiting killers.

But there was nothing.

"Your brother has quite a taste in gardens," he said.

"Parral?" Sofia was puzzled. "He doesn't know about this. I designed it."

The situation had gone awry slightly. Sten lowered Sofia to the grass, then stood again. She put both hands behind her head and eyed him quizzically. Sten lifted one boot behind him and touched a bootheel. The tiny indicator light stayed dark. How odd. No monitors.

For Sten, the situation was very rapidly getting out of hand.

He knelt beside Sofia, one leg curled under him, his hand ready to bring out the knife. She was still staring at him.

"Did you know Parral ordered me to dance with you?"

Sten hesitated, then nodded.

"You did?" she said, slightly surprised. "And did you know he wanted me to wait for you, outside the library? And I was supposed to take you—take you to my chambers?" Her voice was suddenly fast, confessional.

Sten was starting to realize that, at least in this case, *Covert Operations* Manual was a tad lacking. He had the sense to keep his mouth shut.

"Do you know what Parral wanted me to do?"

"I can imagine."

And Sofia stopped.

Embarrassed, Sten suddenly realized that he had carried his basilisk act a little too far.

He swung a leg over Sofia and, balancing himself on his knees, slowly brought both hands down the sides of her face, down across her chest, moving to the side of her breasts, across her stomach.

Sofia sighed gratefully and her eyes closed.

Sten's hands moved gently back up, then down, caressing her bare arms and hands.

Sofia's hand moved blindly to the catches on her gown and snapped them free. Sten, moving very slowly, slid the gown down to Sofia's waist, and her erect nipples on small breasts gleamed in the reflected laser-light from the waterfall.

He kissed her then, on the lips, on the throat and then down across her breasts to her stomach.

Then stood and dropped away his uniform.

And there was no sound except the whisper of her gown coming away from her body and the arabesque of two bodies meeting.

CHAPTER TWENTY-FOUR

IT WAS MINUTES before dawn as Sten, now clad in black coveralls, moved from dying shadow to alleyway through Nebta's main street.

It ain't the killing, he thought sleepily to himself, that makes sojering hard. It's the fact the bassids never let you go to bed.

He preferred not to reflect—not then, anyway—on making love to Sofia. He wasn't sure what it all meant—other than Sofia was the first woman since Bet who had added star drive to her sexuality.

Besides, there was still this clottin' meeting.

After dark no one in his right mind went down Nebta's streets, which then became the province of the killer gangs and the only slightly less lethal night patrols who reasoned (with some justification) that anyone out after dark was either a villain or desperately in need of escort service. Payment up front, please.

Sten slid down an alley that stank of death, garbage, and betrayal. Waiting at the end of the alley was the only other person he'd seen on the streets besides one half-drunk patrol team. A beggar. A scrofulous beggar, whose sores gleamed luminous in the near dawn.

"Giveen me, gentleman, y'blessing," the beggar wheezed.

"Mahoney," Sten said frankly, "you're clottin' hard to bless. Lesions that glow in the dark. Give me a break."

The beggar straightened and shrugged. "It's a new lab gimmick." Mahoney shrugged as he straightened to his full height. "I told them it was too much, but what the hell."

Sten shook his head and leaned against one slimy wall, one eye on the alley mouth.

"Report," Mahoney said briskly.

Sten ran it down—how he'd successfully recruited his mercs, none of whom had yet tried to knife him in the back. How he'd done his first by-the-book raid on the Jann, aimed at getting them into a reactive position and operating emotionally rather than logically. How Parral had opened negotiations to sell Theodomir down the creek.

"No surprises so far," Sten finished.

"What about Sofia?"

Sten's mouth dropped as Mahoney grinned. "You see, m'lad? The day I don't know far more about what's going on than you do is the day you'll take over Mantis. But—"

"Brief me," Sten said.

"Nineteen. Convent—no, you don't know the term—religious/sexual exclusionary training. Parral is trying to marry her off for an alliance. Nonvirgin. Bright, near genius. Prog—looking for her own alliance, which I assume . . ." Mahoney decided to be delicate. Sten decided to keep his mouth shut.

"Sounds as if you're doing quite well, lad," Mahoney went on. "You have only one problem."

"Which is?"

"Unfortunately, our estimates were that it would take three E-years for word of the Eryx discovery to seep out."

"But?"

"But somebody talked. I am truly sorry, m'lad, but current estimates are that within two E-years every wastrel, geologist, and miner in this sector will be heading for the Eryx Region—and coming straight through the Wolf Worlds!"

Sten grunted. "You don't make it easy, Colonel."

"Life does not make it easy, Sten. So your timetable is moved up. The Lupus Cluster must be pacified within one E-year."

"You can ruin a man's entire day, boss."

"After the grotto," Mahoney said gently. "I think it would take a great deal more than me to do that."

And then he was crouched, cloak across his face. He sidled down the alley and was gone, leaving Sten in the shadows, watching the first glisten of the rising sun and wondering how the hell Mahoney knew about *that*.

CHAPTER TWENTY-FIVE

IT WAS A small gray building in a small green glen, located almost one hundred kilometers north of Sanctus' capital. A young man in the blood-red uniform of Mathias' Companions escorted Sten to the entrance, waved him inside, and left him.

Sten entered, somewhat tentatively.

To a tourist the glen would have looked deserted. But Sten had heard rustling in the undergrowth as he and his escort had passed through. And the smell of many campfires. And the forest was silent — a sure clue to human presence.

The walls on the inside of the little building dripped with the sweat of the high-humidity water world that was Sanctus. No one waited for him inside.

He moved through what seemed empty administrative offices filled with desks, coms, and vid-file cabinets, then was brought up short by a glass wall.

Through the glass he could see Mathias.

Except for a modest breechcloth, the young man was naked. Sten watched quietly as Mathias inserted his hands into two metal rings, attached to three-meter-long chains. The chains themselves seemed to hang from nothing, but were grav-bonded into position.

Mathias' body was all one gleaming, rippling muscle. And even Sten was impressed as the Prophet's son lifted himself effortlessly on the rings, supporting himself on upper-body strength alone. The young man's stomach muscles knotted as he lifted his legs straight up above his head and did a handstand on the rings. Mathias did an unbelievable number of arm presses, then swung his body in a long, slow, 360-degree loop. Again and again, and then he let go, doubling himself into a somersault. He landed perfectly on his feet as if he were on a low-grav planet.

Sten whistled to himself softly, and then opened and walked through the glass door.

Mathias spotted him instantly and shouted a greeting. "Colonel. Your presence is our blessing."

Mathias grabbed a towel from the floor and began to wipe away the sweat as Sten moved forward to meet him.

Sten shook his hand, eyed the rings then the young man as he pulled on a plain, rough-clothed robe. "Pretty impressive," he said.

"Oh"—Mathias smiled—"my friends and I believe in the fitness of our bodies."

"Your friends?" Sten remembered the smell of campfires.

"The Companions," Mathias said, taking Sten by the arm and leading him toward the back door. "You know about them?"

Of course Sten did. They were the six hundred young men—all very wealthy and all very religious—who were Mathias' couterie. They delighted in all forms of sport, physical deprivation, challenge, and prayer. They were totally devoted to Mathias and the ancient ways of the religion of Talamein.

"Yes, I know about them."

He was on Sanctus at the mysterious request of Mathias, a polite plea for a visit. An important one, Mathias had assured him. Sten didn't have the time, but he thought it was politic to go.

"I have been following your exploits," Mathias said as they exited the door and started down the path into the fern forest.

Sten didn't reply. He was waiting.

"I must say, Colonel, I'm impressed." And with just enough hesitation to qualify for an afterthought: "As is my father."

Sten just nodded his thanks.

"I have been thinking," Mathias continued. "You and your men are bearing the brunt of this fight yourselves. For which we are grateful. But it isn't proper."

If Sten had *really* been a mercenary, he would have agreed. Instead he made a polite protest. Mathias raised a hand to stop him. "If we are to be truly victorious," Mathias said, "Sanctus must dare to spill its own blood. Not just that of—if you will forgive me—beings who might be viewed as mere hirelings."

A self-deprecating smile to Sten.

"Not that we are not convinced that all of you are committed to the cause of Talamein. And that of the True Prophet—my father."

Sten accepted his apology. Very wary now.

"And so, I have a proposal for you, Colonel. No, an offer."

They turned the corner of the path, which spilled into a broad glade.

Mathias pointed dramatically. Drawn up in line after blood-red line were the Companions. Six hundred young men in their spotless ceremonial uniforms. Without an apparent signal, they all raised a hand in salute.

"MATHIAS," they shouted in unison.

And Sten gave a slight jolt as Mathias shouted back: "FRIENDS."

The young men cheered deafeningly. Mathias, all smiles, turned to Sten.

"Colonel Sten, I offer you my life and the lives of my companions."

Sten wasn't quite sure what to say.

"What the clot could I do?" Sten asked Alex.

The big man was pacing back and forth in the control room on the Bhor ship.

"But the'r't nae professional, lad."

Sten slumped into a chair. "Look, Mahoney has moved the whole operation up one entire year."

"We'll recruit some more men," Alex responded.

"No time," Sten said. "Right now we need bodies. Anyplace we can get them."

"Cannon fodder," Alex said.

Sten shook his head. "They're not professionals, but the Companions have trained—after a fashion. And they will take orders. All we have to do is form them into our mold."

"An Ah dinnae ken wh'll be trainit' them," Alex continued suspiciously. "Ffillips? Trainit th' lads ae commandos? Th' nae be't time f'r thae."

"Possibly Vosberh," Sten said, keeping his face straight.

"Nae, nae. Tha' be't e'en more silly."

Sten grinned at him. "Then we have the answer."

Alex was aghast. "Me," he said, thumping a meaty thumb into his chest. "Y'nae be't suggestin' ae Kilgour wae y'?"

"I thought it was your idea."

Sten handed Alex a fiche. "Now, I was thinking, Red Rory of the Advertisements, you should begin their training with . . ."

CHAPTER TWENTY-SIX

ALEX KEYED HIS throat-mike. "Ye'll be awake noo an' be lookit across yon field."

Fifty of Mathias' Companions were dug in across the military crest of a wooded hill. Most of them looked puzzled, having no idea what the purpose of the exercise was.

It wae, Alex thought to himself, a wee bit ae argument against heroism. He tucked behind a bush as, far across the brush-covered field, another fifty of the Companions came into sight, weapons ready. They were spread out in standard Guard-type probe formation.

He yawned and scratched, waiting for the soldiers to come closer. They did. A Companion next to Alex lifted his rifle, and Alex back-handed him on his shrapnel helmet. The Companion thudded down, unconscious, and Alex reminded himself yet again that the wee light-grav folk had to be treated with ae gentleness.

Wait . . . wait . . . wait . . . and then Alex hit the airhorn's button. The blast rang down the hill, and the entrenched Companions opened fire.

With blanks.

Down on the flats, some of the Companions dove for cover, others began howling and charged.

The firing doubled in volume. Alex let it continue for six

seconds, then bounded up and down into the open. With his mike open.

"Cease fire, y'bloodthirsty reeks! Cease FIRE!"

The popping died away. On the flats, the probing Companions, following instructions, froze in place—in the exact positions they were stopped in when Alex gave the ceasefire signal.

Alex waved the other fifty out of their hidey-holes and down onto the fields. They trailed out and assembled in two-platoon formation. Each man carried a plas target. The plan was to replace the real men with the targets. After that, Alex chuckled to himself, the real fun would begin.

Alex walked around the attacking formation. A Companion who'd sensibly found cover was replaced with one type of target—if the cover he'd found would withstand projectile fire, the target was only part of a man's head. But if, on the other hand, he'd ducked behind a bush (which worked fine in the livies), a full head-and-shoulders replaced him.

The slow-to-react or stupid, who'd merely flattened on the ground or, still worse, stayed erect when the airhorn went off, had man-size silhouettes in their place.

Finally, the howlers-and-chargers had oversize targets targets that were half again the size of a normal man.

By now the entire company of Companions was standing at the hill's base. Alex motioned them back up into the defensive line and had them take firing positions.

Companion squad leaders now passed out live ammunition.

"Lock an' load ae mag'zine," Alex bellowed. "On command, begin . . . firing!"

The hillside rocked to the thunder of weapons. This time Alex waited until all trainees had fired their weapons dry (the projectile weapons used by the Companions and mercs had fifty-round banana magazines, nowhere near the capacity of the unobtainable Imperial willyguns with their 1400-round AM2 tube mags).

Then he brought the Companions out of their holes, checked to make sure all weapons were unloaded, and went back down the hill. If God gae us tha gift ta see ourselves as others see us, came a misquote from Alex's overly poetic backbrain. He led the hundred men from target to target.

"Noo, y'ken wha' happens whae ae mon dinna find shelter encounterin' ae enemy," he explained. "Yama lad, y'dinna find naught to hide behind. Ah' y'see whae would've recked wi' ye?"

The trainee looked at the riddled silhouette, gulped, and nodded.

Alex saved the charging fanatics for last and then gently tapped one of "them" on his shredded plas.

"Ae dinna be knockit heroes," he said. "But a wee hero who's dead afore he closes wi' the enemy be naught but ae fool, Ah think."

The Companions, who'd now had a chance to see exactly what an enemy unit could do to them—and had done it to themselves—were very thoughtful on the run back to the training camp.

A fortieth-century explosive mine looked like nothing much in particular except possibly a chunk of meteorite. It would float innocuously until a ship of the proper size came within range. It then ceased to be innocuous.

The problem with mines, as always, was remembering where they'd been planted and being able to recover them after the war ended. For Sten's mercenaries, however, who had no intention of hanging around the Wolf Cluster for one nanosecond after payday, it didn't matter.

A combined platoon of Vosberh's and Ffillips' men had scattered half a hundred of such chunks of rubble in orbital patterns that Egan's computer boys had suggested, near one of the Jann main patrol satellites. Then they'd withdrawn on the Bhor ship, as silently and unobtrusively as they'd arrived.

The first mine didn't detonate for almost a week. It was fortunate for Sten's purposes that the first one happened to ignite when a full fuel ship was making its approach to the satellite. The small nuke not only took out the fuel ship but its two escorts and the pilot vessel from the satellite.

Mines, properly laid, are extremely cost-effective weapons.

It was nae thae the Companions sang everywhere they went, Alex decided. It was thae they had such bloody awful taste in their music: doleful hymns; chants describing how wonderful it would be to meet death killing Jann.

Ah, well, he realized. Wi' m'own race's history, Ah dinnae hae a lot to complain aboot.

"Seventy seconds," one of Ffillips' lieutenants said. Egan and his bustling computer people paid no attention.

The twelve of them, with two teams of Ffillips' specialists for security, had taken over one of the Jann observation satellites. The three Jann manning the post had been disposed of, and Egan and his men had gone to work.

Wires, relays, laser-transmitters, and fiberoptic cables littered the satellite's electronics room, and now the Lycée people waited while Egan caressed keys on a meter-wide board he'd lugged onto the satellite. He tapped a final key then pulled his board out of circuit. "Very fine," he said. "Let's blow it."

Ffillips' lieutenant saluted and his men began planting demo charges.

The Lycèe gang had used the terminal on the satellite to patch straight into the Jann battle computer. They'd lifted all logs of the mercenary actions from the computer records.

That, Egan thought to himself, will make it a bit hard for the bad guys to get any kind of tac analysis. A good day's work, he realized, as he headed for the Bhor ship hanging just beyond the lock.

He didn't bother to tell anyone that he'd also removed any mention of the Lycée people or Egan himself from the records, and added a FORGET IT command just in case any entry was made. A soldier, after all, has to protect his back—and there was no guarantee that the good guys would necessarily win.

And so the raids continued. A suddenly vanished Jann patrol ship here or a Jann outpost that broadcast pleas for reinforcement before signals shut down. Merchant ships that failed to arrive at their planetfalls. A few "removals" of Jann administrators.

A man is much larger than a mosquito—and Sten's entire force was less than one-millionth the strength of the Jann. But a mosquito can drive a man to distraction and, given enough time, bleed him dry.

Sten was slowly bleeding the Jann.

"You're sure?" Sten asked dubiously.

"Aye," Alex said. "Th' Companions are as trained ae Ah can makit 'em. We're ready to go to battle, lad."

Excellent, Sten thought to himself. Now all I have to do is figure out where and when.

CHAPTER TWENTY-SEVEN

STEN EYED SOFIA with extreme interest, what she was holding with extreme skepticism, and where they were about to go with extreme terror.

One of the more fascinating things about Sofia—besides how a woman that young could come up with such unusual ways of passing the time when the candles were blown out—was that her body, from the eyebrows down, was completely depilitated.

And so she stood, naked and smiling on a black volcanic sand beach, waiting for Sten. Beside her were two three-meter-long pieces of hand-laid clear plas. The boards went from their knife-tip to a curved, half-meter midsection to a suddenly chopped stern. Hanging under each board's tailsection were twin, scimitar rudders.

Sten, whose "culture" had taught him that the best place for water was in a glass with a healthy dollop of synthalk, had trouble understanding the Nebtans' fascination with see-through watercraft.

"You are hesitating, O my brave Colonel."

"Clottin' right," Sten murmured as he turned from the exotic spectacle of Sofia to stare down that beach into the ocean.

Though Nebta normally had mild tides, there were certain places where sharply shelving sea bottoms and undersea reefs made waves build and double on themselves. Such was this beach—one of Parral's seemingly numberless hideaways. Back in the tropic foliage was a small cottage. The beach swept the base of the tiny bay, possibly four kilometers wide at its mouth. And the waves walked in—building to ten- and twelve-meter heights before they crashed into the shore.

One such wave broke, perhaps three hundred meters from the beach, and spume flew high and the air boomed and the ground trembled somewhat and Sten winced.

Sofia had kidnapped him for a three-day break. Sten was quite kidnappable, despite Mahoney's announcement that the timetable was now very, very short—he still hadn't figured out exactly what depredation he and the mercs planned next.

"This is a sport?" Sten questioned. "It looks more like ritual suicide."

Sofia didn't answer; instead she dropped one of the long planks on the sand, picked up the other, and dashed into the surf crawling on the shore.

Why, Mahoney, do I have to kill myself practicing these quaint local customs? Sten wondered. He picked up the second board, ran into the water, flat-dove on top of the board, and paddled after Sofia through the surf.

Sten, in spite of Sofia's giggled harassment and example, was not naked. He wore a pair of briefs, having semi-successfully argued that he would not need a third rudder even if he was dumb enough to try this.

But still, he thought as he awkwardly paddled out behind Sofia's board, the view was worth it. And suddenly the backwash caught him and suddenly the board was on top of him and suddenly he was wading back to the beach to pick up his board.

Looking out to sea, he then noticed how Sofia caught her board in both hands and rolled upside down when a wave came over her.

Learning is such fun, he thought as he began the long paddle out again.

And somehow the gods were kind and somehow the waves were quiet and somehow Sten ended up sitting on his board, outside the breaker line next to Sofia.

"Oh, Princess," Sten began, sputtering out water that tasted very salty, "this is a wonderful sport which you have shown me. Now I assume we sit out here until UV rays burn us, paddle back in, and do what all sensible animals in their mating season do. Correct?"

As a wave swept in behind them Sofia laughed and started paddling vigorously. The wave caught her board and picked it up. The wave grew to seven meters in height, curling, cresting, and—Sten never having been around the ocean much—sounding an ominous boom as it drove toward shore.

You could get killed doing this, Sten thought in astonishment as he saw Sofia get to her knees, then her feet, riding the wave as her board skimmed down its face. He watched Sofia as she back-and-forthed on the board, always keeping it just ahead of the breaking wave as it self-destructed.

Impossible, Sten's mind told him flatly. You are expected to mount a piece of flotation gear, riding an ocean current as it moves toward shore at perhaps 80kph, stand up, maintain your balance, and also be able to do what . . .

Sofia had her toes curled snugly over the board's front edge, still as her board curved up and down on the still-unbroken wave front.

And then the wave broke and somehow Sofia was out of the wave, and behind it and waving Sten on.

Why in the Emperor's name, Sten whimpered to himself, did I have to fall in love with a macha woman?

And then he dropped back on the board, hearing his words echo in his mind. Love? Sofia? You are here on the Emperor's Mission. Sex is one thing. Love? Sten, do you know what love is?

Indeed I do, his mind answered. I remember you mourning for Bet when you thought she was dead. I remember Vinnitsa. And then Bet's being alive. But also remember the love fading with Bet and you suddenly finding yourself as friends.

Nice thinking, another part of his mind mocked. Good way to keep you from having to do what Sofia did. There is no way that this can be done without a meta-balance computer, Sten's mind continued as he dug for the next wave.

And it built and Sten crawled cautiously to his feet and suddenly he was standing and just as suddenly the wind was roaring like the wave below him and Sten wondered why all the excitement since this wave is not moving me all that fast and suddenly he moved his board to the top of the wave and it crested and . . .

The wave curled and smashed, carrying nondescript bits of debris with it, several logs, Sten, and his board.

The board was on top of Sten, then Sten was on top of the board, then the board was lost and Sten was quietly chewing sand and small beach creatures, then he was picking himself up in the spume and quiet of the beach and Sofia was laughing at him.

He spat a mouthful of seaweed and waded to the shore.

"Ready to try it again?" Sofia asked.

"In a moment," Sten managed. "But first let's have a taste." And he staggered up the beach toward their picnic outfit, with Sofia behind him. With luck, wine, and a certain amount of technique, Sten felt sure he would never have to get near that killer ocean again.

CHAPTER TWENTY-EIGHT

STEN AND MATHIAS walked out onto the floor of the massive hangar where Sten's mercs and the Companions were assembled.

"People of the Prophet," Mathias roared, and Sten wondered where the extra set of vocal chords came from as his boyos thundered their agreement.

"Now we strike against the heart of the Jann," Mathias shouted. "Against Ingild. We shall destroy the heresy. We go forth to die for Theodomir and the True Faith of Talamein."

While Sten listened to the howl of glee from Mathias' legions, he wondered if he was riding another wave of the kind that Sofia had seen him destroyed on. He almost discarded the notion, but over the years, Sten had learned never to scrap that kind of thought. He filed it away to ponder later.

Then Mathias smiled and bowed to Sten. "Our Colonel. Our leader. The man who has led us in victory. He will now tell us how we shall destroy the falseness—the evil—of contra-Prophet thinking that is the empire of the Jann and Ingild."

"Aye, Colonel," Alex semiwhispered from behind him. "How you plan ae bein' ae braw hero ae tha, Ae dinna ken."

Hell if Sten knew, as silence fell in the huge hangar. Hoping for inspiration, he eyed the wall-size sit chart that showed, in multicolor projections, the garrison worlds of the Jann. And then he had what might be an idea.

And slowly began composing the battle plan . . .

CHAPTER TWENTY-NINE

OTHO POURED STEN and Alex another liter of stregg, rumbled a laugh, and said, "No. I don't want to hear it the way you presented the situation to those fanatics. But since you're here, and all . . ." His voice gurgled off as he downed the liter. Alex followed suit.

Sten carefully ignored the mug. "Situation, Target—Urich. The Jann shipbuilding world. The only world they've got that can produce starships."

"Och," Otho agreed.

"This is our target. We'll take out this entire complex." The plot board hummed into life and the holographic projection vibrated into existence.

"Urich," Sten continued. "Ship docks are"—he touched a control—"in green. Landing facilities, blue. AA lasers, surface-to-air missiles, and multibarrel projectile weapons in red."

Otho stood and peered down at the projection. Then belched thoughtfully. "By my mother's beard, but the black ones guard themselves well.

"Having none of your knowledge, Sten," Otho went on, "and being but a simple trader, I would have no idea of how you humanoids could capture such a place."

"We aren't. This is another smash-and-destroy run."

"You'll use nuclear hellbombs?"

"Negative."

152

"If I were a warrior," Otho said, "which, praise the beard of my mother, I am not, I would need a host of Bhor and several planetary cycles to destroy this Jann nest."

"We aren't going to take everything out," Sten said. "Just this."

His finger went through a huge, imposing structure in the center of the complex. One kilometer by two kilometers long by one kilometer.

"This is the engine–hull mating plant. Destroy it, and the whole port's nothing but a yacht repair yard."

Another control fingered, and the plotting board cleared, then refocused, this time with only the mating plant on the board. A brooding, dark-gray mass.

Above the projection hung a list of the plant's vital details. Ti-ferroconcrete construction, tetra-beam reinforcement. The walls were, at their base, fifty meters thick, tapering to a thickness of twenty meters at the roof curve. At either side of the structure were huge clamshell doors, with control booths centered in the midpoint of each panel.

"Environment controls, damage controls, and admin are in a long tube, running lengthwise down the plant's interior, halfway up the walls," Sten continued.

"You're a world of information about this, Sten," Otho said admiringly. "Could I wonder your sources?"

Alex preened slightly. "In th' propit light, Ah look quite dashin' ae a Jann."

Otho touched mugs with Kilgour, and they downed the contents and refilled the mugs.

"I can feel the time-winds touch me," Otho said as he gazed intently at Sten. "What will you require of the Bhor?"

"Two things. Most important, fifty planetfall lighters, with pilots."

"Which will be used for?" Otho was growling now.

"You'll land the unit. Then you and your pilots will provide supressing fire."

"No." Otho pushed his mug away and hunched, beetling face now locked in merchant/skeptic/negative expression. "Perhaps you do not understand the Bhor position," he growled. "Admitted, we are not fond of the Jann and, when possible, find an excuse to alter their existence cycle. But we are still only minor body parasites to them.

"And while we admire your cause, Colonel, we must be . . . your word I believe is 'pragmatic' about the situation.

"Sometimes the cause of righteousness does not win, as I am sure you are aware. And if you lose . . . and by the fortune of your fathers survive, you and your soldiers will merely lick your wounds and move on to another war.

"But we—the Bhor—must remain to reap the wrath of the Jann.

"We will convoy you and your forces, Colonel, quite willingly. We will even provide resupply. Both functions are those of a merchant. But join your war?—No."

Alex purpled and was about to say something but Sten quickly shook his head. "I understand, Otho. You do have your people to worry about."

The hulk looked puzzled, then relieved. As Otho reached out for the mug, Sten added quietly, "Your people—and your ancestors."

Otho glowered and took his hand off the mug.

"My apologies, Otho. Now if you will excuse us . . ." Sten stood and Otho rose also, moving slightly reluctantly toward the port.

"We have our own streggans to fight."

And before Otho could react, Sten eased him out. Came back to the plotting board.

"Ae m' gran' said, y'catchit more haggis wi' honey thae vin'gar," Alex said, with mild admiration. Sten frowned then shrugged and sat back down at the table.

Then, swinging a computer terminal down from the ceiling and eyeing the plotting table's holography, he began writing his operations order.

The port slid open and Otho loomed in the way.

"Your streggans indeed! By my father's icy buttocks!"

He stalked back to his half-finished mug, drained it, refilled it, drained it again, and then growled, "If the Bhor must take sides, then at least we must have all information," and hovered over Sten's terminal . . .

OPERATIONS ORDER 14

EYES ONLY. DISTRIBUTION LIMITED TO FOLLOWING OFFICERS AND CONCERNED INDIVIDUALS. ALL RECIPIENTS TO SIGN RECEIPT THIS ORDER. ALL RECIPIENTS TO ACKNOWLEDGE RECEIPT ON ACCEPTANCE. OFFICERS INVOLVED ARE DIRECTED TO READ THIS ORDER IN PRESENCE OF ACCOMPANYING GUARD. NO COPIES PERMITTED. UPON COMPLETION,

THIS ORDER TO BE RETURNED TO ACCOMPANYING
GUARD FOR RETURN THIS HEADQUARTERS.
Distribution: STEN, OC. BN-2 SECTION, FFILLIPS, OIC
FIRST COMPANY, VOSBERH, OIC SECOND COMPANY.
Note: Eyes Only: Involved indigenous personnnel
(committed Bhor tac/air personnel, Command structure,
MATHIAS' COMPANIONS) will be verbally briefed by OC.
This order is not to be discussed in their presence.

Situation:

Since the first operational commitment of FIRST STRIKE
FORCE, now operating in conjunction with MATHIAS'
COMPANIONS, Intelligence estimates of a high order
suggest that JANNISAR command elements and hierarchic
elements of INGILD's theocracy have accepted a defensive
posture. Destruction of THE CITADEL, a primary part of
JANN morale, must be considered a factor, as well as this
conflict, which has lasted for several generations, and now
is entering an active phase.

The above have produced not only tactical inertia on
the part of the JANN but a significant increase in officer
suicides among JANN ranks. Four systems previously
lightly garrisoned by JANN patrol wings have been
abandoned as JANN elements regroup in force on main
garrison worlds. Intel-estimates suggest a JANN offensive
will be mounted in sixty Standard days (estimate plus-
minus: four days). Such an offensive will most likely be
directed either at NEBTA or SANCTUS. Such an offensive
will not be allowed to occur.

The mission:

The operation against THE CITADEL was effective in
partially destroying esprit among the JANN. This operation
will destroy the JANN ability to physically patrol systems
under their control. The target world is URICH, the center
of JANN fleet activity. (See FICHE A for Planetary Details
of URICH.) FIRST STRIKE FORCE, operating with
MATHIAS' COMPANIONS, will force a landing on URICH
and destroy as completely as possible URICH's fleet
support, ship construction, fuel, and maintenance
capabilities.

EXECUTION:

This assault will be a combined operation:
Initial transhipping to 4 planetary diameters off URICH will
be provided by Armed Merchant shipping, to be provided
by PARRAL. (Details—FICHE B). These ships will deploy
assault and tac/air elements, assume an out-atmosphere
orbital pattern, and, on completion of strike, will land on
URICH to pick up assault and tac/air elements. Combat
deployment will be provided by 50 modified Bhor planetfall
lighters. Lighters will be assault armed with available
medium-range weaponry (Details—FICHE C), provisioned,
maintained, and manned by provided BHOR personnel
(Details—FICHE D). Mentioned BHOR lighters will both
land second element assault units and provide active
suppression of enemy fire. (Details on strike formation and
specific tac requirements—FICHE E.)
The Main Strike element will be quartered on a heavily
modified PRITCHARD-class freighter, ex-MS ATHERSTON
(Modification details—FICHE F). This ship will be crewed
by volunteers, as well as selected first-strike assault
troops. In addition, Command Headquarters will be located
on it. The freighter will be lead element, first wave, and
will make a direct crash-assault on Target One, the Jann
engine–hull mating plant. The freighter will be provided
with extensive demolition capability and triggered to
detonate less than one hour after strike forces land. In
addition, deployed assault troops will provide demolition
on selected other targets, engage ground troops, and
attempt to aid Bhor tac/air in supression of enemy surface/
air launches.

COORDINATION . . .

And Sten shut down the terminal. "Coordination" on this
cobbled-together mess, he thought. First I'm going to take a
bunch of Parral's cholesterol-heavy traders, get them to take
us into the heart of the Jann empire. Then I'll manage to offload
my surly thugs onto the Bhor lighters, somehow without having
a grand melee between the Bhor, my mercs, and Mathias'
fanatics.

If I get away with all that, then I suicide-dive the clottin'
freighter—which I still haven't seen—right into the middle of

this bloody great hangar, somehow live through the crash, somehow come out shooting, and somehow hang on and be an active menace for the Jann until Parral's ships heave down to pick all of us up.

This will not work, Sten, my friend, his mind told him. Of course it won't. You got any better ideas?

Go see what Sofia's doing, his mind suggested. And, since Sten couldn't find any argument with that, he put the security lock on the computer and headed for a grav-sled and Parral's mansion.

Maybe I'll come up with something better after a few hours lurking in her grotto.

CHAPTER THIRTY

PARRAL SCROLLED THROUGH Sten's latest reports. Everything was going exactly as the man had promised. The series of lightning raids had the Jann reeling. And now the young colonel was preparing for the master stroke: a daring attack to gut the Jann's resolve to continue the war itself.

Parral chuckled to himself. Yes, he thought, Sten had proven to be a remarkable investment. Of course, Parral didn't believe for a minute that the man would honor his entire contract.

The young fool. Doesn't he realize I know that when the final battle is won, Sten will do exactly what I would: seize the cluster for myself?

It was a final move, Parral had to admit, that any businessman would admire.

He sighed. Too bad. He was really beginning to like the man.

Parral keyed up the analyses his spies had put together and checked them once to see if any details had been omitted, any scenario untried.

No, there would be only one possible solution to Sten's forthcoming challenge. He and his mercenaries would all have to die. And as for Mathias? Another misfortune of the business of war.

Parral also congratulated himself for making sure there could be no possible threat from the Jann—or whatever would remain of them after the final raid. He thought fondly of the powerful armored combat vehicles he had secretly purchased and turned over to his own men. They could crush any attack from any source.

Parral flicked off the computer, pleased with himself. Then he poured a glass of wine and toasted Sten and the men who were about to win him a new empire.

CHAPTER THIRTY-ONE

STEN THOUGHT THE freighter gave ugly a bad name.

Pritchard-class freighters were one of those answers to a question no one had asked. Some bright lad, about one hundred years earlier, had decided there was a need for a low-speed, high-efficiency deep-space freighter that also had atmospheric-entry capabilities.

The designer must've ignored the existence of planetary lighters, high-speed atmo-ships for the more luxurious or important cargoes, and the general continual bankruptcy-in-being of any intrasystem freighter company.

The *Pritchard*-class ships were well designed to be exactly what the design specs stated, so well that it was nearly impossible to modify them. Therefore, they trickled down from large-line service to small-line service to system-service to, most often, the boneyard.

This particular example—the *Atherston*—had cost somewhat less than an equivalent mass of scrap steel.

The Bhor had towed the ship to a berth in a secluded part of Nebta's massive equatorial landing ground, and Parral's skilled shipwrights and Bhor craftsmen, directed by Vosberh, had gone to work.

The *Atherston's* looks hadn't been improved any by the modifications. Originally the ship had a lift-off nose-cone and drop-ramps for Roll On, Roll Off planetary cargo delivery.

The nose had been solidly filled with reinforced ferroconcrete, as had fifty meters of the forward area, so that the drop-ramps were now barely wide enough for troops to exit in double column. The command capsule had been given a solid-steel bubble with tiny vision slits, and the bubble was reinforced with webbed strutting. And finally, just to destroy whatever aesthetic values the tubby rustbucket had, two Yukawa drive units were position-welded and then cast directly to either side of the ship's midsection. Steering jets made an anenome-blossom just behind the nosecone.

"Beauty, isn't it, sir," Vosberh said briskly. Sten repressed a shudder.

"Best design for a suicide-bomber I've ever seen," Vosberh went on. "I figure that you'll have a seventy–thirty chance when you crash into that plant."

"Which way?" Sten asked.

"You pick." Vosberh smiled. Then he turned serious.

"By the way, Colonel. Two private questions?"

"GA, Major."

"One. Assuming that you, uh, miss, and by some misfortune pass on to that Great Recruiting Hall in the Sky, who have you picked as a command replacement?"

Sten also smiled. "Since both you and Ffillips will be grounding with me on the *Atherston*, isn't that a pointless question?"

"Not at all, Colonel Sten. You see—a little secret I've kept from you—I believe I am immortal."

"Ugh," Sten said.

"So the question is very important to me. Under no circumstances shall I turn over command of my people to Ffillips. She is arrogant, spit-and-polish, underbrained..." and Vosberh ran momentarily short on insults.

"I would assume that Ffillips feels about the same toward you, Major."

"Probably."

"I will take your first question under advisement. Second question, Major?"

"This raid on Urich. Is there any chance it will end the war?"

"Negative, Major. We'll still have scattered Jann to mop up—and Ingild to deal with. Why?"

"I warned you once, Colonel. The minute that Parral or that

stupid puppet prophet he's running get the idea they're winning . . ." Vosberh drew a thumb across his throat.

"Mercenaries," he went on, "in case you haven't learned, are always easier to pay off with steel to the throat instead of credits in the purse."

"Good thought, Major. Answer—as I said. This war has not even begun."

Vosberh saluted skeptically and turned away.

"What is that supposed to be, Sergeant?" Mathias asked, staring up at the wood-plas-concrete assemblage in front of him.

"Yon contraption's ae fiendish thingie, Captain," Alex said. "A' tha' Ah'm supposit t' tell ye is it's som'at nae longer needs t' exist. Ye're trained noo, Captain. Takit y'r squad an' destroy yon device."

Mathias scowled but obediently shouldered the demopack filled with plas bricks weighted to simulate demo charges and cord that simulated fusing and primacord.

He motioned his squad forward and, as Alex stepped back, they swarmed up the structure, hesitating at certain key points to lay "demo charges" and connect the fusing and primacord.

Alex checked his stopwatch and grudgingly admitted to himself that even fanatics can be good. The mockup was actually one of the tube-latches that the raid was intended to destroy on Urich.

Mathias and his men dropped off the structure and doubled up to Alex. Mathias and one other man were trailing simulated det fuse. Not even breathing hard, Mathias snapped to a halt and saluted.

"Well, Sergeant?"

"Ah reckit y'r times fair," Alex said. "Noo. Twicet more an' ye'll hae i' doon pat. Then, t'night, w' comit back an' run th' drill again. Wi'oot light."

The landing field was scattered with more of these practice structures, and, on each of them, a mixed group of mercenaries and Mathias' Companions rehearsed what they would have to be able to do drunk, wounded, gassed, or blind when the strike force hit Urich.

Otho's howls of rage were moderately awesome, Sten realized, listening to the Bhor rage on about what had been done to his trading lighters.

"Armor! Projectile cannon! Shields! Chem protection! By my mother's beard, have you any idea how long it will take us to reconvert our lighters to useful configuration?"

"Don't worry about it, Otho," Sten said. "Probably we'll all die on Urich and then there won't be any problems."

"Och," Otho agreed, brightening and slugging Sten on the back. "By my grandsire's womb, I never thought about that. Shall we share some stregg on the thought, Colonel?"

"Mathias?"

"Six hundred trained men, present, ready."

"Vosberh?"

"We're ready."

"Ffillips?"

"All teams trained, aware of targets, ready for commitment."

"Egan?"

"Intelligence, ECM, sensors all on standby."

"Sergeant Kilgour?"

"No puh-roblems," Alex purred.

"Order group number one," Sten said. "All troops are restricted to base camp area, effective immediately. You may inform your troops that Parral's units are patrolling our perimeter with instructions to shoot on sight any soldiers attempting to take French leave.

"We board ship in two days. I expect all men to be fully converted to all-protein diet, water-packed, and all equipment to be double-checked and shock-packed. We will board ship when Mathias and I return from Sanctus.

"That is all, gentlemen."

CHAPTER THIRTY-TWO

STEN STOOD AT full attention before the tiny altar in the Prophet's study. Next to him was Mathias. Theodomir was chanting a steady stream of prayers and waving the incense wand to all points of the compass.

Finally he approached Sten himself and stopped in front of him. "Who brings the candidate?" he intoned.

"I do," Mathias answered.

"Have the proper purification rites been performed?"

"They have."

"And has this man proven himself worthy of Talamein and all we hold holy?"

"This I swear," Mathias said.

"Kneel," the Prophet commanded.

Sten did.

Theodomir touched the wand lightly to each of Sten's shoulders, then stepped back. "Rise, O Faithful One. Rise as a Soldier of Talamein."

Sten barely had time to climb to his feet before Theodomir had palmed the switch that slid the little altar out of sight. The Prophet slopped a chalice full of wine and guzzled it down. Sten thought he caught a quickly masked flash of distaste from Mathias.

"Drink, Colonel, drink," the Prophet said. "An honor like this does not come every day."

Sten nodded his thanks and poured himself a cup of wine and sipped at it.

Theodomir beamed and rubbed two hands together. "Tell me, Colonel. What runs through a soldier's mind on the eve of battle?"

Sten smiled. "As little as possible."

The Prophet nodded in what he thought was understanding. "Yes, I imagine all thoughts would be of an earthly nature. Thoughts of the flesh. Personally, as your spiritual leader, I could not agree more.

"And Colonel, a little advice. Man to man. I know that there are any number of young women, or . . . ahem . . . men . . . on Sanctus who would be willing to share your last hours."

Again Sten thought he caught a faint look of displeasure from Mathias. "Thank you for your advice, Excellency." Then, after a moment: "Now, if you will excuse me, sir, I have many things to do."

The Prophet laughed and waved his dismissal. "Go to it, Colonel. Go to it."

Sten bowed, saluted, wheeled, and exited. Theodomir's smile vanished as the doors hissed closed, and he looked thoughtful. "You know," he mused to his son, "that could be a very dangerous man."

"I assure you," Mathias protested, "he is fully committed to our cause."

"Still," the Prophet said. "During the heat of battle, if you should have the opportunity . . ."

Mathias was appalled. "What are you saying, Father?"

The Prophet's eyes bored into him, reminding the young man of his place. Mathias stood nervously, but with a determined expression on his face. Finally the Prophet chortled and refilled his wine cup. "Just a thought. I'll take your word on Colonel Sten's dedication."

Then he waved his son away, and Mathias left. The Prophet began chuckling, drank down his wine and poured more.

"You have a great deal to learn, my son. A great deal indeed."

CHAPTER THIRTY-THREE

URICH WAS AS well designed and laid out as any Imperial Guards Division depot. It was the only development on an otherwise deserted world. From two hundred kilometers overhead, it looked like an enormous U. At the open end of the U was shallow ocean, useful for engine testing, a fixed approach pattern, and also, of course, a "soft" place for crash landings.

At the curve of the U lay the shipyard itself and, at its center, the enormous bulk of the engine–hull mating plant. Alongside that plant were the machine shops, shielded and bunkered chem-fuel dumps, steel mills, and so forth.

Along one side of the U were docked the major elements of the Jann fleet—a few former Imperial cruisers, some rebuilt light destroyers, and a host of small in-atmosphere and patrol ships. Plus, of course, the necessary support craft—tankers, shopships, ECM ships, and so forth.

On the other side of the U were endless kilometers of barracks for the Jann troops when they were off-ship. As the raiding force approached Urich, there were approximately nine thousand Jann on Urich, an equivalent number of yard workers and yard security, and General Suitan Khorea, the commanding general.

CHAPTER THIRTY-FOUR

OTHO WATCHED THE screen time-tick seconds until dropaway with half his attention. The other half was listening to the droned story from behind him, coming from the humanoid that Otho sometimes found himself wishing to be a Bhor:

"Ahe," Alex went on. "S' th' Brit gin'ral hae order't ae squad up tha' hill f'r Red Rory's head. An' aye, a pickit squad wan' roarin' upit tha' hill.

"An tha's screekit an' scrawkit' an' than, bumpit, bumpit, bumpit, doon tha' hill comit th' heads ae th' squad.

"An' th' Brit gin'ral lookit up tha' hill, an' on th' crest still standit thae giant.

"An' he skreekit, 'Ah'm Red Rory ae th' Glen! Send up y'r best comp'ny!'

"An' th' Brit gin'ral turnit a wee shade more purple, an' he say, 'Adj'tant!'

"An' th' adj'tant sae, 'Sah!'

"An' th' Brit gin'ral sae, 'Adj'tant, send up y'r best comp'ny! *Ah wan' that mon's head!*'

"The adj'tant sae 'Sah!'

"An' he sendit oop th' hill th' reg'mint's best comp'ny!"

And the timeclick went to zero and Otho touched the button. Alex cut his story off as the Bhor captain got busy.

"By Sarla, Laraz, and . . . and all the other gods," Otho muttered, then swiveled his shaggy head to eye Sten.

"You know what's going to happen, Colonel. Those chubbutts who brought us here will probably skite for safety the minute we enter Urich's atmosphere."

"I doubt it."

"Why not?"

"Because I haven't paid them and because Parral will have them thin-sliced if they do."

"But what happens if they do do?" Otho heard what he'd just said and grunted. "You see, Colonel, you try to make me a soldier and then I lose everything. Pretty soon I'll be grunting primordial Bhor."

"Which is ae differen' frae th' way y' talkit noo," Alex asked interestedly. Otho just sneered.

Otho, three Bhor crewmen, Alex, Sten, Mathias, Egan with two com specialists, and the ever-present Kurshayne overfilled the control room of the *Atherston*. Packed safely away in shockmounted compartments were the first wave, two companies of Mathias' troops and Vosberh's men.

Hanging in space around them were the fifty Bhor lighters, filled with Ffillips' commandos and the remainder of Mathias' force.

Otho stared at Sten, as if waiting for him to say something noble. Sten had a mouth too dry for hero speeches; he just waved, and Otho ratcheted the drive to full power and targeted the ship toward Urich's surface.

The Jann picket ships were quickly destroyed by low-speed interdiction missiles that the Bhor lighters had launched two hours before. They had no chance to warn the planet below.

The first clue the main base had was when five one-kiloton nukes flared, just out of the atmosphere. No fallout, no shock, no blastwave, but a near-continuous electromagnetic pulse that, momentarily, put all the Jann sensors on *burble*.

By the time the secondary circuits had cut in, the *Atherston* and the Bhor assault lighters were in-atmosphere, coming in on a straight, no-braking-pattern approach.

As the attack alarm blatted, Jann gunners ran for their posts. One Jann, faster or better trained or more alert, reached his S/A launch station and, on manual, punched five missiles up into the sky.

Above him, a Bhor tac/air ship banked, turned through ninety degrees, and, at full power, blasted toward the field. Its pilot had only time enough to unmask his multicannon before the first Jann missile went off, spinning the lighter sideways.

The gee-force went over 40. Too much even for the massive Bhor. The pilot and copilot blacked out. A millisecond later, the second and third Jann missiles impacted directly on the lighter.

A ball of flame flowered in the morning sky as other ships dove in to the attack.

"Your mother had no beard and your father had no buttocks," a Bhor tac pilot grunted as he brought his control stick back into his gut, and the lighter flattened out, barely a meter above the landing field. The pilot locked a knee around his stick and both hands flashed across the duck-foot cannon mounted in the lighter's nose.

Fifty mm shells exploded from the duck-foot's six barrels, then the weapon recoiled, dropping the first set of barrels down into load position and bringing the second set up.

The antipersonnel shells from the cannon, warheads lovingly filled with meta-phosphorus and canister, ricocheted off the thick landing ground's concrete and exploded, shrapneling through the Jann running for their combat stations.

The pilot lifted at the end of his run, keeping the stick all the way back, and the inverted lighter came back for another pass, the pilot's laughter roaring louder than the slam of the cannon firing.

"We should be receiving fire by now," Otho said cheerily and dumped the ship atmosphere. Sten swallowed hard as his ears tried to balloon—they were still some six thousand meters off the deck.

There was a dull crash from somewhere in the stern, and indicator lights turned red. The internal monitor terminal scrolled figures that everyone ignored.

A radar belched and flames began curling out.

Sten keyed the ship's PA mike. "All troops. We are taking hits. Minus thirty seconds."

In the troop compartments the soldiers tucked themselves more tightly into their shock capsules, tried to keep their minds blank and their eyes off the man next to them, who probably looked as scared as they were.

* * *

Below them, on the field, most Jann AA stations were manned and coming into action, in spite of the intense suppressive fire from the strafing Bhor ships.

Missiles swung on their launchers, sniffing, and then smoked off into the air. Multibarreled projectile weapons nosed for a target.

There was only one good one:

The chunky, rusty mass of the *Atherston*, now only four thousand meters above the field, drive still billowing heatwaves into the air, crashing toward them.

"Station three . . . we have a compartment hit. All units inside counted casualties," a Bhor officer said.

"Whose?" Vosberh asked. Before he heard the reply, a missile penetrated the control bubble and exploded. A meter-long splinter of steel split his spine just above the waist.

Sten pushed the body out of the way and checked Otho. The Bhor's beard was bloody and one eye seemed to be having trouble. But his growl was loud and the grin was wide as he reversed drive on the two Yukawa drive units that had been added for braking force.

"Two hundred meters—"

And Sten dove for his shock capsule.

As it drove downward, the *Atherston* looked as if it were held aloft on a multicolored fountain of fire, and every weapon on the field swung and held on the unmissable target. Quickly the *Atherston*'s compartments and passageways were sieved; Bhor and men died bloody.

Otho's second in command dropped, blood gouting from a throat wound as he slumped over the controls. Kurshayne was out of his capsule, staggering against the gee-force and at the panel. He ripped the dead Bhor away from the controls, then flattened himself on the deck just as one Yukawa braking unit, still under drive, was shot away from the ship and skyrocketed upward.

Most of the Jann guns and missiles diverted onto the drive tube as it arced up into the sky.

And then there was nothing in Sten's eyes but the massiveness of that huge hangar as the ship closed and the doors rose up toward him and became the center of his world and his universe and:

The *Atherston* smashed through the hangar's monstrous doors as if they were wet paper. The ship hung, impaled in the concrete, and then, as if in slow motion, the doors to the engine–hull mating plant broke away and tumbled the ship down into a ground-shuddering impact on the field itself.

"Come on! Come on!" Sten was screaming as he heard the det charges blowing the crumpled nose cone away and then the dry grinding of broken-toothed gears as they tried to lower the landing ramps.

Alex had Otho over one shoulder and was pushing a limping Kurshayne ahead of him as they dropped out of the control room, into the swirling mass of Mathias' and Vosberh's soldiers as the latter ran out onto the landing field.

But no panic, no panic at all. Sten watched proudly as the weapons came off the men's shoulders and the perimeter specialists hit it, set up their crew-served weapons and began spattering return fire into the Jann units.

A vee-bank of Bhor lighters swept across the field at the height of a man's chest, cannon and rockets pumping and fire drizzling out of their sterns.

Smoke began roiling up from the Jann positions.

"Let's go! Let's go! Move! Move!" And why the clot can't I do anything more inspiring than shout as Sten and his team doubled around the corner of the hangar, toward their own assigned demo targets.

And why the hell am I shouting when it's so quiet? Clot, man, you're deaf. No, you aren't, as Sten realized that the only fire was coming from his own troops as they moved out, blindly following the assault plan.

Alex was shouting for cease-fire, and Otho grumbled his way toward Sten, bloodily grinning.

"We have one hour, Colonel, and then by my mother's beard this whole world of the black ones will go down and down to hell."

Less poetically Sten decided that Otho was telling him he'd set the timer on the ship's charges—conventional explosives, but enough to equal a 2KT nuke.

Khorea briskly returned the salute as he entered Urich's main command post. The command staff in the bunker were calm, he noted with approval, and all observation screens were on.

"Situation?"

"We have approximately one thousand invaders on the ground," an officer reported. "No sign of major support or assault ships entering atmosphere. All ships are tac/air support. No sign of potential nuke deployment."

"The invaders—the mercenaries?"

"It would appear so, General."

"And that"—he gestured at the screen, where the crumpled hulk of the *Atherson* lay, still buried in the mating plant's shattered doors—"was their mission?"

"Yes," another Jann said. "Evidently their intelligence incorrectly estimated the thickness of those doors. No plant damage is reported. In fact, General, after the raiders are removed, we can have the plant operational in three, perhaps four cycles."

"Excellent."

Khorea mused to himself as he sat down at the main control board. The cursed of Theodomir have tried another raid. This time they failed, but they will try to commit as much damage as possible. With no pickup ships reported, they must expect to be able to take and hold Urich. Which means they expect us to surrender.

Impossible, his mind told him. The mercenaries cannot know so little about the Jann. So they are suicide troops? Equally impossible. Well, possibly not for those—he eyed a screen—red-uniformed ones we have heard reports about, who call themselves Mathias' Companions. But the others are mercenaries. Mercenaries simply do not die for their clients.

Therefore—analysis complete. Further input needed, Khorea's mind told him as he issued a string of orders intended to close the Jann circle about the raiders and destroy them utterly.

"Out. You people must get out of here," Ffillips chided. She stood, weapon ready, over a cluster of workmen kneeling in one shop. Behind her two of her teams reeled det wire across the shop.

"We do not kill civilians," Ffillips said. "Now you run. Get very far away from here."

The workmen came to their feet and shambled toward the exit. Ffillips sighed in satisfaction and turned back to watch her teams at work.

But one Jann workman stooped hastily near a dead commando and had a projectile weapon up, raised, aimed at Ffillips as the white-haired woman leaped sideways, turning and firing. The spatter of rounds cut the man in half.

Ffillips got back to her feet and shook her head sadly. "But still, you must admire dedication," she told herself.

"Kill them! Kill the Jann!" Mathias raved as a wave of his Companions poured into a barracks door. The barracks, however, was a dispensary. Lying in the beds were the normally injured and sick of any industrial center.

None of them was armed.

It did not matter to Mathias or to his Companions.

The patients died as they squirmed for shelter under their beds.

From overhead, as the Bhor strafing ships dipped and swooped, firing at anything resembling a black uniform, the port of Urich was in chaos. Here smoke or flame flared; there a building mushroomed outward. Troops scuttled from shelter to shelter.

The raid was progressing very well.

"Pretty," Kurshayne said.

They were. Sten/Alex/Kurshayne's own target was the Jann design center, specifically the complex design computers in the building's basement.

But the booths for the designers were hung with sketches and models. Some of them, Sten knew, must have been made by people who loved the clean, swept beauty of interstellar ships.

So? Sten pulled the toggle on the twenty-second timer, and electricity pulsed through the portuguese-man-of-war-swirl that the det blocks and wiring made across the building's floor.

Kurshayne was still staring, fascinated, at one ship model. Sten grabbed the model and shoved it deep into the man's nearly empty backpack. "Move, man, if you don't want to go into orbit."

As the three men doubled-timed out of the building, the charges rumbled and then went off and the center fell into its own basement.

No, Ffillips decided. No man, even a Jann, should die like that.

She and three commando teams were crouched behind a ruined building. Across the square from them was a skirmish line of Jann. And, above them, a huge tank of chem fuel.

Between the two forces one of Ffillips' men lay wounded in the center of the square.

"Recovery!" one of Ffillips' men shouted, and she sprinted out into the open. A Jann calmly broke cover, aimed, and put a shell through the would-be rescuer. Then switched his aim and gut-shot the wounded man.

Which effectively made up FFillips' mind, and she sprayed rounds into the chem tank above the Jann. Liquid fire turned the black-uniformed killers into dancing puppets of death.

"All first-wave units committed, General," the Jann said.

"Thank you, Sigfehr," Khorea returned, and eyed his battle screen. Very well, very well. My first wave has held the mercenaries in place. Now my second wave will break their lines and the third wave will wipe them out.

He was curious as to what possible intentions the mercenary captain had—he still could see no rationale for the suicide raid.

The charges on the *Atherston* were quadruple-fused, just to make sure nothing could go wrong. Even so, two of them had been smashed out-of-circuit in the landing.

But two more ticked away their small, molecular-decay timers.

Brave men of the Jann reinfiltrated back to their AA positions, and slowly the weapons pits returned to life. Suddenly it was worth a Bhor's life for him to lift his lighter higher than the port's buildings.

The commando team edged forward, out of the shadows toward their target. As they moved into the open, a Jann missile lost its intended target—a Bhor lighter—in ground-clutter and impacted into a building.

All those commandos might have heard was the explosion of the missile and then the crumble as the ten-story structure poured down on them.

Their target would not be destroyed, and, for years afterward, some of their friends would wonder, over narcobeers, just what had happened.

The second wave of Jann, Khorea observed, was moving most efficiently. They did seem to be making inroads against the raiders' perimeter.

The third wave, now that the Bhor tac/air ships had to keep their distance, was drawn up in attack formation on the landing field, close to that ruined freighter.

Very well, Khorea thought. Now the Jann will show their courage.

Sten sighted carefully through his projectile weapon's sights and touched the trigger. Eight hundred meters away a Jann Sigfehr convulsed, threw his weapon high into the air, and collapsed.

Sten slid back into the nest of rubble he, Otho, Kurshayne, and Alex were occupying.

Kurshayne had dug out the model Sten had given him and was evidently staring at it in fascination. Sten started to snap something about children, toys, and their proper places when he noticed the small blue hole just above one of Kurshayne's eyes.

Alex crawled up beside Sten, and they looked at Kurshayne's corpse, then at each other. Wordlessly they clambered back up to the top of the rubble heap.

Contrary to the livies, even good men died at the least dramatic time.

A dusty and battered Egan checked his watch, peered out at the wreckage of the *Atherston*, then decided to see how far under the nearest boulder he could crawl.

"Men of the Jann." Khorea's voice rang through the PA.

"You have the enemy before you. I need not tell you what to do. Sigfehrs! Take charge of your echelons and move them to the attack!"

As that third wave of Jann doubled forward—more than three thousand elite soldiers—past the wreck of the *Atherston*, a decay switch ran out of molecules.

For the first time in Sten's experience, Alex had been doubtful about what would happen when charges went up. "Ah ken i' th' door's gone, we'll hae ae wee fireball inside yon plant. But wha'll happit whae yon fireball hits yon *back* door ae th' plant, ah lad, Ah dinna ken. Ah dinna ken."

What did happen was quite spectacular: As intended, the shaped charges on the *Atherston* blew straight out the open-nosed bow of the ship into the engine–hull mating plant, creating a quite impressive fireball—almost half a kilometer high. It rolled forward, at something more than 1,000kps, toward the back door.

But the back door to the hangar did not drop, contrary to everyone's expectations. Instead, the fireball back-blasted, back up through the plant and back out, over the *Atherston* and onto the landing field itself.

From overhead the explosion might have resembled a sideways nuclear mushroom cloud as the now unrestricted blast-wave bloomed across the enormous landing ground. Directly over the charging Jann troops.

About the best that could be said is that it was a very, very quick way to die, mostly from the pressure wave, oxygen deprivation, or by being crushed by debris hurled from the hangar. Only the unlucky few on the blast's edges became human torches.

But in less than two seconds, three thousand Jann ceased to exist. As did the engine–hull mating plant. Nothing less than a high-KT nuke blast could have actually obliterated that huge building. But Sten's demo charges lifted the building straight up—and then dropped it back down on itself.

Some of Sten's men, in spite of specific orders, were too close to the blast area. They died. Others would never hear again without extensive surgery.

Sten's raid was more than satisfactory.

A side benefit—one which would ultimately save Sten's life—was that the Jann command bunker's com net was cut and Khorea, together with what little Jann command staff still lived, would be buried for at least three days.

CHAPTER THIRTY-FIVE

PARRAL LEANED CLOSER to the vidscreen, watching the action from Urich with a great deal of interest. Sten's plan had more than succeeded.

But Sten had done much too well. As far as Parral was concerned, the war was over. Only one final blow was needed, and that Parral would take care of himself.

He switched circuits and keyed the command mike to his transports hanging in space off Urich. "This is Parral. All ships will break orbit. I say again: All ships will break orbit. Navigators, plot a course for home. That is all."

None of Parral's skippers, of course, protested. They were all too well trained. And, as the ships turned on Parral's vidscreen, the merchant prince was mildly sorry he didn't have a pickup down on the planet's surface, to watch Sten's final moments.

He was sure they would be terribly heroic.

CHAPTER THIRTY-SIX

STEN SHOVED A chunk of melted plas off his legs and staggered to his feet. Across the crater, Otho stared in befuddlement as Alex grinned at him.

"Dinna tha' go, lad?" Alex said proudly. "Dinna tha' be't tha most classic-like blast Ah hae e'er set?"

Sten groggily nodded, then turned as Egan stumbled into the crater, his eyes wide in panic. "Colonel," the boy shouted. "They've abandoned us!"

Sten gaped at him.

"We're stuck here! They've abandoned us!"

Then Alex was beside Egan, shaking him and not gently.

"Tha be't nae way to report, so'jer," he reproved. "Dinna y'ken hae t'be't ae so'jer?"

Egan brought himself back under control. "Colonel Sten," he said formally, but his voice was still shaking. "My com section reports a loss of contact with Parral's freighters. Plotting also shows all the pickup ships have disappeared from their orbits."

And then Egan lost it again. "They're leaving us here to die!"

BOOK FOUR

RIPOSTE

CHAPTER THIRTY-SEVEN

"WHAT DO YOU think?" Tanz Sullamora asked proudly.

Clot polite, the Emperor thought. "Slok," he said, quite clearly.

Sullamora's face began falling in stages.

The painting, like the others, was what the Eternal Emperor could have called Russian-heroic. It showed a tall, muscular young man, with dark hair and blazing blue eyes. Good muscle tone. The young man was armed with what the Emperor believed to be an early-model willygun and was using it to hold off a mixed horde of crazed alien- and humanoid-type fanatics.

The gallery itself was stupendous, almost a full kilometer long, and hung with what Sullamora had assured the Emperor was the largest and most valuable collection of New Art in the Empire.

The paintings were all massive in canvas and theme, all painted in the superrealistic style that was the current rage. The medium was a high-viscosity paint whose colors shifted with the light as the viewer moved. Always the same color, but slightly different in tone. The "paintbrush" itself was a laser.

Each of the paintings that the Emperor had stared and then scowled at showed another heroic moment in the History of the Empire.

And each one was so realistic, a cynic like the Emperor wondered, why bother with a paintbrush when a computer-photoreconstruction would do just fine?

Sullamora was still in shock, so the Emperor decided to elaborate. "It's abysmal. A vidcomic, like everything else in this gallery. Whatever happened to the good old days of abstract art?"

Sullamora headed one of the largest entities operating under Imperial Pleasure, a conglomerate that was, basically, a vertical mining discovery-development-exploration subempire. He was very successful, very rich, and very pro-Empire.

Privately his tastes ran to the horrible art the Emperor was looking at and prenubile girls taken in tandem. Which was why he had invited the Emperor to the gallery opening, and which was also why he now slightly resembled a Saint Bernard who'd discovered his brandy barrel was empty.

Sullamora managed to cover his first reaction of pure horror and his second, which was to tell the Eternal Emperor he was a fuddy-duddy with no appreciation for modern art.

Instead, looking at the muscular, mid-thirties-appearing man who was the ruler of stars beyond memory, he backed down. Which was his first mistake. He whined, which was his second. The Eternal Emperor liked nothing better than a good argument, and he loathed nothing more than a toady.

"But I thought you would be pleased," Sullamora tried. "Don't you recognize it?"

The Emperor looked at the painting again. There was something familiar about the man, but not the incident. "Clot, no."

"But it's you," Sullamora said. "When you turned the tide at the Battle of the Gates."

The Eternal Emperor suddenly recognized himself. A little better looking, although he always considered himself moderately handsome and certainly more heroic than he felt. The Battle of the Gates, however, had him stumped.

"*What* battle?"

"In the early days of your reign."

And then, suddenly, the Eternal Emperor remembered. His laughter boomed across the yawning gallery. "Do you think I did that?" he chortled, pointing at the drawn blaster and the screaming hordes.

"But its well documented," Sullamora protested. "It was you who made the final stand during the Uprising seven hundred years ago."

"What kind of a fool do you think I am? Hell, man," the Emperor said, "do you think—when the drakh hit the ducts— I stood out in front of anybody with a gun?"

"But legend—"

"Legend me arse," the Emperor said crudely. "You should know you can always buy a man with a gun. Nope, Sullamora, this is not me. During that Uprising I made clottin' sure I was far behind the lines with the bribes."

"Bribes?"

"Of course. First thing I did was put a price on the heads of the Uprising leaders.

"Like good capitalists, the rebels turned in their own leaders." He smiled at the memory. "It was horrible," he said. "Blood everywhere."

"And then what did you do with the rebel soldiers?" Sullamora blurted out, despite himself.

"What do you think?"

Sullamora puzzled this over and then smiled. He had it. "Execute them all?"

The Eternal Emperor laughed again. Sullamora shuddered; he was beginning to hate the Emperor's mocking laughter. Although he knew it wasn't directed entirely at him, his skin crawled at the feeling that it was aimed at the entire human condition.

In that, he wasn't far wrong.

"No," the Eternal Emperor said, "I hired them. Gave them all double raises. And now, next to the Imperial Guard, they're the most trusted regiment in my forces."

Sullamora filed that odd logic away. Perhaps this kind of personal insight might be of use to him. But, no, it would never work. How could you ever trust men who had tried to kill you? Better to crush them quickly, and get it over with.

He looked at the Eternal Emperor with new disrespect.

"You got anything decent to drink?" the Emperor asked.

Sullamora nodded, boldly grabbed the Emperor by the elbow, and led him to his private chambers.

The Eternal Emperor had been drinking steadily for two hours, telling obscene stories about incidents in his reign. Sullamora forced a laugh at the Emperor's latest joke and, with a great deal of distaste, realized that the Emperor always made himself the butt of all his jokes. The man's a clotting fool, he thought, and doesn't mind anyone knowing it.

Quickly he buried the thought. It was about time to make his move, he realized, noting the fact that the Eternal Emperor had consumed enough spirits to stun a mastodon, without benefit of anti-inebriation pills. With that reminder, Sullamora secretly popped the fourth pill of the evening. He looked at the Eternal Emperor's bleary eyes and decided the time was right.

"I hope this has been a pleasant visit," he ventured.

"Shhure, Shalla . . . I mean . . . Sha . . . no . . . Tanz. That's it, Tanz." The Emperor sloshed out another glass and belted it down.

"Great night. Now. Lesh . . . I mean . . . Let's me and you go hit a coupla port bars. Get into a fight. Get into trouble . . . then finda coupla ladies.

"I know some ladies with figures like"—he made curving motions—"and minds like . . . like . . ." He snapped his fingers—obviously these women were sharp, sharp. "We'll argue all night, then . . . then . . . you know . . . all night." The Eternal Emperor gave Sullamora a sudden, sharp, terribly sober look. It came to the man as a shock.

"Unless," the Eternal Emperor said, "you have something else on your mind."

"But . . . but . . ." Sullamora protested, "this is just a social occasion . . . to show you my new gallery."

The Eternal Emperor laughed that mocking laugh again. "Give me a break," he said and, ignoring Sullamora's bewilderment at the anachronism, pushed on. "You're the head of the largest mining company in this region.

"You got something on your mind. And you don't have the cojones to ask for an audience. Instead you give me all this royal treatment. Clotting artsy garbage—and lousy art at that. Try to get me drunk.

"Now you're just trying to get up the nerve to dump on me."

"I haven't the faintest—"

"Context, Tanz. Context. Clot, what do they teach corporate executives these days? Why, in my time—Hell with it. One more time—what's on your mind, Tanz?"

And Tanz, haltingly, told him. About his company's plans to follow up on the rumors in the Eryx Cluster. His spies (although he did not use that word) had assured him that the gossip about the potentially superwealthy fields was a fact . . . And Sullamora wanted to personally hand in his company's application for exploration to the Eternal Emperor.

"Shoulda asked me straight out," the Eternal Emperor said. "Can't stand a man who hems and haws."

"All right," Sullamora said. "I am asking you—'straight

out,' as you say. My company is willing to invest the credits to exploit this new area."

The Eternal Emperor didn't even think about it. "No," he said flatly.

He took pity on the man, filled up Sullamora's glass, and gave the corporate president time to choke down a huge swallow. "What I had in mind," he said, "was a consortium."

Sullamora spewed his drink across the table. "A consortium!" he gasped.

"Yeah," the Emperor said. "You get together with other big mining companies—I've already put out some feelers," he lied, "put together a consortium and go at Eryx as a unit—then you can exploit the clot out of it."

"But the profits," Sullamora protested. "Too many companies . . ."

The Eternal Emperor raised a hand, interrupting him. "Listen, I've already made my own studies. Any single mining company that attempts to exploit Eryx on its own is heading for bankruptcy. It's a frontier area, after all. Now, if you people pool your resources, you might make a go of it. That's my suggestion."

"Your suggestion?"

"Yeah. Take it or leave it. Just a thought. Oh, by the way— your latest request for an increase in your company's AM2 supply? . . ."

"Yes?" his voice quavered.

"Think about this consortium deal, and I might consider it."

Since the source of all power (AM2) was supplied and controlled by the Eternal Emperor, Sullamora had just been kicked in the place where it would hurt the most.

The Eternal Emperor took another drink. Slammed the glass down, making Sullamora jump about two feet.

"Tell you what," the Eternal Emperor said. "If you like my consortium suggestion, I might even double your AM2 quota. What do you think of that?"

Sullamora was not as dumb as he appeared. He liked that offer very much, thank you.

"Double their quota?" Mahoney asked in amazement.

"Clot, no," his boss said. "I hate these mining companies. They're almost as bad as the Old Seven Sisters . . ."

He waved a "forget it" at Mahoney's ignorance.

"Actually, for old times' sake, I might halve it once they put this consortium together."

Mahoney was aghast.

"You mean you're actually considering letting people into the Eryx Region? Don't you remember how far away we are—"

The Eternal Emperor held up a hand, stopping him. He grinned at Mahoney and mock-tugged at his forelock.

"Where's the congratulations for your brilliant boss? I just bought you more time, Mahoney."

Mahoney was silent.

The Emperor caught it, leaned forward across his desk. Steepled his fingers. "Something wrong, Colonel?"

Mahoney hesitated.

"What's going on, dammit!"

"Our operative. Sten. I can't raise him."

The Emperor sagged back. "Which means?"

"Hell if I know, sir. All I know is Mercury Corps Appreciation: All bets are off."

And the Emperor reached for his own bottle. "Clot! I just may have outsmarted myself."

CHAPTER THIRTY-EIGHT

"HE . . . HE'S . . . DEAD?"

"I'm afraid so, dear."

And Parral bent forward to comfort his weeping sister. Sofia leaned into him for warmth and then jolted away. She wiped away her tears.

"But how?"

Parral gave her his best warm, brotherly smile. "Oh, he fought bravely, as did the other men. But I'm afraid it was just too much for them. A trap. They died to a man."

Sofia held her brother's gaze for a moment, wondering if it was true, wondering if her brother had—no, that was too much even for Parral.

With a great heaving sob she collapsed into his arms.

CHAPTER THIRTY-NINE

"EGAN'S DEAD," THE Lycée girl said in a monotone.

Sten just nodded. There wasn't time or energy to mourn.

"He's dead," the woman continued. "He was just walking out of the shelter for rations and they flamed him."

Viola shut up, and sat looking at and through Sten with the thousand-meter stare. Before Sten could make appropriate comforting noises, Alex had led her away, taken the computer terminal from her pack, and set the woman to figuring out some kind of strength report.

Not that it was needed. The figures were already thoroughly graven into Sten's mind:

TROOPS COMMITTED: 670 (Sten had landed with 146 of his original mercenaries, plus 524 Companions.)

TROOPS REMAINING: 321.

Clottin' great leader you make, Colonel, his mind mocked. Only 50 percent casualties? Fine leadership there. And now what are you going to do?

He heard a scraping sound behind him and turned to see Mathias crawling up. He crouched beside Sten, staring at him intently, his face pale, his eyes full of anger and hate. Hate . . . not at Sten . . . but . . .

"My father," he said. "Did he give the orders to abandon us?"

Sten hesitated and then said quite truthfully, "I don't know."

"His own son," Mathias hissed. "My Companions . . ."

Sten put a hand on the young man's shoulder. "It was probably just Parral," he said. "Parral playing his own game."

Mathias dragged a sleeve across his grimy face. "I should have suspected . . ." His voice trailed off. Sten steeled himself. He had to start thinking, not talking, not feeling sorry for himself.

"Mathias," he snapped, and the young man jolted to semireality. "Get back to your men. Await my orders."

Mathias nodded numbly and slithered back to his position.

Sten cautiously lifted his head above the boulder and eyed the perimeter. After they'd realized Parral's transports had abandoned them, the force had found a defensive perimeter in the four-block-wide chunk of demolished machineshops. They had dug in and waited for something to happen.

They were completely surrounded by the surviving Jann—a force that Egan, in the last estimate before his death, had surmised to be about five thousand.

Only about twenty to one odds. Easy—if you're a hero in the livies. So you have a little more than three hundred troops left, most of them wounded, Colonel. By the way, you forgot the Bhor.

Indeed. The thirty or so Bhor, since they could no longer fly, had fought on the perimeter as berserkers. Sten was only sorry that, evidently, Otho must've died in the original withdrawal. No one had reported seeing him or his body. Add thirty hulks. So, Colonel? What, then, are your options?

There are only four possibilities in battle:

1.–Win.
2.–Withdraw.
3.–Surrender.
4.–Die in place.

It didn't take a battle computer to run the options. Winning was out, and there was no way to withdraw. Surrender wasn't even an option—five of Sten's mercenaries had tried that tactic. Now they were out in the middle of no-man's land between Sten's perimeter and the Jann lines. Crucified on steel I-beams. It had taken them almost a day to die—and most of them had been helped by grace rounds from the mercenaries.

No. Surrender to the Jann was not possible.

So here it is, young Sten. After all your cleverness and planning. Here you are, facing your only option—to fight a holding action that'll go down in history beside Camerone,

Dien Bien Phu, Tarawa, Hue, or Krais VII. Wormfood, in other words.

And then anger flared. Well, and his mind found the phrase from Lanzotta, the man who'd punted him through basic Guards training: "I've fought for the Empire on a hundred different worlds and I'll fight on a hundred more before some skeek burns me down, but I'll be the most expensive piece of meat he ever butchered."

He spun back toward the command circle. "Alex!"

The voice command—and Kilgour found himself at attention.

"Sir!"

"Six hours to nightfall. I want you and five men—volunteers from Ffillips' unit—standing by."

"Sir!

We have location on the Jann command post?"

"Aye."

"Tonight, then. We go out."

And a smile spread slowly across Alex's face. He knew. Indeed he knew. And it would be far better to die in the attack than huddled in this perimeter waiting for it.

CHAPTER FORTY

IT HAD TAKEN almost two days to dig Khorea and what little remained of his command structure out of the bunker. They'd found him, huddled under a vee-section of the collapsed ceiling, deep in trance state.

The Jann medics had quickly brought him out of it, and Khorea had refused further aid. He'd insisted on taking charge of the final destruction of the mercenaries.

Khorea was probably still in minor shock, delayed battle stress. He had ordered the slow death of the mercenaries who'd deserted and insisted that all Jann be ordered to take no prisoners. He was determined to wipe out the far-worlders who'd shamed the Jann—to the slow death of the last man and woman.

Khorea now sat behind the hastily rerigged computers and screens in the command post. He hated them and longed for the days when a leader led from the front.

Then he half smiled. Realized that all of his electronics, all of his analysis, produced only one answer—the mercenaries would not, could not, surrender.

He shut down his command sensor and stood.

"General!" An aide.

"Tomorrow. We will attack. And I will lead the final assault."

The aide—eyes wide in hero worship—saluted.

"Tonight, then, assemble my staff. We shall show these worms what Jann are, from the highest to the lowest. But tonight—tonight we shall assemble for prayers. Here. One hour after nightfall."

CHAPTER FORTY-ONE

"... BUT BEFORE WE could stalk the streggan," the ancient Bhor creaked, "there was preparation. We fasted and considered the nature of our ancient enemy. And then, once we had determined our mind upon him, we feasted. Then and only then would we set out across the wave-struck ice to find him, hidden deep in his lair. ..."

Ancient, Otho thought, wasn't the word for the old Bhor. One sign of approaching death for a Bhor was for the pelt on his chest to begin turning gray. Shortly thereafter, the Bhor would assemble his family and friends for the final guesting and then disappear out onto the ice to die the death, lonely but for the gods.

This Bhor, however, was almost totally white-haired from curled gnarly feet to beetled brow. He was, as far as anyone knew, the last surviving streggan hunter.

And so they listened in council.

Just as the council had patiently listened to Otho, still being bandaged from the wounds incurred as he'd pirouetted his lighter up and out-atmosphere when he heard of Parral's abandonment.

Just as they had listened to the youngest Bhor discuss why the entire Bhor people must immediately support the marooned warriors.

Just as they had listened to the captain of a merchant fleet discuss calmly—for a Bhor (only two interruptions and one

193

hospitalization)—why the mercenaries should be abandoned and attempts made to reach reapproachment with the Jann. The merchant also happened to be Otho's chief trading rival.

But the council listened, as they would listen to any Bhor. The Bhor were a truly democratic society—any of them could speak at any council. The decision, which could take weeks to reach and involve several minor brawls, would have been discussed, argued, fought over, and then settled.

Once decided, the Bhor moved as of one mind. But the time it took! For the first time—and Otho realized his inspiration was a corruption gotten from those beard-curs't humanoids—Otho wondered whether his was an excessively longwinded and indecisive society.

And the ancient droned on, making no point at all, but telling the old stories. Normally Otho would have been the first to sit at the ancient's right, keeping him full of stregg, fascinated by talk of the old days. But his friends—friends, by my mother's beard, friends who are humanoid—were dying.

Otho ground his fangs. The debate might continue for another four or five cycles. Since Robert's Rules hadn't penetrated to the Bhor, there was only one customary way to force a vote. And generally it meant the death of the Bhor who did it. By my father's chilly bottom, Otho groaned, you owe me, Sten. If I live through this, you owe me.

The ancient creaked on. He was now describing exactly how you tasted a streggan's fewmets to determine whether the creature was seasonable or not.

Otho rose from his bench and stalked into the center of the council ring, his meter-long dagger leaving its belt harness.

Without warning, Otho pulled the long, trailing beard straight out from his chest and, with a dagger-flash in the firelight, cut it away. He tossed the handful of fur down, into the center of the ring, then, as custom dictated, knelt, head bowed.

To the Bhor, the length and thickness of one's beard signified personal power, much as the length of other appendages has signified similarly to other cultures and beings. To chop off one's beard, in-council, meant that the issue was life-defining.

And, since none of the Bhor appreciated threatening situations, normally the beard-cutter lost his measure and, shortly afterward, his head.

Grumbled comment built to a roar covering the ancient's reminiscences.

Otho waited.

And now—the issue on whether or not to support the human soldiers would be voted on. Otho would most likely lose and then a volunteer would separate Otho from his head. Most likely the volunteer will be his Jamchydd-cursed competitor.

But, contrary to custom, someone spoke.

It was the old streggan hunter.

"Old men"—and his voice was rumbled whisper—"sometimes lose themselves in the glories of their youth. Most of which, I recollect by the beard of my mother, are lies."

Bones creaked as the old Bhor rose. And then, in a blur, his own dagger flashed and the long icefall of the ancient's beard fell onto the flagstone's atop Otho's own beard.

The council was silent as the old Bhor knelt—nearly falling—beside Otho, head bowed.

CHAPTER FORTY-TWO

THE SNAP OF the man's neck was not all that audible, Sten knew, watching as Alex let go the first Jann's helmet and snap-punched a knuckled paw against the second man's face. Still, it *sounded* loud.

He lay to the side of the Jann observation post, flanked by the five volunteers—Ffillips' men, including their commander—waiting for Alex to finish his minor massacre.

The tubby man from Edinburgh made sure both Jann were dead, then rolled out of the OP.

They crawled on.

The Jann, very sure of themselves, had structured their defense line as a series of strongholds, with possibly fifty meters between posts. Sten wished that he had Mantis troopies instead of mercenaries and somewhere to go—it would have been simple to exfiltrate an entire battalion through those lines.

But he didn't and he didn't, and low-crawled on, below the unsophisticated EW sensors, pressure traps, and command-det mines that linked the strongholds.

Two interlocked Jann lines had been established, but the raiders had no trouble penetrating both of them.

Then, behind the lines, Sten and Alex eyed each other.

Sten wondered what Alex was thinking—and wondered why he hadn't found any words before they left the perimeter.

The second would always remain unanswered and it was as well for Sten's battle confidence that the first wasn't either.

Because, Alex was crooning, in his mind's voice, his death song:

"Ah sew'd his sheet, making my mane;
Ah watch'd the corpse, myself alane;
Ah watch'd his body, night and day;
No living creature came that way.

"Ah tuk his body on my back
And whiles Ah gaed, and whiles Ah sat;
Ah digg'd a grave and laid him in,
And happ'd him with the sod sae green . . ."

The raiders came to their feet and moved toward the command bunker. The low murmur of Khorea's vigil filtered through the entrance as they moved toward the structure.

Of the two sentries proudly braced at attention before the entrance, the first died with Sten's knife in his heart. The second caught a seeping circle-kick as Sten whirled, kicked, recovered, and drove a knuckle-smash into the sentry's temple.

And then Sten was standing above the bunker's steps, watching Alex's ghoul grin as he pulled a delay-grenade from his harness.

And then the Bhor arrived.

Their ships hurtled in low from the east, landing lights full-on. They burst over the ruined spaceport barely ten meters above the ground. Fire sprayed from their every port.

An efficient atmosphere trader also makes a fairly decent gunship, Sten realized, when all the off-loading ports are open and there are a dozen Bhors using laser blasts, multibarrel projectile cannon, and explosives.

Sten had time to wonder where their intelligence came from as the ships banked, curving just above the Jann lines, hosing death as they went, before the world exploded and Jann officers came tumbling up the bunker steps and Alex had the grenade among them and was spraying fire from his weapon and then the shock of the firewaves caught Sten and he was pitched forward, into the softness of corpses and tumbling down the steps and then . . .

He was inside the bunker.

Sten rolled off a sticky body, to his feet, then went down

again as he caught sight of the black-bearded Khorea, weapon at waist-level, and a burst chattered across the bunker at him and the lights went out.

Above him, Sten could hear the howls and screams of battle. Forget it. Forget it, as he moved softly forward in the blackness.

In the hundred-meter-square bunker there was no one but Khorea and himself.

Sten's foot touched something. He knelt and picked up the computer mouse. Tossed it ahead of him, and then nearly died as fire sparked out of the blackness not at the mouse's thunk where it hit something, but in a level arc behind the sound.

Sorry, General, Sten realized. I thought you were dumber than you are.

Lie here on the concrete and think about things. Ignore the war going on topside. You are here and blind in the dark trying to kill a blind man who has designs on your body.

Breathing from the diaphragm, eyes scanning emptiness, Sten crawled forward, knees and hands coming up, sweeping down, feeling for obstructions. Ah, a microphone with a cord attached . . . Interesting . . . A long cord.

Sten moved to a wall support and looped the cord around the support. A strand of the cord ran through the trigger guard of his hand weapon, and there was enough extension for him to slither five meters away.

The weapon was now lashed to the vertical beam. Sten pulled the cord experimentally. The weapon flashed, and the round ricocheted wildly off the ceiling, floor, and walls.

And Khorea triggered a burst at the flash.

Sten yanked the cord as hard as he could, and the weapon went back to full-automatic, and the darkness became a strobe-flare of flashings as the hand weapon spurted its magazine into the bunker and Khorea came up from behind a terminal, aiming carefully at the flashes and was aiming for the shot that would end the duel in blackness having only time to catch the blur of Sten in the air toward him and the flicker of the knife in Sten's hand and the knife drove into the side of his head and Sten smashed into the dead general and then painfully into a careening table.

And then there was no sound except from outside as the Bhor began their victory chant and grenades and small-arms fire resounded and Sten could hear the howl of his mercenaries and the Companions as they broke out from their death perimeter and came in for the final slaughter of the Jann.

And then Sten hooked up a chair with his leg and sat in the blackness, plotting his revenge against Parral.

CHAPTER FORTY-THREE

THE MEETING WAS on neutral ground—a planetoid in the Lupus Cluster's no-man's land. It was a Holy of Holies. It was the first place the founder of the religion, Talamein, landed when he fled to the cluster.

It looked a bit like a park, with broad meadows, gentle streams, and woods thick with small game, and one small chapel, the only building on the planetoid.

Two sets of troops faced each other from opposite sides of the chapel, with ready weapons and nervous trigger fingers. The soldiers were the personal guards of the two rival Prophets. After generations of fighting and atrocities on both sides, they were waiting for the signal to leap at each other's throats.

First Theodomir and then Ingild stepped away from their bodyguards and began the slow walk across the grass toward each other. Both men were edgy, not knowing what to expect. They stopped a meter or so apart.

Theodomir was the first to break. A huge grin on his face, he threw out his arms in greeting. "Brother Ingild, what joy it brings my heart finally to see you in the flesh."

Ingild also smiled. He stepped forward and gently hugged his rival, and then stepped back again. Tears streamed from his eyes.

"You said 'Brother.' How appropriate a greeting. I too have always felt as if you were my brother."

"Despite our difficulties," Theodomir said.

"Yes, despite them."

The two men hugged again. Then turned and walked arm and arm toward the chapel, before which was a small table covered with a white cloth. Shading it was a small, colorful umbrella. And on either side of the table were two comfortable chairs. There were documents on the table and two old-fashioned pens.

The two men sat, smiling across the table at each other. Theodomir was the first to speak.

"Peace at last," he said.

"Yes, brother Theodomir, peace at last."

Theodomir did the honors of pouring the wine. He took a chaste sip. "I know that at this moment," Theodomir intoned, "Talamein is smiling down on us. Happy that his two children have heeded him and are laying down their arms."

Ingild started to take a large gulp of wine, then caught himself. He took a very small, priestly sip. "We have been very foolish," he said. "After all, what are our real differences? A matter of authority, not theology. Mere titles."

You lying sack of drakh, Theodomir thought, smiling broader.

You great bag of wind, Ingild thought, smiling back and reaching a hand across the table for Theodomir to clasp.

"Brother," Theodomir said softly, his voice thick with emotion.

"Brother," Ingild said, tears dripping down his nose, equally emotional, wishing for all the world that he had dared to trank up with a few narco leeches.

"Our differences are so easily settled," Theodomir said. He shot a glance at Ingild's guards, wanting so badly to grab the wizened little drug addict by the throat and choke the life out of him.

"It came to me in a flash," he continued. "From the very lips of Talamein."

"Odd," Ingild said. "At that very moment I was thinking the same thing." And he thought of his awful casualties, and, more important, the terrible cost to the Holy Treasury. For half a credit he would gut the cheap piece of drakh right now.

"So," Theodomir said, "I propose a settlement. An ecumenical settlement."

Ingild leaned forward in anticipation.

"We cease all hostilities," Theodomir said, "And each of

us assumes the spiritual leadership of our rightful regions of the Lupus Cluster.

"Both of us will be called True Prophets. And each of us will support the claim of the other."

"Agreed," Ingild said, almost too quickly. "Then we can end this stupid bloodshed. And each of us can concentrate on his primary duty. Our only duty."

Ingild bowed his head. "Saving the souls of our brethren."

And in two years, he thought, I'll raid Sanctus with half a million Jann and burn your clotting throne to the ground.

Theodomir patted the documents in front of him. They were treaties, hastily drawn up by his clerks for the meeting.

"Before we sign there, brother," he said, "shall we celebrate together?"

He pointed at the small chapel.

"Just the two of us," he said, "in front of the altar, singing our prayers to Talamein."

Oh, you slime, Ingild thought. You heretic. Is there nothing you're not capable of? "What a marvelous suggestion," he said.

The two prophets rose and walked slowly into the chapel.

Parral eased back in his chair, watching the two on the monitor as they opened the door, disappeared inside, and closed the chapel door behind them.

Tears of laughter were streaming down his face. He had never seen anything so funny in his life. Two sanctimonius skeeks with their "brother this" and "brother that." Hating each other's guts.

He rang a servant for a jug of spirits to celebrate. What a master stroke. Theodomir had fought him when he had suggested the meeting. He'd screamed, almost frothed at the mouth.

And then he had become suddenly silent, when Parral explained the rest of the plan.

Parral leaned forward as the hidden monitors in the chapel picked up the two men inside. This is going to be very interesting, he thought.

He congratulated himself once again for having the foresight to remain on Nebta. Because, despite his assurances to Theodomir, he wasn't too sure how things were going to work out.

The two prophets were nearing the end of the ceremony, their chanted prayers echoing through the little chapel. It was taking way too much time, Theodomir thought. Normally a

High Joining took about an hour to go through. But each man was trying to outdo the other, keeping the prayers slow and solemn. Each word was enunciated as if Talamein himself were listening.

He thanked Talamein that only the moving of the book and the blessing of the sacrifical wine were left. The two men turned to the altar, out of time, of course, and waved their incense wands at the huge book, which sat in the center.

Then they took two steps forward, both lifting the book at the same time. Ingild started to move toward the right. Theodomir the left. Suddenly the two men found themselves in the middle of a tug-of-war.

"This way," Ingild shouted.

"No, no, you fool, to the left."

Then, almost at the same moment, they both realized who they were. Nervous glances around the empty chapel. Theodomir cleared his throat.

"Uh, excuse me, brother, but on Sanctus the book goes to the left."

"Is it in the treaty?" Ingild asked suspiciously.

Theodomir covered his impatience. "It doesn't matter," he said with difficulty. "In the spirit of ecumenism, you may put it where you like."

Ingild bowed to him. And shuffled off to the right, pleased with the small victory.

They moved quickly to the last part of the ceremony: the blessing and drinking of the wine. The golden chalice of wine sat inside a small tabernacle with a slanted roof. They opened the tiny doors, pulled it out, and then quickly chanted the last few prayers.

Theodomir pushed the goblet toward Ingild. "You first, brother," he said, urging him to drink.

Ingild eyed him, suddenly suspicious. Hesitated, then shook his head.

"No," he said. "You first."

Theodomir grabbed the cup impatiently and chugged down about half of its contents in a very unprophetlike manner. Then he shoved the cup at Ingild.

"Now you," he snapped.

Ingild hesitated, then slowly took the goblet. He raised it to his lips and sipped cautiously. It tasted fine. He drained the rest of the cup and then set it carefully on the altar.

"It's finished," he said. "Now should we sign those..."

He began to cough. A slight one, at first. Then it came in ever increasing frequency. His face purpled, and then he grabbed his sides and began to scream in pain.

"You fool, you fool," Theodomir cackled. "The wine was poisoned."

"But . . . but . . ." Ingild managed through his anguish, "you drank, too."

He toppled to the floor, writhing in agony, blood streaming through his lips from his bitten-through tongue.

Theodomir began dancing around him. Kicking him. Screaming at him.

"It was sanctified for me," he shouted. "Sanctified for me. But not for an addict. Not for an addict."

Ingild tried to struggle to his knees. Theodomir booted him down again.

"Who's the True Prophet, now, you clot? Who's the True Prophet now?"

Parral laughed and laughed and laughed as he watched Ingild's dance of death.

Then he flicked the monitor off. It was over. Oh, indeed it was over.

For a moment he wished young Sten were sitting in front of him. He thought the colonel would have appreciated his plan. There are so many ways to win a war.

And then his heart froze, and he unconsciously ducked, as rockets screamed overhead and sonic waves boomed and jolted his palace.

CHAPTER FORTY-FOUR

"GAD, COLONEL," FFILLIPS said dryly. "The villians have armor."
The woman appeared absolutely unworried as the mercenaries
and Companions took up fighting positions.

The Bhor, now seeing the commercial potential of backing
Sten, had gleefully agreed to help in the landing on Nebta.
They had scattered enough window and diversionary missiles
over Nebta's capital to confuse even an Imperial Security screen.
The Bhor transports had then slammed into the outskirts of the
capital. Sten thought that the Bhor skippers had deliberately
tried to take out as many monuments, mansions, and memorials
as they could.

For once, Sten was glad to note, he'd made an invasion
with no casualties—other than one of Vosberh's men, who'd
managed to get drunk on stregg and fall headfirst off the landing
ramp.

The three hundred soldiers had quickly formed up in battle
formation and moved toward Parral's mansion. And then tracks
had clanked and the ground rumbled and Sten realized that
Parral had given himself a second line of defense. Men against
armor.

Panic-factor for any inexperienced soldiers. But for the
trained? Sten tried to remember where he'd seen the centuries-
old illo of two crunchies staring at a track and commenting,

"Naw. Not for me. A movin' foxhole attracks the eye." And then turned to a grinning Alex.

"W'doomit," the man reported. "Parral's troopies hae fifty wee recon tracks an' twenty or so ACVs. Shall w'ae surrender?"

"Try not to hurt 'em too bad" was Sten's only comment.

The Battle of Nebta—the first and probably only one—lasted barely an hour as the vee-formation of tracks clanked into the attack.

Alex picked up a crew-served, multiple-launch, self-guiding rack, carried it forward until the point of the vee-formation was almost on him. Then he triggered the missiles. The small rockets huffed out the tubes, shed their compressed-air launch stages, turned themselves on, and went hunting. Five of the rockets promptly homed on different tracks and turned them into fireballs. The sixth, for reasons known only to its idiot computermind, had decided that a statue of one of Parral's ancestors was a more important target and had taken that out.

The ACV vehicles had been short-stopped by a quickly massed wire screen, two meters high. They'd bumped up against the wire, then drifted back and forth while their only semitrained drivers fought the controls and then those drivers had been calmly sniped down by Sten's soldiers.

The two command tracks had lasted a few minutes longer—as long as it took the ten remaining Lycée kiddies to cut off all commo and for Sten and three men to slip behind them and launch line-of-sight rocketry into their unarmored rear boarding ramps.

It wasn't much of a battle, Sten realized as he saw Ffillips jam a huge crowbar into one assault vehicle's tracks and step back as the crowbar turned into filings and Ffillips commented disappointedly, "Some of my older manuals swear that an obstruction in the idler wheels will stop any track," before she flipped a fire grenade onto the greasy engine exhaust and the track became a bonfire.

And then the tracks were halted and their crews were piling out and Sten now knew why conventional soldiers still wear white undertunics as Parral's last line of defense began surrendering en masse.

"So now, Sten thought, it is time to deal with our friend Seigneur Parral . . .

CHAPTER FORTY-FIVE

PARRAL WAS RUNNING out of alternate plans. His great scenario calling for the Jann and the mercenaries to pull a Kilkenney cats on each other had somehow failed. Even his high-tech defense scheme with the imported armor was a bust. So Parral was supervising the loading of the last few art treasures into the ship.

The ship—a modified short-haul, high-speed freighter—had been set down in the middle of the mansion's grounds and the most portable and easily convertible of Parral's treasures stowed on board.

His new plan was to get off Nebta, hunt up some habitable world, and go to ground until the screaming and skirmishing stopped. If it ever did. Because with Ingild dead, the Jann no longer a factor, and his own power-play circumvented, the Lupus Cluster faced the threat of peace for the first time in generations.

He was pretty sure that Sten would turn over Parral's trading routes to the Bhor. Which would leave Parral somewhat less than necessary.

Oh, well, he consoled himself, under no circumstances can that drunk fuzz-kleek Theodomir hold things together for very long. Sooner or later he'd need expert help, money, and someone who could stay sober for longer than two hours. The mansion and Nebta could be rebuilt.

The last servant loaded the last painting, and Parral hurried up the ramp. He could hear the rifle fire approaching closer and closer. So? Let them loot the mansion. As the port closed, he managed a tiny moment of concern for his sister, Sofia, who'd disappeared some hours before. Then he shrugged. Perhaps she thinks she can do better with her bedmate Sten than with her brother.

Parral headed for the control room. The exec had been holding the ship on thirty-second–takeoff point for almost an hour. As Parral sank into the acceleration couch, the pilot began final countdown.

Outside, a haze built from the Yukawa drive, and the carefully sculpted gardens of Parral withered and died.

Five seconds and counting . . .

"Talamein has blessed us," Mathias crooned as he focused the helmet sights across the mansion grounds. "We are chosen by Talamein for his purpose." His fingers touched ready-buttons on the firing panel.

Mathias and ten of his Companions had hastily set up the S/A missile ramp on the avenue behind Parral's mansion. Mathias closed the helmet face, and his viewpoint became the restricted dual-eyes of the missile, the launch-tube looming to either side, and, visible at the center, the heat-waved trees of the mansion gardens. "I have it," he announced.

His hands went around the twin joysticks of the missile control panel. "Launch on command sequence."

"Standing by," a Companion announced.

"Systems on standby. All systems on ready condition."

Mathias felt the tremble as, a thousand meters away, Parral's ship lifted from the estate. Prematurely he keyed the launch button on top one of the joysticks, and suddenly his vision became broad and fish-eyed as the missile came out of the tube, hissing fifty meters up into the atmosphere.

Mathias kept his other thumb poised on the number-two joystick's primary drive switch. The launch button now automatically became the manual-det switch.

Mathias orbited the missile, waiting for Parral's ship to come out of ground-clutter, and then, as the sleek torpedo swept back around, he had the missile's sensors on IR visual.

"Normal vision," he snapped. A companion flipped the switch on the primary switch and the missile howled up through Mach 8, crosshairs centered on the nose of Parral's ship as it clawed for height. The gray steel closed in Mathias' eyes until there was nothing but the heat-shimmer and the metal and then his eyes went blank.

Mathias yanked the helmet from his head in time to see the fireball sweep down the nose of Parral's ship, catch the fuel tanks, and become an elongated cigar of flame, debris slowly pinwheeling back down toward the ground.

His Companions were cheering as Mathias dropped out of the command seat. Mathias allowed himself a laugh, then turned his face serious.

"Not I," he said as the cheering suddenly stopped. "But Talamein. I count myself blessed that Talamein has chosen me as the tool for his vengence, for the beginnings that shall make the Faith into the fire-hardened sword the Original Prophet intended. For this—which I vision as merely the beginning—we shall give thanks."

Which was why, when Sten and Alex burst through the brush, they found the ten men knelt in prayer, seemingly to an empty short-range portable missile launcher.

CHAPTER FORTY-SIX

SOFIA SAT ON a small boulder just at the water's edge. She was staring out to where the huge waves she loved were still continuing their thunder, regardless of man's change.

Twenty meters behind her, just on the fringe of the black sand, Sten waited.

He'd found Sofia in hysterics in the mansion as his troops swept through, moving the servants out from the wall of flame that Parral's crashed ship had started. He'd slammed a med-shot trank into her arm and ordered her moved to his own headquarters. Then, and it was very hard, he forced his mind back to business, to the endless details of what happens when you've won a war and what to do next.

The first, of course, had been a chain-coded message sent on Parral's high-power transmitter, to a clean transponder on some worldlet just outside the Lupus Cluster. The message, a short series of code breaks, read:

> GOOD GUYS CHOSEN AND VICTORIOUS. GOOD GUYS ARE THEODOMIR. PHASE A & B COMPLETE. APPROPRIATE ACTION IN YOUR DEPARTMENT NOW.

Within three Imperial hours, the message had been through

the Mercury Corps chain and was in Mahoney's and the Emperor's hands. And a return message went back:

> STAND BY. IMPERIAL CONFIRMATION ON WAY. DO NOT EMBARRASS THE EMPEROR. LAYING ON OF HANDS WILL COMMENCE IN ONE WEEK. DO YOU PREFER PROMOTION, MEDAL, OR LONG LEAVE? YOUR PERFORMANCE DEEMED IN THE SNEAKY TRADITION OF MANTIS.

Which left only minor details until the Emperor and his entourage showed up to confirm Theodomir as the rightful Prophet and leader of the Lupus Cluster. Minor details like burying the dead, nurturing the sick, keeping the mercenaries from outrageous looting, and . . . and Sofia.

And so they had gone to that black beach. Neither Sofia nor Sten had said anything until the grav-sled set down. Then Sofia dropped her clothes and paced to the boulder where she had sat silently for almost two hours now.

Suddenly Sofia rose and walked back to Sten. She curled down onto the sand beside him.

"You did not kill my brother?"

"No. I did not."

"Would you have if you had the chance?"

"Probably."

Sofia nodded. "You and your soldiers will be leaving now."

"Yes."

"I will go with you."

Sten hesitated—he didn't think it would be a good idea for Bet to meet Sofia even though Bet was no longer his lover. And explaining that Sten was neither a colonel or an ex-soldier would prove interesting.

Sofia shrugged. "You will be taking a vacation with your pay?"

"Probably."

"I will spend it with you." Baronial habits die hard. "And then," Sofia went on, "I shall go. I have always wanted to see the Imperial Court."

Sten covered a slight sigh of relief. Love is wonderful, but it does not last as long as soldiering. Unfortunately.

"For a while, at least, I will not wish to see Nebta," Sofia finished. Sten had no comment. She took his hand, and they rose and walked into the small hut on the edge of the beach.

CHAPTER FORTY-SEVEN

FIVE *HERO* CLASS Imperial battleships hung in stationary orbit above Sanctus. The hovering sharks were attended by a cruiser squadron and three full destroyer squadrons. The formation was backed by a half fleet of auxiliary ships, planetary-assault craft, and two battalions of the First Guards Division.

When the Emperor came to dedicate a building or to legitimatize a conqueror, he preferred to have no surprises—least of all those that began with a bang and directed some sort of projectile in his direction.

The fiche that the courier ship had delivered weighed almost a full kilo and contained everything there was to know or do about its subject:

Protocol Manual for Imperial Visits.

It included such pieces of information as to what weaponry an honor guard could carry (no crew-served weapons, no individual edge weapons, individual weapons with their firing-section disarmed, no magazines in weapons); length of welcoming speech (no more than five minutes); number of people permitted to speak on landing (three maximum); quartering requirements for Imperial security (one barracks plus apartments adjoining the Imperial suite); dietary requirements for security element (normal Imperial diet for plainclothesmen; dhal, rice, and fowl or soyasteak for Gurkhas); and so on and on, endlessly.

Embarrassingly thorough and detailed, the fiche was one of the reasons why the Emperor had survived—by his personal estimate—more than 160 assassination attempts, only three of which had been successful.

It was, of course, one of Sanctus' few sunny days. On an island continent, this also meant it was muggy enough to swim in.

The assembled hierarchy of the Church of Talamein, who'd been standing on the reviewing stand in their full formal robes since an hour before dawn, collectively and silently wished for a good dense fog or perhaps even a snowstorm.

The Emperor—by deliberate policy—was keeping them waiting.

The worthies stood on the kilometers-square landing ground, with ranked Companions in their full dress uniforms around them. Across the field, behind guarded perimeters, were those lucky citizens of Sanctus permitted to view the first Imperial visit to Sanctus. Or, for that matter, to the Lupus Cluster.

Mathias and his father stood side by side, sweating ignobly. Neither of them found any reason to talk to the other.

And then the crowd murmured as, high overhead, five specks materialized and hurtled toward the field.

The specks grew larger and became cruisers. The crowd began to cheer—the cruisers were the Emperor's advance guard. The ships sonic-crashed to a halt a thousand meters above the field, then sank slowly, one to each corner of the landing ground and the fifth directly opposite the reviewing stand.

Landing ramps slid out, and uniformed troops double-timed down them, drawing up into line formation across the field. They were Guardsmen, and their locked-and-loaded willyguns were at the ready.

From the fifth ship two other formations ran down the ramp toward the reviewing stand. All of them were in the fairly plain brown livery of the Imperial household. And all of them were former Guards, Mercury Corps, or Mantis operatives.

Swiftly, without worrying about anyone's dignity, they checked the Companions' weapons to make sure they were, indeed, unloaded.

Another squad, murmuring apologies, came onto the re-viewing stand and ran mass-detectors over the dignitaries.

Theodomir was humiliated. One plainclothesman even had the temerity to confiscate the tiny flask of wine that Theodomir had in an inner pocket as an emergency resource.

Then the head of security took a small com unit from his belt and keyed it. Spoke in an unintelligible code. He listened, shut the com unit down, and turned to Theodomir. He bowed deeply.

"You will prepare to receive the presence of the Eternal Emperor, Lord of a Thousand Suns."

And Theodomir, reluctantly—he was the anointed Prophet of the Faith of Talamein!—found himself bowing back in awe.

"Colonel," the Emperor asked, a trifle plaintively, "would a single drink matter to these clots?"

"Nossir," Mahoney said—but made no move to the decanter in the dressing room.

Neither did the Emperor.

"One of these eons," the Emperor continued, "I shall come reeling down that ramp, declare in a high falsetto that this bridge is now open, and proceed to circumcise the first dignitary I see with the ribbon-cutting scissors. Then I will vomit over the rest of whatever noble thieves are greeting me."

"No question at all," Mahoney agreed blandly. "Excellent idea."

"Oh. One thing. Your operative, this—"

"Sten."

"Sten. Yes. He and his mercenaries have been instructed?"

"They're out of sight, sir. You won't see any of them."

"There were no problems?"

"None at all. Theodomir is embarrassed by them, and a good percentage of the mercenaries are deserters from the Guard. Also, since when did a soldier like to stand at attention until he passes out?"

"Colonel," the Emperor said, checking for the nineteenth time whether the button-line on his midnight-black tunic was even, "you know about psychology and all that. Why do I still get nervous doing this kind of thing—after a thousand years?"

"It's your constant youthfulness," Mahoney said. "Your charming naivete. The awareness that makes all of us love and serve your Eternal Worryship."

"Bah," the Emperor growled, and touched a button. "Captain. Land this bucket. I'm getting tired of waiting."

* * *

The five battleships, each nearly a kilometer in length, hissed down toward the field, and their black shadows merged and blocked Sanctus' sun.

Four of them hung a hundred meters overhead, but the fifth, the *Vercingatorix*, dropped to ground gently on the landing field. And then, following orders, its captain cut the McLean generators and the ship proceeded to sink twenty meters into the field itself. It was the Emperor's own way of autographing a world.

The side of the ship dropped open and became a twenty-meter-wide ramp.

Theodomir waved wildly, and his band began playing. Twenty bars into the song, the band broke off, as no one had yet appeared at the ramp's top. Just as the band squealed and ground to a halt, the Emperor walked down the ramp. Three beats after him, two Gurkha units came down behind him. As the small brown men spread out to either side, the Emperor walked toward the reviewing stand.

The Emperor gives good ceremony, Mahoney thought to himself, watching the solitary man walk toward Theodomir's stand. Two turrets on the *Vercingatorix* swiveled to cover the stand itself.

The Emperor stopped in front of the stand and waited.

And the hierarchy of Talamein dropped to its knees. Even Theodomir, recognizing he was committing some enormous breach, went down.

Only Mathias stayed on his feet, eyeing the muscular man standing below him.

The Emperor keyed his larnyx-mike and, on the *Vercingatorix*, techs found the symp-frequency of the landing field's speakers and patched the Emperor to them.

"I greet you, O Prophet," the voice echoed and reechoed across the field. "As your Emperor, I welcome you and your people back into the fold of Imperial protection. And, as your Emperor, I recognize the heroism and truth of your beliefs and the long martyrdom of your founder, the Original Prophet Talamein."

Then the Emperor flipped his mike back off and started up the steps to the stand, wondering how long he could make these fools sweat in the sun before he had to let them move on to the next, totally predictable stage of the ceremony.

* * *

"And this," Theodomir said proudly, "is a replica of the very gun station Talamein himself manned on the Flight for Freedom."

Mathias, the Emperor, and Theodomir were deep in the heart of Sanctus' inner fastness, touring the treasures of the faith.

The Emperor was preceded by plainclothes security men to each station, plus leap-frogging squads of Gurkhas. Behind them by about forty meters was an awestruck draggle of dignitaries and Companions.

"You know," the Emperor said conversationally, "I knew Talamein. Personally."

Theodomir blinked and Mathias now felt an urge to kneel. The Emperor smiled at their confusion.

"I found him . . . interesting," the Emperor continued. "Certainly it was unusual to find so much dedication in a man so youthful."

Mathias blinked—the only holos he'd seen of Talamein showed him as an elderly, bearded man. He was not sure which was the greater shock—to realize that, indeed, Talamein had walked the face of the Galaxy as a man, or that the soft-spoken man across from him had actually spoken to the First Prophet.

Far behind the group there was a stir as one Companion heard the echoed words of the Emperor, gasped "heresy," and scrabbled for his weapon, momentarily forgetting it was deactivated.

Before his hand touched the holster snap, the razor steel of a Gurkha kukri was at his throat, and he heard a soft hiss: "Remove your hand, unbeliever. Instantly."

The Companion did just that, and the young havildar-major smiled politely, bowed a bit, and resheathed his long knife.

The Emperor chose to make his announcement after the services, on the broad steps of the inner fortress itself. This time his speech was recorded and patched into a cluster-wide broadcast.

"I have visited Sanctus," he said. "And I have seen the fruits of Talamein and found them worthy of belonging to my Empire.

"I further have known and listened to this man, your prophet Theodomir, and find him both good and wise.

"For this reason, I declare that the hand of the Emperor is extended over the Lupus Cluster and its people, and shall assist in whatever means requested.

"And I declare that this Prophet, Theodomir, is the legitimate ruler of the Lupus Cluster and that he and his descendants, until I choose to withdraw the hand of support from over their heads, are the legitimate rulers of this region.

"May the powers of the universe and the First Prophet Talamein bless and approve this decision."

And then there was mass cheering and hysteria and the Emperor wanted more than anything else to get back to the ship, shed his robes and have several—no, many—drinks.

But he couldn't. Now the banqueting would start.

CHAPTER FORTY-EIGHT

MAHONEY COUNTED TOMBS as he crept down the Avenue of Monuments. He found the specified crypt and waited. No sign of being followed. No one waiting for him. He came to a crouch and moved into the blackness of the crypt entrance.

"Colonel," Sten's voice came out of the darkness, "I think we might have a problem."

"GA," Mahoney said flatly.

"No hard data."

"I said report."

"Feelings, rumors. There's talk of a holy war. It's nothing I can pin down."

Mahoney was somewhat grateful for the darkness. Sudden shock is not the appropriate reaction to display before one's underlings.

"Theodomir?"

Sten shrugged.

"How?" Mahoney asked. "He's an alky. Corrupt. No drive."

"I know," Sten said. "It doesn't make sense."

"How about Mathias?"

"It's possible," Sten said. "Look, I told you it was just talk. Still, it bothers me. I just wish you would have given it more time to settle out."

Mahoney considered a moment, and then nodded. "You did ask for more time," he said.

Sten didn't say anything.

"You were right, lad. We should have waited for the situation to settle out further. I cannot tell you why, but there was no time."

"All right," he continued wearily. "You're the man on the spot, Lieutenant. Prog?"

Sten fingered the lump in his arm that was the knife and thought hard. "Damfino," he said frankly. "But I'd better find some way to keep my mercs together for a while. All I can think of is to hang tough in the situation.

"You realize what might happen in a worst-case scenario— aside from a half-million slaughtered miners, full-out war in the Lupus Cluster, armed prophets spreading through the Universe, and full committment by the Guard—don't you? I mean to you and me, lad, to mention the important things."

"I go to a duty battalion and you go to a field command."

"Wrong. We both will be swinging pulaskis on some swampworld. You as a private and me as a sergeant," Mahoney said. "That's providing, of course, the Eternal Emperor doesn't use our guts for our winding sheets.

"At this stage of the game, though, I guess your prog's right. Hopefully, if the worst comes down, you and your troops can figure a way to shortstop the problem. But I doubt it."

He shook his head sadly and started out of the crypt.

"Colonel?"

"Yes, Lieutenant?"

"A favor. Actually, two of them?"

Mahoney stopped dead. Lieutenants do not ask personal favors of their commanding officers, not even in Mantis Section. But lieutenants also normally lacked the temerity to tell their commanding officer his battle plan was full of drakh.

"What?"

"I had a man serving with me. A Private William Kurshayne. He died during that last raid on the Jann."

"Go on," Mahoney said.

"He was ex-Guard. First Assault. I'd like him reinstated posthumously. And a medal wouldn't hurt, either. If he's got any people it might make them feel better."

Mahoney didn't ask if it was deserved. Still, he shook his head. "How do I find his records, Lieutenant? Do you know how many Kurshayne's we must've had in the guard?"

Sten grinned.

"You'll find the right one easily, sir. Busted fourteen times and recommended for the Galactic Cross about four times."

Mahoney reluctantly agreed. He would do it.

"And what's the other favor, since I'm evidently picked as your dogsbody, Lieutenant?

Sten hesitated. "It's more personal."

Mahoney waited.

"It's about Parral's sister," Sten finally said. "Sofia."

"Beautiful woman."

"Take her out with you. She wants to be presented at court."

"You think the situation is that close, lad?"

"I don't know, sir."

Mahoney considered, then shrugged. What the hell. He'd do that, too.

"Tomorrow night, Lieutenant. Start of third watch. Have her report to the *Vercingatorix*. Ramp C. I'll take care of her."

"Thank you, sir."

CHAPTER FORTY-NINE

THE ISLAND CONTINENT of Sanctus seemed to shudder as the Imperial fleet lifted from the ground, hovered for a moment parallel with the reviewing stand where Theodomir and Mathias stood flanked by the Companions. Then the ships hazed and vanished straight up into blackness.

Far down the field, behind a hangar, stood Otho, Sten, and Alex.

Sten waved good-bye to Sofia. She had taken the news of her imminent departure with little surprise. At least she had said very little. But then neither of them had in their last wild flurry of lovemaking before Sten escorted her to the landing ramp of the huge Imperial battleship.

He put that part of his life into his backbrain and turned to Otho.

"You humans have such a love of farewells," the Bhor began.

"Not now, Otho," Sten said. "I want you to get one of your combat lighters fueled and on ten-minute standby. And I want two ships standing by off Nebta.

"For the lighter, I want two of the gunners you used on Urich as crew and yourself as pilot."

Otho's brow beetled upward. "Impossible, Colonel. With the war over, I have my mercantile interests, which I've already had to—"

221

"This is important. Because if you don't, there might not be any Bhor mercantile interests ever."

Otho grunted, then seemed to understand. "You have no reasons for this?

"None I can tell."

"Then I do understand. It is your weird."

It was Sten's turn to look perplexed.

"It shall be done. I will have the ships off Nebta in five days. I assume they will be used in case your soldiers need immediate shelter."

Sten sighed in relief. Now, at least, he'd set up a back door for himself and the mercenaries.

Unfortunately his weird, his fate, would be determined in less than twenty hours. Far too soon for Otho's ships.

CHAPTER FIFTY

STEN GROUNDED THE gravsled at the end of the dirt track, climbed out, straightened his uniform, and walked on.

Beyond the track led the path to the camp of Mathias' Companions, a path now newly blazoned with their scarlet banner. And, as he walked past the hanging banners, he remembered something that Mahoney had told him, about there being nothing more dangerous than a soldier who's gotten his first hero ribbon.

"Ten-hut!"

Mathias, flanked by two Companions, was waiting at the path's last bend. The three were drawn up at full attention, holding salutes. Sten, in return, gave them the almost-limp, afterthought salute of a ranking officer.

"As you were," he said, and the Companions relaxed.

Mathias strode forward, hand outstretched, his face one huge smile. "Colonel," he said. "I am truly happy you could come."

Sten allowed his hand to be pumped and fixed Mathias with a straight stare. "The war's over now," he said. "I have no official rank, no titles with you." He dropped the hand and took a slight step back. "I took your invitation as a command." Then, after a moment: "Or did you mean it otherwise?"

"I meant it as an invitation to a friend," Mathias said, taken somewhat aback. Then he took Sten by the arm and guided him to the tiny gym. "We have a great deal to discuss."

Sten raised an eyebrow.

Some changes had been made in the tiny gym's office. A huge, semiheroic picture of Mathias had been added, and an equally large photo of the officers of the Companions—Mathias in the center. And, Sten noticed, a very small portrait of Mathias' father, Theodomir. A large bulletin board had been added, and it was crammed with very military advice, announcements, and orders from Mathias.

You've been a busy boy, Sten thought. I taught you well. He forced a smile as Mathias poured himself a goblet of water and nodded Sten toward a decanter of wine. Sten ignored the wine, reached for the water, and filled a cup. He raised it in toast to Mathias. "To victory," he said, and gulped the water down.

Mathias returned the toast.

"To victory," he said, sipping at his water. He sat, nodding for Sten to relax as well. Sten sat and waited, something he was becoming very good at.

"You have changed the history of this cluster," Mathias finally said.

"With some help." Sten nodded to Mathias.

Mathias looked at Sten across the desk, struggling with something. Suddenly he rose and began pacing the room. "I look around me," he said, "and everywhere I see evil. I see hypocrisy. I see empty mouthings of faith."

Sten knew Mathias was speaking of his father and kept silent. Mathias whirled on Sten. "I—we can change that."

"I'm sure you can," Sten said. "Someday you'll be Prophet. When your father dies."

Mathias gave Sten a look that was almost begging. "It's still all wrong right now," he said. "The war isn't over."

"I don't know what you mean," Sten said. "As far as I am concerned—and apparently the Eternal Emperor as well—it's over."

He pushed through Mathias' halting objection. "Be patient," he advised. "In a few years—twenty or thirty at the most—you'll inherit this whole thing." Sten waved his hand around the gym, but he meant the entire Lupus Cluster. "Wait until you have the power to change it."

"But the unbelievers—" Mathias blurted out, and then caught himself. Swiftly he changed the subject.

"What are you going to do next, Colonel?"

Sten shrugged. "Find somebody else to hire me." What will you do now, Lieutenant? Get your tail back to something resembling civilization where you don't have to check your compartment for bugs or assassins before you pass out every night. Get back in uniform. Go on a roaring drunk with my Mantis people. Pat a tiger or two. Listen to Doc's latest hatred for everything, Ida's schemes to buy up a galaxy, and maybe see if Bet's got the wanderlust out of her.

Suddenly Sten realized he was very, very tired and very glad the assignment was just about over. "Mercenaries drift a lot," he said, to cover his silence.

Mathias took a breath and then said, "Join me." He sat down quickly, turning his eyes away but waiting for Sten's answer.

Sten took a moment, as if considering. "There's nothing to join."

"The Companions," Mathias pled. "Join the Companions. I know that deep inside, you are as religious a man as we are. I'll give you rank. I'll give you money. I'll—"

Sten raised a hand to stop him. "I'm a mercenary, Mathias. Understand that. And a mercenary requires wars. And I've learned as a mercenary it is best to get out of your employer's way when the war is over."

Sten grabbed the wine and poured himself a drink. He sipped and waited again.

"But it isn't over," Mathias said.

Sten just looked at him. He drank the rest of his wine and rose. "Yes, it is. Take my advice. Let it be. This cluster is good for a thousand years of peace. When you become Prophet you—and your descendants—can do as you like."

He patted Mathias on the shoulder, a young man playing father to another youth. "And if it doesn't work out then," he promised, "let me know. And I'll be yours."

Sten walked from the room.

Very well, Mathias thought. I am sorry. So sorry for what I am going to have to do.

CHAPTER FIFTY-ONE

THEODOMIR HAD JUST finished the last prayer of the Joining. He rushed down the aisle, not even waiting for his aides or guards. Theodomir needed a soothing drink in the worst way. He glanced at the people still in their pews and laughed to himself. Just sheep, he thought, and boomed through the temple doors.

Theodomir clacked down the steps, feeling a little light-headed. With Parral gone, he was the Man in the Lupus Cluster. Sanctioned, even, by the Eternal Emperor. There was nothing he could not do. His merest suggestion was law over a thousand light-years.

But what he wanted just then, most of all, was a drink. And then he would think about the evening's entertainment. Who would he choose? he thought. Which child would he take to his bed? The boy dancer? Or the girl singer?

Both, he decided.

And then his son loomed up in front of him. Theodomir gave him a quick smile and started to push by.

"Father," Mathias said.

Theodomir paused on the steps, impatiently wondering what his dolt of a son wanted.

He started back as the young man drew a dagger. And, for the first time, Theodomir realized that Mathias was only one

226

of a half-dozen men, all dressed in the blood-red uniforms of the Companions.

"Can't it wait?" he complained, "I'm busy." Oddly enough, he knew what the dagger was for. But it was like a dream. Somehow he couldn't interfere.

Then he noticed that the other men also had unsheathed their daggers.

Theodomir screamed as his son plunged the dagger into his chest. And screamed and screamed and screamed as the others took turns stabbing knives into every available area of flesh.

Theodomir's guards thundered up, weapons out, looking wildly at Mathias and his Companions. Mathias looked down at his father. A final moan, a shudder, and the Prophet was dead.

"He is dead," Mathias informed his father's personal guard.

A moment's hesitation, and then there was a clatter as the men dropped their weapons and began to cheer.

Mathias was the True Prophet.

CHAPTER FIFTY-TWO

ANOTHER VAGUE MANTIS law: When in Doubt, Give Yourself an Escape Hatch.

Alex had set up the escape hatch immediately after Sten had returned from his meeting in the woods with Mathias. He had no prog but knew something was about to come down.

Since they were quartered in the Temple itself, the back door had consisted of two strands of granite-dyed climbing thread, hung out one window.

Inside a nearby urn were the figure-8 descenders and locking caribiniers necessary to get down that thread in a hurry. Both Sten and Alex had taken to wearing swiss-seat harness under their uniforms, hoping that when it hit the turbines they would be long gone offworld.

They were wrong but they were ready.

So, when the howling/mourning for Theodomir started, Sten and Alex were in motion. The first twenty ambitious Companions who'd come hurtling through the door had run into one of Alex's less pleasant surprises.

He'd hand-cast directional vee-mines, hooked them to sensors, and mounted them on either side of the portal. They made a significant mess, enough of a mess to delay the next wave of Companions.

The pause allowed Alex and Sten to hook the descenders onto the thread and back out the window. Neither of them found great exit lines as they pushed off, straight down the vertical wall of the Temple.

No one but a fool springs ten or twenty meters per leap on a long rappel—no one but a fool or an outgunned Mantis soldier.

They hit the ground at the bottom, Sten slamming down the last fifteen meters and thudding to safety with an oof. Then they shed their harness and were running.

"C'mon, lad," Alex urged. "W'nae hae truck wi' thae fruit-bars nae more."

And then they were out the gates of the Temple and running toward the town below, swinging into the backstreets toward Sanctus' landing field, where, Sten desperately hoped, Otho had the lighter waiting.

"Dinna worry," Alex flung back cheerily. "A' w' hae t'do is get away frae th' fanatics, gie oursel's offworld, an' then nae worries save th' wrath ae Mahoney an' th' Eternal Emp'ror."

And then a platoon of Companions was running down the alley. They spotted the two men and ran forward. Alex went down on one knee, weapon coming out of its pouch, and double-handed autofire into the men.

Then they were back up, running into a side passageway and Sten thinking, If I can only live through the next fifty minutes I can handle anybody's anger.

BOOK FIVE

FLÉCHÉ

The Further Adventures of Tabitsu... Idrya

CHAPTER FIFTY-THREE

MATHIAS, THE ONLY True Prophet of Talamein, stood before his Companions, a red sea stretching out before him in row upon orderly row.

The Prophet had been talking for three hours, retelling recent exploits, reaffirming their faith in him and Talamein, whipping them into a frenzy. Their voices were hoarse from shouting, their faces flushed, and in a few places there were gaps in the line where Companions had fainted.

Mathias had told them of the betrayal by Sten's mercenaries, who, in league with his father's guards, had foully conspired to assassinate his father.

Theodomir was a martyr to Talamein. Mathias assured the Companions that as long as he lived his father's name would never be forgotten.

Then he had led forward the traitorous members of his father's guard. The guards were silent, beaten. A few were weeping. One by one he had them executed, and the Companions cheered wildly as each man died.

Now Mathias was building to the final moments of his speech.

"This is not the death," he shouted, "that I plan for the mercenaries of the Traitor Sten. They are awaiting their fates at this moment in my cells, deserted by their two leaders, Sten and Kilgour, who made cowardly escapes."

"Kill them," the Companions screamed.

Mathias held up a hand for silence. "Not yet. Not yet, my brothers. First we will try them, so all the Empire will learn of their foul crimes. And then we shall convict them and execute them."

He smiled at his young troops. "I have appointed a committee of Companions," he said, "to determine how they shall die."

A small pause for effect. "And I promise you they shall be long deaths. Agonizing deaths. We shall squeeze from them every drop of blood possible to repay them for my father's death."

The Companions roared their approval.

Mathias lowered his voice, ready now to play his final card. "Lupus Cluster is ours now, my friends. And I dedicate my life as your Prophet, that all men may worship Talamein and bask in his glory."

"S'be't," his men shouted.

Mathias tensed, leaned forward, his eyes seeming to bore into every man's soul. "But there are huge forces now at work against us. Forces that deny Talamein."

A low moan of dismay swept the Companions.

"At this moment, our enemies are gathering. Creeping to our gates."

Another long pause from Mathias.

"I say we should fight," he shouted.

"Fight. Fight. For Talamein," they screamed back.

"I declare a holy war. A war against heresy. Against treason. Against all who blaspheme against the name of Talamein."

The men were in ecstasy, breaking ranks and rushing forward to lift Mathias up and carry him away in triumph.

CHAPTER FIFTY-FOUR

COLONEL IAN MAHONEY, still commander of the Mercury Corps, stood at attention, his heels locked, his face red, his spine a steel bar. He was receiving the chewing out of his life, a dressing down delivered by the all-time master of dressings down.

"Colonel Mahoney, I do not know what to do with you. I do not know what to say."

Mahoney refrained from noting that the Emperor had been at no loss for words for at least an hour.

"Do you *realize* what has happened, Mahoney? I have just given my blessing to a fanatic. A fanatic who calls me a heretic. *Me*. ME!"

Mahoney was wisely silent.

"Clot it, man, I hung myself out there like a babbling fool. State visit. Empire-wide vid coverage. I clotting declared the Lupus Cluster open."

He leaned across his antique desk. "And when I declare something open, by all that is holy in this silly sorry Empire that I was dumb enough to found, I expect it to *stay open*. Do you understand, Colonel?"

"Yes, sir!"

"Don't yessir me!"

"No, sir."

"Don't nossir me, either." He glared at Mahoney, trembling

235

with anger. Then a long sigh. "Ah, clot it, Mahoney. Siddown. Pour us a drink. Something nasty. Something poisonous. Something that will get me good and clotting drunk."

Mahoney sat—but did not make the mistake of relaxing. If it was possible to sit at attention, he did it. He reached for the Eternal Emperor's latest batch of experimental scotch and poured drinks. He sipped at his with as much military bearing as a man could possibly sip.

The Emperor noticed the scotch. Gave Mahoney a thin smile. "You never did like this drakh much, did you, Mahoney?"

Mahoney made a noncommital noise. And waited for the Commander in Chief of the greatest military force in human history to finish speaking his mind.

The Emperor shot back his scotch, shuddered, and poured himself another.

"I'm a reasonable man, Mahoney. I know how things can go wrong. All right. So I'm up to my butt in alligators. So what? I've been there before."

He drank.

"I only have one question," he said in his most reasonable tone of voice.

"Which is, sir?" Mahoney asked.

The Eternal Emperor rose to his feet.

"WHO PUT MY ARSE IN THE SWAMP, MAHONEY? WHO? WHOSE IDEA WAS THIS DEBACLE?"

Mahoney couldn't tell his boss it was, after all, the Emperor's idea.

"I take full responsibility, sir," he said.

"You're clotting right, you do, Mahoney. I'm gonna . . . I'm gonna . . . Colonel, I want you to think of the worst command in my empire. A hell hole. A place you won't be guaranteed to survive in for more than a week."

"Yes, sir."

"I want a full report on it by tomorrow."

"Yes, sir."

"Now, who's that other fellow. Lieutenant what-his-name?"

"Sten, sir. Sten."

"Right. Sten. Is he still alive?"

"Yes, sir."

"That was his first mistake, Colonel. Now, Sten. For him I have special plans. Do I still own Pluto, Mahoney?"

"I believe so, sir."

"No. No. Too soft. I'll think of something. You just leave

that Sten to me, Mahoney. You'll be too busy finding that hell hole I'm going to send you to."

"Yes, sir."

The Eternal Emperor eased back in his chair. Closed his eyes. Almost as if he were asleep. Mahoney waited a very long, very uncomfortable time. Finally the Emperor opened them again. He gave Mahoney a tired look. For a moment Mahoney could almost see just how very ancient the Eternal Emperor was.

"I'm counting on you, Ian," the Emperor said softly. "Solve it. Get rid of this Prophet for me. Get rid of Mathias."

Mahoney came to his feet, knowing that he had finally gotten the Emperor's orders. He snapped his best salute.

"That, sir, will be my extreme pleasure." He wheeled and began to march out.

"Mahoney?"

The Colonel stopped. "Yes, sir?"

"Just don't embarrass me again. Please? As a favor to an old drinking buddy?"

"I won't, boss."

"Being embarrassed is just one of those things I'm lousy at. Funny thing is, the older I get, the worse I am at it."

He looked up at Mahoney. "You'd think it would be the other way around, wouldn't you? You'd think by now I wouldn't give a clot."

"I wouldn't know, boss."

"Well, I do, Mahoney. I do care."

And the Eternal Emperor closed his eyes again. Mahoney silently crept out.

CHAPTER FIFTY-FIVE

AT THAT MOMENT, the prospect of exile on Pluto—or worse—
was the least of Sten's worries. He and Alex were hunched
over a com in Otho's castle, the coldest, grayest, dankest building Sten had ever been in. The two of them had been freezing
their behinds off for weeks and trying to endure the worst food
known to beingkind.

They had been notified two hours earlier to stand by on the
com. Mahoney was about to issue his orders.

"It'll be tha gibbett, lad, Ah just know it," Alex said.

"No," Sten replied. "Mahoney won't let us off with anything
as easy as death."

"Me mither always said Ah should'na be a soldier."

They froze as the com line crackled and Mahoney's scowling
face swam into view on the screen.

"I've just been to see the Emperor. He is not pleased."

"I can understand that, sir," Sten said.

Mahoney softened. "Ah, well, at least the two of you are
alive."

He peered out at them through the screen. "I tried to do the
best I could for you, gentlemen," Mahoney said. "But . . ." He
shrugged. It was the kind of shrug that did not bode well for
careers.

"What do we do next, sir?" Sten asked.

"*You* don't do anything," Mahoney answered. "Just sit tight.

Don't get into any more trouble. I'll have a ship pick you up in a few weeks."

"But Mathias—"

"Don't worry, Lieutenant Sten. We'll take care of Mathias. By the time you're home, I'll have inserted another Mantis team, and it should be over. One way or the other."

"Sir," Sten blurted. "Let me do it. Give me back my team. Team Thirteen. We'll settle Mathias for you."

Mahoney frowned. Alex gave Sten a warning nudge.

"Revenge, Lieutenant? I thought we had trained you better than that."

"No. Not revenge. We just have a better chance. I know Mathias. I know Sanctus."

"Can't take the chance, lad," Mahoney said kindly. "Among other problems, all the mining and exploration certificates were personally approved by the Emperor *before* Mathias decided on patricide. There's a whole fleet of miners heading for the Eryx Region. Straight through the Lupus Cluster."

"Mathias will kill them all," Sten said. "It's even more important that you let us handle it."

"I don't see how," Mahoney said.

"I have a plan." And he began talking quickly. Laying it all out, to an increasingly surprised Mahoney.

CHAPTER FIFTY-SIX

IT WASN'T THE first time Ffillips had been dragged, restraints chinking, up from a dungeon by thugs and hurled to her knees in front of Mathias.

But, the woman wondered, as she did a body-tuck, side-rolled away from the expected kick, and came back to her feet, it could well be the last.

The late and less-than-lamented Theodomir's throne room had seen considerable change, Ffillips realized as she glanced around. The tapestries and exotic statues were gone, as were the pillows on the stone chair.

The vidmap of Sanctus was now shadowed by an overlay of the Faith of Talamein—twin hands clasped in prayer, centered over a bare sword.

Only the twin torches to either side of the map remained.

On the stone throne sat Mathias, wearing the newly official uniform of undecorated red Companion full-dress. Ffillips bowed her head respectfully and kept her mouth shut—a delaying tactic that had worked quite well years before at her court-martial.

"I speak in the name of Talamein," Mathias intoned.

"S'be't," echoed the Companions ringing the bare walls.

"Here, in the most sacred place, seat of the faith of Talamein, I, Mathias, chosen by the Flame as Talamein's True Successor, I charge you, Major Ffillips, in the absence of your leader the arch-antideist Sten, with treason. Treason against our State, our Faith, and My People."

Come, boy. Can't you find a more original charge than that? Ffillips thought to herself.

Ffillips knew it was most important to stall for time. Death—which is the usual result of a treason trial—tends to be long term and without much recourse—unless one believed in the hereafter. After service in twenty wars, Ffillips certainly did not.

Ffillips waited a moment, then lifted her gaze to meet Mathias'. Unexpectedly she fell to her knees. A low buzz of surprise ran through the Companions, and even Mathias was startled.

"I do not understand the charge, O Prophet."

"You will be apprised of the particulars, but they center around the assassination of our late and most honored Prophet Theodomir and your desire to overthrow this Most Holy Our State."

"Before you were Prophet, I knew you as a worthy soldier and boon companion. I can only suggest, most humbly, that these charges derive from jealous or misunderstanding underlings."

"You are incorrect, Major Ffillips. These accusations stem directly from my perception, my prayer, and my lips."

Umm. He wants us dead, Ffillips thought. Then she tried another gambit. "Since we are strangers to your system, Prophet, may I ask how judgment of the charges is rendered?"

"In the occasion of high treason," Mathias said, "the court is composed of church elders and the representative of Talamein."

Star chamber with a hanging judge. "Are the circumstances for trial the same for unbelievers as well as members of the Church of Talamein?"

"Major Ffillips, while the sentence could be the same," Mathias went on, sounding slightly unsure of himself, "the manner of execution differs. Those under the Cloak of the Faith are permitted an easier end." And his eyes gleamed slightly. If he understood what Ffillips was leading toward, this could prove him right in his decision and be an even holier coup.

Got you, you fanatical little bugsnipe, Ffillips thought. "I understand. But, Prophet, I do not wish to sound as if, are we indeed guilty, we would attempt to allay our doom. I was merely inquiring because of the curiosity that my soldiers and

I have shown after seeing the bravery and nobility of those who Soldier for the Faith."

"What is your request, Major?"

"Perhaps . . . since I assume you will provide us with advisors to ensure that trial will be fair under the eyes of Talamein himself, who will come to judge both the quick, the slow, and the dead," Ffillips went on, "it could be beneficial if you could find the wisdom to provide us with religious instructors, so we might know more of Talamein and then reach a decision."

Mathias considered, then reluctantly nodded. That would slow the show trial, of course. But if some of the mercenaries would convert—a blessing. Also, if some of the lower-ranking soldiers find it in their hearts to follow the Way of Talamein, there might be a way for them to be spared and to assist in the training of his Companions for the jihad. But not Ffillips, not her officers, nor Sten—assuming the man could be found.

"I will take your plea under study, Major," Mathias said. "I must say it merits consideration. I will inform you of the Prophet's decision after the Prophet prays, fasts, and asks for confirmation from the aetherian heart of Talamein."

Ffillips bowed as Mathias stood, arms spread.

"We thank you, Talamein, for overhearing this session, and we pray that justice was and shall be performed. S'be't."

"S'be't," came the amen as Ffillips was dragged back to her feet and back to the dungeon. Shambling along, faking a limp, Ffillips' eyes swept across the passageways, looking for ideas.

Not too bad, Major, she thought. You've delayed the headsman, got some possibly bribable or corruptible churchmen to come in, and, most of all, some time.

And she wondered just what Sten was doing and whether the man had abandoned his soldiers and simply fled.

Unfortunately the mercenary, battle-trained side of her agreed that the colonel would be a clotting fool if he'd done anything else.

CHAPTER FIFTY-SEVEN

OTHO WAS FAIRLY certain that the mercenary who called himself Sten was a great deal more. There was, for instance, the highly modified radioset that was beam-cast in a direction that Otho, checking secretly, determined was close to Galactic Center. There was also the absolute idiocy of an unpaid mercenary sticking around to worry about his less-fortunate underlings.

So it did not surprise Otho at all when a sentry peered over his crennelated walk and screamed loudly.

Standing outside the castle, in the driving snow, were one slight human female flanked by two huge four-footed bulging-skulled black-and-white predators; a truly obese humanoid woman with an interesting moustache; and a tiny, fur-covered being with flicking tendrils. Plus four bulky, gravsleds.

Who they were, how they managed to insert themselves unobserved on the Bhor world, and why they knew where Sten was, Otho felt would be perpetually unanswered questions.

So he just opened the gates, set out an appetizing first meal of dried saltfish, the grain-filled, spiced and baked stomach of herding animals, and what remained of the last night's feast animal then sent an underling to wake Sten and Alex.

CHAPTER FIFTY-EIGHT

THE REUNION WITH his Mantis team was brief and, wild. Munin even rose to its hind legs and licked Sten's face. Hugin, the other, and Sten felt brighter animal, purred once, then jumped on the top of the table and inhaled an entire platter of saltfish.

"Y'see, you overstrong lump of suet," Ida rumbled to Alex, "you can't get along without me?"

Alex choked on his grain dish, but admitted that he was, indeed, quite glad to see the hulking Rom woman.

Bet pulled Sten aside. Concern on her face. "What went wrong?"

"We had to move too fast," Sten said grimly. "I'll give you the full briefing in a minute."

Doc was oddly subdued. Sten managed to hug Bet twice, which brought up some interesting thoughts about what they did in the earlier days of their relationship, then he walked over and knelt to get eye-level with the koalalike Altairian.

"Your revenge is a terrible one, Sten," Doc said glumly.

Sten looked puzzled.

"Do you know what Mahoney had us doing after you were detached? Do you know what his idea of On His Majesty's Imperial Stupidity consists of?" Doc's voice was rising toward a falsetto.

Sten knew Doc would tell him.

"Easy duty," the team's anthropologist went on. "Perfect

for an understrength team, Mahoney told us. A tropic world whose government some local humanoids were about to overthrow. All we had to do was guard the embassy."

"Mahoney said the Emperor thoroughly approved the revolution," Bet went on. "We were supposed to keep all the Imperial servants—and their families—from getting fed down the same grinder the government was about to disappear into."

"We did it," Ida added. "For one thing there was no comscan I could figure out that wasn't monitored. Do you know how many credits I lost? Do you know how many of my investments—our investments—have turned to drakh because we were stuck on that armpit?"

"That was not the worst," Doc continued. "We were disguised as Guards security—and we even managed to convince those clots who call themselves Foreign Service people that Hugin and Munin are normally part of a Guards team.

"Pfeah," he sneered, ladling an enormous steak down his maw. And chewing.

"It was hilarious." Bet took over as Doc glumly chewed. She was trying, without much success, to keep from laughing.

"The indigenes took the palace. Besieged the embassy. Usual stuff. We fired some rounds over their heads and they went home to think about things."

Through a rapidly disappearing mouthful that looked more suitable for Hugin, Doc said, "We had, of course, prepared an escape route—out the back gate, through some interconnected huts, into the open, through an unguarded city gate and then walk twelve kilometers to a Guard destroyer."

"So," Sten wondered, "what was the problem?"

"The children," Doc said. "Ida, who somehow has time-in-grade on me, ordered me to be in charge of embassy dependents. Nasty, carnivorous, squeaky humanoids."

"They loved him," Ida put in. "Listened to his every word. Made him sing songs. Fed him candy. Patted him."

"With those *sticky* paws of theirs." Doc grunted. "It took me three cycles to comb out my fur. And they called me"—he shuddered—"their teddy bear."

Sten stood up, keeping his face turned away from Doc, and thumped Hugin off the table. He composed himself and turned.

"Now that you've had your vacation, would you like to get back to work on something nice and impossible?"

Doc levered himself another steak, and the team squatted, listening as Sten began the back-briefing.

CHAPTER FIFTY-NINE

THE ESCAPE PLANS were going extremely well, Ffillips thought. Those mercs with any experience at losing war had secreted some kind of minor edged weapon on their uniforms. These had been put into a common pool, and those most suitable for digging or cutting assigned to the smallest, beefiest, and least claustrophobic of the mercs.

The flagstones that made up the dungeon floor had taken only two nights to cut around and lever up, and the digging had commenced. At each prisoner count and guard shift change, they were dropped back into place and false cement—made from chewed-and-dried bread particles—went around them.

Viola, who'd taken over the Lycée section after Egan's death, had triangulated a tunnel route using trig and what little could be seen from the barred windows at the upper portion of the huge dungeon.

Some of the more devout mercenaries and those who could sound religious had entered study groups with Mathias' instructors.

While listening, asking intelligent questions, and pretending to be increasingly swayed, they also pulled loose strings that held their uniforms bloused over boot-top and scattered earth from the tunnel across the pounded-dirt courtyard.

It was going *very* well, Ffillips thought, as one shift of naked, grimy soldiers oozed out of the hole and was replaced

246

by another. The first team immediately began swabbing themselves clean in the last remains of the liter-per-day wash-and-drink water ration that their captors allowed.

Very well indeed, Ffillips thought. We have only three-hundred-plus meters of rocky earth to dig through before we stand the possibility of being beyond these walls. Then, once we break out, which should be in the cliff edge, all we need to do is figure out how to rappel down one hundred meters of rock and disappear into the heart of Sanctus' capital. All of which we can easily accomplish given, say, ten years.

Sten, Sten, where are you, Colonel? Ffillips shucked her tunic and, in spite of fairly pronounced claustrophobia, dropped into the tunnel and crawled toward its face, past the sweating, pumping airshaft workers, to begin her own digging shift.

CHAPTER SIXTY

THE TEAM SAT, considering. Each was working, in his or her own mind, possible alternate solutions to the one Sten had presented. The tigers had thought out the prospects through their somewhat single-track minds, had presented paws with claws out, had the kill-everything plan rejected, curled up, and started cleaning each other's face.

Ida summarized the situation: "A fanatic. With soldiers. Declared religious war. After our awesomely perceptive Emperor blessed any little atrocity they would want to commit, unto the seventh generation, amen.

"We have mining ships on the way—ships that shall surely be ambushed by these Companions."

"Ae braw summation," Alex agreed.

"One solution," Doc tried. "We wait until the mercenaries are tried, sentenced to death, and brought out for execution. Your Mathias will undoubtedly attend, and it will unquestionably be a public ceremony. At the height of the roasting, or however he chooses to kill your former subordinates, we take him."

"Negative," Sten declared flatly. "The plan depends on saving as many of them as we can."

"Does Mahoney know you're figuring it like that?"

"No," Sten said. The other members of the team dropped

the subject. Secretly all except Doc agreed with Sten's romanticism.

"Agreed," Bet said. "The only option is to take out Mathias before the holy war can start."

"Joyful day," Ida said dubiously. "By the way, as long as we don't know how we're going to get onto Sanctus, let alone how the clot we'll slither into the capital, has your brilliant mind considered how we'll get into this Temple fortress to take out Mathias, assuming we can do all the rest, O my commander?"

"Not my brilliant mind," Sten said. "My cold butt."

"What?" Ida asked.

"My cold sitter—plus Mahoney sent a geo-ship over Sanctus three days ago, for a seismochart."

"You realize none of us has the slightest idea what you're talking about, Sten."

"Of course not, Bet."

"All right," Bet shrugged. "That'll be your department. My department—I just figured out how we get onto Sanctus and inside the capital.

"No creepy-crawly, by the way," she went on. "First of all, it's hard on my delicate complexion."

"Ah dinna ken whae y'be goint," Alex said. "You pussycats, Doc, an' th' braw gross fishwife be hard to hide in th' open."

"Not when we're completely in the open," Bet said. She tried to keep a straight face and failed. "Boys and girls, we are going to have a show."

Puzzlement, and then Sten and Alex got it, and the room dissolved in laughter, except for the tigers, who looked upset, and for Doc, who had no idea what they were talking about.

"You have it," Sten said when he stopped laughing. "Also, do you know what that gives us?"

"Of course," Bet said. "You set things up for what happens after we burn Mathias, his Companions, and the Faith of Talamein into ashes. The solution to the whole Lupus Cluster."

Sten shrugged. So his thunder was stolen. He'd never believed much in the livie detective who said "ah-hah" and then everybody else sat listening in awestruck wonder.

"Otho is going to love this," he said, heading for the door.

"By my mother's beard," Otho roared, and one chandelier swung and two suits of streggan-hunting armor rocked on their stands, "you are making a fool of the Bhor and of me."

"My apologies," Sten said. "But it is one solution and, should it work, it will keep you from having buttocks as frozen as those of your father."

"I will not do it," Otho said.

Sten poured two stregghorns full and pushed one to Otho. He knew the shaggy Bhor would eventually agree. Sten just hoped he'd be able to handle the hangover that was about to be constructed.

Sten huddled in the bed under the heavy furs. His mind was fuddled with too much stregg, but he couldn't sleep. His mind wouldn't shut off as he reviewed the plans for the hundredth time.

He heard the soft-scraping sound outside the door and then came fully awake as it creaked heavily open. His fingers curled for his knife and then relaxed as the small figure stepped in.

It was Bet. She shut the door, walked to the bed, undid her robe, and let it slide to the floor. She was naked under it.

Sten had almost forgotten how beautiful she was. Then she was under the furs and cuddling up to him.

"But I thought . . . we were going to be just friends."

"I know." She laughed. "I was just feeling—"

Sten gulped as she began kissing her way down his bare chest.

"—Real friendly."

With logic like that, who was Sten to argue?

CHAPTER SIXTY-ONE

THE BEARDED MAN stood at the mouth of the beach, his net and fishing pike across one shoulder. He stared without much curiosity at the odd assemblage on the edge of the surf. Then he thoughtfully sucked at a tooth and ambled forward to the brightly painted cluster of boxes in front of which stood the Mantis team and a glowering Otho.

With a single island continent, it had been very easy for a Bhor ship to make planetfall on the far side of Sanctus. Sten and his people had then offloaded to a lighter that had blazed only meters above the sea to land them on a beach near the northern tip of the island. Sten knew that was the easy part— any merchants as skilled as the Bhor would also be capable smugglers, easily able to insert anyone almost anywhere without triggering a radar alarm.

"Yahbee ghosts, Y reck," the fisherman said, unsurprised.

There were far more people on Sanctus' main island than just church officials and Companions, and, Sten hoped, they would provide the key for the success of the operation.

Mostly the residents were illiterate rural or seacoast providers. Peasants. And, as with peasants everywhere, they had the virtues/failings of suspicion, superstition, skepticism, and general pigheadedness. However, this fisherman was a little more superstitious and stupid than even Sten thought possible.

Sten figured that if he himself was a fisherman and wandered down at dawn to his favorite fishing spot to find a short bear, a large hairy being, two oversized cats, and four humanoids, the most logical option would be run howling to the nearest church of Talamein for shriving.

Instead the local sucked at his teeth again and spat, almost hitting Hugin, who growled warningly.

"No, gentle sir," Sten began. "We are but poor players whose coastal ship was wrecked early this morn. Fortunately we were able to salvage all our gear, though, alas, our faithful ship was lost."

"Ahe," the fisherman said.

"Now we need assistance. We need help in assembling these our wagons—and can pay in geld. Also we shall need beasts of burden, to draw the wagons.

"In return, not only shall we pay in red geld, but shall perform our finest show for the folk of your village."

"Shipwrecked, y'sah?"

"That we were."

"Stick to beint ghosts," the fisherman said. "It hah a more believable ring to it."

And, as Alex's hand slid smoothly toward the miniwillygun slung under his red/blue/green tunic, the fisherman turned.

"Y go t'mah village. P'raps one hour b'fore Y hae beasties an' workers for you." He spat again, turned, and trudged, still without panic or hurry, back the way he had come.

Puzzled, the Mantis soldiers and Otho looked at each other, then they started breaking down their gear—five ten-meter-long wagons, hastily built by Bhor craftsmen. They were loaded with the various properties needed for Bet's "show," plus detset lockboxes full of full-bore Imperial weaponry, including tight-beam coms, willyguns, and exotic demo tools.

Theirs was no longer a deniable operation, Sten knew. Either he would succeed, and it wouldn't matter, or he would die. In which case, within six months the Emperor would be forced to commit a full Guard assault into the Lupus Cluster.

And if that was the necessity, something as minor as a blown Mantis team would be the least of the Emperor's worries.

Besides, Sten told himself, if the worst came down, they'd all be dead anyway.

CHAPTER SIXTY-TWO

THE CAMPAIGN THAT Doc projected had a twofold aim. First and most important was to provide a means for some extremely odd-looking beings to be able to insert themselves into Sanctus' well-guarded capital in time to lift the mercs and end Mathias' dreams of a holy war. One of the most effective ways to run a clandestine operation is to run it in plain sight, since the opposition generally figures no one can be *that* stupid and obvious. Covert-ops specialists frequently lose themselves in a maze of double-crosses and triple-thinking.

The second purpose was to emphasize the increasing split between the people of Sanctus and their church. So the jokes, the play, and the afterperformance casual asides were designed to make the Companions and the hierarchy look abysmally stupid—so stupid and corrupt that no self-respecting peasant would give a damn if the regime fell. At least no self-respecting peasant who hadn't been able to figure a way to get his paws on some of the graft.

Doc knew that in a largely illiterate, partially repressed culture, a good joke or whispered scandal would spread almost as fast as if it had been broadcast on a livie.

If the campaign succeeded and most peasants were chuckling over the latest anti-Companion joke, and the Mantis section successfully penetrated the capital to start the shooting, hopefully the local populace would stay neutral. If they rose up in support of Mathias, Sten, all his team, and the prisoned mercs would probably have very brief lifespans. And of course, if they decided to overthrow the palace in support of Sten, the result could well be civil war, and a civil war with religious overtones can last for generations and totally waste a culture.

Doc had spent long hours with his computer before the Bhor inserted the Mantis team. Working within the 28 Rules of Humor (Doc, like other Altarians, had less than no sense of humor), his innate dislike of humanoids, and his massive contempt for any cause beyond basic selfishness, Doc had come up with half a hundred jokes, some fairly juicy scandals, and one play.

The play was less normal drama than a cross between the Medieval Earth mystery cycles and the early, crudely humorous commedia dell'art, with a great deal of improvisation.

Casting the play was somewhat of a problem. Since Sten and Alex were well known by the Companions, their onstage and off-stage presences had to be disguised.

For the play, it was easy. Sten and Alex were force-cast as the troupe's clowns and were completely unrecognizable under white-mime makeup, black-outlined facial features, and fantastic fright wigs and costumes. Offstage, though, there was a bit of a problem.

A basic rule of makeup is that it's unnecessary to change much of a person's features for him to be unrecognizable. And Mantis knew those rules very well indeed. So Sten shaved his head and put a rather unsightly blotch on one cheek. Alex grew a walrus moustache and trimmed his hair into a monkish half tonsure.

The plot of the play was idiot-simple. Bet played an orphaned village girl whose virtue was threatened by a corrupt village official (Alex, with a long beard and a battered non-accent), in cahoots with a somewhat evil churchman of the late and not-much-lamented regime of Theodomir. The official was played by Ida in drag.

Bet's only hope was her handsome lover, who had left the village to join the crusade of Mathias and his Companions against the evil Jann. By then official doctrine wasn't admitting that the mercs had done anything but sit on their duffs, pinch chaste women, and swill alk.

The lover would never be seen, which was a relief since the casting potential was running a little slender.

About twenty minutes in, after appropriate menacings by

the official and the churchman, the girl, sobbed and caterwauled and sank in prayer to Talamein. And the Voice of Talamein— Ida again—spoke from offstage and told her to flee into the forest.

There she was menaced by hungry tigers and saved by a shipwrecked mendicant Bhor, played by Otho—who roared when told that he would have to make nice noises about what he considered to be a ridiculous faith, and then roared louder when told that he also had lines suggesting that *all* the Bhor felt the same about Talamein.

Then the Bhor mendicant led the girl to the shelter of two clownish woodsmen, Sten and Alex.

Somehow, through a plot twist Doc could never figure out but one which didn't bother the audience at all, the tigers turned into friendly tigers and did amusing stunts to keep the lonely girl laughing between chanted hymns while the woodsmen were out being woodsy.

She was threatened by an evil fortuneteller (Ida again), and only saved by a mysterious cute-and-cuddly furry creature (Doc, despite his howled protests).

More chanting, more prayers, and then the Voice of Talamein spoke again, saying that the evil official and prayerman were coming into the forest with their private army (Sten and Alex, playing peasants drafted as soldiers).

The army killed the woodsmen (very deft rolling from the wagon's stage into the curtained-off backstage and slapped-on steel helms for Sten and Alex), leaving the girl doomed to submit to the embraces of the official.

But then, once again Talamein spoke, the tigers and Otho roared onstage, ate the villians, the soldiers recanted their ways, then, in a blinding finale, word came of the success of Mathias' Crusade against the Jann. Unfortunately, Bet's lover had been killed, doing something unspeakably heroic. But the Faith of Talamein was triumphant. Amid chanted praise, clown rolls by Sten and Alex, prancing tigers, the play came to a close, and *exeunt omnes* amid applause.

Then, of course, Sten and Alex would move among the crowd doing simple magic gags, clown stunts for the kids, Bet would stroll with her tigers, and Ida would set up the fortune-telling booth while Doc barkered.

And it went over in every village, from the opening performance in the fishing town through the farming villages even to a couple of command performances before rural clergy.

Not that it had to be that great to succeed, when the only "entertainment" available to the villagers was the drone of the Talamein broadcast in the village square screens, church worship, and getting as drunk as possible on turnip wine.

Slowly the troupe moved closer to Sanctus' capital.

"We're two kilometers from Sanctus' gates," Ida announced from inside the cart.

Sten nodded politely at a glowering guard team of Companions as they passed in their gravsled, then tapped the reins on the hauling beasts' backs. They grudgingly moved from a stagger into a slow walk.

"An' noo," Alex said, "w'be't goint into tha' tiger's maw."

"Hugin and Munin's maw's back on Prime World," Bet added from her position, sitting just behind Alex and Sten, who were on the cart driver's bench.

"Sharrup, lass," Alex replied. "Ah'm dooncast. Ah fearit this scheme wi' nae workit oot f'r th' benefits of Kilgours."

"You're probably right," Sten agreed. "We're doomed. And doomed without hearing the last of Red Rory."

"Red Rory, aye?" And Alex brightened. "W'noo. Wh'n last w'sawit Red Rory, an entire Brit comp'ny wae chargint up thae hill, a'ter his head, aye?"

Sten nodded wearily. The things he did to keep morale up.

"So tha' screekit, an' scrawit, an' hollerint, and ae kinds ae goin' on, an' then heads come doon thae hill, bumpit, bumpit, bumpit.

"Anh't' thae Brit gin'ral's consid'r'ble astonishment, here's his wholit comp'ny, lyin' dead in thae dust.

"But b'fore he hae a chance to consider, yon giant on tha hillcrest screekit again:

"'Ah'm Red Rory ae th' Glen! Send up y' entire rig'mint!'

"An the gin'ral turnit sa red hi' adj'tant fearit he gae apoplexy. An' he holler, 'Adj'tant!'

"'Send up tha' wholit blawdy reg'mint! AH WAN' THA' MON'S HEAD!'

"An' tha' whole reg'mint fixit thae bay'nits an' thae chargit up thae hill. An' thae's screamint, an' screekit, an' shoutint, an' carryint on, for aye half ae day.

"An' thae's dust, an' thae's shots, an' thae's aye battle.

"An' th' gin'ral's watchint frae doon below.

"Ah sudden, thro' thae dust, he see't his adj'tant comit runnin doon thae hill.

"An' tae adj'tant screemit. 'Run, sah! Run! It's ae ambush! Thae's two ae 'em.'"

Very complete silence for many minutes.

Finally Sten turned to Alex, incredulous. "You mean, *that's* the story I've been waiting for, for the last year?"

"Aye," Alex said. "Dinnae it b'wonderful?"

Even more and longer silence . . .

CHAPTER SIXTY-THREE

MATHIAS WATCHED AS they led another of Ffillips' mercs into the chamber. The man was naked and sweating heavily under the bright, revolving interrolights. His body was covered with bruises and cuts from many days of beatings. The soldier was exhausted; his eyes were rolling in fear.

Mathias nodded at the chief interrogator, and the man was muscled into a chair and strapped down. Coldly and efficiently, an interrogrator's aide snapped electrical leads to the prisoner's body.

The Prophet stepped forward, looming over the man. Then spoke gently. "Son, don't let this go on. It grieves me to see a poor sinner submit to such an ordeal. End it for yourself. I beg you in the name of our gentle Father, Talamein."

He leaned closer to the man.

"A simple confession of your sins and the sins of your leaders is all we require...Now, will you confess? Please, son."

Weakly the soldier shook his head, no.

Mathias nodded for the inquisitor to start. And the first screams ripped from the soldier's body.

An hour later Mathias walked from the chamber, a tight little smile of satisfaction on his lips.

* * *

From a crystal decanter, Mathias poured himself a goblet of pure, cold water. Its source was one of the clear mountain springs that he had recently declared holy.

It was night on Sanctus, and Mathias was alone in his spartan chamber. Outside the room he could hear the faint sounds of the pacing guards.

Mathias reviewed his plans once more before going to sleep on the small, hard, military cot he favored.

He realized unhappily that his plans for the resettlement of Sanctus was not proceeding as swiftly as he would like.

The idea had come to him like a vision. He saw a series of small, isolated spiritual communes, devoted to reflection and worship. To create these communes, he would empty the cities and villages. Move the peasants off the farms.

The latest reports said that the idea had met a huge amount of resistance, especially from the farmers and artisans. Who would till the land? they complained. Who would mix the mortar and build the buildings?

This kind of small, ungodly thinking would have to stop, Mathias decided. He would not let the unenlightened of his planet stand in the way of a glorious future.

He scrawled an order for Companions to sweep into the villages. What he could not do with reason, he would accomplish by force. He added a suggestion to the report: Burn the homes and destroy the farms. That way the peasants would have no place to return.

Mathias was more pleased with his progress involving the matter of the mercenaries. Of course, he had personally handled that. He had scheduled the public trial to begin the following day. Enough mercenaries had confessed to insure its success.

One by one, each man would be found guilty. And Mathias would order their executions. Those, too, would be public.

It would be a solemn occasion, followed by a great celebration. Mathias had already announced that some of the rules of Talamein behavior would be relaxed during the festival.

A wise Prophet, he told himself, had to understand that his people were only weak human beings.

Mathias began to scrawl a few notes concerning the planet-wide month of purification that he would declare to take place immediately after the festival.

He had some interesting ideas on this subject. Floggings, for instance—all voluntary, of course.

CHAPTER SIXTY-FOUR

FFILLIPS STOOD AT stiff attention before her ragged band of men. They were drawn up in the temple's central courtyard. Ffillips could sense the hidden vidmonitors that were broadcasting the event across the planet. Around them were row after row of spidery bleachers filled with red-uniformed Companions. Seated in front of the bleachers were the ten judges handpicked by Mathias from his officer corps.

On one side sat the Prophet himself. He was seated on a small onyx throne. He wore a simple uniform, with only two small golden medals—the torch symbol of Sanctus—to mark his rank.

The evidence had been given—mostly, the humiliating confessions forced from men and women who couldn't bear up under torture. The judges had weighed the verdict. And it was about to be delivered.

Ffillips knew she was dead.

Mathias raised a hand for silence. Instant hush. He leaned slightly forward in his throne. His face was serene, almost kindly. "Do you wish to say anything in your behalf?" he asked Ffillips. "In the interest of justice?"

Ffillips looked coldly at Mathias and then at the judges. "I don't see her here."

"Who?" Mathias asked.

"Justice," Ffillips said. "Now, as one soldier to another,

I'll ask you to end this sham. My men and I await your decision."

But before Mathias could give the signal, Ffillips shouted: "DETACHMENT, TEN-HUT."

And her sad, ragged troop suddenly became soldiers again. They snapped to, throwing off the exhaustion and fear. Even those crippled by torture drew themselves up. A few had to be helped. Some grinned at Mathias and the Companions through broken teeth.

Mathias hesitated, then turned.

"What is the verdict?" he asked the judges.

And the same word hissed out along the line of ten.

"Guilty . . . Guilty . . . Guilty . . ." And so on until the last judge pronounced their fate.

Mathias rose, bowed to the judges. "I have agonized over this," Mathias announced. "The evidence was overwhelming, even before the trial. And, as you all know, I counseled compassion."

He paused for effect.

"No doubt," Ffillips said, loudly enough for the vidmonitors to pick up.

Mathias ignored her.

"But," the Prophet continued, "I must bow to the wisdom of the judges. They know best the desires of Talamein. I can only accede. And give thanks to our Father, for his guidance."

He turned to Ffillips and her men. "With great sorrow, I must pronounce judgment—"

Ffillips shouted the order: "TROOP, RIGHT FACE."

Her troops wheeled as one. Proud men and women ready to go to their deaths. Their guards broke rank and dignity, rushing over to them, shouting, waving their weapons.

Mathis had to rush out the words:

"You are all sentenced to die," he shouted. "Within five days. Before the people of Sanctus, and—"

Ffillips broke through his ranting: "FORWARD . . . MARCH . . ."

And the soldiers stepped out in perfect time, heading back for their prison and their doom.

"And Talamein . . ." Mathias screamed.

Ffillips shot him the universal gesture of contempt. And, in her best parade-ground voice: "CLOT YOU."

All was confusion. As the mercs disappeared, Mathias was

yelling instructions at his guard and fruitless explanations at the vidmonitors.

Ffillips might have been a dead woman, but she knew how to go out in style.

CHAPTER SIXTY-FIVE

THE GIANT FUNERAL chimneys of Sanctus belched out ash, smoke, and fire, working overtime as the very wealthy and highly nervous ruling class of the Lupus Cluster poured in their donations to the new Prophet.

Sten, Bet, Alex, and the others jockeyed their gaudily painted wagons through the crowds that were pouring into the holy city.

Red-uniformed Companions made cursory attempts to check out the pilgrims. Here and there they pulled people aside to run scanners over their bodies and belongings. But mostly they were just waving the hordes of people through, barely able to keep up with the traffic, much less look for malcontents.

Once they got through the gates, Sten waved his people to one side. He took a fresh look at the Sanctus of Mathias.

To either side of the Avenue of Tombs and its eye-ear-nose-and-throat-polluting monuments spread the city itself. Sandwiched between the mix of small homes, tenements, and the occasional gabled mansion were the narrow streets and alleyways. Sanctus' capital had evidently not had much of a planning commission.

And now the barely passable streets were roiling with visitors. Sten's back prickled as he realized that all of them, whether peasants, artisans, or merchants, were in their colorful best clothes. Also, Sten noted, here and there, other entertainers' wagons.

The chaos was worrisome. It was a perfect cover, to be sure, but the spontaneous partying meant that Sten and his team had less time than they thought. None of them had seen or heard about the sentencing cast, but from the festive tourists, Sten realized he would have to act quickly.

Bet slid across the seat toward him and nuzzled his neck. "Mathias acted more quickly than we thought," she hissed. Sten forced laughter and pulled her close for a kiss. A Companion stared at them curiously for a moment, then moved on. A drunken beggar stumbled past, waving a sheaf of tickets.

"THE EXECUTIONS," he shouted. "SEE THEM IN PERSON...STILL A FEW SPACES LEFT IN THE PUBLIC SQUARE."

He staggered on.

"SEE THE EXECUTIONS . . . THE TRAITORS OF TALAMEIN . . ."

His voice was finally drowned out by the crowd. Bet broke away from Sten and slid off the wagon seat. Sten gave her a slap on the rump.

"See what you can find out," he whispered.

Bet nodded and laughed lustily, then jumped down onto the roadway. In a moment she had disappeared into the throng.

Alex stuck his head out from the wagon's interior, then slid up on the seat beside Sten.

"Best be movin', lad," he said.

Sten took another look at what faced them before he gigged the beasts into motion.

The Temple sat at the end of the Avenue of Tombs, atop a gently rising hill about three hundred meters higher than the city gates. Its spire towered over thick, protective walls. Below the Temple was what had been a monastary. Years past, it had been a place of silent devotion for Talamein priests. More recently Theodomir and now Mathias used it as a prison.

Sten pointed it out to Alex.

"Tha's whae th' be't keepint our Ffillips," Alex said. He passed Sten a wineskin. Sten upended the bag, letting the wine pour into his mouth. Then it went back to Alex, who raised it, eyes scanning the landscape over the tanned leather.

"Over there," Sten said, nodding to the skeleton of a building going up beside the old Talamein monastery/prison. "That's our way in."

Alex peered at it for an instant, then turned away.

What he had seen was a slim, towering needle of steel, very much out of place next to the ancient monastery. They had heard it was going to be the new barracks Mathias was building for his Companions. Ironically, it was also to be named for Theodomir.

They noticed there were no workers around the building. Obviously they had been given time off for the holiday. They also noticed that although most streets were filled with partying citizens of Sanctus, the area around the prison was carefully being avoided.

Down the hill from it, still on the Avenue of Tombs, they spotted the main armory for the Companions. That area, too, was deserted.

"Got it?" Sten asked Alex.

Alex considered for a moment.

"A wee dicey, lad," he said finally. "But it'll hae t' shift."

Sten gave the signal, then his wagon and the others rumbled forward, deeper into the Holy City.

On a side street farther down the hill from the Companions' armory was what had once been a park. Before Mathias it had been a small green area for pilgrims. A place to rest and, after worship, to picnic after the long fasting. It was three-quarters screened by a ring of tall, slender trees.

But the Companions had put it to a more practical use. Where once had been a sprawling green lawn was now a sea of well-churned mud. The park was filled with small, tracked self-propelled cannon, whose honeycomb armor allowed them high speed and maneuverability. The tracks were built for two men, had small, open turrets, and were armed with quad, full-auto 50mm projectile cannon.

They were powered by old-style low-friction engines that gave maximum performance to a fairly cumbersome little package.

Milling and relaxing in the myriad aisles between the track columns were Companion drivers, mechanics, gunners, and general gofers. Though most of them were pretending to be busy at their duties, they were actually rubbernecking at the crowds of fun-seekers cavorting a hundred meters or so away in the street.

Ida and Doc broke out of the crowd. A few giggling children followed them for a moment or two, delighted at the spectacle.

But as they wandered toward the track park, anxious parents called them back.

Ida was dressed in her rainbow gypsy best. And she was dragging Doc along on a short, silver leash.

"Alley-oop," she shouted.

And Doc did a ponderous somersault.

They paused near one SP. A few curious Companion privates moved forward a bit to see better.

"Play dead," she said.

Doc flopped to the ground and stiffened his limbs. "Don't go too far!" he hissed.

"Your idea," Ida whispered back, enjoying every minute of it.

A few young men, glancing nervously over their shoulders for superiors, came closer.

"Now, beg," Ida commanded.

"No," Doc whispered. "I don't do begging."

Ida jerked the leash while she glanced around the park, instantly filing layout, security, and, most important, eyeing the track's individual locks.

"I *said* beg." Ida smiled sweetly.

Doc did as he was told, trembling on hind legs and waving his paws. He swore to himself that Ida would die many deaths for this disgrace.

"What are you doing here?" shouted a Companion lieutenant.

Instantly young Companion privates jolted in their boots, looked nervously about and started to drift away.

Ida looked at the young lieutenant, then at Doc.

"It's a new act, sir," she said. "He's a bit wild yet. Don't know how to behave."

Before the glowering officer, she half-dragged Doc away on the leash.

"Next time," Doc hissed when they were out of earshot, "you go on the chain."

As they melted back into the crowd, Ida noticed that the lieutenant was still watching them. Just for cover, naturally, she gave Doc a little kick.

CHAPTER SIXTY-SIX

THE SMALL GRAVSLED hissed up to the Theodomir Barracks-to-be. On it was an untidy assortment of crammed tool boxes and chaotic mounds of electrical spare parts.

Sten and Alex stepped off and, ignoring the guards, began to fill two duffle bags with tools and spidery electrical parts. A bored chief guard wandered over.

"Here now. What're you two doing?"

Sten just grunted at him. Alex handed the guard a grease-stained permit. Both grease and permit had first met less than an hour ago. The guard peered at the permit.

"Says here," he commented, "they got problems with the welder on floor fifteen." He glared at the two men, trying on his cop-suspicious look.

"I ain't heard about that," he said.

Sten wrestled on his toolbelt.

"Whaddya expect," Sten said. "It's a clottin' holiday, ain't it? Nobody don't hear nothin', unless you're like my partner and me.

"Clots. We were gonna party tonight. But no. Whadda they care? We spend all those credits on some approved quill. We gotta couple ladies lined up. We're gettin' heated up. Then we get the call. Problems with the clotting welder on the Theodomir building.

"Fix it, they say. I say send somebody else. They say fix

267

it or don't show up tomorrow. So here we are. And we're gonna fix it and get back to the party."

The guard was a bit stubborn. He, too, had a party planned and hadn't expected the day to be a duty day.

"Still," he said. "I wasn't notified. No work done 'less I'm notified."

Sten shrugged. He and Alex climbed back into the gravsled. Sten keyed a report on the tiny onboard computer, then printed it and handed the hard copy to the guard. "Sign it."

The guard stared at it, his eyes widening.

"This says I refused you entrance. You're blaming me 'cause you can't fix the welder."

"Gotta blame somebody," Sten said. "Might as well be you. Look. Be a nice guy. Sign it. We leave. And then it's party time tonight."

The guard handed the report back, shaking his head. "Go do your work."

"Ah, come on," Sten said. "Give us a clottin' break. I wanna go home."

But the guard was firm. He pointed at the building. "Fix it."

Reluctantly Sten and Alex climbed back out of their gravsled, loaded up their tools, and, with a few "clots" thrown over their shoulder, began the weary climb to the fifteenth floor.

Ida and Doc piled over the turret top, into the track. On the ground beside it, the Companion lieutenant was moaning into unconsciousness. After the two had done a quick fiddle with one of the Mantis Section's Hotwire Anything Kits, they'd crept back into the track park. It was unfortunate—for the lieutenant—that he'd come around the wrong corner at the wrong time. Ida'd forearmed him in the gut and Doc had tranked the man, but not before nearly biting through his leg.

Ida fumbled the box out of her purse, looking at the controls.

"Over there," Doc said, pointing at the SP cannon's security/ ignition case. Within seconds Ida had the box epoxied on the case, and the box had analyzed and broken the three-sequence number code that brought the track to life.

As Ida fired the engine up, she settled into the gunner/driver's seat then pushed the track controls forward and hunched a little.

"Hang on, Doc. This is gonna be a clottin' great ride."

The SP cannon's tracks raised great gouts of spray, and then, as Ida yanked one control stick all the way back, the track spun in its own length and churned out of the park toward the armory.

* * *

Alex allowed himself one genteel Edinburghian wheeze as he and Sten dumped their duffle bags on the wooden planking covering the Theodomir building's fifteenth story.

Sten fished through one bag and took out a grapnel gun. He fitted the spool line to the grapnel's shaft while Alex neatly coiled cable from the second duffle bag.

Then Sten took careful aim at the prison's roof below through the gun's vee-sights. He fired and with a whoosh the grapnel drifted toward its target, spooling out light silver line.

Bet signaled the tigers. Hugin and Munin flashed forward out of the alley mouth, bounding in rippling shadows toward the gate of the armory. A few meters from it, they split and darted unnoticed to either side of the gate. They slipped into shadows and became invisible, the only movement an occasional flash of a whipping tail.

Bet patted Otho on his hulking shoulder. She walked out from the alleyway and began ankling toward the steel guardshack.

She was wearing her most prim-but-revealing peasant costume. A summer dress that hugged her body but allowed her long limbs to flash out freely. She acted unsure, vulnerable, little-girl-lost. Without hestitation she walked straight toward the guardshack.

A young, handsome Companion stepped out. "May I help you, sister?"

She opened her eyes as wide as they could go. "Oh, yes, sir. I'm hoping you could. I've never been to the Holy City before, and . . . and . . ."

"You're lost?"

Bet gulped and gave a shy nod.

"We were all with the village priest," she gushed, all over-explanation. "The Talamein youth group—and one of the boys got, well, you know . . . too friendly, and—and . . ." Bet stopped, doing the galaxy's best blush.

"You left the group." The guard was all understanding, and protective.

Bet nodded.

"And now you need to know how to get to the hostel?"

Bet nodded again.

The guard pointed down the street. "Just down there, sister. A few hundred meters."

Bet gulped her thanks and began, with an innocent wiggle, to head for the hostel.

"I'll stand right here," the young Companion shouted after her, "and make sure you're all right."

Bet waved her thanks and moved on, tentatively, slowly. Tripping over little potholes—all Princess and the Pea. She heard gates clang open behind her and then the sound of boot-steps. The changing of the guard was right on time.

She nodded at the mouth of the alley. A moment later Otho staggered out, a shambling, stumbling drunken Bhor. He bleared at Bet, gave a huge smile, belched, and trundled forward. "By my mother's beard," he shouted. "Here's a find."

Bet shrieked, tried to run, and caught a heel in the cobble-stones. She fell heavily. An instant later Otho was falling on her. Laughing and gathering her up in his huge and hairy arms. The theory was that no one dumb enough to be a Companion would be bright enough to realize that, to a Bhor, breeding with a human was only slightly less revolting and impossible than with a streggan.

Otho pretended not to hear the shouts from the onrushing Companion and the other guards.

"Just my luck," he chortled at Bet. "Now, don't be afraid, little lady. Otho is going to—"

He grunted in pain as the Companion slammed into him. He twisted off Bet, wrapped a mighty arm around the Companion and there was a sharp crack as the man's back broke.

Just behind him, a second Companion gaped in surprise. Bet shot him and he dropped without a sound.

Shouts. Clanking. Sounds of confusion. Bet looked up to see the guards gaping. There were about twenty men pointing and yelling. Weapons were coming up.

Bet put two fingers in her mouth and whistled loudly. The entire street seemed to rumble as the tigers roared and bounded out of their hiding spots, straight into the guards.

Guts trailing, three men went under before the rest knew what was happening. Hugin and Munin bounded among them, ripping, clawing, and tearing. There was immediate panic.

Guns went off, and bullets ripped into Companions instead of tigers.

Then, as a melée, the Companions fled back into the guard tunnel, fighting each other to be first.

It was a long, narrow tunnel with gates at each end. The one on the street side had been opened for the changing of the guards.

Security required that the other—the only other exit—be closed.

Companions on the inside of the armory gaped in horror as their friends charged toward them and beat on the bars helplessly as Hugin and Munin tore into them.

Panicked men were climbing the portcullis, trying to squeeze through the slots. And being dragged down.

A guard on the inside violated orders and slapped a button to open the interior gates. As the few Companions still alive spilled through, the guard raised his weapon to fire at the tigers. Before he could shoot, his head exploded.

Bet and Otho ran yelling and firing into the interior courtyard. The way to the armory was open.

Sten and then Alex clipped wheeled guides to the slender cable. The monastery was about twenty meters below them and about one hundred meters away.

Sten tugged experimentally on the wheel's tee-handles. Then held on tight and, without a word, he lifted his feet and began the long, fast slide down toward the monastery roof. He held his breath as his speed grew with every meter of drooping cable. Behind him he heard a low hum as Alex followed.

The roof was coming up fast, and Sten got ready for the shock of landing. Just before he hit, he was textbook-perfect limp and ready. As he slammed into the prison roof, he heard alarms begin to howl. He tumbled back to his feet and was scrabbling a grenade from his pack as he heard the loud thunk of Alex's landing.

Alex did a shoulder roll, Sten pointed, and they sprinted across the roof.

One roof guard got a shot off at them, and Alex cut him in half with a burst from his willygun. They paused about thirty meters from the roof's inside edge. Sten quickly checked for the proper vent, making a mark on his mental map.

"This one," he yelled, simultaneously spinning the timer wheel on the grenade's primer to seven seconds. Alex had three more grenades out of his pack and ready. They dropped the cluster down the shaft and double-timed away.

Four, five, six, and the grenades exploded. The blast sent Alex and Sten sprawling, their ears thundering. Smoke billowed as they ran back to the hole in the roof.

Alex dug a can of climbing thread from his small backpack, anchored one end on the roof, and, holding the can, "sprayed" himself down into the prison.

Sten snapped a special figure-8 descender on the thread—it would have cut through any conventional piece of abseiling gear—and followed. He dropped the last few meters clear, landing beside the heavy-worlder. Then Sten was up and running down a long, stonewalled corridor.

Through the thick walls they could hear the drumming of booted feet. A door smashed open, a confusion of men rushed out, firing.

Bullets splattered around them as Sten and Alex opened fire at the same instant. Sten leaped over dead and dying men and sprinted toward the end of the corridor.

A solid metal door stood between them and Ffillips. Sten slapped a demo pack to the door, thumbed the button, and ducked. There was an explosion and the door dropped in one molten sheet.

Sten and Alex fired two deadly bursts at a group of Companions behind them and thundered down the corridor toward the main cells.

The alarms were screaming help . . . help . . . help . . . through the emptying streets.

Ida and Doc waited for help to come up the Avenue of Tombs, either for the armory or the prison beyond it. Ida had quickly figured out the simple twin-stick controls and Doc had worked out the loading mechanism of the track's quad cannon.

They shared a bar of protein and, in the eating of the foul stuff, had agreed to not disagree. Then they heard the rumble of the reinforcements coming. Ida started to fire up the track.

"Wait," Doc advised.

Ida buried an impatient obscenity and waited.

Then, through the acquisition scope, Ida saw the reinforcements coming. The first to spin into the street were SP tracks identical to the one they rode in. Next came a mass of Companions on foot.

"Now," Doc said.

Ida shoved the track-brakes/throttles forward, and, tracks-clanking, the SP cannon moved out into the middle of the street. Before the others had time to react, she had begun firing.

The street became a sudden volcano as shell after shell crashed into the oncoming tracks and men.

Doc was a flurry of unending activity as he loaded the guns almost as quickly as Ida could fire. He did wish, however, that he could take a look through her scope at the gore in the streets.

* * *

Sten shoved the tiny demofinger into the cell door and shielded his eyes. A low glow, then a ping, and the door swung open.

Ffillips stepped out and gave Sten a long, steady look. "You took your time coming, Colonel," she said.

"A little close," Sten admitted.

"Excellent. Now we're free. Where are our weapons?"

Sten grabbed her by the arm and led the way. Behind her thronged the other mercenaries.

The mercenaries poured out the gates of the prison. The guards might have been able to handle a break by convicts. But not by trained, experienced soldiers who armed themselves as they went, from dead guards.

Once free, they pounded down the street toward the armory. Just beyond it they could see the blazing track that Doc and Ida were using to hold off the Companions.

Then they were through the tunnel and inside the armory itself. Bet and Otho had already broken open the arms room and they were passing out weapons, grenades, and belts of ammunition.

It was like candy.

Professional soldiers don't have much use for battlecries, but the time spent in Mathias' dungeons had made the mercs a little less than cold-bloodedly professional. Shouting and cheering, they spread out through the gates of Sanctus, always after their ordered goal, but keeping an eye out for humiliations that had to be repaid:

The tortured men;
The beaten men;
The men who had been condemned for their faithfulness.

Ffillips was the first to spot a small company of Companions. She motioned to a squad of her men, and quickly, silently, they slipped forward.

And the mercenaries gave the Companions a far easier death than they had planned for the mercenaries.

It was the same across the city, as the mercs fanned out, killing efficiently and coldly. Hunting out the Companions and swinging their guns aside when civilians stumbled into their sights.

CHAPTER SIXTY-SEVEN

THE COMPANION LUNGED at Alex with a bayoneted rifle. Alex sidestepped the lunge, stopped the follow-through buttstroke, and took the weapon from the Companion's hands.

Smiling hugely, he took the rifle in both hands and snapped it in two. Then as an afterthought he broke the bayonet off its mounting and politely handed the weapon's pieces back to the bulging-eyed Companion.

And then Alex howled and charged.

The Companion, as well as the flanking members of his squad, broke and ran, pelting through the streets of the city. Behind them pounded Alex, some of the mercenaries, and a high-speed-limping Ffillips.

The street dead-ended into a large marketplace, lined with barred shops. Only one, the largest mart, was still open. The Companions dashed toward its entrance but the owner was hastily dropping thick steel shutters over the shop.

"In the name of Talamein," the lead Companion howled.

"Clot Talamein," the shopkeeper growled, and slammed the last steel shutter in their faces.

And the Companions turned as Alex thundered into them. A few of them had the brains to collapse and fake death. But most of them died as Alex's meathooks thrashed through the platoon.

There, finally, was only one left. Alex lifted him in one

hand, started to practice the javelin throw, and then considered. He lowered the man and turned to Ffillips.

"M'pologies, Major," he said. "Ah thinkit's y'r honor."

"Thank you, Sergeant," Ffillips said. "The man is someone I remember. You"—turning to the Companion—"were the person who thought it humorous to fill our water supply with drakh, were you not?"

Without waiting for a reply, Ffillips fired. The highpower slugs cartwheeled the Companion into a blood-red spray of death, then Alex and Ffillips were headed back down the street, toward the Temple and the fleeing Companions.

Mathias breathed deeply. Find the Peace of Talamein, he told himself. Find the Truth of the Flame, he reminded, watching as his Companions retreated through the gates of the Temple, far below him.

This is but a challenge. Talamein will not fail you, he thought as the gates crashed closed and he saw the ragged, limping mercenaries take positions around the walls of the Temple.

Talamein will prove my truth, he told himself, and turned from the window to soothe his panicked advisors.

Situation:

One temple. A walled, reinforced fortress, built on a ridge. Defended by motivated, fairly skilled soldiers. Provisioned for centuries and equipped with built-in wells.

A civilian populace outside was desperately trying to stay neutral.

A small band of soldiers, besieging that fortress, armed only with personal weapons and light armor.

Prog? A classic siege that could go on for decades.

Without the nukes the Eternal Emperor forbade, it should have been.

Sten was determined to break the siege and end the war— and Mathias—within a week.

CHAPTER SIXTY-EIGHT

A GIVEN FOR any port city, and most especially for one on an island continent, is that the watertable will be quite close to the surface. This makes building anything over three or four stories an interesting engineering problem, particularly if there's any seismic activity, as there was on Sanctus.

Not only was the water level barely fifty meters below ground level (which meant about 350 meters for the Temple itself), but the ground composition was mostly sand. Which, in the event of an earthquake and in the presence of water, goes into suspension and becomes instant quicksand, a flowing, unstable, gluelike substance.

But tall buildings must still be anchored, which means columns must still be buried deep in the earth. This is, however, not an easy solution since, during an earthquake, these columns will react to the shifting, slurrylike sand and water mix, tilting or collapsing.

The solution, then, is to use hollow columns. During a quake, the sand/water mix will flow up the interior of the columns and give increased stability. This very basic element of structural engineering was known as far back as the nineteenth century.

Hollow columns work very well, except that they duct cold air—air that is chilled to the temperature of the water table or outside ocean—straight up the inside of the column to the building above. The hollow columns under the Temple had chilled Sten's buttocks as he shifted before that first, memorable interview with Parral, Theodomir, and Mathias.

And those hollow columns, coupled with Mahoney's geo-survey, gave Sten the way into the Temple.

A few feet away from where he and Alex stood, sewage gushed from an open pipe, down a gully, and into Sanctus' ocean. The gully widened past the sewage pipe (fortunately, Sten thought) and then narrowed, to disappear into a cleft in the sandy cliff.

From his position in Alex's small backpack, Doc peered down into that cleft. In addition to the Altairian, the pack contained a small light matching the one already on Alex's shock-helmet, some comporations, and a spare set of gloves. Clipped to his belt Alex also had a minitransponder and a spraycan of climbing thread.

Sten was similarly equipped. But he also had a vuprojector reproduction of the cave system below the Temple. The system had been mapped by the Imperial geoship, and Sten was fairly sure that it would lead him to one of the hollow columns—and from there straight up into the Temple itself.

The minitransponder was one of those wonderful chunks of high-tech that most soldiers were never able to find a usable situation for. In theory, it worked fine. Plant two or more senders in given locations at least one kilometer and thirty degrees apart. Those senders would transmit and tell the wearer of the transponder exactly when he was going in the wrong direction. It was sort of a compass with a built-in-not-that-way-idiot factor.

The reason that most soldiers were never able to use this wonderful gadget is its designers had never been able to figure a way to plant those senders deep in enemy territory, and therefore the system couldn't work. It was a fortieth-century Who'll Bell the Cat.

Sten flipped on the transponder and touched the SYSTEM CHECK button. They had already planted four transponders around the Temple and should know exactly where they were at any time. However, Sten, having a deep and abiding lack of faith in technology, carried a conventional compass on his belt, as did Alex.

"Ah dinna ken wha w' be't hangin' 'boot, watchin' drakh," Alex grumbled. "Ah'm ready t' test m' claustrophobia."

And he eased forward, down into the cleft. It was a tight

fit, and Doc squealed as they went out of sight. Sten lowered himself into the blackness after him.

Doc's comfortable ride in Alex's pack didn't last much beyond the narrow entrance. The first chest-squeeze in the passage brought a gurgle out of him and a breathless insistence that he was quite capable of walking.

And so Doc scuttled out of the pack and took the lead. Alex went second and Sten behind. Doc could ferret out the passageways, and, with Kilgour second, the team wouldn't enter any passageways they couldn't get out of.

The cave went exactly as the geosurvey map said and was easily negotiable by bear-walking—bent over, moving on hands and feet. Only two sections required descent to hands and knees. They quickly penetrated about one-thousand meters into the cave. It was far too easy to last.

It didn't.

Doc eeped in alarm as the crawlway came to a sudden end a few centimeters in front of him. He dropped to all four paws and shone his minilight down into the blackness.

Far, far below, water gleamed.

Sten and Alex crawled up beside him. Sten moved his head, and his helmet-mounted light flashed across the vertical walls below. "Another passageway. There." He pointed with the light. The passageway started about four meters above the dark pool that marked the water level.

Alex unclipped the can of climbing thread from his belt, checked the hardener at the can's tip, then sprayed a blot of the adhesive on the rock ledge. Then he slid his hands into the built-in grips on the can and wriggled over the edge, letting himself down with short blasts. He dropped until nothing could be seen of him but the bobble of light from his helmet. Doc took two custom-built jumars from his pack, fitted his hands into them, and went down the same thread. Sten, using more conventional jumars, did the same.

Alex kept going down until he was below the passageway, then clipped and glued the climbing thread to the rock ringing the passage before hoisting himself up into it. The other two were close behind.

The crawlway became rapidly worse, the roof slowly flattening down on them, until they were forced to hands and knees, elbows and knees, and then to a basic slither.

The rock ceiling ripped Sten's uniform as he pushed himself along.

"I am no geologist," Doc observed, "but does the fact that the ceiling of this passage is wet signify what I suppose?"

Sten didn't answer him, though the dampness did imply that the passageway they were snaking along had been recently underwater. If it began raining outside (there would be no way for the cavers to realize this in time), the water level would rise. Sten did not want to consider the various ramifications of drowning in a cave.

And then he stuck.

The rocky ceiling bulged and without realizing it Sten had moved under the bulge while inhaling. Stuck! Impossible. That tub Alex made it!

Sten kicked at the sides of the passageway. Nothing. He felt his chest swell and then his muscles started a hyperventilating beat.

Stop it. He began the pain mantra. Panic died. He exhaled and slid easily under the obstruction. And the crawl went on.

Then the cave opened up, its ceiling soaring far beyond the reach of the soldiers' lights. Crystal of a million colors refracted from their lamps as they got to their feet and walked forward, soft, beachlike sand crunching under their boots.

Salt and rock formations climbed crazily around them, here a giant morel, there a spiraled gothic cathedral, still another a multicolor twisting snake.

None of the three found words as they walked through the monstrous room, their light illumining treasures seen by man for this first and only time. And then the treasures fell back into darkness as they went on.

The stunning chamber came to a rapid end with a vertical wall, a roaring waterfall, and a deep pool. No side passages. No alternates. The cave just stopped.

Sten puzzled over his map. According to the projection, the chamber should have a lower passage out. And there probably should be no river and waterfall.

He swore to himself as he realized what had happened. Sometime in the past, an underground river had worn through into the chamber and then dumped straight into the lower passageway. In caver's jargon, it was called a siphon. Naturally the survey by the geoship could not show something as insubstantial as water.

So the cave they had to follow *did* continue. And if the

three Mantis soldiers had gills, they would be in no trouble whatsoever . . . Sten's thoughts were interrupted as Doc shed his tiny pack and dove into the pool, disappearing.

"Ah suggest w'be watchin' our wee timepieces," Alex said. "Since Altairians no ken people dinnae hae th' ability to stop breathin' f'r hours a' ae time."

It was four minutes by Sten's watch when Doc resurfaced and hauled himself, shivering, out of the frigid water. Alex, in spite of protests, shoved the Altarian inside his own shirt to warm him up.

"It goes down three meters, then level for possibly another four. There is one narrow place, but I would think it passable. Then you hulking beings will have to turn your bodies through ninety degrees, into a small chamber with an exit to atmosphere directly overhead."

Sten and Alex eyed each other. Then Sten motioned for Alex to go.

"Na, lad. Y'mus do't. Ah'll bring up th' rear."

Sten took a dozen deep breaths, enough to saturate his lungs but without going into hyperventilation. He unslung his pack and belt, clipped them together, and jumped, feet first, into the water.

Blackness. Muddy water. Light just a glow. Down. Down. Cold. Sten could feel the rock close in as he hit the bottom of the passage, rolled, and kicked himself forward. The floor came up, grinding against Sten's gut, then he was through, his heart throbbing, then his fingers touched rock. He felt to the side and found the tight spot. Sten jackknifed and inched his way into the chamber. Skin shredded as he struggled through, hung in the tiny rock womb, then kicked off from the bottom, hand above his head and through the crack and up through dark waters, eardrums pounding and heart throbbing and lights beginning at the back of his eyes. He surfaced, gasping deeply, then swam for a beach illuminated by his helmet light.

As he crawled up onto the beach something splashed beside him, and Doc flopped onto dry land, then sat, looking miserable, his fur wet and bedraggled.

Back in the passage, Alex was well and truly trapped. His body simply would not bend far enough to make the jackknife turn. Alex wondered to himself why he could never remember times like these when some Mantis quack suggested he could stand to shed a few kilos.

As yet, he was unworried. His enormous lungs had more

than enough air. P'raps, laddie, Ah'll turn aboot an' go back an' consider whae t' do next. P'raps, e'en, Ah'll hae t' let young Sten carry on w'oot me.

Alex then discovered he couldn't turn back around, either. So he kicked forward and tried the jackknife again, with even less success.

Alex realized he was starting to drown.

Th' hell Ah am, he thought in sudden rage. Ee yon mountain comit nae t' Mahamet, he thought, as he brought his knees up to touch the rock wall in front of the passageway, gripped the rock rim, and thrust.

It was not true, despite stories told later in Mantis bars, that the earth moved. But what did happen is a half-meter-square square of living rock ripped free, coming toward the dim glow of Alex's light.

And then he was rolling into the chamber and frogging his way up for air and light.

He surfaced like a blowing whale, then thrashed his way to shore. Sten, sheepishly treading water just above the hole Alex had come out of, had been getting ready for a nonsensical and impossible rescue dive. He swam toward the small beach, in Alex's considerable wake.

"Ah thought Ah sae aye fish't Ah knew" was Alex's only explanation for the delay, and the team continued.

From there it was easy. The transponder pointed them directly to where one of the enormous poured-and-reinforced columns came through the cave's roof. A small demo charge cracked the side of the column enough for the three to enter.

Then it was just a matter of the three exhausted, bedraggled beings chimneying their way up seven-hundred meters of glass-smooth wet concrete.

CHAPTER SIXTY-NINE

IT WASN'T MUCH of a diversionary attack. But then it wasn't supposed to be. But battle plans, including phony diversions, never work out exactly as they should. Mantis section and the seventy-odd mercenaries who weren't immediately hospitalized had planned to assemble outside one of the Temple's secondary gates, snipe any Companion stupid enough to stick his head above the walls, fire all the available pyrotechnics and light artillery at the gates, and, finally, whoop and holler a lot while Sten and Alex went for Mathias.

Even though she probably belonged in an intensive care capsule, Ffillips insisted on being present. She was quite happily functioning as Ida's loader while the Rom woman directed bursts of 50mm fire at one of the Temple's gates.

"Of course I'm not saying there's no place for mercenaries," Ida explained. "It's merely a dumb way to make a credit."

"Some of us," Ffillips managed as she dumped another clip of shells into a loading trough, "don't have any other choice."

"Clottin' hell!" Ida snorted. "There's always a choice."

"Even for a mercenary?" Ffillips asked dubiously.

"Certainly. A good killer would be a wonderful banker. Or diplomat. Or in commodities, which I can tell you privately is a guaranteed mill-credit career."

Ffillips was trying to decide whether Ida was joking when a burst caught the Temple gate on one of its hinges and proved that the contractor who had built the Temple had been no more honest than most public-works builders.

The entire gate pinwheeled into the air, leaving a clear entrance to the Temple. Suddenly the diversionary attack turned quite real as the mercs howled—a long, curdling wolfpack sound—and ran forward.

Lean, bloody men and women with death in their eyes and revenge in their guts.

Ida flumped into the self-propelled gun's seat and cranked the engine. With Ffillips still loading, Ida gunned the SP track into the Temple's main courtyard.

Behind her Bet and the two tigers followed silently.

CHAPTER SEVENTY

"WHICH WAY WILL it blow?" Sten whispered while examining the tiny ring charge that was anchored to the top of the hollow column.

Sten, Alex, and Doc were five meters below the charge that when set off should let them into the Temple. They were locked in place with treble strands of climbing thread.

"Ah, lad, questions ae thae be't whae makit life in'trestin'," Alex breathed as he triggered the demoset.

The column's cap lifted, as did the floorbeams above it and then the flagstone that was the central Temple's actual flooring.

The flagstone tumbled in the air and chopped down two guards, one Companion, and a statue of the late Theodomir.

Alex, Sten, and Doc shinnied their way up the last few meters, and then they were inside the Temple.

They went looking for Mathias.

CHAPTER SEVENTY-ONE

IDA WAS LEANING half out of her seat and completely unprotected by the track's armor when the Companion finished reloading. She was reaching for a banner that looked like it was made of gold when four rounds slammed into the Rom woman's chest. She sagged across the track's bow and rolled sacklike to the ground as the unmanned track stalled. A look of surprise, anger, and vast disappointment was frozen on her face.

Bet cradled Ida in her arms as Hugin and Munin finished their slow savaging of the Companion who had shot her. Then Bet lowered Ida to the ground and jumped to her feet, mind blank and firing, and the ground rocked and thundered as the Anti-Matter-Two rounds poured out of her willygun, exploding the platoon of Companions running toward her.

CHAPTER SEVENTY-TWO

MATHIAS' ADVISORS DIED in the first burst of fire as Sten and Alex charged through the double doors, into the conference room. The advisors had been too busy watching the debacle in the courtyard one-hundred meters below the balcony to hear the deathrattles of the guards outside the chamber. For which minor error they became very dead.

Mathias stood, looking unsurprised at the carnage, as Doc slid out of Alex's pack and unlimbered the hypo. Alex kept Mathias in the sights of his willygun as the Prophet walked slowly forward.

"I have been expecting you," Mathias said. "My best friend and my worst enemy."

He shrugged out of his red tunic and flexed his muscles. His hands knotted into fists. Sten waited.

"And now we decide the Truth of Talamein," Mathias said softly as he came in.

Sten thought of the careful reasonings and appeals to friendship that he'd come up with to avoid this confrontation. Useless. He shrugged out of his pack and moved forward.

As Mathias' hand flashed back, behind him to his belt, and came out with a small projectile weapon. The pistol came up and Sten double-stepped into him, right foot coming up in a sweep-kick, and the weapon pinwheeled out of Mathias' hand. Sten kept the kick moving, then recovered, his back to

Mathias. Sensing Mathias was coming in he crouched, arm high, and half-spun back to face the Prophet, arm raised to block the snap-punch Mathias had launched.

Both men recovered and side-paced.

"You don't have to die," Sten said.

"Of course," Mathias agreed. "And I shall not. Not now, not here, not ever. This is the Test of the Flame." And, gymnast that he was, he came straight in, a mae-tobi-geri flying frontal attack.

Sten one-stepped under Mathias, snap-punched straight up into his thigh, rolled away as the Prophet crashed back down, then recovered as Mathias drove a knife hand toward Sten's head.

Sten flicked his head to the side, and Mathias' killing punch slammed across his temple and ear.

Sten knife-blocked before Mathias could recover and thudded a flat palm into Mathias' temple. Temporarily stunned, the Prophet back-rolled twice and came to his feet, half smiling.

"You *are* a worthy opponent." He drove in again. Sten blocked his swing-punch, and then Mathias' fist-strike came down on Sten's skull.

The world blurred and went double. Sten snapped his blocking hand into Mathias' gut and, contradicting conventional tactics, dove flat-forward, ball-rolling, rising, and turning as Mathias attacked.

A punching attack, blocked twice, in eye-blurring motion. Sten snapped a knee up into Mathias' diaphragm, and the man sagged back.

Then Sten's single, half-cupped hand swung, slapping Mathias' eardrum. A two-hand stroke would have killed him, but the single blow merely sent his mind spinning, and, for the first time, Mathias lost his balance, stumbling backward.

And Sten paced in, step...punch...step...punch... knuckled fist turning and thudding in below the Prophet's ribcage. Mathias doubled.

A final feint as his fisted, coupled hands came up for Sten's face. Sten locked wrists, drove the strike up, and then, howling, leaped straight up into the air, his foot coming up and out and buried into the Prophet's chest.

Mathias back-flipped and struck the floor behind him with a dull *thud*.

Then Doc was at Mathias' side, quickly checking his pulse.

"Adequate, adequate," he murmured, as he pressed the hypo's trigger and the drug sprayed into Mathias' veins.

"You probably broke some bones, but you didn't kill him."

Sten was not listening. He was dropped down into semilotus, lungs sucking in air as he recovered.

CHAPTER SEVENTY-THREE

BET'S FLASHES IN the courtyard: Ida's body; Ffillips calmly sniping down Companions as they came into sight; Otho, evidently trying to find a Companion who could be thrown completely through a stone wall; the tigers, impossibly low, crawling under a firewall of tracers, then darting into a weapons pit. End tracers. Begin screams.

And then she heard the voice—the boom that turned the din of battle into a sudden hush as Companions, mercs, and Mantis people turned, to look up the looming wall of the Temple to the balcony.

On the balcony stood Mathias, with a hailer-mike hung on his chest. "I SPEAK AS TALAMEIN."

The battle stopped instantly. The Companions flinched upward, then recovered, waiting for the war to start again. But the mercenaries were as captivated as any, staring up at the red-clad figure high above them.

The Companions made obeisance as the voice continued. Stiff, metallic, but forceful.

"I have chosen to temporarily inhabit this envelope of flesh to speak to you, people of the Faith and the Flame.

"And I have chosen to manifest myself in this sin-riddled flesh to keep my people from falling into the pit of heresy.

"I, Talamein, took the Flame to give those I love freedom. And though I have passed beyond, I still have love for you, people of Sanctus, and, beyond you, the peoples of the Lupus Cluster.

"But I see you as a spider on a slender thread, hanging over the terrible chasm of destruction. My faith was of a crusader—a crusader who sought peace and also freedom.

"And then, once having found freedom, each of us would tend his own, whether farm or mercantile, each of us tending the Flame of Talamein deep within each of us.

"Because my Faith is that of the person, not of the race of the world.

"I thought, when I chose to pass into the Flame, that I could rest, knowing I had given my own freedom, wealth, peace, and security. And so I rested for half an eon," Mathias continued.

The speech wasn't bad, Bet noticed, watching the frozen Companions. Doc would be very proud of his composition.

"But then, from my resting, I felt a rumbling, a disturbance. And I was forced to remove myself from the warmth of the Flame, to examine my people.

"To my shame, I found destruction looming for my people. And I found a young man who was attempting to speak in my name.

"Not an evil man was your Prophet Mathias. He did suppress the heresy of the Jann. But he was a man who went beyond his mission.

"But now I, Talamein, do declare the error of his ways.

"I, Talamein, order my people to lay down their arms and return to seek happiness and their homes. Because only in peace and security can the true beliefs of Talamein come to fruition.

"Only in freedom and security will the Flame of Talamein blossom through the universe.

"I now declare anathema the man or woman who picks up arms in my name.

"I declare anathema the man or woman who attempts to convert an unbeliever by any means other than persuasion and example.

"I now declare anathema the being who uses the words of Talamein to imprison, enslave, or deprive any other being of those rights that all of us realize in our hearts are due us."

The Companions were, by now, on their knees, heads on the pavement.

"And now I leave you, to return to the Sanctity of the Flame. I adjure you to follow my instructions.

"If you so do, when your earthly envelope decays, I will welcome you to the Fellowship of the Flame.

"I also admonish you not to despise this man Mathias, from whom I speak. Though in error, he sought the truth. In his memory I require you to raise monuments and memorials.

"And now I shall return to the Flame.

"Having used this envelope and therefore sanctified it, I shall also take its occupier with me to the Sanctity of the Flame.

"And we, Talamein and the mortal Mathias, declare this envelope no longer suited to the uses and purposes of the flesh.

"Any such could only be desecration.

"My final blessings, and may peace pass among you."

The hailer clicked off, and Mathias, gaze fixed on the horizon, took four steps forward, off the balcony. His body silently curved downward through one-hundred meters of space to the courtyard flagstones below.

CHAPTER SEVENTY-FOUR

THE COURTYARD WAS empty, save for bodies, the stunned mercenaries, and the arms hastily abandoned when the Companions stumbled past the broken gates, toward the city below.

Bet was slumped against Hugin, carefully digging a piece of shrapnel from Munin's paw, when Ffillips squatted before her.

"Mantis Section, eh?"

Bet covered her reaction, then looked up. "Pardon?"

"I am a logical woman," the battered soldier said carefully. "When a mercenary officer returns to rescue me, my men and women, against all odds, bringing with him some of the— forgive me—oddest beings I have ever had the pleasure to encounter and then wins the war by making its tyrant recant publicly, I hear echoes of things."

"Such as?"

"Such as tales I heard before I, ahem, separated from the Imperial Guards. Are you not Mantis Section, and was this not an Imperial Mission?"

"Clottin'-A, buster," someone croaked from behind Bet. "Now, if someone'll stop playing with their triumphs and get me a medic, I'll be quite satisfied. I got four holes in my chest and investments to protect."

Absolute astonishment, and then Ffillips and Bet were running for the Temple to get Doc as Ida miraculously wobbled up into a sitting position. One of the tigers walked over to her and, purring, began to lick the blood from her neck.

CHAPTER SEVENTY-FIVE

"YOU MUST UNDERSTAND the hesitation of this council," the graybeard croaked as he tottered to his feet. "I mean no contempt, Colonel... I believe you said that was the way to refer to you?

"But you must know the perplexity that the past few years have brought to us, those of us who have recanted the ways of the world to study Talamein in peace."

"I do," Sten agreed.

Sten stood in front of twenty of the most carefully selected theologicians of Talamein—men selected for their age, expertise, honesty, and longwindedness. They were in the former throne room of the Temple. It looked much as it had when Mathias was occupying it, except the two-handed sword over the vidmap was gone. The twin eternal flames blazed alone.

Two other beings were in the room.

"These matters," the elder continued, "must be studied. Must be considered. Certainly none of us is arguing the truth of the appearance of Talamein himself...."

There was a muttered S'be't from the elders.

"What puzzles us is the necessity to consider these actions. The necessity to evaluate them, as to their truth and as to how they pertain to the Truth of the Flame.

"These matters may require some time to consider, and, in that time, what will happen with the ways of the world?

"We assembled here are elders. Men of silence and thought. But we must realize that beyond this Temple and these walls, there are beings and worlds to reckon with. To govern. And, I think I speak for my colleagues, we do not consider ourselves capable of performing this task. I assume, then, that perhaps you . . ." The graybeard let his words trail off delicately.

"No," Sten said. "I am but a simple soldier. A man of the earth. I shall continue on my own path, seeking my own destiny.

"But you are correct," he said, wondering where the drakh he found this smoothness and deciding he'd been too long with churchmen, hypocrites, and noblemen, "in that you and the people of Talamein shall need protection and assistance.

"This shall be my gift to you." And he turned to the two other beings in the chamber.

"This first person shall keep your government honest and your people free from the threat of invasion."

Ffillips smiled.

"And this other being shall handle the necessities of trade, merchandising, and, most important, dealing with those beings from beyond the Lupus Cluster who merely wish sustenance and a chance to pass through."

Otho grunted.

Sten lifted the medallion that Theodomir had given him months before, when he was made a Soldier of Talamein.

"I am a soldier, as I said. But perhaps, when I was made a Carrier of the Flame, I was given a gift to see into the future a bit.

"I see two things: Strangers shall come into the Lupus Cluster. Travelers. Men who seek strange matter, beyond these worlds. I see that your duty is to give them succor and to show them, by example, the peace that Talamein can bring.

"And I see one other thing: Mathias, it was true, followed the ways of ice and cold and flesh. But somehow I sense that in his final moments, he achieved what few men have gifted to them.

"In his words from the balcony, he truly became what he had intended—Talamein reincarnate."

And Sten bowed his head, waited five seconds, then strode for the exit. He needed Alex's jokes, Bet for more interesting reasons, and about five liters of pure alk.

This salvation thing was a thirsty and wearisome business.

CHAPTER SEVENTY-SIX

"NO, MAHONEY," THE Eternal Emperor purred, "I do not wish to read the full fiche. I want to consider what you just told me."

"Yes, sir," Mahoney said in a carefully neutral voice.

"You will kindly stand at attention while I review this, Colonel."

"Sir."

"Your Mantis team, and this young lieutenant..."

"Sten, sir."

"Sten. Yes. He managed, with a handful of mercenaries, to topple a religious dictatorship, to convince its fanatics to go grow whatever they grow out there, and to arrange things so that my miners will be treated well."

"Yes, sir."

"I am correct, so far?"

"You are, sir."

"Admirable," the Emperor went on. "Promote him to Captain. Give him a couple of medals. That is an order."

"Yes, sir."

"Now, leave us consider his solution to the whole mess. He turned over the military and political affairs of this whole stinkin' Lupus Cluster to a mercenary. Correct?"

"Yes, sir."

"A woman, I discovered, who deserted from the Imperial Guard facing court-martial, after stealing an entire division's supply depot and blackmarketing it. One Sergeant Ffillips. Am I still correct?"

"You are, your Highness."

"Very good. And the diplomatic, intrasystem, galactic, and mercantile end of the operation was handed to an alien?"

"Yes, sir."

"An alien who looks like a Neanderthal—don't look puzzled, Mahoney, go to the Imperial Museum and you'll see one—and comes from a race of freebooters. One Otho?"

"Yes, sir."

"I want this Sten on toast," the Emperor said in a low monotone. "I want him busted from Captain—I did promote him to Captain, did I not?"

"You did, sir."

"I also ordered you to pour me drinks, did I not?"

"Sorry, sir," and Mahoney headed for the cabinet.

"Not that bottle, Colonel. The Erlenmeyer flask. One hundred eighty proof. Open us two beers to go with it. I think I may find myself very drunk while I'm trying to find out if I can legally torture one of my officers."

Mahoney was starting to enjoy this. But he kept his smile buried as he poured shotglasses and cut the tips off beerjugs.

"Sten. Sten. Why do I know the name?"

"He killed Baron Thoresen, sir. Against your orders. You remember, the Vulcan affair."

"And I didn't send him to a penal battalion then?"

"No, sir. You promoted him to lieutenant."

The Eternal Emperor threw down the shot, shuddered, and sipped beer as he fed the mission report fiche into his viewer.

"Interesting ideas this Sten has," he mused, sipping beer.

"Overthrow the tyrant and then appoint a council of church elders to study the matter. They should have their report *ex cathedra* in, what, Mahoney? A thousand years?"

"More than that, sir." Mahoney gurgled, still recovering from the pure alcohol. "He said he chose the longest-winded theologicians he could find. More like two thousand."

The Emperor shut off the viewer, got up, grabbed the flask, and poured two more shots. He gasped his down, then mused aloud:

"Mantis Section. Why do I keep you people around, since you insist on doing exactly what I want, exactly in the manner I don't want?"

Mahoney stuck with beer drinking and silence.

"Correction to my last order, Colonel," the Emperor said, smiling in a moderately evil manner. "Do not court-martial this Sten.

"I want him.

"Detach him from Mantis and Mercury. Give him some kind of acceptable hero background in the Guard.

"Ummm," Mahoney insubordinated.

"Captain Sten is now the commander of my personal bodyguard. The Gurkhas."

And Mahoney's shot went across the room and the beerjug gurgled out, unnoticed, on the carpet.

"God damn it, your Majesty, how the clot can I run an intelligence service when you keep stealing my best men?"

"Good point, Colonel." The Eternal Emperor took a tiny order fiche from his desk and Mahoney realized just how badly he'd been set up.

"These are your orders—Congratulations, General Mahoney, and my further congratulations on your detachment and reassignment from Imperial Headquarters to command the First Guards Assault Division."

Mahoney threw the fiche to the floor, which was an ineffective gesture, since the tiny bit of plas insisted on drifting downward.

"You can't clottin' do this to me! I just spent seventy-five years building up this clottin' Mercury Corps, and—"

"And I am the god damned Eternal Emperor," the man growled and came around his desk. "I can do what I clotting well please, General, and congratulations on your new post and am I going to have to whip your ass to get you to drink with me?"

Mahoney considered for a second, then started chuckling.

"No, sir, your Imperial Majesty, sir. Thank you, sir. Since I have no choice, your Imperial Majesty, sir, I accept."

Besides, Mahoney was not at all sure he could take the Emperor. Let alone what would come afterward if he did.

The Emperor grunted and poured more drinks. "You served me well, Ian. I know you'll continue to do the same in your new position. And clot it, don't make things so hard for me when I want to be nice for a change.

"But don't forget this Sten," the Eternal Emperor said, reaching for the flask. "I have an idea he is going to go very far indeed.

"In fact, I'll give you one of my predictions.

"Sten will either end up on the gallows or as a Fleet Admiral."

And the two men drank deeply.

About the Authors

CHRIS BUNCH is a Ranger—an airborne-qualified Vietnam Vet—who's written about phenomena as varied as the Hell's Angels, the Rolling Stones, and Ronald Reagan.

ALLAN COLE grew up in the CIA in odd spots like Okinawa, Cyprus, and Taiwan. He's been a professional chef, investigative reporter, and national news editor of a major West Coast daily newspaper. He's won half a dozen writing awards in the process.

BUNCH AND COLE, friends since high school, have collaborated on everything from the world's worst pornographic novel to over fifty television scripts, as well as a feature movie. This is their second novel.